Mr S and the Secrets of Andorra's Box

D0978602

Mr S and the Secrets of Andorra's Box

ROSS O'CARROLL-KELLY
(as told to Paul Howard)

Illustrated by
ALAN CLARKE

PENGUIN
IRELAND

PENGUIN IRELAND

Published by the Penguin Group
Penguin Ireland, 25 St Stephen's Green, Dublin 2, Ireland
(a division of Penguin Books Ltd)
Penguin Books Ltd, 80 Strand, London WC2R ORL, England
Penguin Group (USA) Inc., 375 Hudson Street, New York, New York 10014, USA
Penguin Group (Australia), 250 Camberwell Road, Camberwell, Victoria 3124, Australia
(a division of Pearson Australia Group Pty Ltd)
Penguin Group (Canada), 90 Eglinton Avenue East, Suite 700, Toronto, Ontario, Canada M4P 2Y3
(a division of Pearson Penguin Canada Inc.)
Penguin Books India Pvt Ltd, 11 Community Centre, Panchsheel Park, New Delhi – 110 017, India
Penguin Group (NZ), 67 Apollo Drive, Rosedale, North Shore 0632, New Zealand
(a division of Pearson New Zealand Ltd)
Penguin Books (South Africa) (Pty) Ltd, 24 Sturdee Avenue, Rosebank, Johannesburg 2196, South Africa

Penguin Books Ltd, Registered Offices: 80 Strand, London WC2R ORL, England

www.penguin.com

First published 2008
1

Copyright © Paul Howard, 2008
Illustrations copyright © Alan Clarke, 2008

Penguin Ireland thanks O'Brien Press for its agreement to Penguin Ireland
using the same design approach and typography, and the same artist,
as O'Brien Press used in the first four Ross O'Carroll-Kelly titles

Set in 13.5/16 pt PostScript Garamond
Typeset by Rowland Phototypesetting Limited, Bury St Edmunds, Suffolk
Printed in Great Britain by Clays Ltd, St Ives plc

A CIP catalogue record for this book is available from the British Library

ISBN 978-1-844-88126-0

www.greenpenguin.co.uk

Contents

'What can't be remembered, can't be left behind.'
Ingeborg Bachmann

'Even Moses was a basket case.'
Father Denis Fehily

Prologue

'Er . . . *run* that by me again?'

'A Divorce Fair,' he goes. And he's, like, totally serious. In the RDS, of all places.

'Divorce and fair,' I go. 'Two words I never thought I'd hear in the same sentence,' which you have to admit is a cracking line. 'Dude, *why*?'

Oisinn's like, 'Why not? We have wedding fairs, don't we? Getting divorced is a bigger step than getting married. Definitely more expensive . . .'

I stare at the road and say fock-all. Don't even want to think about it.

Fionn pipes up then from the back seat. 'It's certainly a step no one should take without the best advice. I think it's a great idea.'

Then he goes back to reading an orticle about – get this – loop quantum gravity.

'Well,' Oisinn goes, 'I can't claim all the credit. Erika was the original inspiration.'

Erika. Jesus. Even the mention of her name and I'm harder than Sébastien Chabal. 'What's the, er, connection there?' I go, trying not to sound jealous.

He's like, 'She just rang me. I think she had the idea when she was in New York that time. They actually have actual divorce parties over there . . .'

'I can understand how they could be quite cathartic,' Fionn goes. Cathartic? That's definitely made up. It's like he fills his mouth with Scrabble letters, spits them out and that's a word. I don't pull him up on it, though. The poor goy's been through enough this year, what with Aoife and everything? The word is he's not going back teaching either.

'Erika's still focked up about her old pair breaking up,' I go. 'A lot of people would say it's the reason she's never acknowledged her true feelings for me – fear of getting hurt, blahdy blahdy blah . . .'

They just ignore it.

Oisinn's like, 'Two things that Erika knows a lot about – divorce and partying. So she thought she'd set herself up as a divorce party-planner. That's when she rang me.'

I'm there, 'No offence, dude, but why you?'

Fionn's like, 'Because he's twenty-six and worth a reputed twenty-eight million euro. She might have reasoned that he knew a thing or two about business.'

It's like, fair enough – I only asked.

'So,' Oisinn goes, 'I helped her set it up. Suddenly, she's getting fifty, sixty Ks a time to throw these parties for people. I would never have believed there was so much money to be made from other people's unhappiness. It was then that we hit on the idea of the Divorce Fair.'

Fionn's like, 'Erika's always had a good head on her shoulders, though. Very smart girl.'

I'm there, 'It's those lips I'd be more interested in. She could suck the nuts off an alloy,' and then I'm like, 'By the way, who the fock is this J. Oker?'

There's a cor in front of us doing, like, forty Ks an hour and refusing to pull into the slow lane. It's supposed to be the Stillorgan dualler. I'm there, 'Oisinn, flash your lights at him.'

He's like, 'Ross, it's a cop car,' like that means something.

I'm there, 'Two Honours in the Leaving gets you into

Templemore – it doesn't entitle you to drive like an old-age pensioner.'

The focking turnip-muncher eventually gets the hint and lets us pass.

When we get to JP's gaff, his old man opens the door and his face lights up like a knacker on the Nitelink when he sees us. 'Been too long,' he goes, a rolled-up copy of, presumably, *Juggs* or *Adult Stars* in his hand.

I'm there, 'We thought we'd see did JP fancy driving around all the local dole offices with us shouting, "You focking mendicants!" at the people . . .'

'Excellent,' he goes. 'It's just what he needs.'

Mr Conroy's never really got over the shame of his son turning his back on a career in property for – of all things – God. I think when JP had his breakdown and decided not to, like, join the priesthood after all, his old man thought two weeks in a darkened room with plenty of hot 7-Up and he'd be back at Hook, Lyon & Sinker before you could say *the spirit of gracious living.*

Fionn speaks for us all when he goes, 'So, how is he?'

'He's stopped babbling,' Mr Conroy goes, leading us through the house to the kitchen. 'The Psalms and Leviticus quotient is definitely down.' He stops at the window. 'We're still worried about him, though.'

We follow his, like, line of vision out to the gorden, where JP is wearing – get this – green overalls and digging what looks very much to me like a hole.

I just blurt it out. 'Jesus, Manual Labour! What the *fock* is he doing?'

'It's called . . . landscaping,' he goes. Then he shakes his head like he thought he'd never have to say the word. 'He's turning that half-acre there into a contemplation garden. My son with a shovel in his hand. If this gets out, I won't be able to hold my head up in Shanahan's again.'

'Fock!' I go and I look at Oisinn and Fionn for, like, back-up? 'You can't say that that's right. That goy went to Castlerock – that used to mean something in this town.'

'I don't see anything wrong with it,' Fionn goes. 'I mean, if it helps him find inner peace . . .'

Glasses. Ridiculous. I have to actually bite my tongue, though.

Oisinn puts his hand on Mr Conroy's shoulder. At least *he* can see how much this is tearing him up inside. 'Look, we saw a lot of this shit at school. Taking a year out after the Leaving to work for, like, non-profit organizations – Simon, St Vincent de Paul, that whole crew. They all copped on when they found out how much do-ray-me there was in fund management.'

At last – someone's talking sense. It seems to do the trick as well because suddenly Mr Conroy perks up. 'So you think this is purely temporary?' he goes.

Oisinn's like, 'Look, trust me – six months and he'll be back at his desk, using pictures of women drinking champagne and men putting on cufflinks to sell homes in some ant farm on the M50.'

Mr Conroy shakes his head, the smile back on his boat. 'So it's not all doom and gloom, then . . .'

It's not. Oisinn's talking total sense. But still, seeing the goy I know as one of Ireland's greatest ever fullbacks at underage level holding – of all things – a work tool totally weirds me out of it, and when we go out to the gorden I end up approaching him with my hands up, as if to say, basically, stay calm, we come in peace.

'Hey, Ross,' he goes, apparently delighted to see me. 'Fionn, Oisinn – this is a surprise . . .'

It's like, never a truer word . . .

'We just wondered did you fancy haranguing social welfare recipients,' Oisinn goes. 'Like old times?'

JP pulls a face. 'No can do, I'm afraid. I want to finish digging this out while the soil's still moist . . .'

I just nod like he's just said the most reasonable thing in the world. He's still a mate.

'What's it going to be,' I go, 'as in, when it's finished?'

He's like, 'An introspection pond. I'm going to dig about a metre down. Fill it up. Put some nice fish in it – koi are beautiful – some waterlilies. Maybe some stepping stones.'

I'm there, 'Cool.'

'I know what you're thinking,' he suddenly goes. 'JP's off the Richter – Ross, I can see it in your face.'

I'm there, 'I make no apologies for being worried about one of my best friends. The word is you haven't even bought your Leinster season ticket yet.'

He sort of, like, pokes at the ground with the shovel, a bit embarrassed, by the looks of him. Then he suddenly looks up and he goes, 'The greatest gift of the garden is the restoration of the five senses.'

I can't, like, hold my tongue any longer. I'm there, 'That better not be God you're quoting. I thought we'd heard the last of him.'

He laughs at that. He puts the shovel down and moves over to this little, I suppose, gorden bench. I sit down beside him, roysh, and Fionn and Oisinn stand around.

'I never said I lost my faith,' he goes. 'Okay, so I'm not going to be a priest. It doesn't mean I've stopped believing in God.'

'Sorry, I just don't get that.'

'It's like Shane Byrne,' he goes. 'He's off playing for

Saracens, but do you think for one minute that he's stopped loving Leinster?'

I focking love Shane Byrne and JP knows that.

'I can't believe how uptight I was before I found gardening,' he goes. 'It's so calming and so rewarding. It's like balm – balm for the wounded soul.'

He looks up at Fionn. He's like, 'How are you doing?'

Fionn goes, 'Like the cliché says, one day at a time,' and JP nods like he understands.

Then Oisinn changes the subject because it's getting too heavy. 'Speaking of overweight rugby legends who are plying their trade abroad, what do you think of this dude?' and he flicks his thumb at me.

Overweight? That's pure focking muscle.

JP smiles at me. 'When are you off?' he goes.

I'm like, 'Middle of November. Looking forward to it as well, even though it's a big ask. I mean, Andorra – it's where knackers go to ski. Wouldn't say they've a focking clue about rugby. It'll be like teaching monkeys how to type. You know me, though – I love, like, a challenge and shit?'

'If you're going to put koi in there,' someone suddenly goes, 'you're going to need an aerator.'

We all look around and there's Fionn, roysh, staring into the hole that JP's dug.

'One step ahead of you,' JP goes and he points at this sort of, like, pump contraption that's just been taken out of its box.

Fionn, like, considers this for a few seconds, then goes, 'You know what would look good? A bank of clipped yews, sloping down to the water's edge. And over there maybe an organic vegetable garden. Unusual stuff – kohlrabi, physalis . . .'

Something passes between JP and Fionn. More than just a smile. It's, like, an understanding.

6

Without saying a word, Fionn picks up a hoe and I don't mean that in, like, a good way?

Me and Oisinn instantly know that we're going to be leaving here today without either of them.

Doesn't physalis sounds like an STD?

1. For the people on the edge of the night

She's, like, pretty surprised to see me, though not as surprised as I am to see her, standing there under a banner that says MOUNT ANVILLE CLASS OF 1997.

I had literally no idea.

She looks amazing in what I'm pretty sure is her gold Reem Acra dress with the Sergio Rossi shoes I let her put on my credit cord and, I think, Dolce & Gabbana's *The One*, which she never used to wear – and straight away when she cops me, it's like, 'What are *you* doing here?' as in she's *not* a happy bunny to see me?

I'm there, 'Er, *hello*? It's Ron Blacks, Sorcha, in other words a public place?' and then – possibly a bit, I don't know, childish this – I let my eyes sweep the bor and go, 'One or two familiar faces in here, it has to be said.'

Of course, that goes down like a focking turd in a toybox.

'Hordly surprising,' she goes. 'You went through my year like a pathogen,' which is, like, *way* Jodie, if you ask me – even though I don't know what a pathogen is.

Did I mention that she looks amazing?

I'm just there, 'Well, you can relax, babes. You don't have to worry about me *being* with any of your friends in front of you any more. I'm actually going out with someone, *and* it's pretty serious.'

There's not even a flicker of interest from her.

I'm there, 'Her name's Melanie, before you ask. Wouldn't say you know her, though, she's from, like, Malahide?'

Still nothing. Of course, I can't just leave it at that.

'I suppose, looking back,' I go, 'you'd have to say our marriage failed because we both wanted, like, different things out of life?'

'Yes,' she goes, while at the same time giving me an absolute filthy, 'I wanted to abide by the vows we made to each other on our wedding day and you wanted to have sex with our daughter's nanny.'

It's, like, of course it's going to sound bad if you say it like that.

I go to put my orm around her, roysh, but she swats it away with the force of a woman who's been playing tag rugby for pretty much the entire summer. '*Oh* my God,' she goes, 'you *actually* need to get over yourself, you know that?' and she storms off, and of course every set of mince pies in the place is suddenly on me, everyone thinking, looks like the old Rossmeister's up to his old tricks again – that girl'll never be over him.

I turn back to the bor and order another pint of the Dutch stuff. I'm tanning it in a major way, it has to be said. The next thing I hear is a bird's voice going, 'Hi, Ross.'

It's Ellie Banaher, as in Ellie who played the lute in the joint production we did of *Annie Get Your Gun*? Or maybe it was the balalaika.

Whatever. I've had my sweaty way with her once or twice down through the years. She has a great boat race, it has to be said – a little bit like Rumer Willis – though the bod wouldn't be the best, we're talking two breasts short of a dinner-box here. Her bra fits her better worn backwards.

I ask her how she is, which of course isn't a question – it's, like, a figure of speech? – but all of a sudden she's going, 'Aportment, job, cor . . .' and she's, like, counting these things off on her fingers. When she reaches her fourth, as in her ring finger, she wiggles it at me, showing off this diamond that's probably visible from space, and goes, 'Engaged,' and I'm thinking, that's the problem with these school reunions, you ask a simple question and you end up getting a focking PowerPoint presentation.

I grab my beer and slip over to where Erika, Chloe and Sophie are standing and I hang off the edge of their conversation. Chloe is saying that skobies love Argos so much because the little pens remind them of being in the bookies.

Sophie, meanwhile, is skulling the Gerry Thornleys in a major way. 'My Miu Mius are cramping my feet,' she says when I catch her eye. 'It's either take them off or drink through the pain.'

Erika just stands there, looking bored and beautiful. She eventually acknowledges my presence. 'Ross, what are you even *doing* here?' she goes. 'It's all a bit desperate, even for you.'

I'm there, 'Well, for your information I'm actually going out with a bird – a good-looking one as well,' and Erika's like, 'Spare me – you're following Sorcha around like some lovelorn teenager. You know Cillian is here?'

I shrug. It's a boozer. I've as much right as he has.

'You look incredible,' I tell her, 'even by your standards,' and she smiles for the first time since about a month ago, when she found out that Claire from Brayruit was working in Caddles Irish Gifts.

'Yes,' she goes, 'I do, don't I?'

I put my hand on her bare shoulder and she tells me to move it or she'll break my fingers, which she probably would.

I tell her fair focks to her about the Divorce Fair. It's pretty cool that she's taken her anger and bitterness towards her old man for doing a legger and channelled it into something, like, positive?

She doesn't answer me, just stares at me, then has another sip of her mint julep, while Sophie says, *Oh my God*, did you see who Riley Coren brought? Simon McCourt, as in Michael McCourt's *little* brother, which, she says, is, like, *totally* random and Chloe says she's doing a total Rhys Ifans on it, which is like, oh *my* God?

The next thing, roysh, I notice that Sorcha's stood on a low stool, with a microphone in her hand, going, 'Can everyone hear me?' and immediately there's, like, total silence in the bor.

'Thank you all *so* much for coming,' she goes. 'It's hord to believe that it's been fifteen years since we entered into Mount Anville, all young girls unsure of ourselves and our place in the world. Today, we gather as adults and it's great to see that everyone's looking so well and doing so well for themselves . . .'

Everyone claps.

She goes, 'I, for instance, have a beautiful baby girl and I'm running my own fashion boutique in the Powerscourt Townhouse Centre, with exclusive Zak Posen and Betsey Johnson lines . . .'

Not a Charlie Bird about getting married to me, of course – probably doesn't want to have to go into the whole separation thing.

'Last year I met one of my all-time heroes – apart from obviously Aung San Suu Kyi and Ayaan Hirsi Ali – and that was Stella McCartney . . .'

Another round of applause – you can see *why* she was headgirl now? They lap this kind of shit up.

'We were very lucky to have a year in which everyone got on *so* well and it's no surprise that so many of us have stayed in contact with each other. I really value my friendships from my time in school, as I'm sure all of you do.

'A couple of girls have sent apologies, which I promised I'd read out. Bryana Kavanagh sent a cord and it says, "Sorry, I can't be there tonight. But just to let you know, after getting my BA in Business Management (Leisure and Recreation) from DBS, I got married to a really, really nice guy called Barry. A stylist who used to work with Ken Paves did my hair for the wedding . . ."'

A lot of *wows!*, more than a few *oh my Gods* and then more clapping.

'You probably all remember Sarah Moore,' Sorcha goes. 'She left at the end of fifth year to go to the Institute. She says, "Hi, everyone. Sorry I can't make it. I'm actually writing this e-mail on a yacht in the Mediterranean, drinking a strawberry daiquiri. I've lost two stone since most of you saw me last and I've got seventy-two friends on Facebook . . ."'

Another big clap for that. God, Mounties are *so* focking polite.

Then Sorcha tells the room that in a few minutes there'll be, like, trays of food coming around – we're talking miniature Mediterranean quiches, we're talking caramelized onion and Soignon goat's cheese tortlets, we're talking parmentier potatoes with shallot butter – and everyone should eat as much as they can because the biggest threat to the Earth in terms of CO_2 emissions is rotting food and not discarded plastic and glass, as is popularly believed.

Then she says thank you and steps down off the stool and as she does, roysh, she smiles at someone in the crowd and does this little girlie wave and I follow her line of vision across the bor and there he is – *he* as in Cillian – giving it loads, clapping horder than anyone else and basically *begging* me to go over there and deck him.

He's in his focking work suit as well, a Magee job – Dorce's crowd – and he's got his security swipe card hanging from his belt loop, like the knob that he is. Of course, I can't resist moseying on over there to try to, like, wreck his *actual* head?

'Hey, Ross,' he just goes, like we're actual mates or some shit. 'How's life?'

'Life's LL Cool J for me,' I go, 'don't you worry about that. You know, if it gets any better, I'm going to have to hire someone to help me enjoy it.'

It's mad, roysh, but whenever he's around me, Cillian always pins his shoulders back and puffs up his chest to try to make himself look bigger.

I can't believe the birds think he looks like Jake Gyllenhaal.

'What are you doing at the Mount Anville reunion?' I go. 'I didn't know you were raised as a girl,' but he tries to ignore me, the smug prick.

I'm there, 'Is that, like, Dolce & Gabbana perfume Sorcha's wearing?' letting him know I was up close and pretty personal with her earlier on.

'It is, yeah,' he goes, secretly bulling.

I'm there, 'Weird – she never *used* to wear that?' and he's like, 'Well, we *all* move on, Ross,' which is a definite dig at me.

I'm there, 'Well, I certainly have. I'm seeing this new bird, as in Melanie? I don't want to be writing my own reviews here, but the sex is so good that the people next-door light up a cigarette afterwards,' which is actually horseshit, roysh, because after three weeks she still hasn't let me into her pants.

'Lucky her,' he goes and before I can hit him back with, I don't know, some really, really funny line, Sorcha arrives over and gives him this big, like, kiss on the lips – putting on a performance basically.

'Have you one for me?' I go.

She looks at me like I'm cryptosporidium. 'You're drunk,' she goes. 'Why don't you go home, Ross – get a taxi outside.'

I'm like, 'Oh, I didn't realize you still cared so much.'

Cillian steps in between us and it has to be said I'm impressed. I honestly didn't think he had it in him. But then I realize it's only because there's a bouncer behind me.

A hand tightens around the top of my orm and a voice in my ear goes, 'The girl's giving you good advice,' and I'm suddenly dumped out onto Dawson Street before I even manage to say that the girl happens to be my actual wife.

I've worked out, roysh, that it's not the smell of the Joy I hate most, it's actually the attempt to disguise it. Two hundred cream crackers making the effort for the day – it's like someone filled the sprinkler system with *Shh* by Jade Goody and *Adidas Urban Spice*, then switched the focking thing on.

The trick is to get into the visiting room and over to the table before the focker cops you and makes a holy show of you in front of, like, two or three hundred people. I've never managed it. Twenty yords is as close as I've got.

Today, he actually cups his two hands around his mouth and goes, 'Here he comes – like a bad penny!' and then, turning to various randomers around him, he's like, 'Fasten your seatbelts, ladies and gentlemen. We're about to experience some ribbing, joshing, *with*, I dare say, a little good-natured raillery thrown in for good measure . . .'

I sit down – totally morto – and I'm there, 'You know, according to Ronan, it only costs five Ks to get someone whacked in here. All I'd have to do is sell that Ronald Ossory Dunlop original in the study, find the right man and . . .' I make the shape of a gun with my hand, put it up to his forehead and go, '. . . *Poosh!*'

The old man sort of, like, stares at me for a few seconds,

then bursts out laughing and tries to get everyone else in on the gag by going, 'See what I mean? It *never* ceases!'

When he settles down, he mentions that he hasn't seen me all summer and I mention that I've got better things to do than sit staring across a table at a sad sack of shit like him, especially now that he's Keith Flint and I've found another sucker to bankroll me.

'Of course,' he goes, 'you'll have been busy with this new job of yours. When are you leaving us?'

'Middle of November,' I go. 'Can't come soon enough.'

Again, roysh, he can't let it be just me and him – he has to bring everyone else in on the conversation. 'You're looking at the new national rugby coach of Andorra,' he goes to Lex, who has a visit from his solicitor. 'Ever been to Andorra, old chap?'

Lex is there, 'The brutter was – skiing,' which makes total sense.

I look at my watch. The focking time in here drags. Five minutes. Would it be rude to just leave now?

'So,' the old man goes, trying to come up with shit to talk about, 'they're finally closing the Berkeley Court . . .'

I look at him as if to say, and this affects me *how* exactly?

'A sad day,' he goes. 'I, er, went to see your friend and mine in here. John. Ask about maybe getting some compassionate leave, just a few hours. Has somebody died, he said. Quote-unquote. Frankly, yes, I said – a way of life. They are closing down the Berkeley Court. Now, John, I said, I know you're a humanist and you'll treat with the most scrupulous fairness my request to spend just a few final hours in the bar with my two favourite Hennessys, i.e. Coghlan O'Hara and XO . . .'

I'm there, 'Are you saying he let you? I'd have organized a focking picket of the place if I'd known.'

'Alas not,' he goes. 'The – inverted commas – powers-that-be wouldn't wear it. Didn't technically qualify as the passing of a close family member, according to John. Do your time, he said, you haven't long to go.'

He stares into space then.

'They're selling it all off, you know. Fixtures and fittings and so forth – auctioning the lot. I'm wondering who'll end up with our famous stools. People would come in, you know, sit in our little spot at the top of the bar and they'd be told – chaps, you're more than welcome to sit there, but it's absolutely mandatory that you vacate them in the event of Charles O'Carroll-Kelly and his world-famous solicitor, sidekick and long-suffering golf partner turning up. That, by the way, is when the real show starts.'

I'm there, 'It's amazing how, in a few months, I forgot what a total and utter penis you are.'

'Of course, Hennessy wasn't there that famous night in 1990 when I shared a drink with the famous Chairman of the Board . . .'

I make the mistake of going, 'Who?' which is exactly what he wants me to say.

'I'm talking about Mr S,' he goes. 'The Voice. Old Blue Eyes himself . . .'

'Horseshit.'

'Frank Sinatra . . .'

'You're talking out your hole.'

'It happened, Ross, just as sure as I'm sitting here, languishing away in Joshua Jebb's folly!'

'Talk focking English. What happened?' I go, like a fool, actually *inviting* him to bore me to death?

'Well, he *stayed* there, Ross. He was playing Lansdowne Road, you see. With Sammy and Liza. Deano wasn't with them, of course. Well, Hennessy left early that night – had a case the next day, assault occasioning bodily harm or some such.

'I'm sitting at the bar, thinking, I'll have one more before I venture home to your mother. Then in he walks. "Gimme some gasoline," he says to your bar chap. Gasoline was his *word*, you see, for – what's this he drank? Oh, Jack Daniel's! Jack Daniel's, if you don't mind.

'Chairman, I said, put your money away. I would consider it a signal honour to buy a drink to wet the throat that sang "Last Night When We Were Young", full point, new par.

'What does he do next? He sits down next to me on Hennessy's stool. "Cheers," he says. "You're platinum, Charlie." I thought he knew my name, maybe he'd heard one or two stories around the place. Turns out that's what he called you if he didn't have a name for you.

'Well, it seems he couldn't sleep. All those years getting up to all sorts with this Ratpack of his, I expect his body didn't know day from night. Three hours we sat there, me and Mr S, putting the world to rights.'

I'm like, 'Three *hours?*' refusing to believe anyone could spend that long in a bor, in my old man's company, without glassing the focker. 'What would *you* have to talk to Frank Sinatra about for three hours?'

'Everything,' he goes. 'Life, love, how to eliminate glitches from your upswing . . . You could say we bared our souls to one another that night. He told me secrets, Kicker, that I'll take to the grave with me. And I told him things that I'm sure were never repeated outside of that bar.'

I'm there, 'Some loser who stuck his hand in his pocket to buy him a drink – do you think he gave two focks about anything you had to say?'

He pretends he didn't hear it. He's like, 'Oh, we tired ourselves talking. When it was time to go – I'll never forget this – he drained the last of his Jack Daniel's, shook my hand and said, "Eighteen karat, Charlie." I'll always remember that. Eighteen karat . . .

'He never stopped loving Ava Gardner, you know. And he bedded them all, Ross. Or so they say. Lauren Bacall. Jackie Kennedy. Marlene Dietrich. Angie Dickinson. I mean, Marilyn, for heaven's sake. But on this point, we agreed – we all have just one true love . . .'

For a few seconds, he's, like, totally lost in thought.

'Pity yours was a focking hog,' I go.

She's on the phone, showing – it has to be said – absolutely zero interest in her granddaughter. She's on to Penguin, the scabrous beast, wanting to know why she hasn't had her mug in the paper or on television in the past week, as if one look in the mirror couldn't answer that question straight away, the focking grouper.

I can hear her in the old man's study. 'I'm the biggest selling author in Ireland,' she's going. 'We should be reminding people of that every second day. Or *every* day, if need be.'

Honor's chatting away to me. Or trying to. She has no actual words yet, though I thought I picked out 'powder-blue stoneware' from her constant stream of babble and, given the amount of time her mother spends in Meadows & Byrne, I wouldn't be altogether surprised.

It's obvious what this is about, by the way – the old dear just can't stand the competition. There's a new face on the scene and it's a lot easier on the eye than hers. Everyone is suddenly talking about Charlotte McNeel, the new popular fiction writer who is currently banging on the door of stardom and also banging the old dear's former agent and squeeze, Lance Rogan. It's all too hilarious for words.

Indian Summer is in the window of every bookshop in town. You know the story. Neeraja, a young Indian girl, flees Mumbai to escape an arranged marriage to a man she's never met. She ends up in Clonskeagh and meets a young medical student called Ashok, who also left India to avoid an arranged marriage. They fall hopelessly in love and of course the twist is that theirs was the marriage their parents were trying to arrange all along.

It's the biggest piece of shit ever squeezed between two covers, but *TV Now* has already called it charming, while *Company* called it funny and touching, and I only know that because I absolutely insist on reading every review to the old dear, personally.

This morning I told her there was talk of a movie, with the bird from *Bend It Like Beckham*, which is the real reason she's on to that crowd of hers now.

'You must be able to get me on something,' she's going. 'What about *The Restaurant*? I can't believe I haven't been asked on that yet.'

Speaking of books, I must get one or two for the gaff here, just to have for Honor when I have her here. For now I'm having to make do with a Mitchell & Sons Wine Merchants catalogue that I found on the old dear's dresser, the soak.

Honor doesn't care, of course. It's all about the pictures at that age. I'm leafing through it for her and she, like, puts her hand on each page and I go, 'Château Angélus 1995', or 'Château Ducru-Beaucaillou St-Julien', or whatever it happens to be and she cracks up laughing.

She has an amazing laugh. Really, like, giddy. When you hear it, you can't help but laugh yourself and it's funny, roysh, because for the first twelve months she couldn't look at my face without, like, bursting into tears.

It took us, like, ages to bond, though in fairness I never really made the effort. I'd be told to, like, take her out for the day, to give Sorcha some me-time, and I'd just bring her to Dundrum Town Centre, thinking, if she takes after her mother, she's going to end up spending ninety per cent of her life in here, so I might as well get her acclimatized to the place.

I suppose I should admit it – most of the time I just dropped her into the crèche for the afternoon and focked off shopping. Once – the famous day of the Hugo Boss sale – I actually went home without her, and it was only when I was hanging my new black Rossellini Cinema suit in the wardrobe that I remembered her.

The staff in the crèche have nicknamed me Not With-out My Daughter, which I have to admit is funny. But ever since that afternoon – well, *and* evening – I haven't let her out of my sight and, it has to be said, I've discovered the joys of, like, bonding with her, as in *actually* bonding with her?

Now she can't stop laughing – at pretty much everything I say.

'You're not going to end up a dipso like your granny,' I'm going, tickling her under the chin.

Ha ha ha ha.

'Are you? Are you going to end up a dipso like your granny? An ugly, gin-soaked sot . . .'

Ha ha ha ha.

'With a face like a melted welly.'

I can't remember what life was like before Honor. *Or* Ronan. Just that I hadn't a bog what it was all about. It's probably a sign of, like, growing maturity or some shit, but I think family's, like, so important.

'Will you keep your big focking air-raid siren voice down?'

I shout in to the old dear. 'No one in this room's interested in hearing your bullshit.'

But the old dear's too busy going, 'You're Penguin, for God's sake – I expect you to ruin this girl. Dig up *something*.'

Any word from Christian, he wants to know – obviously hasn't heard the news. The dude rang me from the States the day before yesterday, in focking tears.

Oisinn's pint stops in midair, just before it reaches his lips. 'The baby?' he goes.

'No,' I tell him, 'that's all fine. I mean, Lauren's pretty tired – the usual story – but everything's cool that end. No, they were, like, tears of happiness. See, George Lucas, roysh, is opening up, like, a *Star Wars* themed casino in Vegas and – get this – he's asked Christian to be, like, the project manager for it?'

'Shit the bed and kick it out,' Oisinn goes, speaking for pretty much both of us.

So I'm there, 'I mean, they're not actually moving to Vegas until, like, the baby arrives. But we'll have some focking holidays over there when he does. On the big-time lash – you, me, Alan Titchmarsh and Diarmuid focking Gavin.'

He cracks his hole laughing, in fairness to him. Then he just shakes his head. 'I gave them a bell earlier,' he goes, 'to ask did they fancy having one or six with us tonight? They were in – wait for it – a garden centre!'

I'm like, 'What – together?'

He nods. 'Buying pyracanthas and hibiscuses.'

'Fock! And they're not worried about how that looks?'

'Apparently not.'

'Because it looks pretty focking fromage frais from where I'm standing. Jesus!'

Kiely's is pretty rammers for a Wednesday, it must be

said. I don't agree with showing soccer on TV in pubs – it tends to attract the peasantry. Actually, I don't agree with soccer, full stop. It's one of the few things me and the old man agree on. I loved that slogan he had when he ran in the local elections – 'tough on soccer, tough on the causes of soccer'.

'You still going out with that Melanie?' Oisinn goes over the din of people ordering cider.

I'm there, 'Er, *seeing* her, yeah.'

He was actually there when I first met Melanie.

'I mean, she's a ringer for Sarah Chalke,' I go, for some reason feeling the need to justify myself.

'Sounds . . . great.'

'Yeah, it is actually. I mean, she even wants to meet Ronan. The three of us are going late-night shopping tomorrow.'

'Whoa,' he goes, 'sounds like that's getting serious.'

I'm there, 'Well, I need to hit the Great Outdoors – get some clobber for going away. Ro wants a balaclava as well. With the eyes and mouth cut out. Of course, he's only saying that to freak the shit out of me. Although with him, you never know.'

I get the round in. Two more Vitamin Hs.

'I want to show you something,' Oisinn goes, suddenly producing this, basically, cardboard roll. It turns out it's a poster.

In big letters, it's like, 'Unhappy Ever After?' and then underneath, 'Find Out How to Untie the Knot at Ireland's First Ever Divorce Fair – November 4 & 5, RDS Simmonscourt', and smack in the middle there's, like, an old black-and-white wedding photograph from, I don't know, the sixties or something and it's, like, ripped in two.

'Pretty impressive,' I go.

It'd be fair to say, roysh, that I've never seen Oisinn this excited, even about *Eau d'Affluence*, his scented holy waters, or any of the various orcs and cyclopses he's gone out with over the years.

He says it's all Erika's doing and my back is, like, immediately up.

'She's just full of ideas for exhibits,' he goes. 'Obviously we're going to have, like, lawyers there, answering questions about alimony, child access, people's rights and obligations. But there's, like, two or three dating agencies taking stands as well.'

'Dating agencies?'

'Yeah, for people who want to make a new start. Trapped in a sexless marriage for years, you're going to want your Bob Dole.'

I'm there, 'I have to say, in my case, the sex got even better after I got married.'

'Yeah,' he goes, 'it's a shame Sorcha found out about it, though,' which earns him an instant high-five, even if it is *slightly* out of order? 'Then there's, like, divorce *cruises*.'

'You're shitting me now?'

'Seriously. Erika said they're, like, huge in the States. You take your ex for a few hundred Ks, then you're cruising the Caribbean with your b'atches.'

'Fock. I hope she hasn't told *my* ex that.'

'Divorce,' he goes, 'is from the Latin word meaning to rip out a man's testicles through his wallet. I think it was Robin Williams said that. Erika's going to have it put on, like, a brass plaque for the office. Did I tell you we're getting an office together?'

I can't tell you how jealous that suddenly makes me feel. 'Oh, *very* cosy,' I go, like a focking child. I could be back in Wez.

'Yeah,' he goes, not picking up on it, 'on Stephen's Green there. Huge place.'

'Bit, er, risky, isn't it? I mean, the property morket's supposed to be slowing up. The economy, blah blah blah . . .'

He's like, 'Ross, the divorce rate in this country is only going to increase – so is the number of newly single women with enormous five- and six-figure payoffs, just waiting to be spent in a frivolous manner.'

'Sounds like you two have it all worked out,' I go.

He's there, 'Of course there's a serious side to marital break-up as well – I don't want to seem insensitive here . . .'

'Hey, it's cool.'

'We're going to have, like, financial advisers there. Estate agents – obviously JP's old man's going to have a pitch. Experts in the whole area of midlife crisis. Private detectives. Even a DNA lab offering paternity test results within twenty-four hours.'

I'm only half listening now. It's that wedding photograph – could be wrong, but it looks very much like . . .

'That's not Erika's old pair, is it?'

Oisinn's like, 'Yeah, it is – why?'

'On their wedding day?'

'Yeah.'

I actually laugh out loud. 'She's going to go focking Hertz Van Rental when she sees that.'

Of course I end up nearly falling off the stool when he says that Erika did the posters herself.

One of the, I suppose, nicest things about having kids is, like, watching them when they don't *know* you're watching them? As in, standing there while they're engrossed in, I don't know, whatever it happens to be, looking at their little faces – their excitement, their sadness, whatever – and thinking, oh my God, I'm *actually* responsible for giving that person life.

Ronan's watching *The World's Dumbest Criminals* and he's, like, so glued to it he doesn't even know I'm in the room. He's sucking the last bit of pleasure out of one of his famous rollies and sort of, like, tutting to himself whenever a cor chase or an ormed robbery ends badly, then giving his verdict – either 'Fooken amateurs' or 'If you pay peanuts, you'll get monkeys.'

'*Ro!*' I suddenly go, at the top of my voice, and the poor kid gets such a fright he ends up pretty much levitating.

'Ye doorty-looken fooker,' he goes then, trying to catch his breath again. 'Thought me number was up, man.'

I'm there, 'Sorry, Ro,' and he sits down again.

Hilarious.

He goes, 'Were you folleyed?'

I'm like, '*Hello?* No offence, Ro, but who in their right mind would follow someone into an estate like this?'

That seems to, like, satisfy him.

'Reet enough,' he goes. 'Sorry, Rosser – new Super on the Manor. Has me paranoid to fook, so he does. I've already had to postpone one or two blags I had going down.'

I sit down on the sofa, although I think these people call it a settee. 'So you've finally met your match?' I go, basically playing along with him.

'You're tellin' me,' he goes, pressing the last of his cigarette into the ashtray, then immediately lighting another. 'He's not only smart, Rosser, he's lucky.'

'Some combination.'

'Better fooken believe it. Kind of fella walks into a revolving door behind you and comes out in front – know what I'm saying?'

'Pretty much. Anyway – are you ready?'

'Ready?'

'Yeah, we're going late-night shopping. With Melanie, remember?'

He stares at me blankly for a few seconds, then suddenly smiles. 'I like your style,' he goes, like it's the first time he's heard this. 'Filth would never open up on me with a lemon in the picture,' and he gives me a little wink.

At the bus-stop, he suddenly turns to me and tells me I got lucky. 'When you snuck up on me like that . . .'

I'm like, 'Or maybe, Ro, you're just losing your touch?' and straight away I regret saying it because he sort of, like, looks into the distance, sadly, and goes, 'Happens to the best . . .'

Melanie's waiting for us at the entrance to the Stephen's Green Shopping Centre. Before we hit the Great Outdoors, she wants to get, like, a pink cover for her Vaio. Ronan lays on the chorm in a major way, telling her he doesn't know what a girl like her would see in a goy like me and that she'll eventually see sense, like all the rest, and drop me like a hot snot.

You can tell that he's not at all what Melanie expected.

'He's kind of, like, *old* for his age,' she says to me when he stops to talk to the security guard outside Knickerbox. 'He's very cute, though,' and I'm like, 'What can I say? It's in the genes.'

She laughs then, but at what I said, not at me. It's great to find someone who likes me for who I actually am.

'I love kids,' she goes. 'I've got two nieces and one nephew – Dylan, *oh* my God, he's *so* cute – and I absolutely dote on them.'

I'm like, 'What ages?' showing an interest, which is obviously important.

'Daisy and Molly are twins and they're, like, six? And Dylan's fourteen months.'

I'm there, 'Wow, same as Honor. They're amazing at that age.'

'They're amazing at any age,' she goes.

'I do this thing with Honor and it's like, round and round the gorden, like a teddy bear . . .'

'Oh my *God*, my mum used to do that with me . . .'

'She loves it. I mean, the squeals of her when I tickle her under the orm. Actually, it's even before that? It's, like, the anticipation of it more than anything?'

'That brings back – *oh my God* – so many memories for me.'

'The other thing,' I go, 'is that it's a major attraction for birds – seeing a goy with a baby.'

She suddenly stops walking. Looks me up and down. 'Sorry?' she goes, though not in, like, a pissed-off way? Even after a few weeks she's already used to me putting my foot in it, roysh, and she actually enjoys me trying to squirm my way out of it.

'I'm just saying . . .'

'*What* are you saying, Ross?'

'Just that.'

'Just what?'

'I mean, it's the whole strength *and* sensitivity thing – that combination. Kind of bloke who could, I don't know, fix your boiler, then write you a poem.'

'Fix your boiler?'

'Doesn't *have* to be a boiler.'

'Then write you a poem?'

'Well, yeah. I mean, you *all* love that, don't you?'

'I don't know – you're obviously the expert.'

'I'm just saying, that's all.'

'I don't think you know what you're saying, Ross.'

'Well, it's, like . . . do you remember that poster? *You*

must have had it. That dude with the big muscles holding the baby. You must have. I've been in a lot of girls' bedrooms over the years – ninety per cent of them had it on the wall.'

'I know the poster you're talking about,' she goes. 'What about it?'

'Well, I saw this documentary about the actual dude in the picture? I mean, he spent his life . . .'

'What?'

'You know . . .'

'I don't – what?'

'Basically banging like a barn door in a hurricane.'

She suddenly cracks her hole laughing. Of course, I'm all embarrassed now as well. She puts her orm around my shoulder and goes, 'You're right, Ross – it's your strength *and* sensitivity that I fell for,' and even I have to laugh then.

I wait outside the Sony Centre because I hate going into shops with birds, especially when they're shopping for themselves.

So I'm standing outside, roysh, basically checking out the forty-inch Bravia in the window, when all of a sudden – *whoof* – my old dear's big pilchard face is suddenly filling every inch of the screen.

I actually take a step backwards, it's *that* horrible to look at. She's bad enough as it is, but you should see her in HD. Someone's focking botoxed her as well – you could fit a coathanger in her mouth sideways – and she's tarted up to the nines as well, the ugly smelt. Monica John has obviously had a visit.

I don't believe it. She's on *The Restaurant*.

For some reason I can suddenly feel my actual blood boil, to the point where I can't even hear what's being said. All

I'm picking up is, like, odd words and phrases. *Not cooking but passion-cooking . . . Food suited to the way you live . . . Lightly blistered halloumi . . .*

She's cooking what I immediately recognize as her Lebanon Ramadan Half Moon Pancakes with peach and plum habanero salsa, and I'm hoping that Doorley dude hates them. Which he won't, of course, because she's an unbelievable cook, the focking Grendel.

Right enough, he ends up milling into them like they're the last bit of food on, I don't know, Earth – and so does the other dude, with the beard.

I even hear the word 'triumph' used once or twice.

Then it's back to the kitchen, where the old dear's already storted on dessert and it's, like, key lime meringue torte by the looks of it.

'I try to cook every day, even when I'm writing,' she goes. 'Actually, I probably should mention that I'm currently working on a new book and it's one that I think has been crying out to be written in this country. It's a love story set against the backdrop of the new multicultural Ireland, focusing on the relationship between Dermot, a truck-driver from, I don't know, Ballybrack or one of those wretched places, and Nadia, a Romany girl who lives with her extended family on a roundabout on the N3 . . .'

While she's saying this, roysh, she's cracking eggs and separating the yolks with her actual hands, letting the slime dribble through her fingers and it looks like – I don't even want to *think* about what it looks like – and worst of all, she's giving these dirty little smiles to the camera, like Nigella Lawson, or a bird from a cheap meat flick.

'So the story will follow their efforts to form a relationship in the face of almost insurmountable social and cultural obstacles. Not to mention basic sanitation.

'Okay, I've sliced the lime in two and now I'm spearing both halves. Now, when you're doing this, don't be afraid to really *disembowel* the lime . . .' and she really drags out the word.

I hear a couple of sniggers behind me and I whip around, roysh, and realize she's drawing a focking audience here. There's, like, six or seven blokes and they've all got dirty big grins on their faces.

'She's a fine thing, isn't she?' I hear one of them – this total bogger – go.

I can't help turning around and going, 'I *hope* you're joking.'

He's like, 'No, beggorah, the woman who writes the bukes – jaysus, she's a fine thing,' and there seems to be, like, general agreement among them that it's true.

'Maybe if you're from Cavan or somewhere. Look at the head on her. When *she* walks into the bank, they turn *off* the cameras.'

She storts mixing the sugar and the egg whites then. And while she's doing it, she gets her dig in about Charlotte McNeel.

'I think too many of our so-called writers have ducked the whole multicultural issue,' she goes. 'But I think as artists we're *required* to look and see that there's a new Ireland, a modern Ireland, with a growing immigrant population, and we must ask ourselves, how can we represent that? I think the one or two writers who have attempted it have gone off and done it half-cocked . . .'

Half-cocked. The lads love that word. They stort yahoo-ing, like they're at a focking GAA match.

'Big mickey lips on her,' one of them goes and before I get a chance to deck him, the old dear suddenly stops mixing and licks the spatula. Not just licks it either – fixes the camera with what she obviously thinks is a sexy look, then puts the entire blade in her mouth and slowly pulls it out, running it down the length of her tongue.

The old Malcolm's doing focking somersaults.

'Are you okay?' a voice suddenly goes. It's Melanie.

I'm there, 'Er, yeah . . .'

'Ross, you're white as a sheet.'

'Think I need some air,' I go. 'Can we get out of here? As in, now?'

What are *they* doing here?

The funny thing is, I can see them asking each other pretty much the same question. 'What's *he* doing here?'

Then *he* comes over, the tosser, in his good Bugatti coat, giving it, 'Well, well, well . . .' and of course loving the sound of his own voice.

I'm there, 'Mr Lalor, how the hell are you?' thinking, you know, it's nice to be nice.

'Much happier now that you're out of my daughter's life,' he goes. 'You know, I really thought I was going to have to kill you to get you away from her. So it's all worked out rather well in the end.'

I give Sorcha's old dear and her granny a wave, thinking, let's keep it civil, but the granny turns her big grey Afro head away in pretty much disgust and the old dear stares straight through me. Then the two of them sit down, about six rows ahead.

'I gather you've been bothering her again,' Sorcha's old man goes, for some reason taking a sudden interest in the tip of his umbrella.

I sort of, like, shift in my seat. 'I'd hordly say *bothering*,' I go. 'I didn't even know she was going to *be* in Ron Blacks. I was pretty hammered as well, in fairness to me. You know me,' I go, still trying to keep it light, 'know the one that's one too many, and make it a double!'

He can't actually believe I'm knocking out one-liners at a time like this.

'You listen to me and listen good,' he goes. 'Family law is what I do, and I do it well. So remember, you're in *my* arena now. And I'm going to ensure you never, *ever* bother our daughter *or* our granddaughter again.'

I'm like, 'Oh, you're going to stop me seeing my kid, are you? Hennessy'll make shit of you before it ever gets to court.' Which is true. Hennessy's an animal when it comes to this sort of shit.

It's fair to say, roysh, that Sorcha's old man has come close to killing me loads of times, but never closer than at that exact moment. He looks over my shoulder and it's like you can hear what he's thinking: too many witnesses.

It's the Berkeley Court, for God's sake.

He eventually focks off to his seat, stopping once or twice to give me major filthies over his shoulder. I go back to my brochure and it's only when I go to turn the page that I realize my hand is, like, shaking – and we're talking big-time shaking here.

I try to concentrate on the various, I don't know, lots, I think they're called. They're flogging off pretty much everything – corpets, paintings, bed linen, even the crockery, but what I want is on page . . .

Suddenly, there's, like, two loud bangs – one after the other. The sound of the dude banging the hammer to stort the auction.

It's a good hour-and-a-half before my lot arrives, by which time Sorcha's old man, I notice, has bought a ninety-six-piece Denby dinner service and a William John Leech original sketch, but lost out – to Michael O'Leary, of all

33

people – on a crystal chandelier styled on the famous Lyman Frank Baum one from the dining room in the Hotel del Coronado, if all that means anything to you, which it doesn't to me.

All I know is the bidding got serious and the dude couldn't take the heat.

'The next item,' the auctioneer goes, 'is a pair of stools from the hotel bar,' and you can tell from the general, like, hubbub in the room that no one's really interested. They're all still talking about the five-figure war they've just seen between two Clongowes old boys over basically a light.

'Do I have fifty euro?' the dude goes and up goes my hand.

He's like, 'Fifty – I have fifty. Do I have any advance on fifty? Seventy – anyone?' and no one stirs.

'Okay, fifty it is,' he goes. 'Sold to the gentleman there in the baseball cap. Going, going . . .'

But then, roysh, at pretty much the last minute, up goes Sorcha's old man's orm. 'Er, one hundred,' he goes and you can see Sorcha's old dear looking at him as if to say basically, *what the fock?*

It's pretty obvious what's going on here. It was the second the goy mentioned my baseball cap.

'A hundred and fifty,' I go.

But then Sorcha's old man raises me another fifty and suddenly there's a serious buzz in the room again.

'Do I hear two hundred and fifty?' and I think about it for a minute and give him the nod.

The focker cranks it up another fifty and I can see Sorcha's old dear turn to him and, like, wave her finger at him, obviously not a happy camper.

People sitting around me are, like, egging me on. 'Go on,' they're going, 'take him,' so I go to three-fifty, but he immediately raises it to four.

He actually turns around in his seat at that point and looks back at me.

'Wipe that focking smile off his face,' someone behind me goes and it sounds very much to me like Michael O'Leary. So I give him the nod for four-fifty.

Then it's five.

Before I know it, the bid is up to nine hundred sheets and all eyes are on me.

It's at that stage, roysh, that I decide to wuss out. Seriously, I wouldn't pay the guts of a grandington for two stools even if Hilary Duff and Lindsay Lohan sat on them knickerless.

Having said that, one of the things that made me potentially the greatest Irish out-half ever back in the day was my ability to spot openings that didn't appear to be there. I look at Sorcha's old dear and she's getting ready to stand up.

'Nine hundred euro *is* the bid,' the goy goes. 'Do I hear nine hundred and fifty?'

'Keep going,' people are whispering to me. 'What's fifty quid to anyone?'

'Do I hear nine hundred and fifty?' the goy goes.

'Go on! Do it!'

But I don't move a muscle. I sit perfectly still and remember the concentration exercises I used to do, back when I made penalty kicking look as easy as a BESS fresher with two vodka-and-cranberries in her.

I manage to block out everything and everyone in the room – the auctioneer, the clamour, the pressure – everything except Sorcha's old dear, who I watch closely as she rises, in slow motion . . .

'Nine hundred euro *is* the price.'

. . . then helps Sorcha's granny up out of her seat.

'Nine hundred euro for the final time?'

Timing is everything here.

'Nine hundred euro . . .'

Sorcha's granny links her and they make their way out of the row, with apologies to everyone for having to move their knees. Sorcha's old man follows them with his eyes. His mind is no longer on the game. His wife is . . .

'Going . . .'

Out the door. And he'll find her, sulking in the 7 Series, the two of them, her *and* her old dear, madder than a barefoot woman in a roomful of rocking chairs.

'Going . . .'

Not worth it, he's thinking, as he takes a look at them disappearing out the door, both with a strop on. Not worth the Hoff. Aggravation times two. Surround-sound nagging all the way back to the Vico. So what does the hot-shot divorce lawyer do?

He pisses his pants.

Well, not *actually*? He stands up. The second he does, I shout, 'Nine hundred and fifty,' and suddenly there's this, like, spontaneous round of applause. It's not usually allowed, but people can't help it – what can I say, they appreciate a player with the big-match temperament.

Sorcha's old man stops in the aisle and for a second he thinks about getting back in the game. But he knows it's over. He shoots me one last filthy – a big-time one – then he's out the focking door.

I can honestly say, roysh, I haven't felt an adrenalin rush like it since I lifted the Leinster Schools Senior Cup. People are coming up to me and they're all, like, high-fiving me and whatever else.

The next thing, roysh, I feel this hand on my back and this voice goes, 'I see you haven't lost the fire.'

I whip around and it's, like, Sean Dunne. He was always

a big supporter of mine. Used to go to all the games. He told my old man he stuck a grand on in the bookies that I'd be playing for Ireland before my twenty-first birthday.

Actually, I hope he doesn't want that money back.

'Your father's stool,' he goes. 'You know, many's the night I stuck my head into the bar at last orders and there Charles would be, sat with Hennessy, putting the world to rights. At a thousand decibels, of course.'

'Doesn't sound like them,' I go and we both just crack our holes laughing.

'Did he ever tell you about Frank Sinatra?' he goes and I end up nearly collapsing on the spot.

'I thought it was, like, horseshit?'

'Oh, no,' he goes. 'I was there that night – I saw it.'

And he tells me the story, word for word the way my old man told it.

Ten minutes later I'm out in the cor pork and I'm loading the two stools into the boot of an Andy McNab.

I hear *her* before I see *him*. What I hear is, 'Edmund! Don't do anything stupid!'

'Oh, don't worry,' he goes. 'This little ... *rodent* isn't worth that!'

Sorcha's old man's back for afters.

'I've always liked a good loser,' I end up going, not even knowing where it came from. 'You're possibly the greatest loser I've ever known.'

I see his fists just, like, tighten and it's taking every bit of strength he has to stop himself from, like, throwing a dig at me.

'Something's about to happen that's going to wipe that smile off your face,' he goes. 'Permanently.'

I'm like, 'Oh, yeah – as in?'

'Edmund!' *she* goes.

I'm there, 'Tell me.'

But he doesn't. He just goes, 'You'll find out. Soon enough.'

I'm in the gaff, roysh, watching Seoige and O'Shea really getting into this report they had on this nine-year-old victim of a happy slapping who was helped out of a coma by *X Factor* finalists The Conway Sisters.

It's actually pretty moving and I'm still thinking about it, roysh, when they come back from the ad break and announce that they've been joined this afternoon by Ireland's newest popular fiction sensation, the girl who's been described as the new Fionnuala O'Carroll-Kelly – our very own Charlotte McNeel.

And there she suddenly is, full of smiles, great Peter Pan, her humungous chuffed-to-bits hanging out of her silver Mandalay dress, which I happen to know – from personal experience – goes very well with the corpet in this bedroom.

'Charlotte,' Grainne goes, 'you're very welcome.'

'Turn on RTÉ,' I shout at the top of my voice. 'Lance's new girlfriend is on,' and back comes the old dear's response. 'I'm *watching*!' she goes, pissed off before the girl's even been asked a question.

'*Indian Summer*,' Grainne goes, 'your debut novel, has rocketed to the top of the Irish bestseller list. Without obviously giving too much away, tell us a little bit about it,' which is what Charlotte does and it has to be said, roysh, it's a little bit like that *Love Actually*, in that the more you think about it, the worse it actually gets.

'She's really raised the bor,' I go, loud enough for the stupid wrasse to hear. She doesn't answer.

'Now,' Grainne goes, obviously about to bring up something a bit, I suppose, sensitive, 'your success has apparently pricked at least one ego. One or two bitchy comments made about you. It's all happened for you at such a young age – you're still only twenty-four. How do cope with something like that?'

Charlotte just, like, flicks her hair, like she doesn't actually give a shit, and goes, 'Em, I take those kind of comments as a back-handed compliment, really. I think if other writers feel threatened by me, it means I must be doing something right.'

'Focking brilliant!' I shout.

Did I mention that she looks like Holly Marie Combs?

'Let's be specific here,' Grainne goes, 'I read an interview with – I think I can say it – Fionnuala O'Carroll-Kelly, in which she described young writers who were a bit green but who were, as she put it, making all the right mistakes for people with no real life experience. How do you respond to that?'

'I take the high road,' she goes. 'I have no feelings, ill or otherwise, towards Fionnuala. She's the other side of fifty and she's probably conscious of the fact that she only has a limited number of years left and she has to earn what she can now.'

I'm like, 'Whoa – that'll hurt, come winter!'

'Might even be hormonal,' she goes. 'It'd be wrong to judge her. I haven't been through the menopause – I don't know what it's like.'

'I should have married that focking girl!' I shout.

That's it.

I whip out the old Wolfe and I leave her a voice message, telling her basically fair focks to her, the stupid sow had it coming to her and, by the way, just in case you want to slip it into your next interview, she's on the old Leptoprin –

we're talking two hundred yoyos a bottle – to try to lose some of the fat off her orse. 'Well done,' I go again.

I go out onto the landing and give the old dear's door a good bang. 'That put you in your focking box, didn't it?'

But she doesn't say anything. All I can hear is the sound of her crying, the attention-seeker that she is.

2. Better off without a wife

What's the focking deal with the cutlery? The old man and Hennessy are always raving about Guilbaud's, but what would it take for them to put the forks on the table the right way up?

Bernard reads my mind.

'Zees ees how ze French aristocracy lay ze table,' he goes. 'Ze forks wiz ze tines down. You see, zey live een many palaces and zey move from one to zee uzzer. Every night, perhaps, a deeferent table. So it ees always laid in zees way. Zen when zey arrive, zey turn ze fork up – like zees.'

He's so intelligent, but at the same time so cool? It's, like, a really random thing to say, but I wish my old man was more like him.

'How ees your son and your daughter?' he goes, actually interested in *me*?

I'm there, 'Ronan's worried about this new superinten-dent they've got out his way. Honor's great, though. She's up on two feet now, although you have to actually hold her when she walks. Unbelievably intelligent as well. Fock, listen to me – I said I'd never become one of those fathers who can only talk about his kids.'

'I have two girls from my first marriage. Ees very special bond between a fazzer and a daughter, yes?'

'Big time,' I go. 'I'm only learning.'

He's like, 'My wife, Conchita. She lose her fazzer when she ees a leetle girl – very sad.'

'Conchita?'

'Yes, she ees from Spain.'

A bowl of ice cream is suddenly put in front of me. I haven't even had my Atlantic turbot yet.

'Zees ees basil ice cream,' he goes, 'for freshening of ze palate. So, you are excited about zis challenge we have for you, yes?'

I'm there, 'Very. I wish it was, like, tomorrow. I'm pretty bored at the moment. Feel like I'm just killing time. Getting myself into trouble – story of my life, blah blah blah!'

Bernard smiles. 'Eet will come soon enough,' he goes. Then he reaches for his briefcase at his feet. He whips it open and puts, like, three DVDs down on the table.

'For now, you can look at zees. Some of our matches – against Luxemboorg, Leethuania and Toulouse second team. You can see, we are not so bad. For you I have also wreeten a leest of ze players and zer positions and a leetle beet of background on zem.'

I'm there, 'Cool.'

'Remember,' he goes, 'we are not asking for meeracles. Ze long-term aim for Andorra ees World Cup qualification in perhaps twelve years. For now we just look to eemprove.'

I'm there, 'Cool. By the way, I'm pretty grateful to you for, like, coming over here to see me. I know how busy you are.'

'Well,' he goes, suddenly slapping his two hands together, 'I have uzzer reason to be een Dubleen and I tell you now. What do you theenk if I say to you zat Ireland will come to Andorra to play a game?'

He can tell by my Ricky Gervais what I think because he quickly goes, 'Not a fool team – we are not ready for zat, I understend. But Ireland A . . .'

I can feel my hort actually quicken.

I'm like, 'When?'

'On ze last day of December.'

'As in, like, New Year's Eve?'

'Zis afternoon, I met wiz ze great Michael Bradley . . .'

I'm like, 'Jesus – did he say anything about me? Just to warn you, he wouldn't be a fan, always thought I was too fond of the syrup.'

'He has nussing but kind words for you,' Bernard goes, 'as a player and as a coach. He says Ezzie O'Sullivan also has a lot of respect for you, going to anuzzer country, like he deed wiz George to learn hees trade.'

I'm like, 'Seriously?'

'Yes. So ze IRFU, zey call me a week ago and zey say zey want to feet an extra game into ze calendar before ze Seeks Nations. One or two players ze coaching staff are not so sure about wiz ze feetness. One or two uzzers zey would like to take a look at to see are zey up to it.'

I do, like, a rough calculation. I don't get my team until the second week in November, which only gives me, like, seven weeks.

It's amazing, though. I should be kacking it, but I'm actually excited.

'I sought you would be,' Bernard goes. 'Zees game, it ees nussing for Ireland. For us, eet ees quite seemply ze beegest game in our eestory.'

I'm sitting in Buckys, roysh, having a coffee and listening to two Drummies talk about what a total bitch Aednat is for taking Caoilainn off her list of top five friends on MySpace.

And I'm looking at Honor, thinking, it's all ahead of you, girl.

It's then that I suddenly spot, like, Fionn and JP in the queue, the steamers. I'm shouting over to them, roysh, but they can't hear me over the sound of the contemporary

Andean panpipes and anyway, they're deep in conversation – presumably going, oh, I saw a lovely flower the other day.

Eventually, Fionn thinks he sees me, at least he's looking in my direction with his face screwed up. You'd have to wonder do those glasses even work.

Then I see him mouth the words, 'There's Ross!' and suddenly they're over with their, I don't know, honey lattes or whatever and it's high-fives all round.

'We're landscaping a garden down near Wesley College,' JP goes. 'Except the woman's driving us mad. Two and a half acres, she has. A good space, but she just can't decide on a theme and stick to it.'

Fionn borrows JP's stirrer. 'One day it's minimalist,' he goes. 'Then she goes and buys all these water features. The next day she's given them all to her sister and she wants a wooded garden . . .'

He stirs his coffee.

'Women!' I go. 'They couldn't find their focking orses in the bath! So, like, you're actually *working* at this now? It's not, like, a hobby?'

'No,' JP goes, looking at Fionn, 'we're partners now, aren't we?'

It's obviously the first time it's been said because Fionn suddenly looks delighted. I suppose it's, like, what else is he going to do with his life? He's got that many qualifications, he's fock-all use to anyone.

'I would never have believed how much I'd enjoy working out of doors,' he goes. 'And there's a great sense of fulfilment in taking a piece of ordinary land and turning it into an actual living space.'

An actual living space – you never heard shit like that before the SSIA.

'Look at the size of *her*,' JP suddenly goes, leaning down

and picking Honor out of her stroller. He's good with kids, JP. His sister – the one who looks like Jennifer Meyer – she's got one, a girl as well, I'm pretty sure. 'Ross, the last time I saw her she was a helpless little bundle. Now she's, like, a little person. Aren't you?' he goes to her. 'Yes, you are!'

I'm there, 'And that's in, like, a matter of months. Every weekend I see her, it's like there's something different about her, some new trick she does that I haven't seen before. They're amazing at that age.'

JP stands her up on the floor and she holds onto the table and lets, I suppose, a delighted squeal out of her, getting the attention of the Drummies at the next table, who say *oh my God* a few times, then tell me that her Juicy Baby clobber is *so* cute.

'Kids are amazing at any age,' JP goes. 'Look at your Ronan,' and we suddenly stort reminiscing about that Saturday a couple of years ago when we took him to Herbert Pork, just to, like, throw a rugby ball around. Of course, Ro gets bored after, like, five minutes and it ends up being just me and JP, practising our passing, discovering that the old magic's still there, while Ro sits on a bench talking to passers-by. It was only afterwards we found out that he was cracking on – to total strangers, remember – that we were a gay couple who'd adopted him.

'I don't have a mommy,' he'd say with that sweet and innocent look he does so well. 'I have two daddies.' Then he'd point at us.

It's still hilarious, even now. The three of us are practically on the floor laughing here. There's no doubt he's going to make a great big brother for this little one.

Fionn asks me what I'm up to tomorrow night, as in Sunday? I tell him I'm doing fock-all. Melanie, her sister and

two of her friends have gone on a painting holiday to Andalusia. It's funny how I'm always attracted to the orty type. Sorcha won a Special Merit Award in the Texaco competition at school for a picture of a seal with its head basically caved in, and a speech bubble out of its mouth, going, 'Why?'

'It's Aoife's three-month anniversary,' he goes. 'Her mum's asked me round, but I find it a bit . . .'

'Awkward?'

'Yeah, on my own. I just find it easier if it's a thing for friends.'

We haven't always seen eye to eye, but deep down he knows I'd actually do anything for him. I'm like, 'Dude, I'm there.'

JP suddenly grabs the top of my orm. 'Ross!' he goes, sending the total shits up me. 'Quick!'

I look up, roysh, to see Honor walking, as in *actually* walking, not holding onto the edge of the table, but taking her first steps, without anyone holding her hand. We're all suddenly quiet, roysh, because she's obviously pretty unsteady on her feet and we're scared that if she hears our voices, she'll get excited and fall over. She's actually heading for the Drummies. I whip out my phone and stort filming it because this is, like, a huge moment in her life and I actually feel guilty that Sorcha's missing it.

She walks five, six, seven steps and suddenly the Drummies stort encouraging her on, going, '*Oh* my God, come *on*! You're *so*, like, nearly there?'

She eventually makes it and I run straight over to pick her up and tell her how proud of her I am. I'm pretty sure I have actual tears in my eyes.

'Aw, look at her little cordigan,' one of the Drummies goes, 'it's like the pink terry tracksuit top that Iseult brought

48

Melissa back from the States,' and I'm just there thinking, these are the days.

'Wow,' Sorcha goes.

But it's weird, roysh, because it doesn't sound like she means it?

I tell her I wish she could have been there, then I hit replay, but she doesn't even look at it the second time around.

'We should show this to her on her eighteenth birthday,' I go and she smiles like it's a big effort.

But I shouldn't be too hord on her. Aoife was her friend since they were, like, five years old. It must be tough for her being in the gaff, seeing her old pair, seeing pictures of her everywhere and *her* not being here.

Oisinn walks into the sitting room. 'Some mover, isn't she?' he goes. I've made him watch it, like, ten or eleven times. 'She'll play rugby for Ireland one day.'

I'm like, 'Whoa!' because I'm not having that. 'She's *way* too good-looking. It'll be hockey or nothing, right, Sorcha?'

She doesn't answer me.

'I need to talk to you about something,' she suddenly goes. 'As in, outside?' and every conversation in the room suddenly stops.

Sorcha leads me out of the room, through the kitchen and out into the back gorden, where the girls are standing around in the freezing cold in just T-shirts, smoking Marlboro Lights.

A bird called Doireann is telling Chloe and Sophie that Coldplay's lyrics are *actually* really political, if you listen to them. Chloe and Sophie don't seem to *give* a shit one way or the other? When they see us, they immediately go back into the house, like they know what's going down.

49

'Aoife's mum's aged about ten years,' I go. 'I mean, she lived through ten years of her daughter, I don't know, not eating. And then at end of it . . . I suppose none of us can imagine what it feels like to lose a daughter.'

'Cillian and I are going to America,' she goes, straight out with it, just like that.

I'm like, 'America? America as in the States?'

'America as in California,' she goes.

I'm there, 'For a holiday?'

She takes a sudden interest in the patio furniture cover, smoothing the – I think – polyester down with the palm of her hand. 'Cillian's been offered a twelve-month secondment, learning the ropes from the director of internal audit and risk management over there . . .'

'Twelve *months*?'

'It's a really good opportunity for him to skill up in the areas of engagement management expertise and client relationship . . .'

I'm there, 'I hope you don't think you're taking Honor?'

She gives me the big cow eyes, roysh, obviously thinking she can sweet-talk me here.

I'm like, 'I have rights, you know.'

'I *do* know,' she goes. 'I can't do anything without your agreement. But I'm asking you to be understanding, Ross. To be reasonable . . .'

I'm there, 'Oh, it's suddenly *reasonable* to watch your wife and kid be taken off to some other country by some focking –'

'Whoa!' she goes – because Sorcha can turn just like that. 'You don't have *any* say in whether *I* go or not. I'm your wife in name only . . .'

I suddenly remember something. 'This is what your old man meant.'

'Ross . . .'

'At the auction, last week. He said something was going to happen that'd wipe the smile off my face.'

'He hates you, Ross. There's no surprise there . . .'

'Chloe, Sophie, Amie, they obviously knew, too. So when are you going?' I go. And then I'm like, 'Sorry, when do you *think* you're going?'

She can't even look me in the eye. She's like, 'The second of October.'

'The second of October? That's . . .'

'Tomorrow week.'

'Tomorrow week? Oh, I get it – keep me in the dork until the very last minute – no discussion, nothing – until there's pretty much fock-all I can do about it. *His* idea, I presume – focking auditor.'

'There's more,' she goes.

'*More?* So what else?'

She fixes me with a look I recognize from that course she did in the Michael Smurfit School of Business a few years ago on how to deliver bad news. Then she goes, 'I want a divorce.'

A divorce? I must say it, like, ten times before I eventually go, 'Are things really that bad?'

She's like, 'They're really that over,' but not in, like, a bitchy way?

I end up just, like, staring into space, not knowing what to say, trying to, I suppose, arrange my thoughts.

See, last week I went for a bit of physio, deciding that if I'm going to be taking training sessions in Andorra, I'm going to have to get my famous *ligamentum nuchae* problems sorted once and for all.

I was in the waiting room, roysh, bored out of my tree and, believe it or not, I storted *reading*, as in one of the magazines – *Time* or one of those – and there was this, like, orticle in it about Steve Wynn, the billionaire casino-owner and hammer man – a man after my own hort, basically.

It said in the orticle that he rang Donald Trump up one day and went, 'I just want you to know – my wife and I are getting divorced.'

Of course, Donald Trump was like, 'Hey, I'm sorry to hear that,' but Steve Wynn was there, 'Hey, don't be sorry. It's cool – we're still madly in love. We just don't want to be married any more.'

So five years later the two goys bump into each other in Vegas and Steve Wynn goes, 'Hey, did you hear – Elaine and I are getting remarried?'

So obviously Donald Trump was there, 'Oh – what about the divorce?'

And Steve Wynn goes, 'Oh that – well, it just didn't work out.'

I thought me and Sorcha were going to be like that.

I'm there, 'What are you going to do in the States?' which I suppose means I'm not going to stand in her way. 'For, like, work and shit?'

'Well, I'm not *going* to work?' she goes. 'I'm going to be, like, a full-time mum? And I'm going to use the year as, like, a fact-finding opportunity. I'm thinking of restyling the boutique along the lines of Kitson – as in Kitson in Los Angeles? It's where they *all* shop – Heidi Montag, Katharine McPhee, Vanessa Minnillo . . .'

For no reason at all, roysh, I just burst into tears, we're talking proper, full-on crying here. Sorcha just, like, throws her orms around me and sort of, like, cradles my head to her chest. I'm crying that way you cry when you're a kid – you know when you're trying to talk, but you can't, like, catch your breath to string the words together and it comes out as, like, hiccups?

'I just . . . want things . . . to go back . . . to the way they . . . weeeere.'

'Ross, that's never going to happen,' she goes, stroking the back of my neck, like she always used to when I'd get, like, stressed about shit. 'You've got to look forward now. Ross, if what happened to Aoife convinced me of anything, it's that life is, like, *Oh! My God!* We don't have a minute to waste on this Earth . . .'

'I'm pretty . . . sure I can . . . change.'

'We owe it to ourselves to go out there and chase our dreams, whatever they may be – whether it's teaching Pilates or moving to the country to set up a rare-breeds farm . . .'

And maybe that's what's upset me – hearing her talk like that and knowing that if she'd mentioned Kitson when she was still with me, I'd have gone, 'What a waste of time,' and crushed all the focking joy out of her, like I always did.

I pull back and I look at her and go, 'You said you'd *always* love me.' It comes out all whiny.

'We both said a lot of things,' she goes.

I'm there, 'Look me in the eye and tell me you don't love me,' which is a bit *Grey's Anatomy*, I know.

But she does it. Or actually she looks me in the eye and goes, 'I *do* love you, Ross – but in the same way that I love . . .' then she looks towards the house and goes, 'Yeah, Coldplay. It's easy to say, but there's no real passion involved.'

I nod. I finally get it.

I stand up and wipe away the tears with my palm. 'I'm not going to stand in your way,' I go. 'With anything. America. The divorce. Whatever . . .'

'I'm not an iceberg,' she goes. 'I know what I'm asking

you here – I'm asking you to give up twelve months of your daughter's life . . .'

'I've, er, got to go.'

'Thank you, Ross.'

I'm there, 'Say goodbye to Aoife's old pair for me, will you?'

Twenty minutes later I'm back home and I'm lying on my bed, all this shit going round and round in my head. What if I'd been more like this? What if I'd been more like that?

I pick up the remote and stort flicking through the channels. Some cracking-looking bird mentions that a graphic side-parting perfectly complements this season's return to minimalism, but I'm barely able to take in the words.

I think about ringing Melanie, roysh, but no bird wants to hear you banging on when she's away with her mates, especially when it's about your ex.

I look at the two bar stools I bought, in the corner of the room, and I suddenly lose it.

I jump up and grab one, by the back. I lift it up over my head, then smash it against the wall.

Two legs snap off.

Then I slam it off the floor.

The other two break off.

I'm suddenly feeling a lot better.

I pick up the other stool and do the same.

Thwack!

Snaps like a focking twig.

Then I kick all the pieces into the corner of the room. Good for fock-all now except firewood.

It's twelve o'clock in the afternoon and I'm in the sack, eating Cinnamon Grahams straight from the box and deep in, I suppose, contemplation about the events of last night, when all of a sudden the Wolfe rings and a little voice on the end of the line goes, 'Rosser – I want to arrange a meet.'

That's one of the things I love about Ro – you'd never be down for long.

I'm there, 'Cool – as in where?' and he goes, 'Not over the blower, it's a party line,' which is working class for the Gords are listening in, which obviously they're not. 'There's a phone buke on the hall table downstairs – go and get it.'

I do what he tells me.

Then he goes, 'There's a page toorned down,' which there is.

The page is, like, pubs and restaurants and he's drawn, like, a big circle with red morker around the name of this café on, like, Capel Street.

I'm there, 'How the fock did you get in here to do this, by the way?' but he just goes, 'Loose lips, Rosser . . . one o'clock.'

I'm there, 'Mariah Carey,' as in, I'll be there.

He's waiting for me when I arrive, sitting at the table furthest from the door. 'Don't want any fooken window-shoppers sussing us,' he goes. 'Know what I'm saying?'

I'm pretty sure a window-shopper is, like, an undercover cop?

I catch the eye of the waitress, who's seriously shmugly in case you're wondering, but, weirdly, has an incredible orse, like two scoops of butterscotch ice cream, shrink-wrapped. Two full brekkies, I tell her.

There's, like, something different about Ronan, something I can't put my finger on, but, after listening to him ranting about police harassment and the CCTV state for twenty minutes, I finally cop what it is . . .

He's got, like, gel in his hair and he's wearing aftershave, a brand that – from my brief knowledge of working-class people and their smells – is called *Blue Stratos*.

I know what's coming even before he says it.

'I'm after meeting a boord,' he goes.

I end up actually punching the air and going, '*Yes!*' as in, chip off the old block. 'You're a sly old dog, aren't you?'

For maybe the first time since I met him, he actually gets embarrassed. He's going, 'Ah, leave it, Rosser – will you?' which makes a change, because it's usually *him* humiliating *me*.

Two breakfasts arrive. I don't know what's uglier – the waitress or what's on the plate.

'So come on,' I go, 'who is she?'

He's there, 'Her name's Blathin.'

I'm like, 'Blathin?' having expected him to say, I don't know, Tracy or Natlee or Shadden. 'Blathin? Where would *you* meet a bird like that?'

'Ah, she's in Mount Anville, so she is. The junior school and that. See, we're doing *West Side Story* with them – modorden day, set in Blanchardstown.'

I'm there, 'Blanchardstown? Jesus!'

'I'm Tony – part was fooken made for me. Blathin's playing Maria. Here, she's from out your neck of the woods. Clonskeagh.'

So I'm sitting there suddenly thinking, oh my God, I know he's only ten, but is it time to have the chat – as in, *the* chat, as in the *actual* chat?

I mean, it's important that kids are given the facts, so that when they grow up they have a responsible attitude to sex and they also know what's what and don't end up, I don't know, trying to stick it in a bird's ear or some shit.

I go, 'Ronan, when a goy meets a bird . . . okay, a man gets his mickey –' but he cuts me off and he goes, 'Rosser,

56

if you knew the foorst thing about the boords and the bees, then I wouldn't be here today,' which is basically true – bang out of order, but true.

He goes, 'Don't sweat it, man, they teach you all that shit in Biology now – a spoorm cell swims through the cervix and across the uterus and fuses with the ovum to form a zygote –'

I'm there, 'TMI, Ronan! T! M! I! I don't know if you've noticed, but I'm actually *trying* to eat a fried egg here?'

Jesus, what was wrong with the way we learned it? It's a man's occupation to stick his coculation up a woman's ventilation to increase the population of the younger generation of this world . . .

I'm like, 'So if it's not the big fatherly chat you're looking for, what am I actually doing here?'

'I just wanted to let you know,' he goes, 'in case you read it in the *Wurdled* on Sunday . . . Rosser, I'm going straight.'

I'm like, 'No!' just playing along with him. 'No way!'

'Afraid so,' he goes. 'Keeping the old snout clean from now on.'

It's at that point that I probably should tell him about Sorcha and Honor, but I can't. Can't burst his bubble. Not today. Instead I ask the question that's been on my mind since he mentioned Clonskeagh. 'Have her old pair met you yet?'

'Yeah,' he goes. 'Why?'

'And they're actually cool with you going out with their daughter, are they?'

He looks at me like I've just dropped here from, I don't know, another planet. 'Are they *cool* with it?'

I'm there, 'No, I just wondered are they . . .'

'Are they what?'

What I really mean to say is – are they like my old pair?

But in the end I don't say anything, just go, 'Are they nice?'

'Sound as a pound,' he goes. 'But I need to ask you a little favour.'

I'm there, 'If it's going bail for one of your mates, you can forget it. What was that last goy called?'

'Apples.'

'Apples! What a focking name! And where is Apples now?'

'Sudurden Hemisphere's all I'm prepared to say.'

'Yeah, while I'm down twenty Ks.'

'Rosser, you'll get it back. With interest. Anyway, it's not bread I'm after. I was wondering – Saturday, what are you up to?'

I'm there, 'Er, watching the Magners League, I presume. Think Munster are playing Ulster. Why?'

'I was wondering would you bring me and Blathin out to Blanch?' he goes.

'Fock, Ro – why would you want to go out there? It's lawless.'

He doesn't flinch. 'Look, my face is well known out there,' he goes. 'Blathin wants to see it, but. Help her get into character.'

'Could she not just watch *Crimecall*?'

'Ah, this drama teacher of hers said she really needs to reccy it for herself. Help find her motivation for the part.'

I look at his little face – with the Indian-ink spot under his left eye – and I know I can't say no to him.

'I'll take the old dear's cor,' I go and he's like, 'Nice one, Rosser.'

I look down. He hasn't touched his breakfast. I nod at it and go, 'The trick is, Ro, to eat it before the fat congeals on the plate.'

'I can't eat,' he goes.

Can't eat. Can't stop smiling.

We've all been there.

'What are all these test tubes for? I thought this thing was, like, a Divorce Fair?'

Oisinn pretty much snatches the box out of my hands. 'It *is*,' he goes. 'We're going to have a stand there offering, like, paternity tests. There's a dude coming over from the States to do it. Knows his shit as well – he used to work for Maurie,' which I suppose *is* pretty impressive.

But there's me, slower than Mass, going, 'Why paternity tests, though?'

He holds his hand up to, like, silence me while he counts the tubes in the box. Sixty-four. When he's finished, he goes, 'Have you any idea how much money you can save yourself in the divorce courts if you can prove your partner committed adultery? Dude, we're talking the equivalent of a thirty-year mortgage here . . .'

'Whoa,' I go, making all the right noises, roysh, but to be honest all this talk of divorce is putting me on a major downer.

I jump down out of the back of the Transit and wipe the dust off the front of my chinos. Oisinn hands me down three boxes, stacked on top of each other.

I'm like, 'So where am I going with these, then?'

'Around the back,' he goes. 'I'm going to store everything in the utility room until they're ready for us.'

Oisinn's new gaff is humungous, we're talking eight bedrooms, we're talking indoor pool, we're talking gym, home cinema, hot tub, blahdy blahdy blah.

He's supposed to have outbid Denis O'Brien for it.

I put the boxes down in a corner furthest from the door. Oisinn comes in behind me. 'Twenty years ago, if someone had said the words "marital infidelity",' he goes, 'you'd have thought of a man caught up to his nuts in the babysitter,' and then he suddenly stops, obviously remembering who he's talking to. 'Ross, I'm sorry,' he goes.

I'm there, 'Dude – ain't no thing but a chicken wing.'

He shakes his head. 'Me and my big Von. I'm so caught up in this thing, I keep forgetting . . .'

'Oisinn,' I go, 'what happened with Sorcha was my own stupid fault. I don't want people tiptoeing around me.'

He looks at me, Scoobious.

'Seriously,' I go. 'Tell me.'

'You don't mind? Because I'm on *Nationwide* talking about this tomorrow – want to get it straight in my head.'

'I want to hear it.'

'Well,' he goes, 'what I was going to say was, these days there's as many married women putting it about as married men. And the post-industrial work environment practically encourages it. See, house prices mean it's now necessary to have not one but two breadwinners in the home. The last ten to fifteen years have seen the labour market in this country flooded with women. And along with that, we've seen the increasing socialization of the workplace . . .'

It goes without saying that he lost me at post-industrial.

'In that environment, the potential for infidelity is huge. All those boozy lunches, leaving dos, summer softball matches, office barbecues – so many opportunities to consummate whatever's been brewing at the coffee station between the woman who no longer has sex with her husband and the team leader in accounts payable . . .'

He's the one with the gaff on Shrewsbury Road and twenty-eight million snots in the bank – who am I to argue with him?

I follow him back to the van.

He's like, 'It's depressing, I know. But will I tell you what's even more depressing? Last year, five thousand men in this country celebrated the birth of babies that weren't even theirs. That's according to this expert Erika's got coming over from Dundee.'

I'm like, 'Five thousand? Fock!'

'Yeah, he does this non-invasive method of testing. Does it from photographs – studies shit like earlobes, widow's peaks, cleft chins. He's got, like, a ninety-eight per cent accuracy rate.'

He hands me three more boxes, then goes, 'We'd better get these put away and the old Gloria Este off the road. Wouldn't imagine they see too many of these around here.'

Just as I'm turning with the boxes, roysh, there's a sudden screech of tyres behind me. At first I presume it's the Feds, tipped off by one of the neighbours that there's, like, a Tiger kidnapping in progress. But when I whip around it turns out it's, like, Fionn and JP and they're in – wait for it – *another* white Transit.

'Snap!' JP goes out the window.

Snap is right. Jesus, we'll all be wearing toolbelts and listening to Christy Moore if this keeps up.

The goys get out of the van. Working outdoors, it has to be said, really suits them. I never knew either of them to have muscles before.

I'm like, 'What are you two doing here?' as we all exchange high-fives.

'Some old dude,' JP goes, 'retiring from the British Embassy, he wants us to build him a traditional English country gorden.'

I'm there, 'As in?' and I'm immediately sorry I asked.

He's like, 'Roses. Hydrangeas. A birdhouse. One or two stone sculptures . . .'

'Representative rather than abstract,' Fionn suddenly pipes up.

'Definitely. Some nice wooden fencing. Aged brick pathways. Or maybe pea gravel . . .'

'I think the furniture should be all floral fabrics.'

'Oh, no question . . .'

I'm like, 'Fock's sake, you two – get a room,' which they both laugh at, in fairness to them.

'I, er, heard about Sorcha,' Fionn goes.

I just shrug my shoulders. 'No skin off my nose,' I go. 'To be honest, it was getting a bit, I don't know, claustrophobic with her breathing down my neck all the time, wanting to know what I'm doing, who I'm being with, blahdy blahdy blah. She needed to move on.'

He nods. They all nod.

'As in, I hate that feeling of being watched all the time?'

The words are only out of my mouth, roysh, when some old dude, who obviously lives on the road, storms up to us, points at one Transit, then the other and goes, 'There'll be a residents meeting about this.'

I don't know what I was expecting. You build a picture up in your head and then . . .

She's pretty. That goes without saying. Wouldn't expect anything else from a son of mine. I suppose she's like a ten-year-old Ashley Olsen. And polite. Whatever you say about Mounties, they're always *so* polite.

The thing that almost stopped my hort when I turned off the Clonskeagh Road into Wynnsward Park and saw the two of them waiting there on the side of the road was the fact that Blathin was in, like, a wheelchair.

Of course it's not a big deal and I didn't make one out

of it. She can't walk. It's, like, so what? I think what really – I suppose – touched me was that Ronan never mentioned it, like it wasn't even relevant to him?

Ro makes the introductions. She calls me *Mister* O'Carroll-Kelly, roysh, and I tell her it makes me sound way too much like my old man, which believe me is a bad thing, so she should call me Ross. 'I'm Blathin,' she goes and I shake her little hand.

Before I ask how we're going to do this thing, Ronan bends down, lifts her out of the chair and nods at me and pushes the front passenger seat back a few more inches. Then he puts her in it and asks her if she's okay and she tells him she's mustard, which is a nice touch. He folds up the chair in, like, five seconds flat and puts it in the boot of the Lexus, and I don't even bother telling him to be careful of the old dear's golf clubs.

It's only as I'm turning the key that I notice Blathin's old pair in the gorden, waving us off, and straight away I'm thinking, why couldn't *they* have driven them out to Blanchardstown? They've only got a focking Prius.

Having said that, it's actually nice to get to meet Ronan's first girlfriend. First of many – providing, of course, Tina's telling the truth and he really *is* my actual son.

'So, Blathin,' I go, when we're well on the M50, 'you're a Mountie, yeah? I'd say you know all about my rep, then?'

She just nods.

I'm like, 'Uh-oh – go on, what have you heard?'

She looks at me – sweet little face – and goes, 'The school had to go to the High Court to get an injunction to ban you from the debs . . .'

'Guilty!' I go. 'Yeah, one or two incidents from previous years that I could tell you about, except you're too young.'

I'll tell you what – for ten, she knows her shit.

'Ah, thanks Bla,' Ro suddenly goes. 'You didn't have to, but.'

I look in the rear-view and I see him with wrapping paper. She must have bought him a present.

'I remember you said you liked it,' she goes, 'that day in McDonald's in Stillorgan?'

I'm there, 'What is it, Ro?'

'Er, you wouldn't have heard of it,' he goes, trying to hide it from me.

Blathin turns to me and she's like, 'Can we put it on?' so it must be, like, a CD? She asks him for it, roysh, and because it's *her*, he hands it over straight away, then she sticks it in the CD player.

James Blunt.

I'm thinking, Ronan, you little focking smoothie.

You're beautiful, you're beautiful, you're beautiful, it's true . . .

I'm there, 'I'd say the boys like this as well, do they, Ro?'

He's like, 'What?'

'Nudger. Gull. Buckets of Blood. All big fans?'

He doesn't answer – got a big redner on him.

'I can play this song on the piano,' Blathin goes.

I'm there, 'You play the piano?' although I shouldn't be surprised. Mount Anville *are* big on, like, extra-curricular shit? I remember in transition year Sorcha did Mandarin and furniture restoration.

'Oh my God,' she goes, sounding suddenly scared, 'it's getting dorker.'

I tell her it's because I've just taken the exit for Blanchardstown and Ro puts his hand on her shoulder and tells her not to worry. Nothing's going to happen to her because thee'd have to go through him foorst and that seems to, like, reassure her.

Does fock-all for me, though. I'm actually kacking it, my knuckles gripping the steering-wheel horder as I watch the landscape change through the windscreen. There's people playing soccer everywhere. Focked fridges dumped at the side of the road. Grown women in tracksuits sitting on walls, eating chips out of bags.

We've all seen the terrible scenes on television.

'Pull over here,' Ronan tells me.

I'm there, 'Pull *over*? Are you yanking my chain? I wouldn't even drop below fifty. These people can strip a cor while it's still focking moving . . .'

'Pull over,' he goes again and – for whatever reason – I do.

He opens the door and gets out. I'm there, 'Are you out of your mind?' but he laughs at me, roysh, and tells me he's one of 'the faces' out here. Then he takes the wheelchair out of the boot and lifts Blathin into it.

I look around. There's a gang of heads staring at us across this patch of, like, waste ground, total Antos, the six of them, with their Air Max runners and their hoods up. They stort making their way over to us.

'Ronan,' Blathin goes, 'will you button up your jacket?' which he immediately does and I'm thinking, it's not the focking flu we need to worry about here.

They're, like, twenty yords away and I turn around to Ro and go, 'Kid, we've got company,' but Ronan goes, 'Just tell them you're a mate of Gull's – no one'll lay a finger on you,' and then he focks off, pushing Blathin down the road, leaving me on my Tobler.

'What's the story?' one of the Antos goes and of course that could mean anything. One or two of them call me mate, but again there's no way of telling whether it's in a good way or a bad way.

They're all, like, sixteen, seventeen, and they must be wearing, like, forty sovvies between them.

'Er, just to let you know,' I go, slowly, because they don't understand you otherwise, 'I'm a mate of Gull's.'

'Gull?' the one who I presume is their leader goes. He's covered in focking acne scors – he's got a face like a par three tee box. 'Gull who?'

Of course I haven't a focking bog. I don't even know if Gull's his real first name. One of the others saves my orse by going, 'Gull Burden?'

I'm there, 'Gull . . .'

He's like, 'Burden.'

That's it. That *is* his name.

'Gull Byrne,' I go. 'Exactly.'

They all suddenly snap to attention. 'Ah, why didn't you say so?' the leader goes. 'How is he?'

Actually, let's call this dude Riff, for the sake of the story. 'How is he?' Riff goes.

I'm there, 'He's Kool *and* the Gang. In fact, this is his cor?'

'Fook me,' Riff goes, admiring it from front to back, then back to front. 'He's doing well for heself, isn't he? And what are you – he's social woorker?'

'That's exactly what I am,' I go, thinking, and I thought *I* was thick. If you cracked this focker's head open, it'd be like a snow globe inside.

I'm like, 'Now, goys, I'm a busy man. Shit to do,' and as I'm saying it, I'm whipping out a wad of notes and peeling off the twenties. 'I'd appreciate it if you'd keep an eye on Gull's little baby.'

'What are ye doing?' Riff goes, suddenly throwing his hands in the air, like he's being served a summons. 'You don't need to do that, man. It's Gull fucken Burden. We'll make sure it's not touched . . .'

It's unbelievable. See, it's just like our part of the world – it's all about connections.

I catch up with Ronan and Blathin in – of all places – Blanchardstown Shopping Centre. Blathin's in the euro store, in the middle of all this tinsel and cheap hair gel, talking to the locals about what it's like to live out here among the Apaches, and they're all *over* her – you know these salt-of-the-earth Dublin types who'd have a whip-round for you if your house got burgled, but who'd probably buy your shit when whoever robbed it came around later selling it on the knocker.

Ronan's outside, just, like, shaking his head in total admiration. He's there, 'Ah, she's great with people,' which is true.

All you can hear is old dears going, 'Isn't she goer-geous?' and, 'Aw, it's luffly the way thee talk, isn't it?' meaning people from South Dublin obviously, not people in wheel-chairs.

I've never seen Ronan so happy. That's why I hate having to tell him what I have to tell him now.

'Sorcha's going away,' I go. '*With* Honor obviously. The good news is it's only for a year.'

He looks confused. 'Where?'

I'm there, 'California. In other words, the States.'

'When?'

'Day after tomorrow. Only for a year, though.'

He nods, but doesn't say anything else.

'I said we'd meet them tomorrow. Say goodbye. Do you want to do that, Ro? Say goodbye to your sister?'

I'm not sure he even hears me. It's so hord sometimes to know what's going on between those little ears, but I presume he's, like, suddenly sad.

'Let's get Blathin out of here,' I go. 'You never know

67

when a crowd like this'll turn. Five more minutes and that focking chair will be up on blocks.'

Blathin says she's – *oh my God!* – *so* happy she came. She never knew there were people like this in the world and she says she's definitely going to get her mum and dad to set up a direct debit with St Vincent de Paul when we get home.

If we get home.

I actually say it as a joke and Ro even gives me a charity smile. But five minutes later, the joke's on me. We get back to the cor to find it in flames and the, I don't know, Jets cheering and telling me to tell Gull he's a fooken dead man walking.

I look at Ro and he pulls a face. 'Forgot,' he goes, 'he doortied his copy buke out here a while back. Should have told you to say Winker instead.'

I stare at the old dear's Lexus, her pride and joy, eighty Ks worth of cor, blazing away like I don't know what.

Ro says we should probably hit the taxi rank before it gets ugly. Blathin suddenly throws her hands up to her face. 'Ronan!' she goes. 'Your CD!'

He puts his hand in his pocket and whips it out. 'Er, I took it with me,' he goes, looking at me, I think the word is, sheepishly. 'Shouldn't leave valuables in your car – especially around here.'

It's, like, eleven o'clock in the morning and I haven't been to bed yet. I'm in an Andy McNab on the way home, after spending fourteen hours straight playing *Guitar Hero* with One F on the old PS 2.

Long story.

I'd promised him the exclusive interview about the whole Andorra thing for the *Building Labourer's Bugle,* or whatever focking rag it is he writes for. So there I was, roysh, setting out my goals and expectations – World Cup qualification by 2011 – when suddenly, ten minutes in, he produces a bottle of Wild Turkey and two shot glasses. Of course, it was a short trip from there to his tearful memories of the first T-54 tank crashing through the gates of the presidential palace in Saigon, and then on to bending the virtual Fender to 'Smoke on the Water' and 'Voodoo Chile'.

On the way out the door, I told him to make up the quotes. 'Just make me sound like a young EOS, though – a no-bullshit merchant. And a total insomniac . . .'

I'm actually just nodding off in the back of the taxi when my phone rings. I check caller ID, as I always do these days – it's a sad day, the day you realize there's more people in your phonebook you want to avoid than actually talk to – but it turns out this is a call I *want* to take.

'You're back!' I go, hoping I didn't make myself sound too desperate. 'How was Andalusia?'

'Absolutely enchanting,' she goes. 'Andalusia is *so* beautiful, Ross, and bathed in this wonderfully luminous light – you couldn't *but* be inspired by it. Our first morning there, they took us to this rock pool and that's where we set up our easels – with our feet in the water, just surrounded by fig and walnut trees. And Alva – she was our teacher – she just said, paint what you see . . .'

It's great to talk to her and I genuinely mean that, although I couldn't listen to her No Frontiers act for much longer.

'I mean, Andalusia is, like, the *real* Spain? You go to Benidorm or Marbella, you could be anywhere. But where we were, around El Cerrillo and Cannillas, it was like, *whoa!* All these white buildings. I got *so* much painting done. A bit too much vino, though.'

Finally, she goes, 'So, how are *you*? What have you been up to?'

I'm there, 'Well, yesterday I went to Blanchardstown . . .'

'Blanchardstown?' she goes. 'Are you okay?'

'Don't even ask. Then I sat up all night drinking with Derek Foley. And tonight, I'm saying goodbye and good riddance to my soon-to-be ex-wife . . .'

'What?' she goes, like she knows it's a major development.

'She's going to the States for a year. It's, like, whatever. Move on. I have.'

'You're not upset? I mean, do you want to talk?'

'Nah, I'm over it. I got married too young, with way too much living still to do. Hey, what are you up to during the week?'

'That's what I was going to ask you. My sister Sarah's having a dinner party on Friday night. Chance for us to show off our watercolours. It's just, like, her and her husband, another sister, Deirdre, and her fiancé and then a few of their friends. It's Sutton. I just wondered would you like to come along? Be my plus-one?'

It's like, does Amanda Brunker sleep on her back?

'Who's going to look after the shop?'

Why did I ask that? Because I'm obviously still trying to put, like, obstacles in her way. It makes her go suddenly quiet, though. See, Aoife would normally have done it.

'Chloe and Sophie are going to look after things,' she eventually goes. 'And Amie with an ie.'

I'm like, 'Those girls? Are you sure? What about Claire – as in Claire from Bray? She has experience of working in a shop.'

'Look, Ross, I'm not being a bitch here? But the girl doesn't know, like, *anything* about fashion? Okay, she can't *help* where she was born, but at the same time . . .'

70

'That's horsh,' I go. 'They sell clothes in Caddles, don't they? Fake Ireland jerseys. Green, white and orange jester hats. *And* she has a certificate in morkeshing from DBS – they don't give *them* out to dipshits.'

'Sorry, Ross, what have you got *against* Chloe and Sophie?'

'They're basically trouble. *You* know that. Fock, you're the one who calls them the Gruesome Twosome.'

'Yeah, well,' she goes, 'they also happen to be two of my best friends,' and there's, like, no arguing with that?

So I change the subject.

'Hey, good news for you. There's, like, millions of Storbucks in the States. Way bigger than this one, as well.'

Of course she already knows – she did a J1er, too. I only mention it because I know she's a major fan. Poor Honor. I look at her there in my lap, smiling and chatting away to me with her nonsense words. It'll be straight from the breast onto the double tall low-fat soy lattes for her.

Ronan's been in the jacks a long time.

'Are you going to meet up with, like, Lauren and Christian over there?' I go.

She's like, 'Yeah – oh my God, they don't live too far away from where we're going to be. Maybe, like, a two-hour drive?'

She looks incredible, I don't know if I mentioned, in that black ruffle trim Elie Saab cordigan I bought her for Christmas – or rather *she* bought and I paid for.

'Well, don't expect them to be nice to you,' I go. 'They're too loyal to *me*. Oh yeah. I think you and loverboy are in for a *pretty* frosty reception,' and I straight away feel bad because that's actually unfair to Christian *and* Lauren?

So then I go, 'Well, you know that's total bullshit – they will be nice to you,' and she's like, 'I know they will, they're nice people,' and she gives me a little smile.

71

Ronan comes back from the TK Maxx. It's obvious he's been crying. Sorcha doesn't cop it, though, because she goes, 'Hey, Ronan, what's all this about you having a girlfriend?'

'Er, yeah,' he goes, lifting Honor up off my lap. 'Blathin.' She's like, 'Blathin? What's she like?'

'Er, nice,' he goes, copping a sly look at me. 'She's nice.'

'That's good to hear — as long as she's good enough for you.'

I'm there, 'Oh, she's definitely good enough. They're actually *our* kind of people? Clonskeagh.'

Ronan puts Honor down on the ground, takes hold of her hands and sort of, like, walks her around the shop. Sorcha mouths the words 'Is he okay?' to me and when he's out of earshot I tell her he's fine, or he *will* be. Hasn't had time to adjust to the idea yet. She's there, 'The time will fly.'

'Yeah,' I go, 'but a year's like a lifetime when you're a kid.'

She knows.

We *all* know.

'What about you?' she goes. 'How are things going with that new girl? What's her name, Melanie?'

I'm there, 'Good actually. *You* seem pretty interested, for some reason.'

'She was actually in the institute with Muireann, my friend from Reiki? She said she's really, really nice.'

'She is — she's just back from Andalusia . . .'

'In Spain?'

'I think so. Doing some ort course — painting, blah blah blah.'

'Wow — that's like, *oh* my God!'

'Yeah, I know. Seeing her Friday night as well. Her sister's having, like, a dinner porty thing?'

72

'I'm really happy for you,' she goes and I'm suddenly looking into her eyes, roysh, trying to read them, to see whether she means it. There's still something there, though it might not be that she still wants me. It might be just, I don't know, regret at the way it all turned out.

'I wonder what he's saying to her,' she suddenly goes, staring in the direction of the condiments table. I turn around. Ronan's holding Honor in one arm and he's, like, talking away to her. Last-minute advice obviously.

I'm like, '*Foorst thing you do when you walk into a room – check your fooken exits . . .*'

Sorcha's laughs. 'I'm going to miss him.'

'What about me?' I go. 'Will you miss me?'

She doesn't answer straight away. She just sips her tall Featured Coffee, then puts her mug down on the table. She takes her Marc Jacobs sunglasses off her head, smooths her hair back, then puts them back on again.

She eventually goes, 'I always miss you when we're not together, Ross – but when we are together, I miss *me* . . .'

Sometimes she can, like, floor you with shit like that. I'm always meaning to Google some of her better lines, find out is she getting them from *The Hills* or *Newport Harbor*.

'Just promise me one thing?' I go. 'Don't ever let her call Cillian daddy.'

She's like, 'I would never do that,' and straight away I know she won't. You can take Sorcha's word to the bank.

Ronan arrives over and he's obviously upset again, so I tell them that we should maybe split. I take Honor from him and I kiss her goodbye and, with my free orm, I give Sorcha a hug. Then I hand Honor to her.

Ronan gives Sorcha a hug where she's sitting and when he pulls away, roysh, he's bawling his little eyes out. He hates people seeing him cry, so he turns, without saying a word, and walks out.

'He'll be fine,' I tell Sorcha. 'I'll see you.'

3. People in glasshouses

I pick up a copy of One F's paper to see if the orticle about me is in it. At it happens it's not, roysh, but the piece on the front page makes me laugh so hord, I actually think I'm going to get focked out of Eason's.

The headline is like, THIEVES TARGET BOOK QUEEN FIONNUALA, and then underneath it's like, 'Millionaire author robbed in her own home'.

The story's like, 'Chicklit sensation Fionnuala O'Carroll-Kelly spoke of her relief at being alive last night after thieves broke into her home in South Dublin's exclusive Foxrock and escaped with her Lexus IS.

'The fifty-two-year-old author, who is famous for her sexually explicit writing, revealed that she almost came face to face with the ruthless gang, who took her car keys from the kitchen of her €20m mansion – while she was in the next room, working on her new book.

'The car was later found burned out in Blanchardstown.'

Then they've got, like, a couple of quotes from her and it's all typical focking drama queen stuff. '"The book is really a multicultural romance story about a working-class truck driver who falls in love with a Romany girl. I'd just come up with the title – *My Beautiful Gypsy Mot* – when I thought I heard a noise in the kitchen.

'"But I thought nothing more of it until a few hours later when the Gardaí called to say they'd found my car burned out in one of these housing estates. It was only then that I noticed it was missing from the driveway. And my blood turned cold because I realized they must have come into the kitchen to get the keys.

"'I'm still recovering from shock, but I'm also relieved to be alive. I was in the house on my own. This gang could have tied me up and done anything to me.'"

Then it's like, 'She was too upset to comment further. Friends said she was devastated not only by the loss of her high-performance car – an 80,000-euro gift to herself after her first book, *Criminal Assets*, became an international best-seller. Her Lorena Ochoa-personalized PING clubs that she used to win the lady captain's prize in Foxrock last summer were said to be in the boot when the car was torched.

'The incident is expected to intensify local opposition to the proposed extension of the Luas to Foxrock. O'Carroll-Kelly – the estranged wife of jailed councillor Charles – has used her position in the past to speak out against the improvement of public-transport links to the upmarket area.

'However, she hasn't ruled out using her terrifying experience in a future book. "It could be good therapy for her," a friend said.'

Okay, let's see can I get this – Sarah and Mark, Deirdre and Gavin. Barry and . . . Pam. Richard and Janis. And Melanie, obviously.

Sarah and Deirdre are the sisters, both older than Melanie, both doctors – Sarah in the Beacon, Deirdre in general practice in, I don't know, Coolock or Sallynoggin or one of those.

Sarah – whose gaff we're actually in – is married to Mark, who's, like, a hospital consultant, while Deirdre is engaged to Gavin, who doesn't say what he does, just that he's, like, *with* McCann FitzGerald.

I don't know what the connection is to the other two

couples, but I think it might be Ashtanga ... or Vinyasa Flow.

Pam is a primary schoolteacher and Barry owns his own IT consultancy, though he's planning to take a back seat for two years to dedicate himself to skiing, of all things, and try to make the Irish team for the next Winter Olympics.

Janis is pretty high up in the Central Statistics Office and Richard is, like, an architect, but in fairness he knows his rugby. 'I saw you play once or twice,' he even goes.

I'm like, 'Lucky you.'

Actually, that's a lie. That's what I *could* say. What I *actually* say is, 'Whoa – that's, like, *such* a long time ago. Making me feel my age now,' and everyone laughs like it's the funniest thing they've ever heard and I look at Melanie – looking *pretty* incredible, it must be said, in a deep blue Nanette Lepore dress she says she picked up in Bloomingdale's last summer – and she looks at me like she's, I don't know, proud of me and totally happy that I'm there.

And I think to myself, I can do this. I can, like, hold my own in this company.

Back and forth the conversation goes.

The point about tailgating is, you shouldn't *have* to do it – if the driver in front is driving slower than you, he should pull in and let you pass. I mean, it's courtesy, isn't it? Hmm. Hmm.

Well, Fallon & Byrne is where you'll get the best globe artichokes – take my word for it. Yes, it *is* wonderful, isn't it? I'm a fiend for their granary bretzel, aren't I, darling?

Anyone want more of the Guigal? Don't mind if I do, Sarah. Your sister's driving.

Oh, this soup is wonderful – you can *taste* the borage leaves, can't you? It's good for stress, you know. Is it? Is it, indeed?

See, my point is, you *can't* blame the HSE – we wanted lower taxes in this country. People marched for them. And unfortunately, you get the health service you pay for. Yaw. Yaw. Yaw.

You know, that whole wine snobbery thing is gone now – you can get really good wine in Lidl. Oh, Lidl. I have to admit – it's one of my guilty pleasures. Ha ha ha.

Ross, *you'd* know this – Hook and McGurk, they always look like they're about to go at it. Is it true they hate each other? No love lost, you say? So it's not an act, then, for the cameras?

Oh, yes – I can shoot the shit with the best of them. They're all looking at Melanie as if to say, you've done well.

She looks focking great with a tan. 'I'm looking forward to seeing these pictures,' I go.

This Richard dude's like, 'Yes, when are we going to see them?'

'After dinner,' Sarah goes.

Mark's there, 'They've spent the whole afternoon hanging them,' and Sarah hits him, like, a playful slap. 'Now, nobody feel under any obligation to buy one,' but I'm thinking I probably will. Providing they're not shit, of course. I hate pictures where you can't tell what they're supposed to be.

How *was* Andalusia, by the way? Oh, beautiful. Just beautiful. I mean, you couldn't but be inspired. Sitting in the *finca*, surrounded by olive and almond groves. There's the most wonderful sixteenth-century church in Cómpeta that Melanie painted. And the colours – yellow jasmine, pink oleander . . .

I think we've bored them enough with our holiday stories. Ha ha ha.

Oh, these lamb shanks. You obviously slow-cooked these, did you, Sarah?

Deirdre, did Pam tell you about the class she's teaching this year? Six languages spoken in the classroom – and that's not even including English. Six? Jesus! And it's *our* children who're expected to adapt. They're learning hello and good-bye in Russian and Urdu. Awful. Awful. Political correctness gone mad.

The best mascarpone in Ireland, you'll get it in Cavistons. Honestly. Yaw. Yaw.

Just going back to what you were saying there about the whole non-national thing. I mean, Deirdre and I are all for it. One negative, though, *we* feel, is the way it's affected the hospitality industry – and by that I mean there are no more friendly Irish faces front of shop, so to speak. I mean, you stop at a petrol station now, ask for directions – the chances are no one will have a clue where to direct you. They're all Chinese. Yeah, yeah.

God, they work hard, though, don't they? I know it's a cliché and everything. Well, it's only a cliché because it's true, Barry.

What was that story that Lorraine had, darling? This friend of Sarah's – she's one of these *vegans* – she works as a public health nurse, does home visits to all these, you know, *teenage mothers* in the inner city. Meets this girl last week – what was she, fifteen? – and she's *real* Dublin, lives in one of these awful blocks of flats. And she has a baby called – wait for it – Pocahontas!

Ha ha ha.

Pocahontas O'Connor!

You're joking, right?

True as I'm sitting here. Pocahontas O'Connor!

Well, I'm not surprised. Fifteen – she's still only a child herself.

True. True.

I need to drop one. I need to drop one in a major way.

'Er, too much information,' Melanie goes.

I'm like, 'Oops – sorry.'

Meant to say it in my head.

'Top of the first flight of stairs,' Sarah goes. 'Mezzanine level. The door straight in front of you.'

Like the rest of the gaff, the can is incredible. Melanie's sister's either got OCD or Mary focking Poppins as a maid. There's, like, eight types of Molton Brown handwash and cream, all equally spaced out on, like, the sink area, with the labels facing out and there's, like, little neat piles of fresh towels as well. Honestly, it's like taking a shit in Brown Thomas.

And when the old butt cheeks hit the seat, I can't focking believe it – it's heated!

The only thing it really lacks is maybe a stack of magazines – a couple of *FHM*s or a *Rugby World* – but at least it gives me time to think about how unbelievably well tonight is going while I'm dropping the kids off at the pool.

There's no doubt Melanie's a ringer for Sarah Chalke, with an even better bod, if that's even possible. But better than that, she's actually really nice, even though I don't usually go for that in birds. And, much as I hate patting myself on the back, they're loving me downstairs.

I fall asleep. I don't know why. The load I dropped was an epidural job – maybe it was the effort of delivering it. But I ended up falling asleep anyway. How long, I haven't a clue. What I do know is that Melanie's suddenly tapping on the door, asking me if I'm okay.

Could have been two minutes, could have been two hours.

I've got my kacks around my ankles and pains down the backs of my legs from sitting on the seat for too long. Actually, I might have focking grill marks as well.

'Yeah, I'm Kool and the Gang,' I manage to go. 'I'll, er, be down in a second,' and she's there, 'Okaaay . . .' sounding a bit Scooby Dubious.

What am I doing falling asleep? Yeah, no, it must be that night with One F finally catching up with me.

I wipe up, whip up the old chinos, give the chain a yank and I don't focking believe what happens.

It breaks off in my hand.

So I'm left standing there with it, looking into the bowl at the focking ugliest, hairiest shit I've ever seen, thinking, okay, no one can know that I dropped *that*.

I take the top off the cistern and fiddle about with, like, the insides, thinking, there's usually some kind of plunger thing that the handle operates and it might be possible to, like, pull it by hand to release the water. I put my hand in and try to pull it, but without the handle I can't get any, like, purchase on it?

There's, like, total silence downstairs. They're obviously whispering and it's obviously about me.

I suddenly feel like I'm in one of those stories – what are they called, urban myths? – the stories that always happen to a mate of your brother's or a dude your best friend's sister works with, but are usually, like, total bullshit.

This one isn't. I can vouch for that.

I sit on the side of the jacuzzi and consider my options, but there are very few. I think about maybe dropping it into the sink and beating it down the plug hole with the toilet brush – but that'll take about two hours and forty gallons of water.

Honestly, this thing is so big it has an observation deck.

The stories, I think. What do they always do in the stories? Wrap it in a bit of tissue paper, then go back to the table, forgetting of course that it's in your back pocket. Squish.

Definitely not. Wouldn't have a pocket big enough anyway.

Throw it out the window. How does that one end? Can't remember and no time to think about it.

I just do it.

The window's one of those, like, frosted jobs that you can't see through, but there's, like, a little window at the top of it that opens out. I reach up and open it, then I wrap a load of jacks roll around my hand so it looks like an oven glove. I reach into the bowl and lift it out.

It's about the same weight as Honor.

Still, it's a good job I'm back lifting weights again, because, when I throw it, I'm pretty sure I manage to get a bit of distance behind it.

Then I close the window again, thinking, that's a load off – literally.

I wash and dry my hands, then I think, fock it, I'll have a couple of squirts of. the old *Blu Maquis* on the strength of that. I'm sure Sarah won't mind – as long as I leave the bottle eyes front.

I'm actually feeling *pretty* good about myself coming down the stairs, thinking, I might even tell them one or two of my Ocean City stories later on.

I go back into the dining room, but there's, like, no one at the table. How many courses did I sleep through? Have they all gone home?

No – there's ten bowls of rhubarb and caramelized almond semifreddo with mocha coulis untouched on the table.

But there's, like, total silence in the house.

The loudest silence of all is coming from the other side of those French doors, leading out into a bigger room.

That's where they are. I can see them through the glass.

The exhibition's obviously kicked off. I'm hoping nobody's bought that church Sarah was banging on about.

I walk through the doors. They obviously had a busy week. There's, like, fourteen or fifteen paintings hung on the actual wall part of the conservatory? Very good as well. I'm beginning to see what they meant about the colours.

'What kind of flowers are they?' I go, but nobody answers.

After a few seconds I notice that nobody's looking at the pictures either.

They're all looking up.

Up?

Up at what? I wonder.

So I look up myself.

No!

Oh, fock!

Oh, fock, *no*!

It's sitting there on the roof of the conservatory.

My . . .

I can't even say it.

My shit. Looking through the glass at us like an alien from *Dr Who* or something.

Everyone suddenly looks at me, but no one says a word. They all look like they're in total shock, like the survivors of, I don't know, one of those terrible things you see sometimes on the TV.

There's no *right* thing to say in a situation like that, but I make the mistake of trying to keep it light.

'I'd love to see the bird who dropped that,' I go.

But no one laughs and, looking back, I can understand why.

Melanie bursts into tears and Sarah says she thinks I should leave. Not that I need telling. I'm already on the way out to the hall to grab the old Henri-Lloyd. See, it's the oldest rule in the book when it comes to women – when there's nothing left to say, you just walk away.

It's the middle of the morning, roysh, and I'm in the sack, really depressed, wondering should I ring Melanie to apologize, maybe explain my side of the story. Or would a quick Hilary Swank cheer me up.

That's when it suddenly dawns on me.

In, like, ten weeks' time I'm going to be pitting my wits against the great Michael Bradley. It just hits me out of the blue and I'm suddenly thinking, I bet *he's* not at home watching *Dance It Off with Vicky Binns.*

So what do I do? I whip out the DVDs that Bernard gave me of the team and also the rowing-machine I bought when I was thinking of going back playing for DLSP.

I take it out of the box and set it up.

Two hours later, I'm pulling stroke after stroke while watching Andorra against Toulouse's second team.

I'm also wondering what the fock I've got myself into here.

We're shit. There's no nice way of putting it. What Bernard didn't mention was that Toulouse put, like, eighty-one points on us – including *ten* tries – and that Andorra got zilch.

Honestly, if you got the old Castlerock dream team of ninety-nine together this afternoon – none of us having played the game for the best part of, like, seven years – we'd still beat them out the gate. Pres. focking Bray would beat them out the gate.

We – and I use the word loosely, because they're fock-all to do with me – are a total shambles.

Obviously, I'm most interested in the outhalf, who, according to Bernard's notes, is an English dude called

Jonny Hathaway, who qualifies under the residency rule. This Jonny, it has to be said, is no Wilkinson. This Jonny couldn't kick away a blind man's stick. His technique is all over the shop.

The scrum-half's name is Ander Acebes and Bernard has written the words 'Be careful – a crazy man' at the end of his little biography. That's pretty obvious to see, though. He spends the first half-an-hour ranting and raving, threatening the Toulouse forwards, throwing himself into ridiculous tackles – and then he's, like, focked tired. For the entire second half, Jonny can't get any decent ball off him.

I like the look of their captain, Toni Moreno – Frodo, they call him, for whatever reason – who's, like, our inside-centre and probaby the one *true* footballer in the team. Even so, he handles like a focking supermorket trolley.

The only decent thing you cay say about the pack is that they're all focking giants. At the same time, they punch well below their weight in the scrum and the line-out.

World Cup qualification within twelve years? In what? Lacrosse?

I can't watch either of the other two games. Not today. This kind of punishment is best taken in small doses. Yeah, the moolah is good, but I'm beginning to think I'd be better off back at Pearse Street Sanitary Services.

It's good to hear the focker's voice, even *if* all he can talk about is work?

He says they're going to have, like, a helicopter landing pad on the roof and it's going to be identical in every detail to the docking bay in Cloud City where the *Falcon* landed. And the chips for the actual casino, they're going to be based on the currency system used by the Hutts, in other words Peggats, Truguts and Wupiupi. And the security staff are all going to be dressed as, like, Stormtroopers, with Imperial Royal Guards accompanying the high rollers to the high-stakes tables . . .

I'm like, 'Whoa, Christian – any chance of getting a word in edgeways here? It's, like, *I'm* paying for this call?' which comes across as, like, really petty, I suppose, and I immediately regret it.

At the same time I'm still thinking, out of all of us, why did Erika fall for *him*?

I ask him how Lauren is and he says great, only sixteen weeks to go now. I tell him to say hello for me and I hear him go, 'Hey, babes – Ross says hi,' and I hear her just go, 'That's nice,' without actually saying hi back.

'I told her,' Christian goes.

'No message for me, no?'

'Er . . .'

'Hormones, huh? Still, sixteen weeks – that's, like, the middle of February, is it? Then your life is over, my friend!'

'No, I'm really looking forward to it . . .'

'Major changes.'

'But exciting ones . . .'

Yeah, who am I kidding? I'd love to go back and do it all again. All differently.

I'm there, 'Christian, don't listen to me. I'm just missing Honor. Like you wouldn't believe.'

'Ross, it's *me* who's sorry. I didn't think.'

'Ah, whatever. I've got, like, three or four videos of her on my phone, you know. Sometimes I'll sit for, like, an hour, watching them over and over again. I didn't think it was going to be this bad. So,' I go, 'have you seen them? As in her and Sorcha?'

'No, but I think we're having them here next weekend. It's only a couple of hours' drive, you know . . .'

'So I hear. Personally, I don't think she's going to stick the States.'

'Lauren's spoken to her on the phone a couple of times. She seems to be loving it, especially the shopping.'

'I think the heat'll get to her eventually, though . . .'

'There's, like, air-con everywhere you go here, Ross.'

'She'll probably get really badly burned in the sun, though. I can see it. Decide, I can't take any more of this. Tell your man, focking Love Actuary, that she's coming home. Her and my daughter . . .'

Love Actuary. I just thought of that on the spot.

'You're okay with them staying with us, are you, Ross?'

I could say no, but I wouldn't do it to him. 'Course I am.'

'They're staying for two nights – Cillian as well.'

He didn't have to say his name.

I'm there, 'Hey, look, we're both free agents.'

He suddenly remembers something. 'How's it going with that girl you were seeing? Melanie?'

'Er, didn't *really* work out?' I go. 'Bit of a disastrous date last night, if I'm being honest . . .'

'How do you know it can't be rescued, young padwan?'

'You know the way you just sometimes know?'

I tell him it's been great talking to him. It's one of those things you say that never really needs to be said.

One of the, I suppose, upsides of having to live under the same roof as that pollock who calls herself my mother is the nosebag. Utter weapon of mass destruction that she is, you wouldn't believe the things the woman can do with a sprig of fennel and a griddle pan.

I get up pretty early on Monday evening, roysh, big-time Hank, and the first stop of course is the fridge, to get myself a bit of breakfast.

You'd want to see what's in there – we're talking Mediterranean lasagne, we're talking pork and chicken terrine, we're talking smoked bacon, blue cheese and pineapple pasta, not to mention a humungous chocolate and amaretti mousse.

So I lay it all out on the island in the middle of the kitchen and stort throwing it into me like there's no *actual* tomorrow.

That's when the old dear walks in. I actually catch the hum of her *Chanel No. 5* first and I look up – my mouth stuffed to the gills with, like, roasted eggplant and tahini – and I go, 'Look who it is – Menopause the Musical! This is focking revolting, by the way. I'd make a better meal with my feet.'

'*Ross!*' she goes, going way over the top as usual. '*My food!* What have you done? Oh, I'm so late as it is . . .'

I'm there, 'You should be grateful *anyone's* prepared to eat your slops.'

She doesn't even acknowledge me, just stares at the mess I've made of her dinner and goes, 'Look at what you've done! It took me hours to prepare!' and it's like, sue me!

'Who are you cooking for anyway?' I go.

She's like, 'If you must know, I'm having some dear, dear friends around for supper.'

There's a huge amount wrong with that sentence. Firstly, who the fock calls it supper? Secondly, she *has* no friends.

She needs reminding.

'I have a great many friends,' she goes.

'Horseshit – who's coming tonight, then?'

'Not that it's any of your concern,' she goes, 'but my *writing* friends,' and as she's saying it, she's picking her way through my leftovers, trying to salvage something to serve them up.

'Your writing friends?'

'Yes, my writing friends. Sheila, Cathy, Patricia . . .'

She manages to pull together a couple of plates of food, which she puts back in the fridge. I actually laugh in her face. They'll all have to hit the focking chipper on the way home if that's what she gives them.

'I think it's nice,' she goes, 'that they're rallying around me – after my ordeal.'

'Ordeal? Would you get a focking life? Your cor wasn't even stolen . . .'

I'm laughing so hord I can hordly get the line out. '*I* took it.'

She's standing at the sink, roysh, with her back to me, so I don't see her immediate reaction. The last thing I expected when she turned around was to see a smile on her face.

It's, like, an evil smile as well.

'I *know* you took it,' she goes. 'I saw you go out in it. But when they rang to say it'd been found burned out, I thought, hmm, this could catapult me back onto the front pages.'

'You played along just to steal the limelight from Charlotte McNeel?'

'You couldn't buy the kind of publicity I've had over the past week.'

I tell her she's a disgrace and a focking shambles of a woman and she tells me she doesn't have time to listen to my unpleasantness. She then announces that she's going upstairs to get ready, on the off-chance that I actually *give* a shit.

She's like, 'Bring the girls into the living room when they arrive.'

I grab a beer, sit down in front of the old Liza and for the next twenty minutes turn my mind to the important question of what order I'd like to do the TV3 *Xposé* girls in. And, as I'm mulling this over, roysh, I just happen to notice the old dear's black, knee-high Gucci Duchessa boots in the corner of the room and I don't know why – might be the beer – but I end up having one of the best ideas I've ever had in my life.

I go out into the hall, stand at the bottom of the stairs and listen. She's having a Paddy Power. Washing that big focking elephant seal body of hers, which means she'll be out of commission for the next twenty minutes or so.

So what I do, roysh, is I grab the boots and throw them down in the doorway of the sitting room, with just the actual foot part of them sticking out into the hall.

Then I do a quick reccy. I go outside and check out how it looks from the front doorstep and it's, like, perfect – just two feet sticking out into the hall.

Then I hit the kitchen, grab the recycling bin and stort whipping out the empties. Holy shmoley – she's been tanning the Châteauneuf-du-Pape, by the looks of it, the focking lush.

I grab, like, eight or nine empty bottles, roysh, and scatter them around the hall, making sure they're all, like, visible from the front door.

Then I go back into the sitting room, where Lorraine Keane's saying that Jessica Biel has revealed the secret of how she keeps her skin so clear – every morning she boils a handful of rice in six cups of water, then drinks the film off the top. It helps get rid of impurities.

Five minutes later – unbelievable timing – the doorbell rings. 'Could you get that?' she shouts down the stairs. 'Tell them I'll be down in a moment – just making myself pretty,' and I'm thinking, yeah, that'd require focking planning permission.

I whip open the front door and the whole gaggle's there and I end up giving them the whole dorky son performance.

'Mum's friends!' I go, clapping my hands together in a gesture that would probably have to be described as bent. 'It's *so* wonderful that you've come to see her! She will be pleased.' Then I go, 'I hate her spending time alone. She has so many dork episodes,' and suddenly they're all staring at me in, like, total bewilderment.

'Your mum?' Cathy Kelly goes. I'd do her in a New York minute, in case you're wondering. 'Fionnuala never mentioned that she had a son.'

You have no idea how actually hurt I am by that.

'Well,' I go, 'I suppose I *was* her son. Nowadays, I think she looks on me more as her carer,' and it's at that exact moment that I sort of, like, step to one side and open the front door wide enough for them to cop the boots and the bottles strewn up and down the hallway.

Suddenly, silence. A porchful of writers and not one of them has words for this actual scene.

They're all like, 'What the . . .'

'Your timing couldn't be better,' I go. 'I was just about to wake her . . .'

Sheila O'Flanagan – I'll tell you what, they're lookers, this lot – goes, 'Is she . . . drunk?' and I'm like, 'Pretty much bladdered, yeah. That's her – fairly lashes into it in the afternoon. She sobers up pretty quickly, though. I'll just go and throw a bucket of water over her,' and I stort heading for the kitchen.

The women stort sort of, like, backing away quickly, the three of them all of a sudden rediscovering the moonwalk.

'Tell her we'll, er, phone her,' they're all going. 'When she's feeling better,' and I'm there, 'Are you sure – it's no Hoff for me to wake her,' watching them disappear up the driveway.

Then at the top of my voice, I go, 'Oh, mum, you've left

the chip pan on again!' and then I slam the door and just collapse with the laughter.

I actually slide down the wall and end up sitting on the floor with tears just, like, streaming from my eyes.

The next thing, roysh, the old dear comes trotting down the stairs, sort of, like, surveys the scene for a few seconds and straight away cops what I did.

Of course I'm laughing too hord to even acknowledge her.

And that's when, totally out of the blue, she goes, 'I want you out, Ross,' and all of a sudden I'm not laughing.

'What?'

'I'm not putting up with your daily hostility any longer,' she goes. 'I want you gone.'

Of course I'm straight on my feet.

'You can't fock me out of my actual home . . .'

'This is *not* your home, Ross. Not any more. You *have* a home.'

'No, I don't.'

'Or *had* a home. Either way, it's not my problem. I don't want to live with your unpleasantness.'

'*My* unpleasantness? Have you looked in the mirror lately?'

'Just be gone by tomorrow evening,' she goes.

It's, like, one of the few things that makes me smile these days – seeing the two of them together, thick as, well, literally thieves. I stand at the door of the visiting room, though it's ages before I approach the table because, to be honest, it's too much of a buzz just watching them, totally engrossed in each other's company, tears of laughter rolling down their faces.

Ronan somehow cops me. 'Rosser, you steamer!' he shouts at the top of his voice and of course the entire focking room's suddenly laughing.

'You lot think it's okay for a ten-year-old kid to talk

to his old man like that?' I go, to no one in particular, as I make my way over to where they're sitting.

Then I think, of course they do. It's Mountjoy, not Mount Cormel.

They're both delighted to see me, of course. 'It's been a few weeks,' the old man goes, like he's been chalking off the days on the wall of his cell.

I'm like, 'What the fock do you expect? It's a major hassle getting here.'

'Well,' he goes, 'it doesn't look like it'll be an issue for much longer – exclamation mark, new par,' and when he's finished, like, punctuating, he turns to Ronan and goes, 'Do *you* want to tell him, little chap?'

Ronan sits up, proud as you like. 'I've just been filling me grandda in on the ins and outs of TR,' he goes, waving a piece of paper at me.

Whatever TR is, I'm praying it's serious.

Terminal something or other.

Rheumatism? Nah.

Rickets? Too good for the focker.

'Temporary Release!' the old man goes, loving the sound of his own voice echoing back at him in this room. '*Full* Temporary Release! Been told I should apply. Tipped the nod, quote-unquote. I've been a mostly exemplary prisoner, you see,' and he says it like he's expecting me to, like, jump for joy or some shit?

'Mostly exemplary?' I go. 'What about your stint up on the roof?'

He laughs. 'Well, I wasn't in possession of my full faculties. I think that rugby at Croke Park business must have got to me. Anyway, the powers-that-be, quote-unquote, are prepared to write it off as a temporary mental aberration, on account of the leadership role I've played here in the prison and my general attitude towards rehabilitation. Ronan here's been explaining the terms of this TR to me. Tell Ross the last one, Ronan – we've been laughing, see . . .'

Ro goes, 'Temporary release is granted subject to certain conditions, including – the requirement that you do not consort or otherwise associate with known criminals . . .'

'I said, that's my friendship with Hennessy down the pan,' the old man goes. 'Good Lord, walking through the door of Shanahan's could be a parole violation in itself.'

I'm looking around me, thinking, it's a focking miracle this goy hasn't ended up in an isolation unit.

'Alreet, Charlie,' Ronan goes then, 'here's another one for you. You'll love this – the requirement to maintain sober habits . . .'

'No Shelbourne Bar!' he goes. 'I'm beginning to think I'd be better off in here, drinking Lex's awful *hooch* . . .'

'Number three – the requirement not to publish or communicate anything to the media . . .'

'What?' he goes, but actually serious this time. 'They expect me to retire the old Mont Blanc for the duration? No more of my world-famous letters to the paper of record?'

I reckon the real reason they're letting him out is because they can't take much more of the focker. He's worn them down. Then I'm thinking, I'll have to, like, ransack his study over the weekend, see can I give the Feds any more goods on him – get him banged up for another few years.

I'm suddenly there, 'Can we, like, dispense with the pleasantries for five minutes and talk about the biggest problem in all of our lives at the moment?'

The two of them look at me, not a focking Eliza what I'm talking about.

'*Your* wife,' I go, 'and *your* grandmother,' looking at Ronan, 'turfing me out on the street . . .'

Ronan looks suddenly serious. He's like, 'Find out about the car, did she?'

I'm there, 'No, she knew about the cor. You're presuming, though, that women need a reason to act the way they do. It's all ahead of you, kid.'

'Where are you living?' Ronan goes.

I'm there, 'Back in Newtownpork Avenue. Keep it to yourself, though. Sorcha's old man finds out and he'll send in the focking sheriff.'

'How's Melanie?' he goes.

I don't give him a straight answer. I go, 'Complicated,' and I hope that's enough.

'I take it,' he goes, 'that you fooked it up royally?'

I'm there, 'And you'd be pretty much right.'

He shakes his head and tells me I'm a tulip. Then he stands up. 'Reet,' he goes. 'I'm splitting. Taking Bla to the pitchers.'

Pitchers is, like, working class for the flicks?

The old man's delighted, of course. 'Ah,' he goes, 'the desire for the company of beautiful women – well, it's in the O'Carroll-Kelly genes,' and I am *so* tempted to go, 'Beautiful women? I hope you're not including that focking scrod you're married to in that.'

But then I think, no, he's in such good form over this Temporary Release shit – wouldn't be fair to piss on his parade.

But then I think, nah, fock him, and I go, 'Beautiful women? I hope you're not including that focking scrod you're married to in that.'

JP comes here, like, once a week. Sometimes with me, sometimes with Oisinn, sometimes with Fionn. Sometimes with all of us, sometimes with none of us.

But *he* always comes. Once a week, to this tiny little bungalow in Rathdrum, in deepest, dorkest Wicklow.

Today's the day he's going to press the doorbell, he says. Mr Breathnach will open the door and JP will say, what?

Hello, Mr Breathnach. You don't actually know me.

No.

Well, I met your son Eamonn once. A couple of times, in fact. I'm sorry I missed the funeral. I only read it in the paper.

Were you a friend of his?

Er, no. In fact, not at all. I'm the estate agent who sold him his house.

In Mullingar?

Well, it was more Cloghan.

I see – and what are you wanting?

Well, I'll tell you what it is. And I know you're going to laugh at this. I was the one who told him that Cloghan was within commutable distance of Dublin. And I couldn't help but notice that the coroner said he likely fell asleep at the wheel of the cor before the crash.

Oh.

So to be honest, I kind of think in a way I'm responsible. I think I killed your boy.

I see.

I recently went completely around the twist thinking about it. Some kind of emotional breakdown is what Dr Lynn said. I thought I'd just drive down here and tell you that.

It's stupid, but of course, who are we to tell him that?

Today is always the day he's going to ring that bell. But then he never gets it together enough to do it.

Today – this particular day – we sit there for an hour-and-a-half, me in the front passenger seat, passing the time texting, Fionn in the back, reading one of his science magazines. And JP sitting behind the wheel, with the engine off, just staring at that door, not even blinking.

'Who'd have thought,' Fionn goes, 'that one of the Earth's biggest biodiversity hotspots would be in an oceanic region with such low nutrient concentrations?'

JP turns the key and storts the engine. He says it's not going to happen today. Sorry, goys. Really sorry.

We tell him not to be stupid. We'll keep coming back for as long as it takes.

I'm lying on Sorcha's bed – *our* bed – sort of, like, browsing through Sorcha's old magazines. I'm six or seven paragraphs into a *Heat* special investigation about how many food miles are in the average fair trade polenta wrap when the doorbell rings.

For a minute, I think about not answering it, roysh, but whoever it is, they're pretty insistent, if that's the word?

I throw on my Leinster training top and my boxer shorts, then tip down the stairs and open the door. It's obviously someone with the wrong address, because it's a bird – eighteen, maybe nineteen – and, without wanting to come across as, like, racist here, she's black.

I go, 'Er, sorry, wrong gaff,' and I go to close the door in her face, but just as I'm about to, roysh, she goes, 'I want to speak to Sorcha Lalor,' except the way she says it, it's like Soar-chah Lay-lor.

She's wearing this really loud, multicoloured sheet thing wrapped around her upper body, I suppose a little bit like the sarongs they used to have here, and also, like, a head-tie.

I'm there, 'Soar-chah Lay-lor's not here – what's all this about anyway?'

'Hello,' she goes, offering me her hand. 'My name is Immaculata Okonjo. I come from Nigeria . . .'

I'm there, 'Okaaay,' like a fool actually agreeing to hear her out.

'My home is a small village called Owu-Ijebu in the Ogun State, a hundred and forty-five miles east of Lagos. My mother and father died when I was a little girl, my mother from tuberculosis, my father from ischemic heart disease. I was six years old when I came to Owu-Ijebu. It is a small community with only twelve houses, a nursery, a primary school and a small clinic . . .'

Lois and Clark is about to stort, so I end up going, 'Is there much more of this?' and she looks at me sort of, like, confused. 'As in, can you get to the point?' I go.

She's like, 'Oh, yes. Now I am finished school and next year I will start at the university. I would like to be a teacher of mathematics . . .'

'But can you explain to me how this is any of my beeswax?'

'Because, when I was six years old, Soarchah sponsored me.'

'Sponsored you? To do what?'

She looks at me blankly.

I'm there, 'Are we talking walk? Are we talking skipathon?'

'I do not understand.'

'Because you're a bit late coming around for the do-ray-me, aren't you?'

'No, no, no,' she goes. 'I mean she sponsored *me*. It was thanks to Soarchah that I was rescued from the streets of Lagos, where there are very bad men . . .'

Suddenly I'm like Celine Dion, as in it's all coming back to me now?

I actually remember her sponsoring a kid now. See, she was always a sucker for those ads on TV, especially if she liked the song – 'You Raise Me Up', 'Flying Without Wings', any of that focking muck. There was always something about Westlife that made her want to set up standing orders.

Anyway, she sponsored her for years. I remember her trying to interest me in one or two of her letters – 'Oh! My God, Ross! They've set up a small farming project, providing cassava and yams to hungry children' – but obviously I'd fock-all interest.

'Sorcha's actually in the States,' I go. 'She's gone for pretty much a year.'

This look of, like, disappointment crosses her face.

For some reason I look down at her feet. She's got a suitcase with her. It all of a sudden hits me that she has nowhere else to go.

'Why don't you come in?' I suddenly find myself going. And it's not what you think. I don't want to score her.

There's at least some decency in me.

The truth is she probably caught me at a weak moment. There's, like, photographs of Honor everywhere you look in this gaff and I have to admit that I'm missing her so much, it's almost like a physical hurt? Which is only natural, I suppose.

Then I'm suddenly face to face with this girl who's, I don't know, probably millions of miles away from home, roysh, with nowhere to go. Looking back, I was probably thinking, on some level – what if that was your daughter? And I'm also thinking, what would Sorcha do in this situation?

And the answer's obvious. She's been sponsoring her for ten focking years – I presume she'd take her in. Which is what *I* do. I even carry her focking case for her.

'I'm Ross,' I go, doing the whole handshake thing.

She's like, 'Yes, I recognize you from the pictures Soar-chah sent to me.'

I ask her if she fancies a cup of coffee. I was going to fire up the Nespresso.

'That would be nice,' she goes. 'You are very kind. Not like Soarchah described you to me . . .'

Whoa! That rocks me back on my heels. I'm like, 'Really? What exactly did she say?'

'She said you slept with her sister and her friend before your wedding. She said you photocopied her notes for her special history topic at school and sold them on the internet. She said you gave her oral thrush for her eighteenth birthday . . .'

Fock – up until that point I was going to ask her to produce her passport, just to prove she *was* who she *said* she was?

I'm like, 'I'm sure she must have told you one or two of the high points as well?' but she doesn't answer.

She just storts mooching around the kitchen and the dining room, looking at shit, going, 'You have a beautiful home. You are very lucky.'

'*Was* very lucky,' I go. 'Me and Sorcha, we're not actually together any more.'

'No!' she goes, genuinely horrified. 'This cannot be!'

She obviously hasn't written for a few months.

I'm there, 'Hey, it's cool. It was, like, mutual?' then I turn around and pop the capsule in the machine, a wedding present from Oisinn and one of the few good things to come out of our marriage.

She's like, 'So – Soarchah is gone to . . .'

I'm there, 'The States. She's gone for a year. You probably should have written.'

She doesn't respond to that because she's sort of, like, drifted into the sitting room, where she's obviously looking at the photograph on the mantelpiece because I hear her go, 'Wow – Honor, she is so beautiful.'

Yes, she is.

Two Livanto cappuccinos. I breathe in the hum and I'm thinking, fair focks to you, Clooney. You were shit in *Batman*, but when it comes to coffee, you know your beans.

Then I have a total brainwave. I whip out a packet of the Fair Trade stem-ginger cookies that Sorcha buys from Oxfam and follow Immaculata into the sitting room.

She's standing in front of the contemporary bookshelf, her head cocked to one side, reading the spines on all of Sorcha's boxsets.

'What are these?' she goes.

I'm like, 'They're called, like, DVDs? They're pretty much like a CD except they've got, like, movies on them and shit?'

She gives me the *duh* look then.

'I am from Nigeria,' she goes, 'not from outer space. What I mean is, I have never heard of these movies. *Nip/Tuck. Dawson's Creek. ER. The OC . . .*'

I'm there, 'The thing is they're not actual movies? They're, like, all her favourite TV programmes.'

'She watches all of these?'

The innocence of it. So cute.

I'm there, 'She does in her Swiss. If we ever experience a nuclear winter, she might get around to it. Yeah, no, the thing with boxsets is you don't buy them to watch, you buy them to *own*?'

She suddenly gets, I don't know, frantic. 'I must watch them all,' she goes. 'I have so much to learn about Ireland.'

I'm like, 'Here, have one of these cookies. The ginger comes from some place in, I don't know, India. They pay the fockers a fortune for it as well . . .'

She takes one and says thank you.

I'm thinking, I could be a good host. 'So,' I go, 'how long are you planning to stay?'

'My ticket is for two months. But I think now I should perhaps go back.'

It's weird, but I suddenly don't want her to go?

I'm like, 'Go back? You've only got here. Why don't you stay. I'm going away myself in a few weeks. Why don't you stay until then? A month. See a bit of Ireland.'

Spare me the psychological evaluation by the way. Because I already know. Later on, I'd come to understand that Immaculata was what cleverer people than me call a surrogate for the daughter I had and lost.

Of course, I only found *that* out after it all blew up in my face.

I made, like, a vow to myself. I was going to show Sorcha and everyone else that I actually can be a nice goy. Looking after Immaculata was going to be my fock-you to all the people in the world who think they know Ross O'Carroll-Kelly – as in the *real* Ross O'Carroll-Kelly – but actually don't?

So that's why I did what I did. Looking back.

'Make yourself at home, Immaculata,' I went. Five words I didn't expect to hear myself say that particular day.

She gives me the most incredible smile then. 'You are a very nice man,' she goes.

I'm like, 'Separate beds, though.'

'Of course,' she goes, looking slightly confused. 'I have a boyfriend.'

I'm there, 'Believe me – there's a lot of birds who've said that.'

I step out of the lift and into, like, a corridor lined with all these framed posters with stuff that famous people said.

So Zsa Zsa Gabor's there going, 'I'm an excellent house-keeper – every time I get a divorce, I keep the house.'

That kind of shit.

I see her through the glass doors, leading into this big reception area. It's Claire from Brayruit.

She buzzes me in.

'So,' I go, 'you're working for Oisinn and Erika now. What happened to Caddles?' unable to resist it.

She's like, 'I just walked out, Ross, in the middle of a shift. I mean, I totally flipped. If I had to listen to "Dublin in the Rare Oul' Times" once more, I was going to hurt a customer.'

I know what she means. Old fockers pissing and pining for the Pillar and the Royal and the whooping cough and the left turn at the bottom of Dawson Street. I'm surprised more Caddles staff don't go postal.

'Anyway,' she goes, 'it was only ever a stopgap until something else came up. At least *here* I'm getting to use my morkeshing experience.'

'Answering the phones?'

'Not *just* answering the phones,' she goes, all defensive. 'I actually have a lot of responsibilities.'

It's at that exact point that her phone rings and she answers it straight away. 'Hi, Erika,' she goes. 'No – I haven't actually hoovered in there yet?' and I crack up laughing in her face. 'Oh, by the way, Ross is here.'

Erika says something, then Claire looks at me and goes, 'Oisinn's not here. He's in Paris,' and I'm like, 'That's cool – it's Erika I'm here to see.'

The whole set-up is pretty impressive, it has to be said. They must have, like, thirty or forty people working for them in this humungous open-plan office and it's buzzing – everyone on phones or banging away on computers.

Erika has her own room at the far end, looking out onto Stephen's Green and all done out in sort of, like, reddish-brown wood. I can see her a mile off – well, what I actually see is her Christian Louboutins up on the desk.

What is it about Loubs that career women love? I think it's the red soles. Make you look like you've trampled over dead bodies to get where you are.

'Cool office,' I go.

She shoots me a look of total contempt. 'Ross, I haven't got time to play,' she goes. 'I'm organizing eight parties for this weekend, the Fair itself is only three weeks away and Oisinn has focked off to France for the week.'

I sit down. I have to – I've a boner on me you could hang a wet coat on.

'Eight!' I go. 'Holy fock! So what do people, like, *do* at these porties?'

She looks at me *wearily*, I think is the word.

'I'm only asking asking because I might be in the morket for one. As you may or may not know, my marital status is about to change . . .'

'Different people want different things,' she goes. 'Some have all-male parties, some all-female. If it's amicable, some even throw joint parties.'

'Serious?'

'All depends on how you *feel* about your STBX. It's rare, though. There's a lot of bitter women out there . . .'

'I'd say.'

'Most of them want the night to end with the ceremonial burning of the marriage licence and/or wedding photographs. A lot of places won't allow it, though. Fire regulations. So we usually arrange a barrel outside.

'Then there's the music. Lot of Carrie Underwood and Lily Allen . . .'

'Jesus,' I go, 'that *is* bitter.'

'. . . Donita Sparks. Some just want a quiet night – a few

friends, canapés and a movie. *Waiting to Exhale*. Or what's that one with Tina Turner?'

I am going to sleep with this girl or die old asking.

'I have to ask you,' I go. 'Would you be interested in getting it on? Not here obviously. I mean, I'd pay for a hotel . . .'

'Ross,' she goes, 'are we going to keep doing this forever?'

I'm there, 'No – just until you say yes.'

'Well,' she goes, 'my answer is still the same. If you were the last man on Earth, I'd breed outside my species.'

I'm there, 'Still worth asking, though,' basically putting a brave face on it.

'Look, why are you even here?' she goes.

So I get straight to the point. 'Do you remember Sorcha sponsoring, like, a kid in Africa?'

Erika sort of, like, throws her eyes up in the air. 'Ross, that girl is *forever* sponsoring things. You know she bought me a mango sapling for Christmas the same year I bought her a Roger Vivier Pilgrim clutch? I wouldn't mind, but it's in Sri Lanka. I get a photograph of it every year . . .'

'Yeah, no, but this was, like, an actual little girl,' I go. 'Her name's, like, Immaculata?'

'. . . I must write to them, tell them to save themselves the postage. Two inches bigger than last year – okay, I get the general idea. Wait a minute,' she goes, all of a sudden, 'why are we even discussing this?'

'Because,' I go, 'she turned up on the doorstep yesterday. As in, this girl . . .'

It's a real conversation stopper, it has to be said. Erika's mouth just, like, drops open, showing off some very expensive orthodontic work.

'She turned up on your doorstep!' she goes, not even *trying* to hide her delight? 'Where is she now?'

I'm like, 'Where do you think? Back in the gaff. She had, like, nowhere else to go . . .'

'*Oh* my God,' she goes, 'you've *been* with her, haven't you?' absolutely delighted at the idea.

I go, 'Am I that bad a focking person that people would automatically think that?'

She doesn't answer.

Doesn't have to.

'So, Ross, you came here to tell me this to, what, cheer me up?'

'No, it's just, well, *as* Sorcha's best friend, I thought you might know a bit about this shit. I mean, what do they even eat in Nigeria? I remember that thing on the ad that used to crack me up – plumpy nut or something. I mean, would the formers' morket have that? Or would I have to go to Sheridan's?'

She's like, 'Okay, this is too weird. Why are you even *doing* this?' but of course she can read me like a book. 'You're pining for either Sorcha or Honor – I'm not sure which – and you're projecting your feelings for them onto this total stranger . . .'

'I wouldn't say that necessarily. Maybe I want people – Sorcha especially, but there's others I could mention – to see that I am an actual nice goy. That I am capable of *not* actually focking up the odd time?'

'Okay,' she goes and she's being genuine when she says it. 'Ross, they only use plumpy'nut in famine-relief situations. This girl would probably slap you across the face if you served it up to her . . .'

'Her name's Immaculata,' I go.

'Whatever – just give her what *you're* having.'

I'm like, 'As in, steak and chips?'

'As in, steak and chips.'

I'm there, 'Okay.'

I tell her thanks and then I stand up.

'For what it's worth,' she goes, just as I'm reaching the door, 'Cillian's not right for her.'

I stop.

She's like, 'He's a bore,' and that totally floors me.

Sometimes the girl is capable of saying the nicest things.

4. The new black

She walks in wearing what I presume is her best clobber – a black suit with, like, a white blouse underneath it. I'm watching the repeat of last night's *X Factor*, trying to get my brain into gear.

I'm about to tell her how well she looks when, totally out of the blue, she says the funniest thing: 'What time do you go to church?'

I must laugh in her face, roysh, because she looks at me sort of, like, confused. 'You are a Catholic?' she goes.

I'm like, 'Er, yeah?'

'And it is Sunday?' she goes.

I'm there, 'I think I know where you're going with this one. But, to be honest, I haven't been to Mass since I was, like, twelve?'

This is the worst thing Immaculata's ever heard, judging from her reaction.

I'm there, 'Look around you. We *have* everything. I couldn't think of a single thing to pray *for*.'

She shakes her head. 'But you do not pray to the Lord just to ask for things. You must pray to Him to thank Him for His wonderful blessings.'

It's the innocence of it.

'To be honest,' I go, 'I'm not really sure I believe in God. Don't get me wrong, I think there's, like, *something* out there? But something that *wants* me to sit around in my boxer shorts on a Sunday morning watching TV and doesn't want me bothering him with prayers, which he'd only have to then answer.'

She still looks confused. It's got to be a major culture shock for her coming to a place like Ireland.

'I'll tell you what,' I go, 'why don't I fix you some breakfast and you can tell me all about – what was it? – Nigeria?'

'Okay,' she goes, obviously deciding, when in Rome . . .

So while I'm lashing the sausages and rashers into the old Manfred, Immaculata disappears upstairs and comes back a few minutes later with a big whack of photographs, we're talking three or four hundred here.

I'm thinking, me and my big mouth.

I put the plate down in front of her. 'This is basically a traditional Irish fry,' I go. 'Also known as slow death on a plate . . .'

She looks at it like it's a puzzle to solve.

I'm like, 'So what would you have for breakfast over there?'

'For breakfast in Nigeria?'

'Yeah.'

'For breakfast in Nigeria, I cook moyin-moyin . . .'

'*Mmm*,' I go, cracking on I've heard of it, so as not to hurt her feelings.

She sees straight through it, though.

'You take some black-eyed peas or some type of beans. You skin them. And you mix with some ground tomatoes and some ground peppers. Some spices. Some minced beef, if you have some – but I prefer to have dried fish. Then you steam it in a large pot . . .'

It sounds focking revolting.

'I will make this for you,' she goes, picking up her knife and fork.

I'm like, 'Er . . .'

'I must,' she goes, 'because you have shown me hospitality. In Nigeria, we cook to show kindness. We have a proverb. To eat from the same pot of another is to take an oath of perpetual friendship.'

Dried fish, though.

'Er, cool,' I go, 'show us these snaps of yours.'

So she storts handing them to me one by one and there's, like, a little story with each of them. But it's weird, roysh, it's not boring? Not like looking at some focker's year in Australia – Oh my God, we totally tore it up out there – look, here's me bungee-jumping *again*.

No, I'm really interested in this and I actually regret never being orsed whenever Sorcha tried to interest me in Immaculata's story before.

She's going, 'This is the youth village where I have lived since I left the children's village when I was eleven. It is a calm haven. There, I have always felt at home.'

'Look at those focking roads,' I go. 'Is it, like, *all* dirt tracks?'

'Where I live, yes. But there are not so many nice cars, like in Ireland. Ah, this photograph here – this is Joyce and Samson Nwanu. This is the director of the youth village and his wife. I call them my second mother and father.'

I'm there, 'How did your actual mum and dad die again?'

'My mother died from tuberculosis. Nigeria has one of the highest rates for this in the world – I think number four. A lot of people lose their mother and their father this way. My father, he had a weak heart – this is how he died.'

'And you were only, like, six?'

'I do not have photographs of them. I cannot remember their faces. This makes me sad.'

I'm thinking, what a life this girl has had. Her old pair

dying when she was just a kid. And look how she's turned out. Really, I suppose, gentle – and such a cool person.

Milling into the sausages as well – Superquinn, you see.

'Without Soarchah, none of this is possible,' she goes. 'That's why I had to come to say thank you. Without sponsorship, there are many thousands of children like me who are vulnerable. The streets of Lagos are not a good place for a child to live. But in Owu-Ijebu I found a sanctuary. This is what I say. I wish you could travel to my village to see for yourself how someone can change a life . . .'

I pull a face that doesn't commit me to anything one way or the other.

She shows me a picture of, like, ten or eleven kids, cooking in a kitchen. There's one little boy – a real dude – who's trying to rub what looks like flour on this other girl's face. 'These are my brothers and sisters. They are also sponsored and mostly orphans, too. What you cannot see in the photograph is the laughter. Always in the village there is laughter.'

She shows me one then of her boyfriend, who looks a few years older than her, in fairness. 'This is Mikel,' she goes. 'He is studying to be a doctor. Final year. He is at the university in Lagos and next year I will go there to study mathematics.'

I'm there, 'And you want be a teacher? You must have brains to burn.'

'For Joyce and Samson,' she goes, 'school is the most important thing, after laughter. Nigeria has very high un-employment, but from the people who come through our youth village, almost everybody gets a job.'

She shows me a photograph of her bedroom then. She shares a bunk with her best friend, Anne. She points out, like, a globe of the world that she has on her locker.

'Joyce and Samson gave me this for my fourteenth birthday.

When you are older, they say, you can travel to every country in the world. Straight away I look for Ireland. I say, this is where I will go first. I will go to Ireland and say thank you to Soarchah. Because she let the Lord lead her to me. Without her, today I would be dead.'

It's the way she puts it. Straight out with it like that. I get up and I'm like, 'Come on.'

She's there, 'Where are we going?'

I must be mad.

I'm like, 'Mass.'

The front page of the Sunday *Wurdled* makes me laugh so much that I end up *actually* buying it?

Charlotte and Lance are getting married.

Of course, they're not actually – Charlotte's way too smort and way too good-looking to marry that fat, ponytailed prick. He's practically fifty. No, sex to Charlotte is – in her words – a means of social and career advancement. As well as very hord on your back.

You can take it for granted that the 'friend' who described their love-making as gymnastic and unrelenting was actually Charlotte herself.

Poor Lance. The second she gets what she wants out of him, she'll drop him like Honours German.

The headline's incredible: Charlotte's Church Date. It's, like, who thinks of these things?

'The news,' the story says, 'is sure to come as a bitter blow to Lance Rogan's former partner, Fionnuala O'Carroll-Kelly, whom he DUMPED to pick up with the stunning writer, who's half her age.

'McNeel's book, *Indian Summer*, has been top of the best-seller list for five weeks now and she is being hailed as the new queen of popular fiction in Ireland.

'Industry sources say that readers are turning away from O'Carroll-Kelly's books, detailing the breathless sexual adventures of South Dublin's affluent upper-middle-class set, in favour of McNeel's slick storytelling, which more accurately reflects the modern Ireland in which we live.

'O'Carroll-Kelly is said to be devastated at having lost her position as Ireland's favourite writer – and her beau. McNeel has publicly mocked her efforts to go after her market with a multicultural tale of her own, reportedly describing the book's plot as "lame".

'"Charlotte feels that Fionnuala should just stick to what she does best," said a friend last night. "As a writer, you've got to find your own voice, not copy somebody else's. Charlotte doesn't know what's eating her. Too much Leptoprin, I'd say."'

I can hordly imagine what a shock to the system it must be coming from somewhere like Nigeria to somewhere like Blackrock.

It's probably like the first time I walked into the Orts block in UCD and realized I was the only white face in a sea of tangerine.

So I suppose I'm pretty sensitive to what Immaculata's *going* through? For three days I'm listening to her banging away about *aksi fura do nono* and the hills of Futa Jalon when, all of a sudden, I go, 'Let's go out again.'

'But where?' she goes.

I'm like, 'Parnell Street.'

While she's getting ready, I phone for an Andy.

'What is this place we are going to?' she goes when we're well on the road. 'You said Parnell?'

I'm there, 'Yeah, I've never actually been there myself, but they call it Little Addis. It's all, like, African, if that

doesn't sound too racist? Well, *all* of those actually – African, Polish, Chinese . . .'

I don't think she really gets it until the driver lets us out at the rank at the top of O'Connell Street and we head down what's known as East Parnell Street and I swear to God, roysh, I think her spirits actually stort to lift.

Now it's my turn to experience, like, a culture shock.

This side of the river has always been a foreign country as far as I'm concerned, but suddenly it's like we've stepped into another world. Everything's different. The sights, the sounds, the smells.

I feel like Dora the focking Explorer here.

We're suddenly passing all these people on the street, men and women, and they're all – I hate to keep banging on about it – but black. There's, like, people in robes and all sorts. And shops selling pretty much everything you want – as long as what you want is powdered yams, your hair braided or your mobile phone unlocked.

And cheap internet as well.

I'd, like, heard about this place, but never thought I'd ever end up seeing it.

'Igbos,' Immaculata suddenly goes, pointing at a sign above the door of a shop. 'This is a tribe of Nigeria. In Anambra, Imo, Abia . . .'

'I mean, this wouldn't be, like, the *real* Ireland,' I try to tell her. 'For that you'd want to go somewhere like Dundrum.'

'They are very hard-working people. Many are traders. Ross, I must see this shop.'

I'm like, 'Er, yeah, cool,' thinking, this is an actual education for me because even though there's, like, millions of them in Ireland now, the only, I suppose, non-nationals I've had dealings with are the ones who've worked for me and Sorcha or for my old pair.

I actually should find out a bit more about that whole *thing*.

There's a big flag in the window – green, white, then green, which I presume is the flag of the actual country.

So we go in.

'Hello!' Immaculata goes to the dude behind the counter. 'I am from Ogun State – Owu-Ijebu!' and the dude – he actually looks a bit like Seal – his face suddenly comes alive, roysh, and he says something that I don't quite catch, then they're suddenly all over each other, hugging each other and talking at, like, ninety miles an hour, both telling their tales of how they ended up here, on the mean streets of Dublin's northside.

I know Immaculata's story back to front, so while they're doing the whole getting-to-know-you routine, I have a mooch around.

It's one of those shops, roysh, that doesn't know what the fock it is. It's actually a bit of everything. You can phone home for fock-all money. There's, like, three or four 'puters there as well for, like, e-mail or whatever. And they also sell, like, clothes and Tupperware containers and food.

Or what to *them* is food.

It's basically cellophane bags of, like, powder and leaves and shit. I'm looking at these printed-out labels, roysh, and it's all ewedu, fufu flour, starch, jero, masara, dawa, shinkafa, cassava . . .

All stuff you wouldn't chance eating, in other words.

All of a sudden, roysh, Immaculata's behind me. 'This is Ben,' she goes, introducing me to her new friend. 'And this is Rosockeral Kelly, the man I told you about.'

He sort of, like, claps my hand in two of his and goes, 'You are a very, very kind man.'

I'm there, 'Hey, there's a few out there would disagree with you – basically critics of mine . . .'

'In Nigeria,' he goes, 'we say this about kindness – when an only kola nut is presented with love, that kola nut carries with it more value than might otherwise be associated with a whole pod of many kola nuts . . .'

I'm like, 'Er, thanks,' at the same time thinking, their sayings don't exactly trip off the tongue. I'd love to see the size of their bumper stickers.

'Look at all of these things,' Immaculata suddenly goes, picking bags off the shelves and, like, examining them. 'They make me so sad for home.'

Then she has an idea. 'Tomorrow, Ross, I will cook a meal for you. Traditional Nigerian food to say thank you for what you have done for me.'

I'm there, 'You don't have to go to any trouble.'

She looks at this Ben and goes, '*Fura do nono*,' and he sort of, like, nods approvingly, then Immaculata storts throwing various bits and pieces into a basket.

I'm not even going to ask what it is. You just take it for granted that any dish with the word *nono* in it is going to have you on the Josh Ritter for days.

Ben's just, like, slapping me on the shoulder, telling me I'm going to like it.

Then he won't take any money from us. There must be, like, twenty squids' worth of shit here and he won't take a cent. 'You have shown generosity to a child of Nigeria,' he goes, as he packs it all up into two brown paper bags, 'and this is my gift to you.'

Then – fair focks to him – he throws in a bottle of what turns out to be palm wine.

I'm looking at Immaculata's face, roysh, then I'm looking at Ben's face, and I'm thinking, you know what? Much as

I hate patting myself on the back, I am pretty capable of making people happy when I put my mind to it.

Anyway, we say our goodbyes and we step back outside and the next thing I hear is the sound of hooves on the road, then a voice that I'd know anywhere shouts, 'Rosser, you fooken ladyboy!'

Now generally, roysh, on average, Ronan does or says one thing a week that makes my mouth just fall open. Even that doesn't prepare me, though, for the sight of him riding up Parnell Street towards town on a horse and two-wheeled cort, which I found out subsequently was called a sulky.

There's a line of traffic behind him as well, and all these drivers are, like, beeping him and telling him he shouldn't be on the fooken road in the foorst place, but Ro just ignores them, then pulls in at a bus-stop just ahead of us.

'Who is this funny little man?' Immaculata goes.

I'm there, 'Believe it or not, my son!'

Ronan looks me up and down. 'Chinos! Are you fooken mad? They'd moorder you over here for less!'

I'm there, 'Ro, how can I put this – what the *fock*?'

He's like, 'Nice, isn't she?' unclipping his legs from the stirrups, then slapping the horse on the orse.

I'm there, 'Where the fock did you get it?'

'Gull owns her.'

'Well, what are you doing with her?'

'Thought I'd get her out on the road,' he goes, 'open her up, see how she's ticking over . . .'

I'm like, 'Er, that doesn't answer my question.'

'It's me new thing,' he goes, then he turns around, wipes his hand on the front of his *Fcek – the Irish connection* T-shirt and offers it to Immaculata. 'Sorry about the other fella's manners,' he goes. 'I'm Ronan.'

'Ronan, Immaculata. Immaculata, Ronan,' I go. 'And

before you say it, Ro, it's not what it looks like. Sorcha sponsored her through one of those charities years ago. She's on holidays. Now what's the focking deal, Ro?'

He throws his eyes up in the air, then goes, 'It's called harness racing. I'm after taking it up, so I am. Me new sport.'

I'm there, 'Oh, so you're giving up rugby, then? Just like that?'

'Keep your fooken G-string on,' he goes. 'Rugby's for school, Rosser. This is how I'm gonna make me name. Racing, man. Lot of bread does be riding on it as well.'

I'm there, 'Oh, illegal gambling? I take it Blathin knows nothing about this?'

Immaculata storts petting the horse. She seems like a friendly enough thing.

'Bla's wide,' he goes. 'She's into what I'm into, just like I'm into what she's into. She's coming to me race on Saturday as well, with her ma and da.'

'Where's it on?'

'Back of me gaff – you know that big field?'

'There?'

'Yeah.'

'And Blathin's old pair are going?'

'Yeah.'

'As in Blathin's old pair from Clonskeagh?'

He's like, 'Are you alreet, Rosser? Have you been sniffing something?'

I'm there, 'No, it's cool,' not wanting to make a big deal of it. '*I'm* cool.'

'Well,' he goes, 'I was going to ring you in anyhow. Me ma's doing tea before the race. Me, her, Bla, Bla's ma and da, then you, you fooken tulip, if you're up for it, like.'

I'm like, 'Mariah, my friend. Wouldn't let you down. Where are you going with this thing now, by the way?'

He's like, 'I've one or two things to get in town. Gonna stick it in the Ilac.'

I suppose all the cor porks on this side of town take horses.

He tells Immaculata it was a pleasure to meet her, then he climbs back onto his little cart and goes, 'I'll see you, Rosser,' and he leaves me, as usual, just shaking my head.

I swear to fock. Every single piece of clothing I own – washed, ironed and put away in my wardrobe. I don't want her to think she has to, I don't know, *earn* her board, but at the same time . . .

'I don't even want to hear it,' Fionn goes when I'm telling the goys the story in Special Ks. 'It's like something from *Heart of Darkness*,' and Oisinn and JP crack their holes laughing.

Of course, it's not a proper slagging if the actual person you're slagging doesn't get it, which means the joke's really on Fionn.

He gets them in, though – aitches all round.

Erika arrives over with Chloe, Sophie and Amie with an ie in tow. Sophie is telling Amie that she is *so* never buying concert T-shirts again because you always end up using them as, like, pyjamas. *Oh* my God, she goes, taking off her DVBs to smooth back her hair, except Keane – she'd definitely buy a Keane one, if *they* ever came.

Erika looks incredible, in what I happen to know is a Roberto Cavalli suit – because Sorcha was always banging on about it – and obviously more Loubs.

'Is he here yet?' she goes.

'Texted,' Oisinn goes, 'to say he's running ten minutes late.'

I tell her she's looking well and she stares through me like I've just told her that Andrew Trimble could be badly exposed against South Africa in two weeks' time.

Every time I see her, I fall in love with her all over again.

I ask Chloe and Sophie how the shop's going and they don't answer, roysh, they just look at each other, then *I* look down and notice that they're both wearing brand-new Citizens of Humanity cigarette-leg jeans and Betsey Johnson ballet flats, which I automatically know they haven't paid for.

'Er, tell me how it's any of *your* business?' Chloe goes and I'm like, 'Because I'm still married to the bird you stole them from.'

The goy that Oisinn and Erika are waiting for turns out to be Dirty Harry, who owns a little basement sex shop on South William Street – we're talking DVDs, crocodile clips, electrodes, all that kind of shit.

Bits of rubber hosepipe, blah blah blah.

He's going to have, like, a stand at the Divorce Fair, which I suppose makes sense when you think about it. Sexually frustrated, single and all that.

When he arrives, roysh, he's exactly as I would have drawn him – short and fat, with big Hot Dog fingers, a well-slapped face, a bad comb-over and two swallow tattoos, one on his hand and one on his Gregory. He's wheezing like a focked boiler as well and there's, like, a sheen of sweat on him and it's no wonder because he's wearing one of those big leather jackets that bouncers wear, in Kiely's as well, which is like a focking steambath tonight.

I immediately hate him, and not just because he's a creamer. It's the way he walks in, like he owns the place. Then, if I'm being honest, the way he looks at Erika, like he's been asked to guess the weight of her thrups, then the way he goes, 'How's my little plaything?' the sleaze, and especially the way Erika just smiles and goes, 'Hello, Harry.'

'Call me Dirty,' he goes, kissing her on the cheek.

Oisinn asks him what he wants to drink and Harry says gin.

Then he turns around to JP and asks how his old man is.

'Er, fine,' JP goes.

'You the priest?'

'No, I, er . . . well, not any more. I'm a landscape gardener now.'

Harry sort of, like, narrows his eyes. 'That slang for something?'

JP looks at me, then Fionn. 'Er, no – I'm an *actual* landscape gardener.'

Harry nods, like he's no opinion on it one way or the other. 'You broke your poo-er fadder's heart,' he eventually goes. 'Hasn't been able to show he's face in the club since . . .'

Club? Christ!

Then Harry, Oisinn and Erika fock off to another corner to talk business.

'What a focking sleaze,' I go. 'If ever I get like that . . .'

No one says anything.

Sophie asks me if what Erika says is true, that I've got the African girl who Sorcha sponsored at school staying with me, and I ask her what the fock it has to do with her, roysh, but she doesn't answer, except to say that she sponsored a little boy called Moses at the same time, but cancelled her direct debit after seeing a documentary about female circumcision and deciding that she was *so* over the whole Africa thing?

If they know, then Sorcha's going to find out – that's for sure.

As if reading my mind, Chloe asks has anyone seen Sorcha's Facebook page? Her and Cillian took Honor to, like, Disneyland and the pictures are, like, *so* cute and – *oh my God!* – they met Anne Geddes there, as in *the* Anne Geddes, and she wants to, like, photograph Honor.

She's being a bitch. Fionn tells her to shut the fock up, which is actually a first – *him* sticking up for *me*.

'Focking Cillian!' I hear myself go. I'm actually a lot more hammered than I thought? 'I can't believe she's gone from me to *that*. Some focking come-down. He's never even played rugby . . .'

Fionn and JP nod. They're good like that.

'Sorcha needs a man,' I go, 'not some focking weed in a suit. What use would he be in a situation?'

Chloe waves her finger at me and goes, 'Oh my *God* – *weirdo*?' then she and the other two fock off.

Fionn puts his orm around my shoulder. 'You want to come out laying decking with us,' he goes. 'Find some peace. Get your parasympathetic system working properly.'

I remind him I already have a job.

JP asks me how they look on the DVDs and I should tell him they're actually a good squad, room for improvement, blahdy blahdy blah. But I've had too much of the truth serum to pull it off.

'They're the worst team I've ever seen,' I go. '*We'd* hand them their orses, as in the three of *us*? Plus Oisinn and Christian, obviously. I mean, I watched them the other night lose to Luxembourg. Focking Luxembourg!'

'Well,' JP goes, 'if anyone can turn them into world beaters, it's you,' and it's a nice thing to say, even if it *is* total bullshit.

I'm like, 'I meant what I said, by the way. About that focking Cillian. Sorcha needs, like, a protector. She can be a total sap sometimes. Like, I remember the time we went to see *Jurassic Park* – the second or the third one, maybe. For, like, two weeks afterwards Sorcha was waking up in the middle of the night screaming – we're talking nightmares, blahdy blahdy blah.

'*I* was the one who sat up with her all night, I suppose

reassuring her. Telling her that dinosaurs aren't real, that they're, like, a Hollywood invention.'

Of course, this is the funniest thing that either of them has ever heard. They're laughing so much that pretty much everyone in Kiely's is looking.

Then all of a sudden JP stops and goes, 'I've just realized that as a practising Catholic, I actually *agree* with Ross,' and then they crack their holes laughing again.

It rings, like, seven or eight times before a girl's voice answers.

'Hello, Ronan's phone.'

I'm like, 'Hey, Blathin – how the hell *are* you?'

She's there, 'Oh, hi, Ross. Fine – I'm practising my lines.'

'Lines?'

'For the play?'

'Oh – you're still doing it? Our little trip out west didn't, like, put you off?'

'Er, *no?*' she goes. 'If anything, it's made me even more determined to do it, to spread the word far and wide that Blanchardstown is an actual place and the people there need our help.'

I'm like, 'Er, I suppose that's one way of looking at it.'

In fairness to Mount Anville, they take that whole social conscience shit really seriously.

'Is himself about?' I go.

I can just about catch the sound of galloping hooves in the background.

She's like, 'He's training at the moment, Ross.'

'Training?' I go. 'Of course – the race.'

'He's just getting to know the horse. They have to trust each other, see. It's like, *oh my God*!'

'So where are you?' I go.

She's like, 'Sandymount Strand.'

In my mind I can picture them. Blathin sitting there in her little wheelchair, memorizing her lines. Ro flying past on his trusty steed, churning up the sand. The two of them exchanging little smiles.

See, I'm, like, a romantic at hort?

I'm there, 'Would you just tell him I said hi?'

Fura do nono turns out to be corn balls with fulani milk yoghurt and, without wanting to come across as, like, anti-black or whatever, it's focking revolting.

I'd rather eat my own socks.

'This is Mikel's favourite meal,' she goes. 'I make it for him for special days.'

Poor focker.

I'm chasing the corn balls around with my fork, to give the impression that I'm actually eating them. At the same time I'm trying to distract her attention from my plate.

'You've told me pretty much nothing about Mikel,' I go. 'How did you goys hook up?'

She's like, 'Mikel lived in my village. He was an orphan also. His mother and father come from Benin. You know Benin?'

'Er . . .'

'It is next to Nigeria.'

'Okay.'

'It is a sad story. His mother died giving birth to him and his father did not want him. He said he was cursed. His mother's sister lived in Nigeria, in Abuja. He lived with her for two years, but then she did not want him. She said he looked too like his mother. Every time she looked at him, it made her sad . . .'

'Jesus.'

'. . . so she took him to Owu-Ijebu. This is where we met.'

'And he didn't mind you, like, coming to Ireland?'

'No,' she goes, 'he encouraged me. He knows this is my dream, all my life, to find Soarchah and to say thank you because without her, I am sure today I would be dead.'

'So, like, what's the age difference between you and Mikel?'

'He is six years older. He would like to get married, but I say no, not until after I finish at the university.'

'But you *do* love him?'

She smiles and stares into the distance. 'When I see him, my heart beats quicker.'

'So we're talking love of your life here?'

She's like, 'He is the only man I have ever . . .' and she lets her voice trail off.

'You're joking?'

'No,' she goes, obviously embarrassed at having told me.

'The only goy you've ever . . .'

'Yes.'

I'm like, 'Whoa – that's pretty special.'

'Yes,' she goes, 'it is,' and then she points at my plate and goes, 'Did you like it?'

What I've actually done is I've piled it all up on one side of the plate, so it looks like I've eaten half of it.

'It was absolutely incredible,' I go. 'Sorry I couldn't finish it.'

'Tomorrow,' she goes, 'I will cook you puff puff with jollof rice . . .'

'You don't have to go to any trouble.'

'This, too, is a favourite of Mikel. It is my pleasure to cook for you, Ross.'

I've a feeling Mackey Ds in Blackrock is going to be seeing quite a bit of my boat over the next few weeks.

She clears away the plates and takes them to the kitchen. It's at this exact point, roysh, that my phone rings and I don't even need to check caller ID to know who it is.

I've been expecting her to ring.

'What have you *done* to her?'

That's her opening line.

I'm like, 'Why is that everybody's automatic first question? The answer is nothing, except put a roof over her head and show her how to use the washing machine and the DVD player.'

'Yeah, *my* roof,' she goes.

I'm there, 'So who told you – Chloe or Sophie?' but she doesn't answer, just carries on having what can only be described as a knicker-fit.

'You shouldn't even *be* in the house,' she's going. 'You know what Dad will do if he finds out?'

I'm there, 'I presume he'd fock me out on the street. Then Immaculata's homeless as well. So I presume you *won't* be telling him?'

That focking softens her cough.

'Ross,' she goes, all of a sudden switching to the tone she uses when she wants something, 'Cillian's going to book her a ticket, Dublin to Los Angeles, tonight. Will you drop her to the airport?'

I don't know why, roysh, but I get the impression that he's standing behind her, massaging her shoulders, trying to keep her calm. And I'm thinking, there's no *way* he's taking Immaculata away from me as well.

It's, like, suddenly we're having the custody battle we didn't have over Honor.

'To be honest,' I go, 'she seems happy enough here? We're getting on like I don't know what. She's cooking all sorts. And she's telling me all about this place she's from. Did you know it's, like, the eighth biggest country in the world, as in population-wise?'

'I can't believe you didn't even ring to tell me about this.'

'Yeah,' I go, suddenly losing it, 'just like I can't believe you didn't ring to tell me about Disneyland and Anne Geddes. I have to get on Facebook to find out about my own daughter. I'm going off my actual rocker without her. You promised you'd stay in touch. You promised you'd send regular pictures, Sorcha . . .'

All of a sudden, Immaculata's at my shoulder. 'Soarchah? You are speaking with Soarchah?'

Sorcha hears her and lets out a squeal that pretty much deafens me. 'Ross, put me on to her!' she goes. 'Put me on to her *now*!' and she's pretty much hysterical.

I hand Immaculata my phone and straight away she launches into this speech, which she's obviously been rehearsing in her head for years, all about how Sorcha's kindness saved her life and how her letters taught her that there was so much love in the world and we must always learn to see it.

And as she's saying it, roysh, I'm actually nodding in agreement, thinking, yeah, no, that's one thing you'd have to say about her – she always saw the good in people.

I don't know what Sorcha says then, but suddenly Immaculata's going, 'No, Ross is sleeping in your bedroom and I am sleeping in the other bedroom . . .'

So much for that focking theory.

'No,' she goes, 'he has not said anything like that to me. No, he has not used any of these lines . . .'

I'm sure Sorcha can't believe it. I'm there, 'Hey, tell her I think I'm going to prove the critics wrong on this one,' and Immaculata does.

They spend, like, an hour-and-a-half on the phone and there's, like, tears and laughter and I dare say, on the other end of the line, more than a few *oh my Gods*.

I rinse off the plates and leave them to it.

I can't say I *always* miss Sorcha, but tonight I miss her so much that it hurts to think.

My phone rings. A number I don't recognize, though for some reason I answer it anyway. It's, like, Angela, as in the old dear's friend from the Funderland campaign? Ringing to say she's worried about Fionnuala. Penguin have, like, ditched her.

'Ditched her?' I go.

She's like, 'Well, she explained it to me – they've decided not to take up the option on her next book . . .'

'No!'

'They say the market's shifted, Ross. They're no longer sure the books she writes are either relevant or . . . what was this phrase they used? *Commercially viable?*'

'Bastards!'

'Oh, she's devastated.'

'I can imagine. The fockers!'

'Ageism – that's what it is. That's my view. This Charlotte what's-she-called – how old could she be? These bits of kids haven't any experience of life. How can their writing be taken seriously?'

'Poor Mum!'

'Now, I know you two had a silly falling out . . .'

'Oh, don't – it seems so ridiculous now, in view of this . . .'

'I'm sure a lot of things were said . . .'

'We *both* said shit . . .'

'Well, it's good to hear you say that because she could really do with your support. You know she's talking about pulling out of this charity milonga event she's been organizing for the victims of Typhoon Xangsane?'

'Whoa – that's crazy talk.'

'The state she's in, I'd say she's capable of anything.'

'That's it,' I go, 'I've got to go and see her . . .'

'It'd mean a lot, I'm sure. Honestly, Ross, I've known Fionnuala for a lot of years and I've never seen her so depressed, so without hope . . .'

'And when you think about it, I'm, like, all she's got.'

'But please don't tell her I told you,' she goes.

I'm there, 'Yeah, no, I won't, but Angela, thanks so much for ringing.'

'It's fine. I'm just worried about her. Worried she'll do something drastic.'

The plan is to go straight to the gaff, roysh, but when I'm in the actual Jo, *something* – call it a hunch – tells me to stop off first at The Gables.

She's in her usual spot, looking shit it has to be said, like she hasn't slept. I walk over to where she's sitting and I go, 'Mum!' and she looks up from her poached eggs with smoked salmon and tarragon Béarnaise, which she's barely even touched. 'I just . . . I just heard the news. Aw, it's too bad, it really is . . .'

She doesn't say anything, roysh, just nods sadly and of course I can't keep it up any more. 'I'm focking delighted!' I go, then I crack my hole laughing, right in her face. 'It's the funniest thing I've ever heard.'

Everyone in The Gables is suddenly looking, but I can't actually stop. I'm in total focking hysterics here.

The old dear just, like, bursts into tears, looking for sympathy – and of course I'm even worse then, just, like, laughing and laughing and laughing, like an actual lunatic, until one of the staff comes over and tells me she thinks I really should leave now or she's calling the Gords.

Tea, to me, is a drink. Where Ronan comes from, tea is an actual meal. See, these people have the main meal of the day at, like, lunchtime. Then, when the rest of the world is having its dinner, they're having a slice of ham, a quarter of a tomato and a couple of slices of beetroot. That's tea to them.

Fock knows what Blathin's crowd are going to make of it. Her old man's, like, an obstetrician, which I presume means he's coining it in. I mean, Clonskeagh, for fock's sake.

Tina's putting her back into it, in fairness to her, though I think running the old J. Edgar around the place would be a better use of her time than buttering slices of what they call pan and cutting them in half, while smoking, of course.

If Ronan's nervous, he's not showing it. He's playing the big man, sitting in his granddad's ormchair with his little Ronnie Kray half-glasses on, reading his *Heddild* and sort of, like, tutting to himself.

'Another dead hero in gangland,' he goes. 'Will these shams *ever* learn?'

You have to give it to him, he's good value.

'So,' I go, 'two families coming together for the first time? Went through this a fair few times myself. And okay, Ro, I can feel the elbow in the ribs – you're looking for some last-minute advice . . .'

'Try not to take a shit out the window,' Tina suddenly pipes up, then her and Ro just crack their holes laughing.

I told Ro that in, like, strict confidence?

I'm like, 'Whatever happened to, *a shut mouth* . . .'

'Sorry, Rosser,' he goes, still laughing, 'I couldn't resist it, man.'

He gets up out of the chair and makes his way over to where Tina's slicing a cucumber. He's, like, nearly tall enough to look over her shoulder now. 'Ma, not too much for me,' he goes. 'I'm apposed to be racing in an hour.'

134

That's when the doorbell suddenly goes. Sorry, the letter-box – there *is* no doorbell.

Tina's not used to being around these kind of people and she's, like, over-compensating in a major way. Her voice is suddenly a good twenty postcodes posher.

'It's lovely to meet you, Dr Roberts,' she goes to Blathin's old man, practically curtsying.

I hang back, playing it coola boola, like I don't even know what a focking obstetrician does.

Which, of course, I don't.

'David,' he goes. 'Call me David.'

Blathin's old dear, I can't help but notice, is actually a bit of a milf. It's hord to know who to compare her with, but if you put, like, a gun to my head, I'd have to say Marcia Gay Harden.

'Hi, Ross!' Blathin goes, genuinely delighted to see me.

I ask her how she is and she tells me she's been asked to play the pipe organ in the Irish National Youth Orchestra's version of Strauss's 'Alpine Symphony' on New Year's Eve. Her friend Kandra is playing the E-flat clarinet.

She actually reminds me a lot of Sorcha, it has to be said.

So when we've finished the whole meet-and-greet thing, Ronan grabs the handles of the chair and pushes Blathin through to what Tina calls the kitchenette, with the rest of us sauntering behind. That's when I notice the chill for the first time – and I'm not referring to the Superser F150 with the focked ignition switch.

Amanda – Blathin's old dear – has a face on her. I actually thought I copped it when Tina first opened the door. I noticed she had her nose in the air, but I thought she was just scared to breathe in. But no, I recognize that look now.

It's disgust.

Tina's forting around, putting the finishing touches to the

famous tea, which means it's left to me to make all the running conversation-wise.

'So, Dave,' I go, 'what do you think of this Andrew Trimble? Is he going to fall flat on his face against South Africa?' but Dave goes, 'Not much of a sports fan, I must confess,' and of course that stops that line of conversation dead in its tracks.

Tina puts the plates down in front of us then and Amanda looks at hers like it's a focking roadkill badger. I look at her and roll my eyes, in sympathy more than anything, but she totally blanks me, then David gives her a look, which I take to mean 'Eat the thing', so she picks up her fork and storts trying to, like, prong one of her pickled onions, which she obviously has no intention of putting anywhere near her mouth.

The silence is, like, seriously painful.

Blathin asks Ronan if he's nervous and he says not really, playing it tougher than a cheap steak. Well, maybe a little, he goes, but he'd be worried if he wasn't because that'd mean he wasn't focused. The kind of shit I used to tell Gerry Thornley back in the day.

Blathin says she bought him another present, then she reaches into the little pouch at the back of her wheelchair and produces this small package, wrapped in shiny red paper with, like, a gold ribbon around it.

He's like, 'Ah, Bla – you shouldna.'

'Open it!' she goes.

It turns out it's, like, a scorf. We're talking blue-and-brown stripes. 'Ah, thanks, Bla,' he goes, at the same time shooting me a sideways look, I think expecting me to stort ripping the piss out of him.

'I bought it in, like, Avoca?' she goes. 'I thought you might wear it in the race.'

136

'I will,' he goes, suddenly not giving a shit what I think. 'It's warm, isn't it?'

'Yeah, it's all natural fibres.'

During this whole time, roysh, there's not a word out of the adults at the table, except when I turn around to Blathin's old dear and go, 'More Heinz Russian salad, Mand?' and even then all I get back is a really quick shake of the head.

I'm thinking, maybe I *will* take a shit out the window – might liven this lot up.

Ronan excuses himself from the table, saying he has to change, then he comes back a couple of minutes later wearing one of those stripy, round-necked jumpers you see in, like, Penny's, a pair of tracksuit bottoms and his Nike Air Maxes. Oh and his scorf of course, wrapped twice around his Jeff Beck.

'Do you need some help clearing this away?' Bla's old dear says to Tina. It's the first time she's spoken since she walked through the door.

'Nah,' Tina goes, 'sure I'll leave them there till the morning.'

The morning! It's half-six at night! Amanda's reaction is hilarious, like she's been slapped across the back of the neck with a wet kipper.

We walk around to the field at the back of the gaff, me pushing Blathin, Ronan walking beside us, yakking away, not a care in the wurdled, Tina, David and Amanda walking a few steps behind us.

Holy fock!

I think I actually say that out loud when we reach the field. There must be, like, three or four hundred people there, waiting for the race – mostly Travellers and Dublin criminal types, it has to be said, standing around this huge

raceway they've, like, morked out in the middle of the field. It must be the size of an actual athletic track.

It's already dork, I don't know if I mentioned – as in *pitch* dork? But there's, like, thirty or forty Hiaces around the perimeter of the track, all with their full headlights on, so it's as bright as Donnybrook on a Friday night.

There's some focking sights as well. All these little huddles of people, smoking and arguing and calling each other every doorty-looken this and doorty-looken that under the sun. There's a fair few out on the actual track as well, down on their hunkers, feeling the ground, suggesting they know shit. And there's plastic bags full of moolah passing back and forth between men with no necks and pitt bull terriers on leashes pulled so tight that the dogs are actually up on two legs.

I'm looking around, roysh, expecting to see Guy Ritchie and a focking camera crew filming it all.

Ronan gives Blathin a peck on the cheek and she wishes him luck. Then he walks over to where Nudger, Gull and Buckets of Blood are standing, with the horse and the little cort. On the back of it, written in what looks very much to me like Tippex, is the word *Honor*, which is a lovely touch, you have to give it to him. There's like, two or three minutes of discussion, then they pick Ronan up and strap him into the little stirrups on the side of the cort. One crack of the whip and off he goes, warming up with the other riders in the race.

Buckets of Blood gives Blathin a little wave.

I turn around to her old pair, standing behind me, and I go, 'Where's your Celtic Tiger now, huh?' trying to keep the situation calm. 'It's only a focking rumour around here,' but neither of them says anything. They're too busy trying to look invisible.

I'm scoping the crowd, roysh, and – unbelievable – I end up spotting the fockers who torched the old dear's cor. They're on the far side of the track – their horse, I notice, is the only white one in the race – and they're giving some obviously last-minute instructions to the jockey. One of them cops me, then nudges one of the others, then suddenly they're all looking over at me, laughing.

One of them even blows me a kiss and I swear to God, roysh, I suddenly want Ronan to win this race more than I want him to win a schools Senior Cup medal.

So whatever, roysh, five, ten minutes later, the horses are all under storter's orders, then someone fires presumably a sawn-off and the race is suddenly under way. Ronan's away quicker than anyone and he takes the first bend, roysh, a good two lengths clear.

'Come on, Ronan,' Blathin's shouting, but, to be honest, roysh, I'm drowning her out, giving it, 'Go on, Ro! You the man!' and the adrenalin is seriously pumping. The thing is, I love live sport – doesn't matter what it is.

Thrump thrump thrump . . .

Ronan's absolutely flying. In total control.

Then he gets an unbelievable break.

Coming up to the stort of the second lap, the horse immediately behind him takes the bend way too fast. The cort actually goes up on one wheel, then, after what seems like forever, ends up toppling over and pulling down the horse.

Of course, the one immediately behind him mills straight into him as well.

All you can see is this, like, dust cloud with horses' legs and bits of broken wood and angry skobie faces sticking out of it.

The other three horses in the race have to take the long

way around and Ronan's suddenly seven, eight lengths clear, with the Blanchardstown horse at the back of the field, looking seriously focked.

Thrump thrump thrump . . .

The crowd is going absolutely Hertz Van and it's suddenly obvious, roysh, that most of the money here tonight is riding on him and the bookies are going to take a tonking.

I instinctively check the quickest way out of here.

Thrump thrump thrump . . .

Further ahead Ronan pulls.

Whacker, Nudger and Buckets are roaring at him.

Tina's going, 'Go on, Ro-nin! It's yo-ers! It's yo-ers!' like she's put the focking TV licence money on him. Which, of course, she probably has.

It's no longer a race. It's, like, a procession, with Ro way out in front now and there's me in the crowd, roysh, turning to total randomers and telling them that that's my actual son out there.

Thrump thrump thrump . . .

Blathin's going, 'Faster, Ronan! Faster! Faster!' and I tell her not to worry, that it's *ins an mála* now, that Ro has the big-match temperament that the O'Carroll-Kellys are famous for, going all the way back to my great-grandfather, who won an Ireland B cap on a development tour to Uruguay in 1931.

Of course, I end up speaking too soon.

One of the reasons why sport is so exciting is that you never know what's going to happen from one moment to the next – it's, like, the unexpected.

And it's at that exact moment that something totally unexpected happens.

By the time Ro passes in front of us the second time, with a lap and a half to go, it's suddenly obvious that his horse is storting to tire. Happens just like that – the fuel tank's suddenly empty.

Now it's like, *thrump . . . thrump . . . thrump . . .*

I remember him telling me on the Wolfe that he had one or two doubts about her staying power, which meant he'd have to go off like – pordon the phrase – a bullet from a gun and just hope she'd enough in her over the last lap.

The white horse is suddenly at the front of the chasing pack and he's, like, eating up the ground, like he knows Ronan's horse has fock-all left, like he knows it in his nostrils.

Ronan's suddenly looking over his shoulder for the first time in the race and he's giving it loads with the whip.

Blathin has her hands up to her face, going, 'Go, Ronan! Oh my God!'

One lap left and there's, like, four lengths in it, which sounds like a lot, but not at the rate this horse is closing.

The lads from Blanch are suddenly giving it loads. 'Go on, ye fooker! Ye have it!'

Thrump thrump thrump . . .

Three lengths.

Two lengths.

Two shorp cracks of the whip from Ronan and it's three again.

Thrump thrump thrump . . .

Then two and a half . . .

Two . . .

They're on the back straight now. I can hordly stand it. The crowd's going totally ballistic. Blathin's screaming, but at a pitch that only the dogs present can hear.

One and a half . . .

Then one.

All of a sudden, roysh, the Blanchardstown horse cuts

inside, giving him the shortest route around the final bend, with Ronan forced to take the outside lane. The manoeuvre takes Ronan totally by surprise and you can see him, like, wheel around in shock, as in his whole upper body, and it suddenly upsets the balance of the cort.

We watch in slow motion, roysh, as one wheel leaves the ground, though it doesn't just topple over like the other one. The whole thing actually snaps away from the horse and the cort is suddenly thrown twenty feet into the air, with Ronan still attached to it.

There's, like, a sudden intake of breath from the crowd.

Then the cort lands with this, I don't know, sickening thud.

Time stands still. For the next few seconds I can hear literally nothing. Then all I can hear is the sound of Blathin screaming. I look down and I realize I'm running, pushing Blathin in the direction of where Ronan landed.

'Let me through,' I hear myself going. 'Let me through,' and I use the wheelchair to cut, like, a path through the crowd.

Blathin's bawling her eyes out, going, 'Ronan! Ronan!' while my hort is beating so hord, I think it's going to, like, burst out of my *actual* chest?

We hear him before we see him. 'Someone tell Bla I'm alreet!' he's going. 'Someone find her, tell her not to worry!'

He's lying on his back, roysh, still attached to what's left of the cort, with Nudger and Buckets undoing the straps. 'Someone find Bla,' he keeps going.

Suddenly, roysh, she's there in front of him and Ronan's straight up on his feet again. People are telling him to stay down, he might have concussion, but he doesn't care. He totally ignores me and throws his orms around her. She buries her head in his chest and just, like, sobs her little hort

144

out, covering his new scorf and his good jumper in fake tan.

The crowd has lost a fortune, but no one seems to *give* a fock?

'Some fooken race, wha'?' seems to be the general verdict.

See, they love their heroes on this side of the city, as much as we love, I don't know, having two last names and wrapping parma ham around shit.

They're all clapping and cheering him as he takes the wheelchair and pushes Blathin through the crowd, limping, nodding sort of, like, humbly and waving with each hand in turn. I follow a few feet behind, watching the crowd port in front of him.

Once or twice I hear people go, 'That's his oul' lad,' and they say it in, like, total awe.

The next thing I see is the Blanchardstown – I suppose you'd have to say – posse, up ahead. They're lined up, roysh, either side, in a kind of gord of honour and they just, like, applaud him as he passes, which is a nice touch, one you wouldn't expect from chip shop filth like them.

As I walk past them, I feel a hand on my shoulder. It's *him,* as in the dude with the lunar complexion, the dude who torched out the old dear's cor.

'Sorry we had to do that,' he goes, except, the way *he* says it, it's obviously *dat.* 'You can tell Gull we're square now, but.'

I tell him I will, but of course at that stage I haven't a focking bog what he's talking about.

Tina greets Ronan like a soldier home from war. David and Amanda just look traumatized. Amanda takes Blathin and goes, 'We really should be going,' and Tina's there, 'Will yiz not come in for some deseert?' thinking, I've a fooken tin of strawberries in there would round off this unforgettable evening for you.

'Afraid we can't,' David goes, cracking on to remember something he's got to do, but not orsed enough to actually make something up on the spot. I'd be focking stunned if they're ever seen north of Dame Street again.

Then it suddenly hits me, as they're putting Blathin's chair into the boot. What that line meant.

You can tell Gull we're square now.

Ronan threw the race. He threw it to sort out whatever shit Gull had got himself into out in Blanch.

'Jesus, Rosser,' he goes, 'I could see *your* fooken gaff, I was trun so high,' but he cops me smiling at him and he immediately knows I know. 'A shut mouth . . .' he goes, his lips not even moving.

Blathin waves at us through the window. Amanda doesn't even do that. She's sat in the front passenger seat, staring straight ahead, going, 'Drive! Just drive!'

From my own experience – not to mention the wheelspin that David pulls – I suspect that this is the last Ronan and Blathin will be seeing of each other.

Unbelievable, roysh – as the cor disappears down the road, Tina actually turns around to me and goes, 'I tink dat went well, didn't it?'

What do you say to that?

'I think you're reet,' Ronan goes, standing, squinting, in the middle of the road until the Prius NHW20 is just a speck in the distance. Then he turns and limps back to the gaff and I can honestly say I've never seen him happier.

So much so that I can't bring myself to tell him about the even horder landing that's coming his way.

How can I tell him how this focked-up world really works? So instead I just sit and stare at him, while he sits and stares at nothing, a little smile playing on his lips, and I wish we could stay like that – even *here* – forever.

Tina asks me if I want tinned strawberries and I tell her damn roysh I want tinned strawberries.

It's, like, midnight by the time I get back to Blackrock and I'm fit for nothing but bed. I walk through the front door to find Immaculata standing in the hall, waiting for me.

She seems pissed about something.

I'm there, 'Hey, is everything cool?'

'Ross,' she just goes. 'Is it true?'

I'm like, 'True? As in?'

'Is it true,' she goes, 'that women have orgasms, too?'

I'm like, 'What are you talking about?' obviously a bit taken aback.

She's there, 'Answer my question!' pretty much screaming at me. 'Do! Women! Have! Orgasms!'

I peg it straight into the living room and check the shelf.

It's gone.

Sorcha's *Sex and the City* Season One boxset.

I whip around and Immaculata's behind me, madder than any bird I've ever met.

'Mikel,' she goes, 'he told me this was a lie . . . only men have orgasms, he said.'

Sounds like me and Mikel are cut from the same cloth.

I don't want to land the dude in it. That'd make me a hypocrite, so I turn away and just, like, stare into space.

'But Samantha Jones,' she goes, 'she has many, many orgasms . . .'

'It's just a programme,' I go. 'It's not *supposed* to be taken seriously?'

'Look at me,' she goes, 'and tell me the truth.'

Reluctantly, roysh, I look at her and, when I do, I realize I can't actually lie to this girl.

'Look, a tiny, tiny minority of women have orgasms,'

I go. 'I mean, *I've* never actually witnessed it myself. But I *have* heard stories . . .'

That focking programme. All it ever did was raise women's expectations to an unreasonable level.

But she seems satisfied by this news, happy almost.

'But bear in mind,' I go, 'that if you haven't had one by the age of nineteen, it probably means you're not, like, meant to?'

'No,' she goes, sitting down, 'I am going to have an orgasm! Like in *Sex and the City*!'

And, as I hit the sack, I suddenly know – just *know* – that this is another story that's going to end in tears. And you can bet they're going to be mine.

5. The three-tiered plate of life

'The shell button.'

I'm like, 'The what?'

I swear to God, roysh, there's times when you'd need focking subtitles to understand this kid.

He's there, 'The shell button. The shell button hotel.'

'Oh, the Shelbourne?' I go. 'Wow! That's a bit . . .' and what I'm about to say is that it's a bit upmorket for *him*, but I manage to stop myself.

'Bit what?' he goes, checking himself out in the window of Laura Ashley.

I'm there, 'Exciting – that's what I was going to say. Meeting Blathin's old pair again. Are you nervous?' and he's like, 'Nervous? It's only Arthur Noon tea, Rosser.'

He looks the part, in fairness to him, though eventually I have to turn my head because my lungs are filling up with *Blue Stratos*.

'And sure, I'm after meeting them loads,' he goes. 'Why would I be nervous?'

It's shit, roysh, because I know the Jack here – the kid's about to get the straight red. The worst thing is, though, I can't bring myself to tell him. I end up wussing out and just dropping hints.

'Life is a bit like afternoon tea,' I go, as we stort walking again. 'When the three-tiered plate arrives, you'll see that some people will go for the smoked salmon and cream cheese, some for the egg and cress. Others might go straight for the scones or the miniature eclairs . . .'

He looks at me like I'm off my rocker.

'What I'm saying is that people have, like, prejudices? They're into, like, one particular thing? And then when they come up against something they're not used to, their minds aren't open enough to realize that . . . egg and cress are pretty focking incredible, you know . . .'

We stop at the top of Grafton Street and I point him in the direction of the Shelbourne.

'A few hundred yords down there on the left,' I go. 'If you've any problem getting in, just mention my old man's name,' and he says mustard, then he tells me he'll bell me later.

'The second it's over,' I go, then I watch him disappear down the street.

I hit the Buckys in BT 2, grab a tall white chocolate mocha and sit in the window, thinking that if I was any kind of father, I'd be in the Shelbourne now, telling Blathin's old pair what an amazing kid Ronan is, even if he *is* from Iffy Valley.

I know my old man would do it for me, the dickhead.

Instead, I sit there for, like, an hour, maybe more, looking at my watch, then at the old Wolfe, wondering what's happening, when's he going to ring.

A girl who's a big-time ringer for Hayden Panettiere is checking out my reflection in the window as she looks for a seat, but I'm too – I suppose – uptight to even think about chatting her up.

Then I'm suddenly thinking, isn't the Shelbourne closed for, like, renovations? When did it open again and why didn't I hear about it?

I order another coffee.

The girl is now sitting at the next table, reading *Heat* and telling her friend that crimson lips are going to be *so* in next year because there's, like, a movement away from girly gloss towards a more womanly appeal.

I suddenly decide I can't wait any longer.

He answers on the third ring. I'm like, 'Ro, where are you?'

He's there, 'I'm on the so-say. Heading home . . .'

He's crying.

'The Shelbourne's closed,' I go.

He's like, 'I know. Blathin's pardents weren't taking us for Arthur Noon tea, Rosser. They wanted me to meet them outside. Blathin wasn't even with them . . .'

'So what happened?' I go, actually *making* him say it?

'They don't want me to see her any more . . .'

My fist suddenly tightens, just like it does when I hear the words 'Declan Kidney'. I want to, like, punch something.

I'm looking around me and I can suddenly understand all those rioters you see on TV trashing Storbucks. I just want to tip over that big stand of Black Apron Exclusives over there.

But I have to, like, *try* to stay calm?

Especially because Ronan isn't.

'Me fooken wurdled's after been torn apart,' he goes. 'I'm going to do something stupid, Rosser . . .'

I'm there, 'Hey, just keep the head, dude.'

'No, I'm a desperate man. I'm capable of anything. I'm thinking of going back on the skag.'

I'm like, 'Ro, you've never *been* on skag. You're ten.'

'Well,' he goes, 'maybe I'll get all liquored up and hit the canal. Get meself a couple of toots – one a looker, one a smashnose . . .'

And of course what can I say, except, 'Ro, I'm really, really sorry.'

*

It's literally weeks since I've had any action. I *have* been up to my towns, I suppose, with Sorcha, Ro, Immaculata, blahdy blahdy blah. But it's not long before the old Rossmeister decides it's time to get one or two items in the in-tray again.

It might sound arrogant, but I wasn't exactly at the back of the line when God was dishing out good looks. And after a Friday night in Café en Seine followed by a Saturday in Ron Blacks, then Krystle, I end up with a lot of women's digits and my love life is suddenly back to the way I like it – a plate-spinning act.

One or two I end up losing – through my own clumsiness in fairness – but by the middle of the week I still have four on the go. As Mickey said to Minnie, it's a sorry mouse who relies on only one hole.

The pick of them, I would have to say, is a bird called Mia McKinley, and that's not just because she's a ringer for Elisabeth Hasselbeck. She has brains to burn, this bird – we're talking second-year Human Resource Management in DBS – but more importantly she's seriously low mainten-ance, knows all about my rep as a ladies' man, but wants no exclusive rights over me.

I know this because she tells me, we're talking ten minutes into what you might call our first date, which involved two 99s from Teddy's and a walk along the seafront in Sandycove.

My knackers are pretty much frozen solid because it's, like, November, but we're chatting away and somehow we get onto the subject of, like, September 11 and she gets pretty upset, telling me that a really, really good friend of an American girl that her flatmate worked with while she was on her J1er was killed when the second tower collapsed.

It's when she goes really quiet that I turn around and go, 'I think you're amazing,' and she's like, 'Oh, *please!*' in a real I-bet-you-say-that-to-all-the-birds kind of a way?

I'm giving it, 'Hey, you really should learn to take a compliment, especially with a face like that. I think you're the kind of girl I could end up being with for a long time – a majorly long time,' and that's when she says it.

'Look, Ross, I know all about your history,' and she would, roysh, because she's originally from, like, Dalkey, even though she has, like, a flat in Blackrock now? 'I'd be flattering myself if I thought I was the only girl in your life right now. But I'm, like, cool with it.'

Of course, I'm thinking, Carlsberg don't do perfect dates, but if they did . . .

I mean, not only does she put her hand in her Davy Crockett to pay for the ice creams, she gives me the green light to keep on trucking.

We end up – of all things – walking around the Joyce Tower. She asks me if I know anything about it and of course I neither know nor *give* a fock? I put my orms behind my back, trying to look all intelligent, and tell her that no one's quite sure who built it or why, but they reckon it might have been, like, Druids or maybe even Brian Boru or one of those.

Of course, it turns out she knows the whole focking history, but luckily she thinks I'm ripping the piss.

I end up throwing the lips on her, just at the Forty Foot, then I'm suddenly warming my hands underneath her pink Abercrombie hoodie. That's when she goes, 'Do you want to come back to mine? For maybe a coffee?'

I'm as horny as a bogger's dog, so the answer is an obvious yes.

It's like putty in the *lámh*. As we stort walking back to her cor, I'm even composing a little condolence speech in my head for her flatmate – God, I was really sorry to hear about that really, really good friend of that American girl you worked with on your J1. It might not seem it now, but, believe me, every day it's going to hurt a little bit less.

At the same time, roysh, there's a little nagging voice in the back of my head telling me that no bird could be this basically perfect. I'm thinking there *has* to be, like, something wrong with her when, all of a sudden – we're talking, out of the blue here – she storts whistling.

We're talking *proper* whistling here, as in whistling an *actual* tune, like a focking tradesman.

I think it's actually 'We All Live in a Yellow Submarine'.

It's weird, roysh – and I don't understand it – but suddenly I have no interest in this girl sexually. It's, like, an instant thing. Fifteen minutes ago I wanted to give her the rattle of a lifetime. Now I feel like – yeah, no, I think *this* is it – I feel like her *mate*? Huck Finn to her Tom Sawyer, you could say, two focking rapscallions kicking tin cans up the street and running away from home in search of adventure.

Of course, I don't want to come straight out and go, er – *what* do you think you're focking doing? So instead I try to be subtle.

I'm like, 'What's that song again?'

Mia suddenly stops walking. 'Oh my God, I am *so* sorry,' she goes. 'It's, like, a nervous thing I have?'

'A nervous thing?'

'I wouldn't mind, but I don't even like The Beatles. It's like, *random*?'

I shake my head, roysh, cracking on that I think it's as cute as she obviously does. But on and on it goes, all the way back to the cor pork, then in the actual cor, twenty-seven verses, the same number of choruses, all the way back to Blackrock, where she lives in one of those huge aportments next to Pill Hill.

I'm chatting away to her, trying to pretend it's not bothering me. I tell her about this African girl I've got staying with me, about her getting her hands on my ex's *Sex and the City* DVDs and how it ended up nearly focking up her head. She's, like, so innocent. When I left her tonight she was four episodes into the second series and fock knows what I'm going home to.

Mia laughs. Then ten seconds later, she goes back to whistling and I'm suddenly worried, roysh, whether I'm even capable of achieving and sustaining now.

Weird as it sounds, it's like I'm about to get up on Oisinn or something.

I follow her into the gaff anyway.

Her flatmate, it turns out, is away on a luxury spa week in Drogheda, which means we've the place to ourselves.

I suggest a movie, roysh, to help get us in the mood, so she lashes on a chick-flick I know my way around, we're talking *One Fine Day*, featuring Clooney as a chorming, wise-cracking newspaper columnist – a role *I* can identify with – and Pfeiffer as a smart but vulnerable architect, who are too busy hating each other to realize that they're falling in love.

Anyway, roysh, I make my move on her at my usual point in the movie. We're suddenly ripping the clothes off each other and showing each other one or two tricks.

But after twenty minutes, nothing's happening, if you know what I mean. Just can't get the focking air in my tyres.

Stunning and all as she is, Mia is just a hord hat and Lithuanian passport away from being a focking construction worker. And, without wanting to be crude here, it's basically like trying to thread a wet noodle through a keyhole.

'It happens to every guy,' she goes after we give it up for a bad day's work.

I get dressed in a hurry and tell her I'll text her. That I might text her.

I'm in the back of a Jo and an ad comes on the radio that sort of, like, jolts me awake. It's one of those ads, roysh, that's supposed to be, like, a conversation between two people?

'Higher that up,' I tell the driver and he does.

It's like, 'Howiya, John – you look a bit down in the dumps?'

'Ah, it's me wife. She's a right bitch, so she is.'

'Why don't you get yourself down to Ireland's first ever Divorce Fair at the RDS?'

'Ireland's first ever Divorce Fair at the RDS?'

'Yeah, Ireland's first ever Divorce Fair at the RDS. They've got all your marital dissolution solutions under one roof. You can get a free consultation from some of the best divorce lawyers in the country, plus advice from some of Ireland's foremost financial and tax planners on how to make your split work for *you*.

'And if your partner's cheating on you, don't get mad – get proof. There'll be private detectives there, showing off all the latest gadgetry to catch your spouse in the act! Not to mention DNA testing with twenty-hour results . . . Hey, where are you going, John?'

'I'm off to Ireland's first ever Divorce Fair at the RDS – to see what all the fuss is about!'

I'm in the sack, roysh, having a nosy through Sorcha's box of private stuff, and I find – of all things – the compilation tape I made her when I was, like, sixteen or seventeen?

It's weird that she kept it.

It was, like, the first present I ever gave her and it would eventually teach me the lesson that the past has a nasty habit of coming back to bite you in the orse.

We've all made birds tapes, of all the songs that remind you of them, the big-time romantic bit, blahdy blahdy blah.

From what I remember, some focking sap had made one for, I don't know, Sophie – or maybe it was even Aoife – and Sorcha decided it was time for me to make one for her. Well, what she did was, she mentioned about three million times that it was like, '*Oh! My God! So* romantic!' and then, when I still didn't take the hint, she went into a sulk that lasted three or four days, until I decided, Ross, you've got to meet the competition head-on, just like you do week in, week out on the rugby field.

So I sat down and basically put together a tape of *our* songs.

Well, I say our songs, but what I actually did was I got this CD that I stole from this bird from Loreto Foxrock, who I was seeing behind Sorcha's back. *Eternal Flame* or one of those love-song compilations.

Anyway, I lashed the entire thing down onto a ninety-minute cassette and Sorcha was none the wiser. For seven focking years she was tapping her toes to 'A Whole New World' by Regina Belle and Peabo Bryson, not to mentions REO Speedwagon's 'Can't Fight This Feeling', never suspecting a thing.

Until, that is, she walked into HMV one day during the sale and picked up a copy of *Eternal Flame* for seven focking yoyos.

She was not a happy rabbit, I can tell you.

So now I'm sitting on the bed wondering why did she, like, hang onto it?

Maybe she actually likes it. Or maybe it's, like, a permanent reminder of what an orsehole I am.

The next thing, roysh, Immaculata shouts up the stairs. She's like, 'Ross, I'm going out,' and of course I'm suddenly sitting straight up in the bed when I hear that. 'Out? As in where?'

I mean, she doesn't *know* anywhere? She hasn't left the gaff since she got here, except with me.

'I'm going to buy a dildo,' she goes.

I end up nearly falling off the bed. She says it like it's a packet of Digestives or a bottle of Cillit Bang.

I'm like, 'You're what?' and I'm suddenly throwing my clothes on.

'I'm going to buy a dildo,' she shouts. 'I'm giving up on men and throttling up on power.'

I'm there, 'Immaculata, wait!' and I finish getting dressed.

'Ross,' she goes, as I'm coming down the stairs, 'the kind of wattage I need you cannot get from a shrivelled dick . . .'

'Jesus,' I go. 'Look, I think we need to have maybe another little chat.'

'No,' she goes. 'I have to find The Rabbit. Carrie Bradshaw said it was wonderful. She said, it nearly burned her clit off . . .'

I'm like, 'Fock! Could you *please* stop talking like that?'

I put my orm around her shoulder and lead her into the living room, where we both sit down on the sofa.

'Look,' I go, 'it's like I told you already – it's, like, a programme? Nothing more . . .'

'No, no, no,' she goes, 'I read that this is the show that broke all of the taboos relating to female sexuality.'

'No – it's actually the show that filled women's heads with a load of shit, if you'll pordon my French.'

I pick up Season Two off the coffee table. 'I mean, it's not even realistic. Look at them! Do you really believe these four grunions are banging their backs out every night of the focking week? It's made up . . .'

She sighs. 'Perhaps you are right,' she goes.

'I *am* right.'

'It's just that in Nigeria we do not have this programme.'

'Well, I think it's only supposed to be watched in, like, *small* doses?'

'Mikel says I am too impressionable.' She smiles then.

'Look,' I go. 'I've actually got some more of those sausages you love in the fridge. How about I cook up one of my world-famous fries?'

'Well, I *am* hungry,' she goes. 'Thank you.'

I'm there, 'Hey, it's not a thing!'

While I'm waiting for the old Jackie Chan to heat up, I send a quick text to Ro. He's not actually answering his phone, so I just want to let him know that I'm basically thinking about him, plenty more where *she* came from, blah blah blah.

So then I'm, like, cooking away, thinking, look at me, taking care of Immaculata, taking care of Ro . . .

And I'm thinking, Sorcha, Melanie, most of the birds I've been with – they don't *know* me, as in the *real* me?

Of course, I'm too busy patting myself on the back to hear the front door open and Immaculata go out and disappear up Newtownpork Avenue.

It'll come as a huge shock to many to hear that there was an actual second date with Mia.

I don't actually *know* why? I think it was, like, curiosity.

See, I've been with a fair few ugly birds in my time. Some of them the original bucket of ormpits. A *real* mess. And yet I never had trouble waking the chubby fella.

Over the years I've been with birds with moustaches, hooked noses, curly teeth, squints, stutters, hunchbacks and skin like focking Braille and it never put me off. I watched a bird pick her nose and eat it once and I still managed to pitch a tent.

So obviously I'm wondering what makes this so different, how a cracking-looking bird doing something as hormless as whistling can instantly be, I don't know, suddenly desexualized – *if* that's even a word.

Call it pride, rosyh, but I'm actually seeing it as a bit of a challenge, as in conquering this? Which is why I decide to give her a second shot.

So I actually *do* text her and she straight away texts me back, telling me she's pretty busy in the evenings with this aroma-therapy and holistic massage course she's doing, but suggesting an afternoon date – of all things, a Zen lunch in Ukiyo.

I make my mind up, roysh, that I'm going to ignore the whistling, maybe use one or two visualization techniques I learned back in my days as a kicker to try to, like, block shit out?

Of course, that's easier said than done.

I'm standing outside the place waiting for her and I actually end up hearing her before I see her, whistling some tune that was obviously never *meant* to be whistled? I'm pretty sure it's Eve's 'Let Me Blow Ya Mind', and I turn around to see her coming up Exchequer Street, looking absolutely stunning, tanned and blonde . . . and her lips working away like a set of focking bellows.

She's wearing, I think, Gold Sign jeans and the exact same Enrico Coveri blazer that Sorcha wanted me to buy her for her birthday last year, but they didn't have in her size.

It would not be an exaggeration to say that nearly every-body who passes her ends up doing, like, a double-take, though there's no way of telling whether it's because of how well she looks or because she's tootling away like a focked kettle.

But I do what I said I'd do. I block it out. We do the whole air-kissing thing and I tell her she looks well, then we go into the restaurant, get seated and make small-talk while we look at the menu.

I bring up the whole September 11 thing again by saying it'd be cool if someone brought out, like, *one* DVD with, like, *all* the footage of the planes hitting the towers, as in from all the various different angles? She says she's thinking of buying a Badgley Mischka hat because you can get them really cheap online.

She's actually *really* easy to talk to.

For storters, roysh, she orders the wonton soup and I ask for, like, the chicken satay skewers, which I tell her I love. Mia says she can't go near satay because she's, like, seriously allergic to peanuts.

After we order, she sort of, like, excuses herself, then hits the old TK, presumably to check the lippy and text her friends to tell them how well it's going.

She's only just gone when all of a sudden Oisinn rings. I haven't seen the focker in a couple of weeks. Been up to his mebs – this fair of his storts tomorrow.

I ask him how it's all going, just for openers.

'Unbelievable,' he goes. 'Erika's had this cake made – it's in the shape of a penis.'

I'm like, 'A penis? As in a dick?'

'Can you believe that? Apparently they're all the rage at these divorce parties. The birds love sticking the knife into them apparently.'

'Fock, I'm in love with that girl,' I go.

'I know you are, my friend. By the way, are you still seeing Roger?'

I'm like, 'Who?' obviously not having a clue what he's banging on about.

'That Mia McKinley,' he goes.

I don't give him a yes or no. I'm just like, 'Er, what's the whole Roger thing? I don't get it.'

He's like, 'That's her nickname. As in Roger Whittaker.'

All of a sudden, I just, like, freeze in my focking seat. I'm like, 'Yeah, no, I only saw her that once. You know me, Ois – get in, gut 'em and get out.'

I haven't a focking bog who Roger Whittaker is, though I suspect it's not, like, a compliment.

'I know a couple of dudes who went out with her, Ross. I mean, she's pretty easy on the eye.'

'Yeah, no, she looks like Elisabeth Hasselbeck.'

'Agreed – but the whistling drove them mental. Hey, where are you now, by the way?'

I'm like, 'Oh, er, I'm in the bank.'

'Bit noisy, isn't it?'

'Is a bit. Yeah, I'm just paying a few Harry Hills – credit cord mostly. Hey, you should see the cashier in here. Looks like Cobie Smulders and she's giving me the deep and meaningfuls.'

'Really?'

'In a big-time way.'

'Great,' he goes. 'So that's not you sitting in Ukiyo on Exchequer Street, no?'

All of a sudden, roysh, I whip around and there's him and Erika, waving at me through the window, him cracking his hole laughing, her just sort of, like, sneering at me, the way she does.

'Where's she gone?' he goes. 'The apple fritter?'

I'm like, 'Yeah,' because there's no point lying. I'm caught by the knackers here.

'Hey,' he goes, 'Erika wants a word,' and he hands the phone to her.

'We're just coming from Dirty Harry's,' she goes.

I'm there, 'Okaaay,' still wondering where this is going.

'Seems your name came up in the shop yesterday.'

'Go on.'

'He had a girl in. Nigerian, she said she was. He got talking to her. Harry never misses an opportunity. He asked her where she was staying . . .'

'Wow,' I go. 'And you're saying it was Immaculata?' still hoping that this is one of those it's-a-small-world conversations.

'She was looking for a vibrator!' Erika goes, delighted, as usual, to have shit on me.

Oisinn, by the way, has got two fingers in his mouth and he's making what could best be described as sheepdog trial noises. People on the street are staring at him.

'I take it you're going to tell Sorcha?' I go.

Erika's like, 'Ross, do you honestly think I care enough to ring that girl?'

'Em, I suppose not.'

'As far as I'm concerned it serves her right for getting involved in the first place. This is what five euros a month gets her.'

'Yeah,' I go, laughing to myself, 'she was always a focking do-gooder.'

'Of course,' she goes, suddenly giving me the evils, 'I can't promise I won't let it slip around Chloe and Sophie. And you know them, Ross, they've got such big mouths.'

She suddenly hands the phone back to Oisinn, who goes, 'Seriously, Ross – lose that girl.' Then he hangs up.

I swear to God, roysh, at that point my blood actually boils.

I snap the phone shut, feeling like I've been, I don't know, taken for a ride here. It's like I think everybody in the world is actually laughing at me and I'm suddenly thinking, this problem of hers, it's something she should have declared at the very stort.

But she didn't and now it's, like, Humiliation *City*?

The storters arrive and I'd say mostly out of anger I end up doing something that, looking back, I wouldn't be a hundred per cent proud of. I remembered her banging on about her peanut allergy and I ended up giving her soup a good stir with one of my chicken satay skewers.

Back she comes from the can and she sits down and asks me what's wrong.

I'm there, 'Er, nothing,' and she's there, 'Oh, good – sorry I took so long, I had to text a friend of mine. She's the one who's thinking of quitting law in-house to teach Montessori.'

I'm like, 'Wow!' but obviously being sarcastic.

I can't even look at her tucking into her soup. I'm storting to feel guilty, but at the same time I'm thinking, okay, how bad could a peanut allergy be? The worst I'm picturing is her leaning up against the wall of The International spitting chunks – and me being home in time for *The Afternoon Show*.

'*Oh* my God, I can't believe the Christmas lights are up on Grafton Street already,' she goes. 'Hallowe'en's only just gone,' and I'm thinking, yeah, but you won't feel the time going before you're whistling Frosty the focking Snowman.

I suddenly look up, roysh, and – I swear, this is not an exaggeration – I actually jump back with fright when I see her boat race, because it's actually like something out of a horror movie. Her forehead has storted to, like, swell, as has her left ear, to pretty much the size of a baseball glove.

Of course, she hasn't copped it yet.

'Is it just me or is it hot in here?' she goes.

I'm about to answer when I suddenly hear a voice behind me go, 'My God – what have you eaten?'

I turn around and this goy – another diner, basically – is rushing over to our table. 'I'm a doctor,' he's going. He's actually shouting now, drawing a fair bit of attention our way. 'I need to know what you've eaten?'

Mia's like, 'Nothing,' looking at *me*, totally confused.

'You've got anaphylaxis,' he goes. 'You must have eaten *something.*'

After that it all happens very quickly. She touches her forehead and realizes it looks like the Cliffs of focking Moher, then she actually storts screaming, as in proper, full-on screaming?

'You're going into shock,' the goy goes.

Mia has her hands around her Gregory and she's, like, kicking her focking legs now, which is pretty scary it has to be said.

'She's got, like, a peanut allergy?' I end up having to go. The doctor looks at me, obviously wanting more information. I'm there, 'And, well, I stirred her soup with one of my chicken satay skewers.'

There's suddenly what would have to be described as a collective gasp in the restaurant.

'Are you insane?' the doctor shouts – actually *shouts* – at me. 'You could have killed her!' and he tells someone, anyone, to phone for an ambulance.

'Focking animal!' someone shouts.

Then, 'What a creep!'

I'm basically being guilt-tripped here, which I suppose is fair enough.

Mia, though, ends up being fine. Someone – one of the other diners basically – goes through her bag and finds, like, an adrenalin pen and twenty seconds after that the drama's pretty much over.

Of course, I'm just sitting there, getting serious focking

daggers from all these people and I have to say, it's something I'm *not* actually enjoying?

When the ambulance arrives they put Mia on a stretcher and she looks at me with her big cartoon face and goes, 'Why? Why did you do it?'

So I go, 'I just didn't know how else to end it,' and there's, like, howls of disgust from all directions.

I hear someone go, 'I'm going to beat the shit out of him!' and I'm thinking, I'll be lucky if I get out of here with this pretty face intact.

'You should have told me about your . . . *problem*,' I go, not unreasonably, I think. '"We All Live in a Yellow Submarine"? For fock's sake . . .'

She's like, 'You absolute wanker,' which is something I've been called a million times before. She's, like, hitting out randomly now, trying to hurt me. She's there, 'Your dick is tiny,' and, well, that's not exactly an original either.

I follow the, I suppose, stretcher-bearers out of the restaurant and hail a passing Jo.

Mia's shouting, 'I'm going to tell everyone you have a tiny dick and you don't know what to do with it!'

I get into the cab and I'm just telling the driver Blackrock when the doctor suddenly knocks on the window. I wind it down, an inch, maybe two, but certainly not enough for him to throw a dig through.

'I *presume* you're following her to the hospital?' he goes.

It's rare that I come up with something really, really funny on the spot, but I have to say I was delighted with myself when I turned around and went, 'No – she can focking whistle.'

I know how it looks, I'm telling her, but this is one of those times when it's *not* my actual fault?

'An innocent girl,' she goes. 'Two weeks under your spell . . .'

'Spell?'

'And she's hanging around sex shops!'

'Not sex shops,' I go. '*A* sex shop. And if this is anyone's fault, Sorcha, it's yours.'

'Excuse me!'

'Hey, *you* left those DVDs lying around. They're basically porn!'

'Ross!'

'No, it's, like, what are you going to do next, Sorcha? Why don't you throw that set of Stellar Sabatier steak knives that Hennessy bought us as a wedding present into Honor's cot?'

The next thing, roysh, the doorbell rings and I'm thinking, *phew!*

'Anyway,' I go, 'I've got to head. Someone at the door.'

She's like, 'It'll be the girls . . .'

'Girls? What girls?'

'I've asked them to do an intervention, Ross.'

'An intervention? *Hello?* You're not back at school?'

'Just tell them to ring me when Immaculata's safe,' she goes, then hangs up.

I'm thinking, safe? *What* the fock?

I tip downstairs, roysh, open the door and suddenly Chloe, Sophie and Amie with an ie push past me into the hall, squealing, clapping their hands together, going, 'Where is she? Where is she?'

She's in front of the TV, of course.

Immaculata hits the pause button when they burst into the living room, as it happens catching a perfect freeze-frame of Miranda flashing a knocker at her peeping-tom neighbour.

Without saying a word to her, Sophie takes Immaculata's

face in her two hands and goes, '*Oh* my God, she looks like Rihanna!' which I don't think she does.

I don't think she looks like anyone actually.

Chloe shoots me a filthy and goes, 'I cannot *believe* you've kept her to yourself this long.'

Amie's like, 'Do! You! Speak! English!'

Immaculata looks at me, sort of, like, confused? Then she goes, 'Of course – English is the first language of my country!' and Amie's there, 'Oh my God – *same*!' and Sophie's like, 'That's like, *Aaahhh*!' and then they all introduce themselves.

Immaculata knows pretty much everything about them already, presumably from Sorcha's letters.

'Sophie,' she goes, 'you wanted to be a midwife like your mother, but you didn't get the points because you didn't do a tap all year. Amie, you play the viola and you are not good-looking, but you make the best of yourself. And Chloe, you had a boyfriend called Steve, but he cheated on you with a girl who is amazing-looking and you couldn't blame him because you are, like, totally passive-aggressive . . .'

'*Oh! My God!*' Sophie goes. 'It's like we've known each other *all* our lives?'

Chloe's staring at Immaculata's orms. '*Look* how thin she is. You have *such* an amazing figure. It's like, *oh* my God – *total* bitch?' and they all crack up laughing, including Immaculata.

Of course, after two weeks of living with just me and barely venturing outside the door, she's suddenly in, like, total awe, big smile on her boat, her eyes shooting from one new bezzy mate to the other.

Amie's giving it, 'Do you know what would look – *oh my God!* – *so* amazing on her? That white and silver Temperley dress in the window. *With* those Brian Atwood slingbacks.'

'No,' Sophie goes, 'What about the J. Mendel form-fitting, calf-length dress – the one that Rosario Dawson was wearing in *OK!*?'

And Chloe's like, 'She'd actually fit into those skinny Sevens – remember the twenty-four-inch-waist ones that Lisa Foden tried on, then left in a snot. It's like, *attitude problem*?'

Sophie claps her hands together in excitement and goes, 'Project!'

I butt in then. 'Speaking of the shop,' I go, 'can you tell me who's actually looking after it at the moment?'

Chloe's there, 'Cop on, Ross, we closed up for the afternoon,' and when I go to point out that they're actually costing Sorcha money, she makes a W with her fingers and goes, '*What*-ever!'

'So, what are the guys like in Nigeria?' Amie wants to know. 'Are they good-looking?'

'Oh my God, I was with a guy, the time I au paired in Paris,' Sophie goes, 'and I know this is going to sound bad, but he was, like, black? And *oh* my God, he was *such* a good kisser.'

'Your country sounds *so* amazing,' Amie goes, even though I haven't heard Immaculata say a Charlie Bird about it.

'Right,' Chloe goes, suddenly all mumsy, 'let's get your things together. Where's your bag?'

I'm like, 'Sorry, *where* do you think you're taking her?' and she acts like it's beneath her even answering me.

'She's going to stay with me,' she goes and before I even get a word in, she's like, 'You're going away next week, Ross – to Andorra?' which *is* actually true. So I can't say anything.

Immaculata does a quick sweep of the gaff, gathering up what's hers. She looks at the DVDs, but Chloe goes, 'Don't worry — I've got *all* those at my place. They're not even opened.'

Immaculata thanks me for everything and says she'll always be grateful and she gives me, like, a peck on the cheek and then — as suddenly as she arrived — she's gone, following the girls out to Chloe's Touareg, looking as excited and as happy as a girl who's just discovered . . . I suppose, the world's greatest dildo.

I cannot believe I wasn't told. I mean, I was only talking to Oisinn and Erika yesterday.

Then again, I should probably have guessed. The dude's, like, a family law solicitor. It stands to reason he'd be here.

It's amazing, roysh, there must be, like, ten thousand people in the Simmonscourt Pavilion and the focker still picks me out of the crowd. I'm standing at this exhibit, roysh, for some private detective agency or other, checking out this pair of night-vision goggles and asking the dude if they're the same kind they use in, like, *Cheaters*.

'Yes, it's, er, the same technology,' he goes, and that's when I get the tap on the shoulder.

I spin around. I've still got the goggles on, but even through the blur I know that it's him.

'Hey, Mr Lalor,' I go. 'Focking rammers in here, isn't it?' but he's in no mood for pleasantries.

'Who gave you permission,' he goes, 'to go back to the house?'

I'm like, 'House?' obviously stalling.

'Tenzin Gyatso House,' he goes.

Yeah, that's what Sorcha's calling the gaff days — the postman must think we're off our focking chops.

I'm there, 'Oh, you heard? Well, it's only temporary . . .'

'You're not supposed to be there,' he goes.

'The old dear focked me out – where am I supposed to go?'

'Under the terms of the separation agreement, you are not permitted to enter the house.'

I'm like, 'Whoa, horsy – can I actually remind you who paid for it?' which, it has to be said, doesn't go down well.

'Sorcha paid for it,' he goes, 'in tears and heartache.'

They love their focking drama, the Lalors.

'Well,' I go, 'it's only for a few more days. Then I'm off to Andorra. Don't know if you heard.'

He smiles at me. 'It's for *no* more days,' he goes. 'Because right now, while we're talking, the locks are being changed.'

I'm like, 'What? But what about all my shit?'

'I told them to dump it out on the road.'

I'm like, 'Oh my God, if any of my good threads are ruined . . .'

But he laughs in my face, roysh, then goes back to his exhibit. I'm spitting nails, of course. The focker's bang triple O and he knows it. And if he doesn't, roysh, I'm going to tell him.

So I walk back over to him, thinking, I'm going to wipe that focking smug look off your boat.

I push the goggles up onto my head and I go, 'Dude, can I ask you a question? Your daughter's got over me – why can't you?'

He looks at me with, like, total contempt and goes, 'I won't rest until I ruin you.'

'But why?' I go. 'Sorcha's cool with me.'

'Fathers have longer memories. You have a daughter – *had* a daughter.'

'Whoa, she's *still* my daughter.'

'And how would you feel, Ross, if someone ever treated her the way you treated my daughter?'

'I presume not good.'

'You made her so unhappy . . .'

'The past is the past.'

'Almost ruined her life . . .'

'But she's flying now.'

'Our little angel.'

'Angel?' I go, then a little voice in the back of my head is suddenly going, don't say it, Ross. Do *not* focking say it. It's actually a cracking line, in fairness to you – but under no circumstances should you say it out loud.

'Let me tell you something,' I hear myself go. 'Your little angel is a devil in the sack.'

I've never seen someone's face change so quickly.

Of course, I can't focking leave it at that. 'So's the other one,' I go. 'Astrid or Orinoco, or whatever the fock you called her. Knows more tricks than David Blaine, that one.'

I'm suddenly looking into the face of a man who's about to commit murder and doesn't give a fock about jail.

So now the whole self-preservation thing kicks in. I'm watching his face and I'm slowly backing away. There's still, like, a table between us, piled high with, like, leaflets and shit, so I'm not, like, panicking yet?

But I am when he suddenly tips the table over and roars, 'I'm going to tear your fucking heart out!'

One of the things that made me one of the best rugby players of my generation was my acceleration over the first ten yords – very few players could live with it. Sorcha's old man, though, is surprisingly quick on his feet.

I'm out of there like a shoplifter from Boots, with him no more than five yords behind me, the two of us suddenly cutting through the crowds, sending people flying out of the way.

You can imagine what goes through my head when

someone suddenly shouts, 'Oh my God, dorling – he's got a *gun*!'

There's suddenly a lot of screaming.

I swing a shorp left into the Singles Cruise Exposition, where I think I've actually lost him. I'm cracking on to be really interested in this brochure on the Mexican Riviera, hiding behind two or three of those Disco Divorcee types you meet in Joys and Bojangles, knocking back champagne and pretending not to be bitter.

Suddenly, roysh, out of the corner of my eye I can see him, scanning the crowd, looking for me, showing his gun to people to clear a path for himself.

I'm suddenly there thinking, no, this isn't how I die – not here, not like this. So I drop the brochure and peg it again. He sees my move and he's straight after me.

Behind me, I hear someone shout, 'Edmund, don't do it!'

Then I hear a shot and I feel wet on the back of my leg and I presume, naturally enough, that I've taken a bullet here, but then I realize, much to my relief, that it was actually a fart and follow-through.

Everywhere, people are screaming.

I turn right and slam straight into this woman holding one of Erika's penis-shaped cakes. I'm still picking bits of icing and light sponge out of my Tony Blair when I take another hord right and head for where the biggest crowd is, thinking I can somehow get lost in the numbers.

It turns out it's the DNA testing area. There's so many people in there, I think I must be safe. So I'm tipping around, checking out what's going down. There must be a hundred, maybe a hundred and fifty people milling around in there – we're talking men, women and children – a lot of them holding little bottles with, like, blood or hair or whatever else in them and there's, like, seven or eight nurses in there as well, struggling to cope with the demand.

I'm wandering around, looking over my shoulder, but at the same time thinking, this is some focked-up, I don't know, commentary on marriage. Most of these people stood at the altar, just like me, and got married to people they basically loved and thought they were going to be with, like, forever. Then this is how it ends, with total strangers looking at blood through microscopes.

And that's when I decide I'm going to walk back out there, roysh, and try to reason with him, say that whatever happened between me and Sórcha was *my* actual fault and I'm sorry and, hey, at least we didn't end up like this lot.

So I *do* step out.

But then I see his face, mad as constipation, and I know there's no talking to him.

He points the gun in my general direction. I automatically duck and stort making my way, pretty much doubled over, through the jungle of bodies in front of me, not having a clue where I'm going, travelling basically blind.

From the commotion, though, I can tell he's still pretty close.

But then all of a sudden I look up and see – smack bang in front of me – an emergency exit.

It's like a gift from God.

I go through those doors like I used to go through Dorce back in the day. I slam them behind me and then – bit of a *Bourne Identity* move this – I grab a table that just happens to be randomly standing there and slam it up against it.

So now I'm standing in this stairwell and I'm about to turn my mind to the job of finding a way out to the cor pork when all of a sudden I hear what sounds very much to me like a man and a woman arguing.

It's coming from up above me, roysh, and I suppose you could say it's, like, curiosity that gets the better of me?

Instead of looking for the way out, I suddenly stort climbing the stairs, slowly, one at a time.

When I reach the first landing, I turn around and see her standing there, halfway up the next flight, make-up all over the shop, but still – for my money – the most incredible-looking bird in the world.

'Why would you say something like that?' she's going. 'With *people* present?'

She's seriously focked off about something.

The dude she's shouting at is some randomer I've never seen before, some tool with a beard and a lumberjack shirt and a focked-up accent. 'It was one of thae things. Ah was just thinking it and then it, likesay, slipped oot, know?'

Now, we've had, like, our differences over the years, roysh, but I would still regard Erika as one of my best friends. Which is the reason I turn around and go, 'Okay, what's the Jack here?'

The second she sees me, she puts her two hands over her eyes and goes, 'Ross! Get! The Fock! Out of here! Now!'

I'm like, 'Not until I know you're okay,' and then I turn to the goy, waiting for him to explain.

'Whae are you?' he has the balls to go.

I'm like, 'I'm one of Erika's best male friends, that's who I am. Why the fock's she crying?'

'Ah cannae discuss it with you,' he goes.

It's at that point, roysh, that I cop who he is. He's this Scottish dude that Oisinn was banging on about, who does paternity tests from, like, photographs? It's one of those times when you immediately know what's coming next, even though you don't, if you know what I mean?

'He says my father *isn't* my father,' Erika goes.

Fock – that's some day's work.

My first reaction, naturally, is to ask the goy if he's *looking* to be decked?

'Look, ah saw the poster for the event,' he goes. 'I'm looking at the photae. Yer man oot there – Oisinn – he says it's Erika's ma and da. It couldnae be, ah says. Couldnae be your father, Erika . . .'

'In front of twenty focking witnesses?' she goes.

'Likesay, I didnae mean it. I was in shoak maself.'

Erika's nose twitches, like she can suddenly smell something foul. Of course, it's me.

I'm there, 'I think the question that's going to be on everyone's lips is, is it true?'

Straight away, roysh, without looking at either of us, Erika's like, 'Yes . . .'

'Nuthen matches,' the dude goes with a shrug. 'None of thae facial characteristics – earlobes, chun, hairleen, ayebrews, set ae the jaw . . . nuthen.'

'I've always known,' Erika goes, staring at the ground. 'Always knew there was . . . something . . .'

I'm there, 'But wait a sec, this test is only ninety-eight per cent reliable, remember?'

It's obviously the wrong thing to say because *he* pulls a face and Erika tells me to get the fock out of here. As in, *now*!

I'm there, 'I'm not going anywhere until I know you're all right,' and she looks at me, roysh, like she's picturing herself crushing my testicles with the heel of her Guillaume Hinfrays.

I find the way out pretty quickly after that. It's back downstairs and at the end of this, like, corridor.

I push the emergency bor. The alorm immediately goes off, but the doors open and I swear to God, roysh, fresh air never felt so good on my face. I'm pegging it across the

Simmonscourt cor pork, thinking I'm home and hosed, when all of a sudden, roysh, I feel my legs disappear from under me and everything suddenly goes black.

I don't know how long I'm out for, though it could be only a few seconds. When I wake up, I'm lying flat on my back, with Sorcha's old man standing over me, pointing the gun in my boat.

If there was anything left in my bowels, there isn't now.

'Repeat for me what you said,' he goes.

He's seriously lost it – you can see it in his eyes.

I'm like, 'I don't think that'd be a good idea, Mr Lalor.'

My left leg is totally dead and I'm wondering what hit me. I sort of, like, turn my neck and realize it was Sorcha's old man's Merc – not the C-Class Saloon either, but the GL-Class Off-Roader he bought during the summer to bring Sorcha's sister to horseriding. It's got a bomper on it that'd make a chorging bull think twice.

'I want you to repeat it,' he goes again. 'If you're going to die, it's important you understand why . . .'

He puts the gun against my forehead.

I suddenly stort gibbering. 'I said . . . Sorcha was a devil in the sack, which I shouldn't have. Not that she isn't, but it was a shit thing to say. Shouldn't have said it. I just felt I was being attacked and I reacted . . .'

'What else?'

'What else? Oh, I said your other daughter . . .'

'She *has* a name.'

'See, the thing is, I can never remember it? I know it begins with, like, an A. Or an O. For definite. Agatha. Orkney. One of them. I said she knew a fair few tricks . . .'

'More tricks than . . .'

'Oh, yeah . . . it was either David Blaine or Stephane Vanel.'

'David Blaine . . .'

'Yeah, no, it *was* David Blaine. Not that it makes any difference. Again, I reacted. I felt cornered. And I'm sorry. And I'm begging you not to do this thing . . .'

He laughs. I shut my eyes tight, expecting to hear a bang any second.

Instead, I hear a woman's voice go, 'Come away from him, Edmund.'

I slowly open my eyes to make out the outline of Sorcha's granny's massive puffball 'fro. He doesn't even look at her. He's like, 'Why should I?'

'Because,' she goes, 'it's about time you got over this thing.'

It's exactly what I told him earlier, but I'm too scared to open my mouth to say it.

'Sorcha's happy,' she goes. 'I daresay Ross is, too.'

She obviously remembers. She owes me. I saved her life the night she nearly choked on a Murray Mint. This is, like, payback.

Slowly, without once taking his eyes off me, he puts the gun back inside his jacket, then walks backwards to the cor.

Sorcha's granny checks if I'm okay, then helps me to my feet. She asks if I need, like, an ambulance and I tell her no, I think it's just bruising. 'I'll get a taxi,' I go.

She looks at the mess I've made of my chinos. She's like, 'If you can get one to take you in that state.'

I tell her thanks. I owe *her* one now. Not really, she says. It was only a storter pistol.

Erika's old man – as in her *real* old man? – turns out to be some Greek dude. She is kind of dork, I suppose. The word is her old dear told her everything last night. Some shipping magnate who's worth a couple of billion. A friend of Aristotle Onassis. Maybe a cousin.

Of course, it would have to be someone who's rolling in it.

It's all anyone in Finnegan's is talking about – Sophie the loudest.

'Apparently it's the *real* reason her dad – *so-called* – left? He, like, found out? *Oh my God*, this new goy, he owns, like, two hundred ships?'

I can't listen to any more. I go back to the bor, where the goys are sitting. 'Good luck,' Fionn goes.

I'm there, 'I'm going to need it.'

In fairness to the goys, roysh, they're always bulling me up. I'd probably have no confidence – or at least very little – if it wasn't for them. 'It's only a second string you're playing,' Oisinn goes. 'No Drico, no Shaggy, no Dorce . . .'

I'm there, 'Yeah, no, but they'll have Gavin Duffy. And Tommy Bowe. And possibly even Jamie Heaslip. I swear to God, you'd have to see us to know how shit we are . . .'

At the same time, I don't want to bring the goys down.

Oisinn's as happy as a man with a kickstand dick. Sitting on another mountain of cash after the weekend.

And as for the other two – it's weird, roysh, I never thought I'd see anyone in my circle *doing* actual work, never mind being cool with it.

I check out Fionn's hands when he's not looking. They're covered in, like, calluses and ground-in dirt, but at the same time the outdoors obviously suits him because he looks really, really well – not that I'd actually say it to him.

JP's a totally different person from the one he was even three months ago. See, he finally did it. He went to see the Breathnachs and this time he pressed the bell. Went by himself. Told Fionn he had some Cornish slate to collect, then he drove down to Rathdrum and did it.

There's balls for you. Balls like planets.

Fehily used to tell us that the hero and the coward

experience exactly the same fear – it's only what they *do* that makes them different.

The dad told him he was being stupid. You sold him a house. Sure that's nothing. Nothing to do with it. Stupid. Blaming this and that. Won't bring him back.

He took him in. Brought him up to see the goy's old bedroom. He had a huge collection of guitars. Played GAA for some local team or other.

That was, like, a week ago and you can see the change in JP. A burden off and all that.

My phone rings and it's Ro. I step out onto the street to take it. I'm like, 'Hey, Ro – are you coming in?'

He sounds shit. 'I won't tell you a lie,' he goes. 'I'm not in the humour for it.'

I'm there, 'Did you get my voice messages?'

'Yeah, I haven't been answering me phone,' he goes. 'You know . . .'

'I do. Listen, Ro, we all remember our first broken hort. I know it's hord for you to hear right now, but it won't be long before *you're* doing it to *them* . . .'

It has no effect on him whatsoever.

He's like, 'I don't give a fook any more, Rosser. I'm going to go and do the big one.'

The big one is Weir's on Grafton Street. I play along, hoping to put a smile on his face. 'Lot of security in there, kid.'

'Well,' he goes, 'I've fook-all left to lose, man. Here, enjoy yisser self away.'

I'm there, 'I'll be back for a few days at Christmas. We'll do something.'

He hangs up and I'm left standing there in the middle of Dalkey, wondering should I ring him back, when all of a sudden along comes Chloe, with Immaculata in tow.

Not that I immediately recognize *her*. The multicoloured blouses and the headscorves are gone. Now she's wearing a pink Abercrombie T-shirt with the collar up and a pair of – of all things – Chloe sunglasses holding back her hair. And Uggs! Fock! That didn't take long.

'Did you hear who Erika's dad is?' is the first thing that Chloe says to me. 'Aristotle Onassis.'

'A friend of his,' I correct her. 'Or a cousin . . .'

She's like, '*What*-ever!'

I ask Immaculata how she's been, roysh, and she looks at Chloe before she answers. 'I have broken up with Mikel,' she goes.

I stare at Chloe, but she refuses to look at me, just takes out her Marlboro Lights, then lights one up.

I turn to Immaculata and I'm like, 'Why?'

'He cannot satisfy me the way I am entitled to be satisfied,' she goes. 'I have decided while I am here that I should keep my options open relationship-wise.'

That's not her talking at all.

I'm there, 'What do you mean, *while you're here*? You're only on, like, a holiday visa? You're supposed to be going back.'

'And what?' Chloe goes, suddenly turning on me. 'You're going to ring Immigration, are you?'

It's lucky for her that Sophie and Amie with an ie arrive outside at that exact moment to have a smoke, roysh, because I don't know *what* I'd have said. I mean, I don't *want* to see her deported, or even ending up in Mosnia.

Sophie and Amie both take turns to hug her and go, '*Oh my God, I heard*! Oh my God – *so* sad!'

'I still think you're mad,' Amie goes. 'Oh my God, he is *so* like Charlie from the *West Wing*. Ross, did you see the photograph?'

I'm like, 'Yeah,' staring Immaculata out of it.

Sophie's like, '*Oh* my God, you are *so* thin in that picture. I've never been that thin. Well, not since I had that Senokot problem?'

I can't listen to this. I give Immaculata a hug and tell her to look after herself and not to forget who she really is and also to, like, stay in touch. Then I stick my head through the door of Finnegan's. The goys are cool. They know I hate long goodbyes. I just, like, raise my hand to them, as if to say, I'm out of here.

And in one voice, they wish me luck.

6. A land where skobies go to ski

My old hort is beating like I don't know what as I grab my bags off the carousel and head for the arrivals gate. I stop just before I reach the electric doors and take a deep breath, bracing myself for what's on the other side, expecting the press to be out in a major way

I'm expecting to be pretty much mobbed here – we're talking TV cameras, all that shit – which is why I spent most of the flight rehearsing a little speech in my head, just saying, basically, no more will Andorra be the laughing stock of the world, blahdy blahdy blah.

But when I walk through the doors, it's obvious that Rossmania hasn't exactly swept this port of the world yet. There's focking no one here, except for, like, five or six people in North Face and Helly Hansen clobber, holding up signs saying shit like Budget Tours and Ski 4 Less.

Maybe Barcelona was the wrong airport to fly into. Maybe I should have gone to, like, Toulouse, where I happen to know they love their rugby, and I'm thinking this while I'm scanning the arrivals lounge, looking for Conchita, Bernard Dussourd's wife, who – knowing Spanish birds and the way they pile on the blimpage in their forties – I'm expecting to be this dumpy little Raphaël Ibañez lookalike with a Ronnie and a fat orse, like two boy scouts fighting in a tent.

'Hello?' I hear this voice suddenly go. 'You are Ross?' and I whip around.

If you told me at that point that the woman standing

there was *actually* Eva Green, I would have to believe you. That's how much she looks like her? In other words – stunning.

'I am Conchita,' she goes, offering me her hand and I swear to God, roysh, from my point of view, it's love at first sight, so much so that I actually forget to let go of her hand and she gives me this sort of, like, embarrassed laugh and goes, 'We must go now. I am parked in a set-down area.'

She's wearing, like, a suit, with the skirt cut just above the knee and a pair of black patent – I would presume – Giuseppe Zanottis because Sorcha has a pair almost identical, and it's doing it for me in a major way.

What else can I tell you? Green eyes. Unbelievable skin. Brown hair pinned up. But none of those descriptions comes close to capturing her. I mean, she totally oozes class and I've a pole on me like a focking guard-rail as I sit into her BMW 6 Series coupé and we hit the road.

My respect for Bernard has, like, doubled, maybe even trebled?

There's not many birds who've ever, like, stunned me into silence, but for the first ten minutes I don't say anything because I'm thinking, what could I possibly have to say to impress someone like her?

Pretty quickly, though, I find my stroke. 'You don't *look* in your forties,' I go.

She's like, 'I am twenty-seven,' which sort of, like, catches me by surprise.

'Wow – same! It's funny, I don't know *why* I thought you were older . . .'

'Because,' she goes, 'Bernard is forty-seven and you find it difficult to believe that a man of forty-seven could be luffed by a woman of twenty-seven.'

I love the way she says that – luffed.

'I wouldn't say that,' I go, but then she turns around and catches me staring at her left hand on the wheel and on it a rock the size of, I don't know, Mars or one of them.

With no warning at all, she puts her foot down on the accelerator and suddenly we're taking the long and winding roads through the mountains at, like, a hundred and forty Ks an hour. It's actually hord to hear yourself think over the noise of the wind.

'Am *I* what *you* expected?' I eventually go and she makes this face as if to say she hadn't actually thought about it.

She's obviously too smort to fall for my bullshit.

'So what do you *do*?' I go, recycling the ball, going through the phases.

She's like, 'You would not prefer to learn something about Andorra, perhaps the history . . .'

I'm there, 'No, actually, I'd prefer to learn something about you. What do you do for a living, for instance?'

'I am a psychoanalyst,' she goes, like it's no big deal.

I'm there, 'A psychoanalyst? As in, like, the mind and shit?'

She laughs. I've always made birds laugh. 'Yes – the mind and sheet . . .'

'Cool! So go on, then – give us your expert opinion on me. Where am *I* going wrong?'

'I prefer to speak about Andorra. You like to ski?'

I'm the one who laughs then.

'Sorry, Conchita, but where I come from, asking someone if they like to ski is like asking Lindsay Lohan if she likes the odd drink. It's basically a skiing hotbed. And I'm pretty amazing, it has to be said.'

'Oh, I bet.'

Whoa – flirt alert!

'I *am*. It's the legs, you see. I played a huge amount of

rugby back in the day. I've never actually skiied in Andorra, though. The Irish who come here are mostly skobes, you see. I hope you don't judge the rest of us based on them.'

'Skobes?'

'Yeah, skobes would probably be best described as skobies? Poor people, knackers, povs. I've done most of my skiing in Verbs – as in Verbier? And once in Colorado. Hey, do you mind if I say something that's been on my mind since pretty much after I touched down?'

'I'm not sure.'

'I thought there'd be a bit more fuss at the airport. I thought me coming here would be, I don't know, major news.'

'Okay,' she all of a sudden goes, 'you want my expert opinion on you?'

'Yeah, go on – this'll be good . . .'

'I think – and this is just a guess, Ross – you might be a narcissist.'

'A what?'

'A narcissist.'

I'm like, 'Okay, what are *they* like?'

'A narcissist, Ross, is . . . Do you look in the mirror and you like what you see?'

'Well, since when is that a crime?' I go, hearing myself getting all defensive.

'But you luff what you see, yes?'

I shrug. 'It's, like, who wouldn't? I'm a good-looking goy – what do you want me to do, slash my face with razorblades?'

I don't know why I react so badly.

There's, like, silence then for a few miles and it storts to rain, so she puts up the roof of the car.

'So,' she goes, as much to break the tension as anything

else, 'Andorra is a principality in the eastern Pyrenees between France and Spain . . .'

We're reduced to this now.

'. . . the two countries shared sovereignty over it for most of its history. Even now, although Andorra is independent with its own prime minister, the President of France and the Bishop of Urgell in Spain are co-princes with joint authority . . .'

I'm sitting there not even listening, instead thinking, Bernard in Paris and her here – how does that work?

After two or three hours of driving through the mountains, she suddenly goes, 'Welcome to Andorra la Vella – capital of Andorra.'

I'm watching all these petrol stations and cheap flophouses zip by the window, thinking, if she'd just described it as like Bray, except with skiing, duty free and fewer burned-out buses, she could have saved herself the twenty-minute history lesson.

My gaff while I'm here turns out to be the penthouse suite of a seven-storey aportment complex on the Baixada del Molí, and it's incredible. It's pretty much what the gaff back home would look like if Sorcha didn't have a limit on her credit cord. Everything is either cream or white, from the three-inch-thick corpet to the humungous sofa, to the cocktail bor in the corner.

'It's like I've died and woken up in a Shayne Ward video,' I go, but it goes totally over her head.

She's there, 'A big apartment for two people, yes?'

Two people?

I'm there, 'Oh my God,' suddenly smiling so much that it hurts. 'Are you saying we're sharing – as in *us*?'

Of course, it *is* too good to be true.

'No, no – this apartment, it belongs to the Sports Council

of Andorra,' she goes. 'You are sharing with Joseba Garmendia.'

Name means fock-all to me.

'He is a very famous boxer. The Little Bull. He is a hero to Andorrans.'

It's cool with me. An aportment this size, we mightn't ever meet.

'Are you free tonight?' I go, just chancing my orm and – whether she meant this or not – the sun through the window suddenly catches her diamond and ends up nearly blinding me in the process.

She fixes me with a look and goes, 'I am not free any night.'

Fock.

'Oh, I hope you don't think I was, like, coming onto you there. It's just, I know Bernard's away Monday to Friday. I just wondered if you wanted company, dinner, whatever . . .'

She decides to just ignore this.

'You should get some sleep,' she goes. 'Bernard will come here for you tomorrow afternoon.'

When she's gone, I go into the bathroom and splash cold water on my face. I'm looking well, it has to be said, even *if* the old Tony Blair needs a cut. I wander over to the cocktail bor, pour myself a JD and Coke and go out onto the balcony. The view pretty much takes my breath away. And I'm not talking about the mountains.

I'm looking straight down at what must be the stadium and it has to be said – Donnybrook it ain't. It's like, I don't know, Stradbrook or some shit, just a few hundred seats and on the far side of the pitch two little perspex-covered dugouts, like you see in soccer. And the surface is in rag order. It's suddenly lashing out of the heavens and the rain has already formed, like, a pond in the centre.

190

But, you know, suddenly the sight of all that water stirs something in me. It reminds me of Januarys in Dublin and the early rounds of the Leinster Schools Senior Cup. Breaking our balls in the mud and the wind and the rain, knowing that the payback, when it came, would be so focking sweet.

I stand there, nursing my drink, thinking about Fehily. See, in a way, I actually believe *he* brought me here and I can almost feel him standing here beside me, giving me advice, playing his old records of Hitler's speeches.

I think about Honor and Sorcha. I think about Ro. I think about Immaculata and the goys and all the chaos of the last few months.

I stare at the puddle in the middle of the pitch and I think, this is it. A new chapter. This is where my life storts to get good again.

That smell. I'm trying to make out what it is. Is it . . . yeah, it's sweat.

Not mine, I might add.

I can hear someone moving around outside the door. It feels early, maybe seven in the morning. Must be this Joseba dude.

I hear the Paddy Power go and I think, of course, I've seen *Rocky* enough times to know that boxers go out running at all sorts of mental hours of the night.

I drift off again and I end up having this dream where I'm in the Leinster dressing-room and for some reason I've taken a Donald Trump in one of Bernard Jackman's Dubes and straight away – I don't know how – he knows it was me and he's not a happy bunny, and he's coming over to where I'm sitting, big Newbridge head on him . . .

Then I wake up with a fright because there *is* actually

someone standing over me, bearing down on me, I think you'd say.

'You dreenk some meelk?' he goes.

I'm automatically like, 'Meelk?' not even knowing who it is at first.

It's Joseba.

'Oh, milk. Yeah, I was pretty porched during the night. All that Jack Daniel's . . .'

'You use a gless?'

I'm like, 'Of course I used a glass,' knowing how funny some people are about that shit.

He's there, 'But where is the gless?'

I go to sit up, roysh, but I suddenly feel this enormous weight pressing down on my chest. It's his hand. 'Where is the gless?' he goes again and I'm suddenly kacking it.

I'm there, 'I, er, washed it. I washed it and put it away.'

'You washed it – where did you wash it?'

I can actually hear my voice tremble when I go, 'In the sink. As in the sink in the kitchen . . .'

'But I look,' he goes, 'after I hear you go beck to bed. I look at it. The seenk, it was dry.'

It's, like, oh my God, total OCD?

'Which means you lie to me,' he goes.

I'm not a hundred per cent sure my mouth would work even if I could *think* of something to say?

He suddenly grabs me by the scruff of my All Blacks training top and, with one hand, drags me out of the bed and throws me onto the floor. Even in the dorkness of the room I can make out his fist and it's cocked, ready to mash me to a pulp.

'Not the face! Not the face!' I'm suddenly screaming and I close my eyes and sort of, like, brace myself for the sound of bones crunching and, well, pain.

But then nothing happens. Joseba suddenly lets go of me, turns and walks out of the room, stopping only to go, '*Malparit!*' which – whatever it means – doesn't *sound* like a compliment?

I lie there on the floor for what feels like half-an-hour, too scared to even move. Eventually, I hear the front door slam, then I crawl back under the sheets and I lie there, staring at the ceiling, kacking it in case he comes back.

'Ross, you look terrible,' Bernard goes when he arrives at the gaff later that morning. I fob him off with some excuse about jetlag, which he doesn't seem to buy. We take the lift down, then we tip around to the old Camp d'Esports del M.I. Consell General. Bernard presses this little clicker and the big black gates just, like, roll to one side.

'Welcome to ze field of dreams,' he goes, which, it has to be said, is taking the complete piss.

The players are already out on the pitch, warming up, and it's amazing, roysh, when they see us walking towards them, through the puddles, they immediately form, like, a gord of honour on two sides and stort applauding me.

'This,' Bernard goes, putting his orm around my shoulder, 'is the new national coach of Andorra.'

So I'm looking around at the players, sizing them up, trying to put faces to the focking muck I saw on those DVDs.

Bernard runs through my CV for them. For some reason, I just happen to look down and notice that his feet are almost totally submerged in water. I'm thinking, whoa, a brand new pair of Mezlans – focked. Then I'm thinking, okay, what am I prepared to give to make this team? And the answer is suddenly . . . everything.

Bernard's going, 'My good friend een Ireland, Mr George

Hook, describes heem as potentially zee best coach zat Ireland has produced since Eddie O'Sullivan,' and the players are suddenly, like, exchanging serious looks. 'Gentlemen, may I introduce to you . . . Ross O'Carroll-Kelly.'

I'm getting ready to say something, roysh, when the player I recognize straight away as Frodo steps forward and introduces himself. What he wants to say is that he's led Andorra on the pitch for, like, seven years, but he'd understand if a new coach wanted to appoint a new captain.

'Whatever you decide,' he goes, 'I will want you to know that I will speel my blood onto this peech here for Andorra rogby.'

'Frodo?' I suddenly go. 'I presume that's, like, a nickname?'

Half the players laugh. Then they translate it for the ones who don't speak English and *they* laugh as well.

'His grandmother gave heem her wedding reeng,' Ander Acebes, who I recognize as our scrum-half, eventually pipes up. 'Before she die. Give it to special girl, she say to heem, to marry . . .

'Every girl he meets, he fall in love with. A girl who drive the snow plough in Arinsal. He know her five meenits. He say, I love you! Merry me!'

Everyone cracks up laughing, including Frodo.

'Adriana, from Pas de la Casa. She work in customs with Engleesh Jonny. I love you! I heff ring! My seester, Lala. Oh, I heff never felt like thees before about any wooman! I must mek you my wife!

'So, you see, this reeng, he has travelled so far with it – thees is why we call heem Frodo.'

That's the ice broken.

'Well, Frodo, I don't care what your name is. Thanks to Bernard's DVDs, I know what you're about.' In other words, he's the only decent player here, though I don't actually *say* that? 'And so, captain – introduce me to your team . . .'

His face lights up like Ballyfermot on bonfire night.

I've a shit head for names. It'll take me a while. The ones that stick in my head are mostly the ones I remember from the Luxembourg and Toulouse matches. There's, like, Jonny Hathaway – English Jonny – who works for the border police, specializing in the area of drugs. This is one number ten who can learn a lot from the master here.

Ander's without doubt the smallest scrum-half I've ever seen, a mental focking midget who spent most of the Toulouse game running into forwards twice his size, gesturing to the crowd and kissing the badge on his jersey, so that by ten minutes into the second half he couldn't keep up with the play.

The third goy who stands out is, like, a new recruit, which means he wasn't on any of the tapes, but he's a focking giant, we're talking six foot ten – a second row who once played basketball for, like, Spain. They call him The Generalissimo.

It's still pissing it down and the temptation, of course, is to get inside. Instead I clap my hands together and go, 'Okay, goys, let's play some rugby,' because fock knows they need it.

I give them various drills to do, some we did with Fehily, some I invented myself – all shit that's new to them – and there's suddenly a real buzz about them. An hour-and-a-half later, they're walking off the pitch, soaked to the skin, focked tired, but – unbelievable this – high-fiving each other because they've done an afternoon's work and they know it.

I tell them I'll see them tomorrow and I'm on a high

because I *know* I'm good at this. It might be the only thing in the world that I *am* any good at.

'A pleasure to watch a professional at work,' Bernard goes, clapping me from the dugout.

We chat for ten, fifteen minutes and of course I end up feeling guilty then for lusting after his wife.

The great thing about guilt, though, is that it passes.

'I must fly back to Paris tonight,' he goes, 'so I will say good-bye. I have not told ze players about zis game weeth Ireland. I thought I would leave it to you, perheps tomorrow, yes?'

I thank him. I thank him for everything.

I'm heading back to the aportment, relieved to be getting out of these wet clothes. Then I remember this morning. I stop outside the building and look up at the top floor, wondering is he home.

It shames me to say it, roysh, but I end up bottling it. I wander back to the cor pork, where Bernard is getting into his cor – a silver Renault Laguna.

He has an actual chauffeur.

He winds down the window when he sees me and goes, 'Ees everything . . . *cool*?'

I'm like, 'Yeah, no, I was just wondering basically, what's the story with that dude I'm sharing with?'

'Oh – Joseba Garmendia,' he goes, spelling out every, I don't know, syllable, like he's talking about a monster that's only rumoured to exist in, like, legends and shit. 'Heavy-weight. Eighteen fights, eighteen wins. No man has lasted more zan two rounds . . .'

I'm there, 'I wasn't so much looking for his record – have you any idea what his actual problem might be with me? I think I sensed a little bit of hostility from him this morning.'

Bernard says something to his driver in what turns out to be Catalan and it goes back and forth between them, then eventually Bernard goes, 'Next week – here een Andorra la Vella – he weel fight Jesús Zapata of Spain for the European title. Beeg fight.'

The driver nods and says something that I don't understand.

'Yes,' Bernard goes. 'Zey say – ze unstoppable force meets ze immovable object. Perhaps he ees just, eh, *comment dites-vous? Nerveux* . . . Nervous? Tense?'

I nod, like I get it.

'Also, you must understand, at football and many other sports, we are not so good now. For two years, Joseba has been ze hero of all of Andorra. Now you are here. Een France, we say *un coucou dans le nid*. Perhaps eet is true zat he is jealous. And from what I see today, he has very good reasons to be . . .'

Instead of going back to the gaff, I end up walking into town along the banks of what turns out to be the Valira.

I sit on a bench, whip out my phone and watch the video of Honor walking that day in Storbucks for, like, the millionth time.

I wander up and down the Avinguda Meritxell – which I suppose they look on as *their* Grafton Street – looking in the windows of mostly duty-free and, like, winter sports shops, which is all there seems to be here.

I think about buying a snowboard, definitely a Burton, but in the end I can't make up my mind between the Blunt – tank-armour construction with a pure hort – and the Twin – grab the line between chaos and control – so in the end I don't bother.

I wander into a couple of duty-free shops and – I don't know why – grab sample bottles of all the various perfumes Sorcha's worn down through the years, we're talking

Sunflowers, we're talking *Tommy Girl*, we're talking *Issey Miyake* – and I roll up my sleeve and spray them on, like, various points of my orm and stort sniffing them.

I have one of those moments when I'm wondering am I off my Jorvis Cocker here – am I bored, am I lonely or am I just homesick?

I get to the bottom of the street and I find a little chocolate and coffee shop called Vives. It's already dork out, so I ask the bird if she's, like, closing and she goes, 'Ten minutes,' in English.

I order, like, a vanilla latte and she also brings me over a plate of, like, macaroons, all different colours, that I didn't even ask her for, which I suppose means she's interested, if not gagging for me.

She's not bad either. Think Joely Richardson without the massive beak.

I realize, roysh, that I need female company tonight, but it's like being back in that board shop – I can't make up my mind whether to hit this one with some of my world-famous lines or to shoot for the stors and ring Conchita.

In the end my mind is made up *for* me when some dude with long hair and a motorcycle helmet under his orm strolls in, leans over the counter and kisses her. Obviously the boyfriend.

I realize I'm taking, like, a serious risk ringing Conchita. For storters, I don't even know if Bernard has left for the airport yet – he could be still with her, saying their goodbyes.

She answers on the third ring by going, 'Ross?' and she says it in a what-the-fock-do-you-want kind of a way. At the same time, though, if she knew who it was before I even opened my Von Trapp, she obviously has my number in her phone, which has to mean something.

'What are you up to?' I go.

Straight away she's just like, 'I am very busy – what is it?' trying to, like, hurry me along.

I'm there, 'I wouldn't mind seeing you.'

I look up. Joely's switching off the coffee machine and the various other bits and pieces while her boyfriend plays with his espresso cup and cracks on he's *not* actually listening in to my conversation?

'See me? Why?'

'I don't know – get to know each other better.'

'I am married,' Conchita goes, in pretty much a whisper. She must be out and about herself. 'And you work for my husband. It is not appropriate.'

I'm there, 'I meant in, like, a professional capacity?' which of course I didn't. 'I wouldn't mind doing that whole, I don't know, looking into the mind thing.'

'You want me to take you as my patient?'

'Er, pretty much, yeah. I mean, are you free now? I could tell you loads of shit over, like, a drink . . .'

'Tomorrow,' she goes, 'three o'clock.'

I'm there, 'I was thinking more in terms of tonight . . .'

'The only session I have that is free is tomorrow at three o'clock. For fifty minutes. One hundred euros. And I don't want to waste time explaining to you about boundary issues, you understand?'

And what else is there for me to say except, 'Later, gator . . .'

I end up nearly levitating when my mobile rings – that's how much of a fright I get. According to the clock, it's, like, five in the morning and of course the only person who ever rings me at this time is One F, to tell me stories about Vietnam and the night he met Bonnie Tyler.

Did I tell you how big her hair was, Ross?

I couldn't take another hour of that. But I check caller ID, roysh, and it's not him at all.

It's Chloe.

Or actually, as I discover when I answer it, it's Immaculata, using Chloe's Wolfe.

I'm still waking up here, going, 'What time is it over there?'

'I don't know,' she goes. 'We are all in Chloe's apartment – we're talking me, we're talking Sophie, we're talking Amie . . .'

Fock, she sounds mullered. 'Have you been drinking?'

'Yes. And I have some joyous news. I have fallen in love. I have fallen in love with a rugby man.'

I actually feel like, I don't know, a father hearing this from his daughter. 'Who does he play for?' I go.

'What is his team?' I hear her ask the others.

Sophie's there, 'Seapoint – but he used to play for Mary's. Tell him that – it'll mean more.'

I'm like, 'You got over Mikel pretty quickly, didn't you?'

'Mikel is my past,' she goes. 'This morning I was like Carrie Bradshaw. I was thinking, how do you bounce back when love batters your belief systems?'

I hear Amie go, 'Oh my God – *hello*? My *life*?'

'Then I found the answer – Krystle. I have never seen somewhere like this nightclub. The men in there were, like, totally A-list. I was like, *oh my God*, these men are too good-looking to be straight.'

I'm there, 'Look, Immaculata, I know life's pretty exciting for you at the moment, new friends, blah blah blah. But don't forget who you are. Father Fehily, our old coach who I told you about, he used to have this, like, saying – be yourself, everyone else is taken.'

'I turned around to Chloe and I was like, who are all these

men? She goes, rugby players. I say, that is it – I am going to get myself a rugby player. Then I see this man, Tiernan, across the floor and it is lust at first sight. He's like, can I buy you a drink? And I'm like, that would be very nice, thank you very much . . .'

Then she goes, 'Wait a minute – Chloe, your bill . . .'

'No, it's cool,' I hear Chloe go. 'It's the same price as, like, a local call? *He* pays the roaming chorges,' and it's like, thanks very much, Chloe.

'So, Ross, I am talking to this man, Tiernan, and one minute later we are making out in front of everybody and it's, like, totally hot. Of course all of the girls are going, be careful, Immaculata, he is a total toxic bachelor. We're talking manthrax here . . .'

Faith Hill comes on in the background and Sophie sort of, like, screams and goes, '*Oh my God*, this song is *so* me driving from Rhode Island to Connecticut on my J1 . . .'

'I remember that Samantha Jones says that men who are good-looking are never good in bed because they never have to be. But this was not the case with Tiernan . . .'

I'm like, 'Wait a minute – you actually *slept* with him?'

Imagine my shock when she turns around and goes, 'There wasn't very much sleeping, I can tell you. He played me like a double-bass.'

I'm there, 'Put Chloe on! As in *now*!'

She passes the Wolfe to her and I'm pretty sure I hear her say the words attitude problem. I'm there, 'Chloe, what the fock? You're supposed to be in chorge of this girl . . .'

'Oh my God,' she goes, 'will you *actually* lighten up? We took her to a nightclub, then we all went back to a porty . . .'

'Where she slept with some rugby guy?'

'Ross, it's not so long since *you* were some rugby guy – so *spare* me?'

In the background I can hear Immaculata go, 'This is the size of Tiernan's cock,' and then lots of drunken laughter.

I'm there, 'Chloe, just tell me – *what* is she holding?' and Chloe goes, 'The pepper mill I stole from Dunne & Crescenzi.'

I don't get back to sleep again. Half-an-hour later Joseba's up and moving about, obviously getting ready for his run. I lie there, trying to judge from the amount of noise he's making what kind of a mood he's in this morning.

I'm staring at the light coming in through the crack at the bottom of the door, watching him come and go from his room. At one point the light disappears and I realize that he's standing outside my door and I'm lying there expecting him to just, like, burst in at any minute. He stands there for twenty, maybe thirty seconds, then obviously thinks better of it and moves away.

And then I realize that, without knowing it, I've been, like, holding my breath. I don't actually breathe out again – not properly – until I hear the front door slam.

I lie there thinking, maybe I'll get a hotel. There's bound to be, like, a Radisson or some shit. But at the same time I'm hating myself for being such a focking woman. I'm thinking, what is it about this dude that has me kacking my pants? It couldn't *just* be physical? I tackled Denis Leamy at school and they had to practically get the fire brigade to cut me out of him.

I remember hearing someone on TV say that what we actually fear more than anything is, like, the unknown? And I suddenly realize, roysh, that I haven't actually *seen* Joseba yet, as in I don't know what he looks like because it was actually dork when he nearly beat me into the pattern of the corpet.

I decide I need to put, like, a face on my fear, so I give him ten, maybe fifteen minutes to get a good distance away, then I get up, throw on the old threads and decide to search the gaff for a photograph of him.

I already know there isn't one in, like, the kitchen or dining room. So the first and only stop really is his bedroom.

I open the door really slowly, just a tiny crack at first, then an inch at a time, trying not to let it creak, though God knows who'd hear it.

I don't know what I'm expecting to find. A punchbag swinging from the ceiling. Two or three women chained to the bed. A couple of half-eaten, I don't know, wildebeest, with flies buzzing around them.

But no.

His room is like the rest of the gaff. Neat and tidy. His sweat gear is on the bed, washed using what I recognize, from my all-too-brief marriage to Sorcha, as Comfort Sweet Almond Oil concentrate, then ironed and folded neatly.

Not exactly Mike Tyson behaviour.

Then I notice a picture frame on the nightstand. It must be him . . .

It's not.

From what I can make out, it's a woman – his girlfriend, I'd say – with two Rottweilers, which I presume are also his. His girlfriend is the one in the middle, although I'm thinking he should probably caption it, save people the embarrass- ment of having to ask.

It's a good line and I'm actually having a bit of a chuckle to myself when I suddenly hear it. Someone moving around in the aportment. For some reason, roysh, my eyes are suddenly drawn again to the running gear on the bed. And of course the light was on in here when I walked in.

He *hasn't* gone out yet.

It must have been the *bathroom* door I heard.

Something – call it, like, survival instinct – tells me to dive under the bed, which is what I immediately do. And not a moment too soon, because at that exact moment the door opens and in he walks.

The first thing I notice is that Joseba growls in the same way that the rest of us breathe. He stands right beside the bed and I'm lying there, with my hand over my mouth, looking at his feet. Yeti feet. Focking huge. I'd say the focker has to put his trousers on over his head.

He forts about for a few minutes, possibly tidying – but tidying what? – then he just throws himself down on the mattress and I have to say, I don't know how the bed doesn't just collapse.

The next thing, roysh, the growling stops and I'm trying to work out from his breathing has he, like, fallen asleep. I'm storting to think about maybe trying to slip out of here when all of a sudden he jumps up off the bed and I swear to God, I think I'm going to have an actual hort attack.

I suddenly remember my phone. It's in the focking pocket of the hoody I threw on. I have to say, I have *never* wanted to hear the *Hawaii Five-O* theme tune less than I do right now. I'm, like, willing it not to ring, focking praying Immaculata doesn't remember some other detail of what this Tiernan did to her.

He storts putting on his sweat gear. Very slowly. And from the noises he's making, he's obviously throwing punches at, I don't know, imaginary people while he does it. He steps into the biggest pair of runners I've ever seen. Victor Costello could sleep in these fockers. He mutters something to himself in, like, Catalan or whatever, then he's gone – for real this time.

*

'Chalmun's.'

'What?'

'Chalmun's,' he goes. 'It's the name of the cantina in Mos Eisley.'

'Well, what about it?'

'I'm saying we're going to have, like, a bar themed on it. We're going to dress the house band as Figrin D'an and the Modal Nodes. George has all the original costumes. Is this a bad line, Ross?'

I'm there, 'Sorry, Christian, I'm just a bit distracted.'

'Is it Honor?'

'A bit of that.'

'You must be really missing her.'

'Pretty much.'

'I saw her yesterday, I meant to say. Had to go into the city. Lauren came and she went shopping with Sorcha for the day.'

'And Honor was with her?'

'Yeah – she's *huge*, Ross. I couldn't believe it.'

'Hey, did you hear about Erika?' I suddenly, for some reason, go.

I haven't a bog why I keep bringing her name up with him. It's like I'm asking him to give me a clue, to give me some, I don't know, insight into how someone like her could be in love for all those years with – no offence – someone like him. Because I'm still focking bewildered.

'Sorcha said something,' he goes. 'She found out her dad wasn't her real dad.'

'Very *Home and Away*, huh?'

'Poor Erika,' he goes. 'You seem a bit wound up. You sure you're okay, young Skywalker?'

I'm like, 'Ah, it's not just Honor, if I'm being honest. This dude I'm sharing with turns out to be a focking lunatic.

And I'm giving the team their first major pep talk today. Have to tell them about Ireland A. I don't know what the reaction's going to be.'

'You don't think they'll be, like, excited?'

'They shouldn't *be* excited,' I go. 'They should be terrified. There's one or two Junior Cup teams back home would probably beat us – never mind Ireland actual A.'

'Ross,' he goes, 'with you coaching them, there's no way they're going to disgrace themselves,' and I suddenly remember why this quite possibly insane man is my best friend in the world.

I can never remember the difference between psychology and philosophy. I suppose they're pretty much the same thing.

'I want to explain to you some of my psychology about rugby,' I tell the players at the end of the session. 'It's a simple game that we sometimes over-complicate. Basically, it's like war. You goys,' I go, pointing to the forwards, 'are the artillery, as in, like, the tanks? Your job is to basically blow the shit out of everything, to open up space for these goys,' and I point to the backs. 'The infantry.' Everyone's, like, nodding and smiling at each other, like they never thought about it like that before.

Now, obviously I've a soft spot for the backs. 'Don't let those pretty faces fool you,' I go. 'The backs are, like, the coolest killers in the, I don't know, regiment,' remembering that the first rule of teaching, according to Fionn, is to keep shit interesting.

And what I have to say next is definitely interesting.

'We've arranged a match for you,' I go and it has to be said, roysh, there's not that much enthusiasm because they probably think it's against, I don't know, some focking dump of a country they're used to playing against.

I'm there, 'It's against Ireland.'

All of a sudden, they're babbling away in a million different languages, too excited to hear me go, 'A'.

'Brian O'Driscoll!' Mariana Albiol, our outside-centre, goes, like a man who's suddenly remembered he left his cor unlocked.

I'm there, 'Well, it'll be more of a development squad. I think Drico's pretty much shown what he can do. Have any of you ever heard of Barry Murphy?'

There's, like, blank faces all round.

The Generalissimo goes, 'What habout Ronan H'Ogara?' – you know the way Spanish people talk.

I'm like, 'Again, it'll probably be Jeremy Staunton,' which means fock-all to them either.

'Whoever they 'ave,' Jonny Hathaway goes, 'they're going to be ten times tougher than anyfing we've ever faced. This is facking great. I'm facking up for this. Are we *all* facking up for it?'

There's a big roar from everyone saying, basically, yes.

Frodo steps forward then and goes, 'This news makes this even more important – Ross, we have a geeft for you,' and he hands me, like, a package wrapped in brown paper.

I look at all their faces and they're full of, like, anticipation?

I rip open the paper and I pull out what I presume at first is, like, a GAA jersey. It's got, like, three horizontal bors – red, blue and yellow.

I look at them, waiting for someone to explain the joke.

'Thees har the netional colours hof Handorra,' The

Generalissimo goes. 'We theenk perheps you whould like to wear thees when we tren,' and then his eyes stray to what I'm *actually* wearing and I'm thinking, yeah, I suppose it'd be wrong for me to keep wearing my Leinster jersey while I'm training them.

So I make a big show of taking it off.

I can feel a lot of respect in the house when they see what kind of shape I'm in.

I fock my Leinster jersey onto the ground, into a puddle as it happens, and go, 'That's the last I want to see of that.'

Then I pull on the new one. It's, like, a perfect fit – even though I wouldn't be seen dead in it back home. Everybody claps. It's actually a great moment and really important for, like, team bonding.

'Same time tomorrow,' I go and they disappear into the dressing-room.

When I'm sure no one's watching, I go back and pick up my Leinster jersey.

'In psychoanalysis, we use this.'

I follow her finger to this big blue sofa taking up half the main wall of her office.

'You want me to lie on that?' I go.

'We use the couch because it is felt that eye contact inhibits truly honest communication. We are too much influenced by the responses of who we are talking to . . .'

'It's just that when Tony Soprano was seeing his one, they were sitting, like, face to face?'

'Please lie down,' she just goes, which is what I end up doing.

She looks incredible, even nicer than I remembered. Some pair of getaway sticks on her as well, with her skirt ending a good three or four inches above her knees today.

I'm horder than algebra here.

'I want to ask you,' she goes, 'what is your objective for these sessions?'

I'm there, 'Objective? Er . . .'

'Okay,' she goes. 'I want to know about your *dramatis personae* – the other actors in your world. Your relationships. Your mother . . .'

'She's a focking pollock, that's all you need to know.'

'Your father . . .'

'A penis. Of the highest order. Next question.'

'This is an unusual way for someone to speak about his mother and father, don't you think?'

I'm there, 'Well, *you* haven't met them. There's also an ex-wife in there as well by the way, as in Sorcha? Well, we're still *technically* married.'

'You are separated?'

'Exactly. I'm a free agent.'

I just wanted to get that in.

'Why did the marriage fail?'

I stare at this weird-shaped knot in the wooden coving. It looks like a giraffe smiling. 'I've often thought about it. I don't think you can say any marriage fails for one *particular* reason?'

'Were you unfaithful?'

She's good.

'Er, you could say that, yeah. Oh, I've kids as well. Honor's my daughter by Sorcha. She's, like, fifteen months. Then Ronan's a kid I had with, well, another bird. He's, like, ten. And I've got a lot of mates. Good mates as well, mostly goys I played rugby with.'

She goes, 'I am more interested in the relationships you have mentioned. Your mother, your father, your wife . . . tell me about . . . you call her Sorcha?'

'Yeah, Sorcha. Well, she's really just an all-round good girl-guide – sorry, that's the way I'd have to describe her. One of these people who's never happy unless she's making the world a better place.'

'And you resent that?'

'Well, it's everything. There always some dude in some country nobody's ever heard of, about to get offed. Always some animal on the verge of, I don't know, extinction. The Hill of Tara. New Orleans. And then the recycling . . .'

'Recycling?'

'Separate bins for everything. Paper. Bottles. Tins. One for compost. I swear to God, if you took a shit, you were afraid to flush in case she had focking plans for it.'

Conchita laughs for the first time. The ice is definitely melting here.

'Sorcha wanted to live in a perfect world, you see. She wanted a perfect life, a perfect home – a perfect husband. And that wasn't me. It *so* wasn't me. It's like, get over it.'

'Describe your mother to me.'

'A focking wrasse. Move on.'

'Ross, it is very important that we talk about this. The most important relationship in a man's life is with his mother. It is physical. You were once inside her.'

I end up suddenly losing it for some reason.

'Okay, you want to know about my old dear? She posed for a yummy-mummy calendar – *so-called* – in her focking raw. She writes these books full of basically filth. Does that sound normal to you?'

'In psychoanalysis,' she goes, 'we do not think in those terms – there *is* no normal. Calm down, please. I am more interested in your choice of language . . .'

'As in?'

'The names you call her – pollock, wrasse . . .'

'Oh, I've plenty more.'

'These are fish, yes?'

'I don't know. Your point being?'

'Many believe – especially in dream interpretation – that the fish is a symbol of sexual repression.'

I'm not a million per cent sure I like where this is headed.

'Your father,' she goes. I hear her turning pages. 'You call him penis . . .'

'Yeah, I also call him dickhead and knob features.'

'But always the fixation with the male phallus. The rival phallus.'

I swear to God, roysh, I go ballistic then. Who wouldn't? I jump up from the sofa or couch or whatever and I'm suddenly pointing at her, going, 'That's bang out of order. And I'm talking *bang* . . .'

'Ross, please lie down.'

'No. You know what, when I first met you at the airport I was thinking, what does a bird like that see in a goy like Bernard – no offence to him, blah blah blah. Now I'm thinking it's the other way round.'

'Ross,' she tries to go, 'we are only getting started here,' but I'm like, 'Er, *hello*? We're actually *not*?' and I end up just storming out of there.

There's very little chat out of Ro. I'm like, 'Hey, how did Ireland get on against South Africa?'

'I don't know,' he goes. 'I think they won,' then he tells me to hang on while he checks it on Aertel. 'Yeah, toorty-two fifteen. Trimble had a stormer, according to this. Scored the foorst try.'

'So you're telling me you didn't go? I left two tickets for you – for you and Gull.'

'Nah, I didn't bother me bollicks in the end.'

He sounds so down.

I'm there, 'Ro, it'll get easier – I swear. But you've got to get out and mix . . .'

'When'll it . . . stop?' he goes, like even *he* can't believe he's asking this shit.

I don't know what to tell him, so I end up telling him a lie. 'Usually six or seven weeks,' I go.

Then I try to cheer him up. 'Hey, there's one or two big banks over here, I'd say you'd love to case them. The Feds have got, like, sub-machine guns. I passed by one today and I thought, I know probably the only man in the world who'd find a way in there.'

Nothing.

He says he's not playing Tony in *West Side Story* any more. He told the drama teacher. Now some other sham's doing it. Sham called Clive.

I ask English Jonny if he'd mind me being honest.

'Facking 'ell,' he goes, 'course not, mate.'

'When you address the ball, you don't do it with any, I don't know, conviction. I mean, when you do end up splitting those posts, you always look like the most surprised man on the field. That's just an observation.'

He thinks about this while sort of, like, spinning the ball in his hands.

'Tell you the troof,' he goes, 'I probably *am* the most surprised man on the field. Got an accuracy rate of abaht forty-five per cent. Can't get it any higher – don't matter 'ow much I practise.'

I'm there, 'See, it's not just *about* practice? You'll get better through practice only if you're practising the right things. If you're technique is wrong, then all two hours of practice is going to do is make you two hours worse.'

It's great – I *know* this shit.

'The first thing you need to get right is your attitude . . .'

'So you mean, stop being scared of the bawl?'

'No, no – *be* scared. You should be – it's not easy what we do. Two points down in time added on, a penalty forty yords out close to the sideline, and the whole crowd silent, looking at you. *Be* scared – just don't *look* scared.

'I'll give you an example – possibly my all-time hero – Ronan O'Gara. When the whistle blows for a penalty, he's immediately looking for the ball. He wants it. The shoulders are back. The chin up. Even when he's looking at the posts, checking the wind, thinking about his angle of approach, he never looks like he's going to miss.'

He nods. He looks pretty convinced.

'Now,' I go, 'what's with the golf stance, like you're teeing up a drive?'

He's there, 'Well, they're awl doing it these days, in't they? Johnny Wilkinson does it . . .'

'But do you actually *play* golf?'

'Used to – nevah any facking good at it.'

'So why do you think it's going to help you? I mean, if you were shit at golf, it'd be, like, a negative association?'

'So what did you do,' he goes, 'when you played?'

'Well, what I was pretty famous for was four steps backwards, hand through the hair, three steps to the side, hand through the hair, blah blah blah. The point is, it's not what works for me or for Rog or for Johnny focking Wilkinson. It's what works for Jonny focking Hathaway. And the answer to that is not in some coaching manual – it's in *your* actual head.'

He goes, 'Well, the troof is I don't like all the little, like, rituals. I find them distracting. Dancing up and down on the spot – all 'at. I don't even like coming at the ball from an angle. If it was up to me, it'd be four steps backwards, then run and hit the facking fing.'

'Let's try it, then.'

'Eh?'

'Jonny, it *is* up to you. Let's try it. But let's try it over here.'

I bring the ball over to the sideline.

'Come on, mate,' he goes. ''Ow abaht a few easy ones to get warmed up an' 'at?'

'Remember, you've got to *look* like you want it.'

'Fair nuff.'

I throw him the ball and he spots it.

'Shoulders back,' I go.

He laughs, but he does it.

'Now, as you're counting your steps back, imagine the kick. Picture what it will look like, sailing through the posts . . .'

He takes four steps backwards.

'Okay,' I go, 'eyes on the spot where you're going to hit it. Imagine your foot as a weight at the end of, like, a pendulum. Make sure you swing it smoothly and as quickly as possible. And remember, the job's not done the moment you make contact with the ball. Follow through – you don't always –'

Before I've even got the words out, he hits what I would almost be forced to describe as the perfect penalty, straight between the posts. It's unbelievable.

I throw him another ball.

'Again,' I go.

He does the same thing. He can't believe it, of course.

He goes – and he actually says this – he goes, 'I ain't never 'ad a coach like you before,' and he means it as, like, a compliment?

The third kick, he misses. He gets the fourth, then misses the fifth. I tell him to keep on practising until he hits five successful kicks in a row.

'By the way,' he goes, as I turn for the dressing-room, 'you fancy going to the fight?'

I'm there, 'Fight?'

He's like, 'Garmendia and Zapata – gonna be a right ding-dong. Ere, you're sharing wiv *'im*, in't ya? What kinda shape's he in? Finking of frowing a few quid on 'im.'

'Believe it or not, I've never actually seen him.'

'You live wiv 'im and you ain't met 'im yet?'

I can't bring myself to tell him that I've been hiding from him. 'Yeah, no, our paths have never crossed.'

'Scary facker . . .'

'You know what – I think I'm actually supporting the other dude.'

He laughs. 'Keep that to yourself arahnd 'ere, mate. Anyway, Frodo says he can get tickets. We was finking it might be nice to go as a team. Build morale an 'at – maybe 'ave a few after,' and of course when he puts it like that, there's no way I can say no.

I have a quick Paddy and throw on clean threads. It's pissing again. Does it ever do anything else in this place?

I'm walking across the cor pork when all of a sudden I hear a beep behind me and I whip around and there, with the engine of her 6 Series ticking over, is Conchita.

She winds down the electric window and I get a sudden blast of what I'm pretty sure is *For Her* by Narciso Rodriguez.

'You following me?' I go, but in, like, a flirty way, just to let her know there's no hord feelings.

'Bernard told me to keep my eye on things,' she goes, but we both know it's horseshit.

She looks amazing, even in just a black Donna Karan bubble jacket, jeans and not a lick of make-up. She has great skin actually, which is always a major thing for me.

'The way we finished,' she goes, 'it was not good. I am sorry – perhaps I pushed you too quickly.'

I think she's genuinely, I don't know, *intrigued* by me?

I tell her I can't stay mad at a face like that and she doesn't mention, like, boundary issues or any of that shit. She smiles and asks me if I want to go for a drink.

We end up hitting the Delta Café on Avinguda de Santa Coloma. 'So,' I go, when we're still standing at the bor, 'you and Bernard – bit random?' because I feel I can actually, like, *say* this now?

'Random?' she goes. 'What does this mean?'

I'm there, 'Look, I'm not saying anything against the goy, but it's, like, you're *my* age. And he's, I don't know, twenty years older. That's what I mean by a bit random.'

'But isn't luff itself random? Isn't that why it's such a mystery to us?'

'Don't ask me. Not sure I've ever actually *been* in love,' and it sort of, like, surprises me to hear myself say it.

'You didn't love your wife?'

She's having a glass of Sancerre.

'I know it sounds bad, but obviously not. I cheated on her, didn't I?' She doesn't say anything, just looks at me, wanting me to say more. 'With the nanny, of all people. Well, there were others, but the nanny was the one I got done for.'

It's amazing, roysh, because she doesn't make me feel like I'm being judged here.

I'm there, 'See, I actually pretty much meant what I said on our wedding day, as in the vows and shit? I wanted all that, you know, settle down with one woman, have kids, be a good husband, good dad, blahdy blahdy blah. But this little chap,' I go, nodding down at himself, 'he had a whole other agenda . . .'

It's meant as a joke, but she doesn't laugh. 'Relationships make you feel trapped?' she goes.

I think about that. 'Yeah, no, it's like when you see the animals in the zoo, isn't it? I took Honor a while back and we were watching this lion and I was thinking, he's actually like me.'

'In what way was he like you?'

'He was, like, right at the fence, roysh, sort of, like, pacing backwards and forwards? See, it doesn't matter how big they make those enclosures, how much space they give the animals, you're aways going to find them right at the edge of the cage.'

'And this is what marriage was like to you – a cage?'

'See, I'm famous for this, thinking too deeply about shit? But yeah, basically, that lion made me think of my marriage. It didn't matter how good I had it in there, it was the idea of being, I don't know, penned in that was my basic problem.'

There's no immediate response, so I take the opportunity to go, 'Enough about me – what's your story?'

'My story?'

'Yeah – for storters, are you actually *from* Andorra?'

'No but close – Garraf. In Catalonia. That is where I grew up. I went to Barcelona to study, then here to practise.'

'What about your olds, as in your mum and dad?'

'My mother, she still lives in Garraf. My father, he was a fisherman . . .'

I click my fingers. 'Ah, that's how you knew so much about fish yesterday.'

'He died when I was eleven years old. So in psychoanalytical terms, you could say I am an open book. I am not difficult to read.'

'Explain that to me?'

'Well, I lost my father as a little girl and so I marry an older man to try to get back what I missed. And it's true – my life is the worst cliché in psychoanalysis.'

I'm wondering is she very subtly lifting the old hemline here. 'It works, does it – Bernard being in Paris and you being here?'

'For now,' she goes. 'Bernard's work is in Paris, my work is here.'

'Are you ever tempted to stray yourself?' I go and immediately wonder is it a question too far.

She's like, 'No,' but she says it way too quickly and I notice she doesn't look at me when she says it, which means it might well be bullshit.

The next thing, roysh, I notice her eyes have suddenly, like, filled up. 'Hey,' *I'm* suddenly going to *her*, 'come on, nothing's ever that bad.'

Anyway, the tears don't come in the end.

'I see someone, too,' she goes. 'When you are a therapist, you must have therapy, too. For three weeks she has been in Portugal,' and then she sort of, like, waves her hand and goes, 'That is all that is the matter.'

I tell her she doesn't need to explain it and that, if I can open up to her, she can open up to me. I ask her if she fancies another glass of Sancerre, but she says no because she's driving.

'I would like you to come back,' she eventually goes. 'I would like you to start again in therapy.'

I'm cool with that.

'I'm certainly prepared to have the chats, find out whatever I can, blah blah blah. As long you promise not to go down that road again. As in my old dear?'

That puts the smile back on her face.

'I mean, if you saw this woman, you'd know I could never, you know, what you said . . . And *I'll* try not to use fish names. I'll say she has a face like an unwired plug. Or a sniper wouldn't take her out.'

She laughs. She can't help herself.

I think she's falling for me in a major way.

It's, like, one o'clock in the morning. This has got to stop. I ring the number back and Sophie answers.

I'm there, 'What's the focking Jack?'

'Hi, Ross,' she goes. 'Did you hear I've decided *not* to move into my new aportment?'

Of course that totally throws me. I'm like, 'What the fock has that got to do with anything?'

'My cousin, who's, like, an accountant, he told me I'd be mad to actually live in it? Said I should rent it out and carry on living at home.'

I'm there, 'Sophie, I just woke up to find a voice message from Immaculata, crying her eyes out. It's like, what the fock?'

'Oh my God,' she goes, 'that's, like, *so* two hours ago, Ross. Tiernan scored somebody else. But it's, like, onwards and upwards. We're in Ed's . . .'

'Put her on,' I go. 'Now.'

I hear Sophie go, 'It's your *dad*,' and then this sudden explosion of laughter on the other end.

Immaculata says hi, like nothing ever happened. I'm there, 'What's going on?'

'I am sorry about the message,' she goes. 'I should have

listened to Chloe and Amie with an ie. They say he was toxic. I think, no, I will change him. I will be the one. Then I see him eating the face off another girl. You know what he said to me – I'm so sorry, I get scared. With you it was too perfect.'

'Oh my God,' I hear Amie with an ie go, 'he is *such* a bastard to women.'

'Amie is right,' she goes. 'He *is* a bastard to women. But now my relationship with him is DNR – we're talking Do Not Resuscitate.'

I hear the clinking of glasses. Chocolate malts being raised in a toast.

'Immaculata, look, I know you're on the big-time rebound, but you're not going to find the man of your dreams hanging around rugby wankers like him.'

'This I know. Because while we were queuing for a table, I thought about Samantha Jones and I had one of those women-should-be-fucking-like-men epiphanies.'

Oh, Jesus.

'I know now, there *is* no Mr Right – just Mr Right Now. With Tiernan, I was just chasing an illusion. The urban relationship myth. He was like – intimacy? *Aggghhh!* But now I just want to get laid.'

'Preferably by someone who *doesn't* have a dick like a bookie's pencil?' I hear Sophie go and they all crack their holes laughing, including Immaculata.

'This is true. He could not give me an orgasm.'

'Those girls,' I go. 'They're a seriously bad influence on you. Believe me, you won't learn anything hanging around them. I can hook you up with one or two nicer friends,' and I'm thinking maybe I'll ring Melanie – might be a way to let her see how much I've changed already in the week I've been away.

'Oh my God,' Chloe goes, 'I *hate* my thighs!'

Immaculata's there, 'Now I have to hang up, Ross. My footlong has arrived.'

The worst thing is, I can't even say for sure that she's talking about a hotdog.

7. A bad penny

'Tell me about Sorcha.'

'Why do you want to know about her?' I go, wondering is it more for her benefit than mine.

'Because she was your wife and your marriage lasted for only, what, eighteen months? I think she is very relevant to the story of you.'

Fair enough.

'Well,' I go, 'there's not a lot to tell, really. Met her when I was in, like, fifth year at school? She was a Mountie.'

'A Mountie?'

'It's, like, a school? As in Mount Anville? The birds are usually pretty hot. Or supposed to be.'

'And Sorcha went to this school, yes?'

'Yeah, a year ahead of me as well, which was a factor, I'd have to say, in me wanting to *be* with her? And of course later, when I was in sixth year, she was in UCD, which was a big, I suppose, status thing as well – as in scoring a college chick.'

'And this was the attraction?'

I'm trying work out if she disapproves.

'The attraction, I would have to say, was mainly physical. I mean, she was, like, really, really good-looking? Any time we were out, she'd have all these goys, like, staring at her, giving her loads . . .'

'In the context of our sexual history, we often give a special status to our first. Was she your first sexual partner?'

'Fock, no! But I was *hers* – and I know that for a fact.

No, *I'd* been at it for years. My first was actually Tina, as in Ronan's mother. That was, like, a cultural exchange programme that went drastically wrong. In fairness to me, I'd a fair few notches on the old tomahawk by the time me and Sorcha hooked up.'

'What was it in you that Sorcha liked, do you think?'

'Well, looks-wise I'm not exactly Neil Jenkins. And I can be quite the chormer when I'm on form. I suppose me being on the Senior Cup team helped as well. Oh, and I made her laugh – that was a major thing.'

I hear her pen scratching away on her pad. 'What kind of things made her laugh?' she goes.

I'm there, 'Okay, let me think. Big pressure here. What kind of things ... Yeah, there was that time she wrote to Nelson Mandela ...'

'She wrote to Nelson Mandela?'

'She wrote to Nelson Mandela. She was a fan – seriously, don't get me storted. Anyway, all I remember is that, years after he got out of the clink, he was getting hitched and she decides to send him, like, a cord. Of course, then it turns into a letter – you're quite possibly my all-time hero, along with Steve Biko, Anita Roddick, blahdy blahdy blah.

'I mean, the thing was, like, pages and pages long. If they'd sent the focker back to prison for twenty years, he still wouldn't have got through it all.

'So what happens next is, about a week later, I get Oisinn to ring Sorcha – he's unbelievable at doing voices, in fairness to him – and he cracks on to *be* Nelson Mandela. As in the *actual* one?

'I swear to God, I nearly had a focking stroke listening to his side of the conversation. Yes, we are having a very nice time on honeymoon. Yes, I will pass on your best wishes to Graça.

'Then he says he'll be in Dublin for some, I don't know, conference or other – Aids or one of them – next week and he'd love to call to see her in the shop that she wrote about so lovingly in her letter. This was when she was still working in her old dear's boutique.

'Now, you can imagine, I'm on the actual floor laughing at this stage. So the following week, she's got the focking South African flag flying outside the Merrion Shopping Centre. She persuaded the management to put it up there, in between the ones for Garfield's Bistro and Nutley Newsagents.

'It was like, suckered! Then I morch in and tell her it was actually me all along, ripping the piss –'

'Ross,' Conchita goes, cutting me off, 'I'm not here to make value judgements about your behaviour, but to me this story contains much cruelty. You say she laughed at this?'

'Em. Laugh is probably not the right word, come to think of it. I thought you just wanted a few stories from me – give you a flavour of what *I'm* like?'

She doesn't respond to that. I hear her rub her hand up and down her leg, the nylon sort of, like, crackling and I get an instant boner.

'Is it safe to bring up the subject of your mother?'

'Yeah, providing you keep it clean.'

'Tell me about her.'

'Where do I begin? You've no idea how much I hate that actual woman.'

'And yet,' she goes, 'I notice you call her the *old dear*?'

'That's, like, an expression where I come from?'

'But it's a term of endearment, no? To me, it's interesting. You must retain some fond childhood memories?'

Horseshit.

'You want to hear one of my typical childhood memories?'

'Please.'

'Okay, it's the day of that Chernobyl thing – the disaster, in other words?'

'You were how old?'

'Five? Six?'

'Okay.'

'So she's just seen it on TV – whatever happened, big explosion and blah, blah blah. I'm sitting there at the kitchen table with, like, a colouring book or a jigsaw or some shit. I go to say something to her, but she cuts me off and goes, "I don't have time, Ross – there's been an accident!" and she suddenly has out the Salter Brecknell.'

'Okay.'

'So she's weighing caster sugar with one hand and she's got the phone in the other, ringing around everyone she's ever spoken to in her focking life, telling them about the traybake and coffee morning she's organizing for the people of, I don't know, wherever the fock Chernobyl used to be . . .'

'Why does this make you mad? Does this not suggest a level of empathy in your mother, compassion for people?'

I'm like, 'You don't understand – she hates *people*, as in *actual* people. What she loves is, I don't know . . .'

'The kudos that come with seeming to want to help people?'

'Exactly. It was only ever about being the talk of the neighbourhood, getting her big bet-down face in the paper, about being the centre of attention.'

'At an age when *you* should haf been the centre of attention.'

'As in . . .'

'You are five years old, Ross. More than anything, you want your mother's luff.'

'Let me tell you something. She'd plenty of time for me later on, when I made the rugby team at school. She used to arrange all the lunches for the Senior Cup mums. Any excuse to drop a grand in Pamela Scott's, then feed her face for the afternoon . . .'

'What is the Senior Cup mums?'

'It's, like, the mothers of all the goys who were on the senior rugby team. It was, like, a social thing? And she had to take over it, of course. I mean, I wasn't even captain that year. They'd meet every Tuesday – get all tarted up, have lunch and be false to each other for a few hours.'

There's, like, silence then and I don't know why, roysh – as in, I don't know where it comes from – but I end up going, 'She put on a lot of weight when she had me.' Then I laugh. 'I've seen photographs,' I go. 'She's an actual blimp.'

'Why do you mention this?'

'Don't know. Just thought of it.'

'Do you think the weight problems associated with her pregnancy caused her to reject you in some way, to resent you?'

'Don't know. Don't care.'

'Well,' she suddenly goes, 'I would luff to have her here on this couch. She would make a fascinating study, I think.'

'Fascinating how?'

'Some kind of change seems to have happened to her around the time, I think, of the menopause. These later things you told me about – the modelling, the books . . .'

'The egg yolks.'

'All of it. Perhaps I am wrong, but she seems to have undergone some kind of sexual awakening – or perhaps reawakening. Do you think that your father had lost interest in her, sexually, I mean?'

'Whoa! I'm not going there . . .'

'Okay,' she goes, laughing. 'Our session is over.'

I sit up. 'You nearly got me there. I'm going to have to be shorp in here.'

'One thing you might think about before the next time,' she goes. 'Ross, I think you have very much anger in you.'

'I'd say that's fair enough.'

'Any time you have a quiet moment, can you think about the ways in which your mother might have contributed to this anger?'

'I'll try,' I go, 'but I'm not sure there's enough hours in the actual day.'

Whatever else I might say about Sorcha, she's been pretty good recently about sending me pictures of Honor and updates.

These ones are obviously from, like, a couple of weeks ago, when they went to visit Christian and Lauren. Christian's great with her, by the looks of it – that's the exact same smile she only ever gives me – and for the first time I can suddenly picture him as an actual dad.

There's fock-all else in my inbox except spam. I end up getting a huge amount of that shit. I scroll down through forty, maybe fifty messages, with subject lines like 'Surprise her with a rock this Christmas!' and 'They won't laugh at your erection any more!' clicking all the little delete item boxes, hordly even looking to see who they're from. That's how I end up nearly deleting a mail from Immaculata.

Well, that and the fact that the subject line was 'The search for the perfect climax continues . . .'

I open it, roysh, and a link directs me to – sweet suffering fock! – her new blog, called, wait for it, 'Sex in Dublin City'! It's, like, written in that style as well and I end up reading it with my jaw on the actual floor.

In Dublin's Fair City, it's the boys who are pretty – and there's nothing like the sight of stockbrokers blowing off steam at the end of a busy week of trading to make you feel alive, alive, oh!

Chloe, Sophie, Amie and I had decided to go to Café en Seine on the night of the Davy's annual table quiz, each of us hoping to find our very own white knight.

Unfortunately, every eligible female working in financial services between the two canals had the same idea. By the time we arrived, it looked like the trading floor of the New York Stock Exchange, except with females outnumbering males by about three points to one. 'What are you girls waiting for?' Chloe asked, strutting confidently up to the bar. 'The opening bell?'

Two hours later, I was sipping my seventh Archers Aqua, wondering whether it would take hand signals to attract male company in here, when I was suddenly the subject of a takeover bid – a friendly one, too.

His name was Rupert Schefter and he was one hundred per cent blue chip. 'Yeah, to be honest, I only ever drive the X5 on Saturdays. *Most* Saturdays – depends, of course, where we happen to be playing. I always call it my really, really expensive golf bag – with star spoke 209s. I suppose my main car, though, would have to be the 6 Series saloon . . .'

In my mind, I ran through the usual inventory and found he *had* the Big Three – looks, manners and money. After ten minutes of playing FTSE under the table, it looked like a merger was very much on the cards when he suggested we go back to his place to check out his member firm.

In the taxi, *I* took off his tie and loosened his shirt, while *he* explained to me just how the stock market works. An investor who believes the share price or market is about to rise is a bull, he said, while an investor who believes it's about to flop is known as a bear.

As he paid the driver, I couldn't help but wonder if the same terms could be applied to our investments in the bedroom: would *he* be a bull or a bear? After five minutes of trading, I had my answer.

'There, there, Rupert – it happens to every man.'

The following morning, in Odessa, I enjoyed a brunch of chorizo scrambled eggs with pico de gallo and a side order of sympathy.

'What?' Sophie said.

'I said – the much talked about flotation was cancelled . . .'

Amie went, 'What she means is, she got Security and Futures Authority out of him.'

Chloe was like, 'I've heard of this before. It's well known that stockbrokers work out all their sexual frustration before they go home. They leave it on the trading floor. A day of rising and falling and the poor little things don't know whether they're up or down.'

Three Kir Royales later, we thought we had found the solution. It was time for a New Issue.

But later, I couldn't help but ask myself, is it just brokers who are Limited Company or am I destined to be a sole trader for life? How many Black Fridays will I have to endure before I experience my own Big Bang? And will I ever receive my cum dividend?

There must be, like, five or six thousand people in here, crammed in, and no one's sitting in their seats. They're standing on them, chanting, 'Jo-se-ba! Jo-se-ba! Jo-se-ba!' at the top of their voices.

But louder than the sound is the smell. Working-class things. Wintergreen. Cheap deodorant. Chewing gum. Clothes dried on radiators.

I've only ever been to, like, one boxing match in my life and that wasn't even intentional. I bought Sorcha tickets to see Michael Bublé at the Point, but somehow managed to get the dates orseways.

By the way, if you ever want to know what Neilstown looks like all gathered under one roof, go to see Bernard Dunne fight.

It was all too much for Sorcha, of course. She ended up fainting.

I turned around one minute and there she was, lying flat on her back in her good Christopher Deane maxi dress, with the Order of Malta elevating her feet and feeding her salty water, while a girl in hoopy earrings, who looked like she'd been hit in the face with a bag of bent euros, was trying to work out a way of stealing her gold Loriblu evening sandals without sawing off her actual feet.

The atmosphere here reminds me of that night and I swear to God, roysh, I'll be on my back myself if it gets any hotter.

'Facking roof's gonna come off in a minute,' Jonny says to me.

I look behind me and one or two of our goys – that Ander Acebes lunatic especially – are giving it loads.

'*Jo-se-ba! Jo-se-ba! Jo-se-ba!*'

Rudi Ayala, our hooker, has draped himself in the Andorran flag and there's great crack between him and The Generalissimo, who's Spanish, of course, and up for the other dude.

The next thing, roysh, some goy in a tux ducks under the ropes and storts saying shit in, like, Catalan into this microphone. It all sounds like makey-up shit to me, but whatever he's saying, the crowd are loving it because they're cheering every line and then I realize, roysh, that he's bascially introducing them to all the various celebrities at ringside – though none of them I've ever heard of, it has to be said.

Frodo leans forward in his seat behind me and says shit in my ear like, 'This guy is the Julio Iglesias of Andorra,' and, 'This guy is a racing driver – he will be bigger than Schumacher.'

All of a sudden, we're talking totally out of the blue, everyone in the place is suddenly looking in our direction and they're giving it loads. The goys all stand up and take the applause and they're loving it, as in *really* loving it.

Then, roysh, I don't know what he's saying, but the dude in the tux is looking straight at me and sort of, like, beckoning me forward and the goys are all pulling me to my feet, telling me that he wants me in the actual ring.

The next few seconds are a total blur. Mounting the steps. Slipping through the ropes. The dude's hand on my shoulder as he blabbers away, then at the end goes, 'Ross O'Cattle-Keeeeeely.'

It would not be an exaggeration to say that the place goes ballistic. It's the closest thing I've felt to hero-worship since before I left school.

Someone drapes a red, yellow and blue scorf around my shoulders and the dude in the tux grabs my wrist, pulls my hand in the air and, in English, goes, 'The hero of all Ireland! The hero of all Ireland!' and I'm thinking, Hooky might have slightly oversold me here, fair focks to him.

I keep on smiling, right until the moment when the room suddenly goes pitch dork, a hush falls and the announcer babbles something or other and, at the end of it, goes, 'Joseeebaaa Garmeeendiaaa!'

The place goes absolutely Baghdad. At the far end of the hall, suddenly spotlit in blue, is this absolute giant – you can see it even from here, he's a foot taller than most of his entourage – and he's sort of, like, rolling his head from side to side, trying to loosen up his big focking tree trunk of a

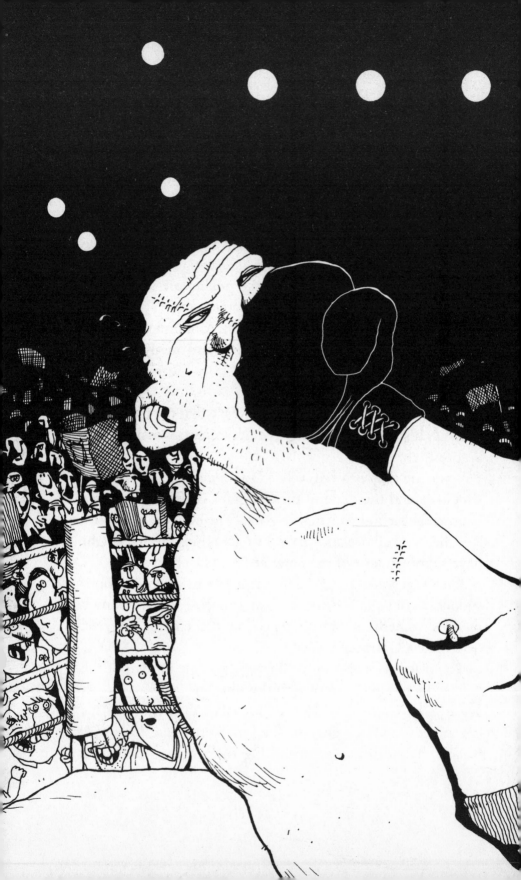

neck. No gown, just black shorts and boots, and muscles on his muscles.

Then, all of a sudden, this music comes on – I'm pretty sure it's Public Enemy's 'Don't Believe the Hype' – and the whole group storts trundling its way towards the ring.

Of course, I'm still *in* the ring. I've suddenly been forgotten about. Nobody's thought to show me out and I can't *find* my way out because it's too focking dork and I'm not even sure I can trust my legs enough to move them.

Honestly, I couldn't be more scared if Serge Betsen came home and caught me wearing his dressing gown, smoking his Gauloises and pissing on his toothbrush.

They're now maybe twenty yords from the ring and I'm seeing Joseba for the first time, full-frontal, and it's a focking horrible sight.

He has a head like a Space Hopper with a focked valve. It's all angles and bits sticking out where they shouldn't, basically a big bald scaldy mass of scar tissue and pure focking anger with – you know the way your eyes can play tricks on you? – an iron bolt through his focking neck.

As he's walking, he keeps pounding his two gloves together and you can hear it, even over the roars of the crowd and the 98 booming with the trunk of funk and the jealous punks trying to stop the dunk and I'm standing there thinking, in about ten seconds that spotlight will be on the ring, he'll come through those ropes and the first face he sees will be mine.

By the time I wake up, my focking clothes will be out of fashion.

All of a sudden, roysh, I feel this hand on my shoulder and someone – I never did find out who, but I owe him my life – guides me out of the ring, just as the whole thing storts to shake with the weight of him climbing the steps and I'm looking back at it, like a man who's just walked out of a burning building.

I'm back in my seat in time to see him punching one of the ring posts and shouting all sorts of mad shit at the crowd.

Then Jesús Zapata is announced and there's nothing but booing and whistling and a few rows behind me someone throws a plastic glass full of beer in his general direction and just barely misses.

His music is 'Put a Little Love in Your Heart' and it's like, er, *random*? It's probably just ripping the piss, but it seems to make Joseba even madder.

Jesús could be, like, a marine or some shit – square jaw, blond hair, nice Peter Pan. The face of a lover, not a fighter. He likes his style as well – big red dressing gown with, like, yellow tassles. He ducks through the ropes and does a bit of a dance, then – how's about this for brass balls? – with his right glove, taps the championship belt hanging around his waist and tells Joseba, presumably, to take a good look because it's the last time he'll be seeing it.

I'm really warming to this dude. I did something similar to three or four of the Newbridge players when I collected my Schools Cup medal, but of course Joseba doesn't turn his head away in shame like they did. He tries to go at him like a focking wild animal and it takes his entire entourage and pretty much all of Jesús's men to hold him back and persuade him to leave it until after the national anthems.

Jesús flashes a big white smile at the crowd and everyone's going ballistic.

'S'awl front,' Jonny goes. 'Prepare to see a man get facking murdered.'

'No, no,' The Generalissimo goes, 'Jesús weel hannihilate heem.'

The bell eventually rings and Joseba tears across the ring to my man, who doesn't even blink, just catches him full on the forehead with a punch that we all felt at ringside, then steps to the right. Joseba is sort of, like, stunned and Jesús walks to the other corner, like one of those bullfighter dudes, waiting for the beast to chorge again.

He's cooler than a bucket of free beer, this dude, standing there, just smiling at Joseba, with his hands down by his side. After what seems like ages, Joseba runs at him again, but at the last second Jesús sort of, like, shifts his weight onto his right foot and catches him coming in with an uppercut that would have put Peter Clohessy into orbit.

Suddenly, there's not a sound in the place. This is a far more interesting fight than anyone had imagined and they're not liking it.

Jesús snaps Joseba's big ugly head back with a couple of straight jabs, then really opens up on him, three or four shots to the body, two to the head and out again before Joseba's even thought about throwing a punch. Then he does it again. Then again. One man fighting in slow motion, the other in, I don't know, real time and suddenly all you can hear from the crowd are individual voices, shouting encouragement, but it's obvious that something's seriously wrong here.

Joseba literally hasn't landed a punch.

All of a sudden – and I'm the first to notice this – the most unbelievable thing happens. Joseba storts crying. I say it to Jonny, of course failing focking miserably to hide my delight.

'Leave it aht,' he goes. 'His eyes is just runnin'. Zapata's got facking caustic on his gloves – he's known for it . . .'

Pretty soon, though, it's obvious to everyone and it's suddenly quiet enough to hear him, like, sobbing away.

236

Then the booing storts.

'The Little Bull,' I hear Frodo go, 'crying like a baby.'

He's not even throwing anything now. Not even defending himself. You can see Jesús turning to the referee, as if to say, are you going to end this or am I going to actually have to?

In the end, roysh, he turns to his corner, shrugs his shoulders, then cracks Joseba on the side of the jaw with the best punch I've ever seen and Joseba collapses like a focking dynamited building.

The referee doesn't bother his orse with the count, just storts his waving his orms like a man directing an airplane in to land and the medics are straight in, rolling the goy onto his side, but he's fine because even over the booing we can hear him still crying.

'A fuckeeng tray tare – I wheel keel him with my own hends,' Ander Acebes goes, all four-foot-eleven of him.

I'm there, 'Can anyone tell me what actually happened back there?'

'Fink he had some kind of breakdown,' Jonny goes. 'Imagine. A facking breakdown, there in the facking ring.'

Ander stops my orm as I go to knock back some of my pint and tells me, pretty angrily, that all Andorrans are not like this and he wants me to know he would rather die than dishonour, well, what is basically a giant outdoor duty-free shop where it seems to piss rain twenty-four hours a day.

Of course you couldn't say that to him.

I get chatting to Rudi, Oscar and Justo – basically our front row – and I'm telling them a little bit of where they're going wrong. Oscar and Justo are twins, both cowherds in Cortals d'Encamp, and haven't a word of English, so Rudi translates for me. As I see it, Oscar's not getting down low enough and Justo, at tight-head, isn't standing absolutely still, so the scrum's not locking basically.

They're lapping up the advice.

They can certainly put away the beer as well. We're all tanning it in a major way.

The Generalissimo asks me what our chances are hagainst Hireland and this time I don't bother reminding them about the A bit.

'Depends on our attitude,' I go. 'Rugby's as much a mental game as a physical one. I remember, like, one year in school, we had a pretty weak S, it has to be said. There were, like, seven of us on it who were in fifth year. We hadn't, like, filled out yet, but it was more about blooding players for the following year.

'Anyway, Father Fehily – who I'm sure you're all tired of hearing about at this stage – he arranges this friendly for us against Mungret College. Muckers from Limerick. Parsnip-chomping savages every one of them.

'Anyway, the word goes round that they're going to do a job on us, that they've promised Cistercian College Roscrea – who we had in the first round of the Cup – that they're going to soften us up, as a favour for their welly-wearing cousins.

'Fehily gives us each a crash helmet and two headache tablets and tells us to defend our line as if our lives depended on it. No one noticed that Oisinn – who was, like, our hooker – was missing. Suddenly he arrives in with this big shit-eating grin on his boat. He'd got into the Mungret dressing-room, put hay all over the floor and the benches, then threw in three or four live chickens . . .'

That gets a good laugh.

'What deed thees cheekens do?' The Generalissimo goes.

I'm there, 'Nothing as such. It just meant that in those

few minutes before the game, the Mungret players were thinking about chickens and hay instead of their gameplan.'

'They were broken – up *here*,' Ander goes, tapping the side of his head. I'm really beginning to warm to the mad focker.

I'm there, 'We won 3–0 in perhaps the worst match in the history of rugby.'

'We must do this!' Ander goes, suddenly excited. 'Oscar and Justo, they will put six fucking Holsteins in the Ireland dressing-room,' and then he turns around to the two boys and storts yacking away to them in the local lingo. Then he turns back to me and goes, 'Six Holsteins, three cocks and two izards. Fucking Irish – no offence, my friend.'

I'm there, 'None taken. But you've got to remember – the rugby crowd, they're not *Irish* as such. Most of them wouldn't know a focking cow if it fell on them. Except Johnny Hayes, of course. I don't actually know what you'd throw in there to psyche that lot out of it – a couple of Shanahan's pork shanks, maybe. A few BT store cords scattered around the place . . .'

Eventually, the night breaks up, roysh, and I head back to the gaff. I stick my key in the door, walk in and I can hear it straight away.

Joseba sobbing his hort out.

The sound is coming from the kitchen. I stand at the door and watch him, his big muscly shoulders going up and down. Crying like a teenage girl.

You'd have to be pretty hord not to feel sorry for him, seeing him reduced to this.

It's bad news for him that I *am* pretty hord.

I walk up behind him and hit him a focking smack across the back of the head. He turns around to me with a look of absolute focking terror on his face.

It doesn't take much to tip him off the chair and onto the floor of the kitchen, where he actually cowers from me, waving his hands in front of him, going, 'Don't heet me! Please don't heet me!'

He must have, like, fifty or sixty stitches in his face.

I'm like, 'Not so focking scary now, are you? How the tables have turned,' and he storts crawling towards the door, going back to his own room, on all fours, like the focking dog that he is.

I give him the most unbelievable kick in the orse. Even just the sound of it – *gock!* – like hitting the perfect shot in the driving range.

I'm thinking, what a focking great thing sport is for sorting the heroes from the zeroes.

I'm on the old Avinguda Meritxell with an hour to kill, when all of a sudden who do I see coming out of Massimo Dutti, struggling with a load of bags, only Conchita.

Of course, I'm straight over, ever the gentleman, offering to help.

She looks incredible, all in black. She's pretty pleased to see me as well – we're talking full eye contact. Then she grabs my hand and tells me I must be freezing. To be fair, it's colder than a witch's tit out. 'You must remember, you are not in Ireland now,' she goes. 'You must wear warmer clothes.'

I'm there, 'Do you fancy a coffee?'

'Yes,' she goes, straight away – doesn't even have to think about it.

'It's just I'm meeting Frodo in the Lizarran and I'm actually early for a change.'

'Let's go,' she goes, and we walk the hundred yords or so to this little taberna.

We sit outside, at one of the little, I don't know, oak tables – just to let her see that the cold doesn't bother me.

The waitress comes out and the two of them end up having a good old chinwag and of course I don't understand a word. Then Conchita turns to me and goes, 'Espresso for you?'

I'm like, 'No, a normal one – whatever you call that,' and I make the shape of, like, a large coffee with my hands.

'Ah, Americano,' the waitress goes.

Conchita turns around to me and she's like, 'In Italy this word is meant as an insult. They spit it out with contempt – *Americano!* The American soldiers who occupied Italy during the war, they could not drink the coffee as the Italians like it – too strong, they say. Add water, add water. *Americano*, the waiters say. Bloody Americans!'

It has to be said, she knows a lot of shit for someone only my age. I don't know what the fock I've been doing with my time. I'm thinking I might actually buy a book while I'm here. There's loads of facts out there I don't know. It'd be good to have stuff to talk to people about.

The coffees arrive and I end up not even touching mine, feeling like a total idiot for ordering it in the first place.

'The waitress,' Conchita goes, 'she says tomorrow it will snow – early this year. I cannot remember the last time the snow came in November.'

I'm there, 'Make a change from all the rain.'

'The people here will be happy. The last four years the snow did not come until late. Tourism is vital for the Andorra economy.'

I'm there, 'Hey, do you fancy going skiing – as in together?'

She's delighted.

'I would very much like that,' she goes. 'We can go

to Ordino-Arcalis. Then I can see how *pretty amazing* you are....'

'Well, I'm not bad,' I go and she laughs, roysh, pats my hand in, like, a patronizing way and goes, 'Pretty amazing is what *you* say. *Foxrock is basically a skiing hotbed.*'

It's a pretty good impression, it has to be said.

Automatically – I don't know why – I go to tickle her and she actually screams, but of course I've never let that stop me. I give her, like, a seriously good tickling, the kind I used to give Sorcha in bed on a Sunday morning, under the orms and the ribs, and we're suddenly fighting each other, her orms and legs flailing and we're both laughing so much I think we're going to explode.

When I stop, roysh, I'm left pretty much on top of her and we're just, like, staring into each other's eyes. Her mouth drops open. It feels like we're about two seconds away from throwing the lips on each other.

That's when Frodo arrives.

Of course, I jump straight up, guilt written all over my face.

He and Conchita seem to know each other well and it turns out that she was in school with Adriana, Frodo's bird, who, for what it's worth, works in Crèdit Andorrà with him.

That's another way that this place is like Bray – everyone is linked somehow. Although here it's not because the gene pool is the size of a focking foot spa.

I turn around to Frodo and I go, 'Hey, I've a present for you,' and I give him a little bag.

See, I rang him this morning and told him I was worried about his ball-handling and it's a mork of how serious he is about his rugby that he was prepared to give up his lunch break to get some tips from the master.

'Juggling balls,' he goes, pulling the little package out of the bag. 'And a book. *Juggling for the Complete Klutz*. This is for me?'

I actually picked it up in a toy shop.

'This is how we all learned,' I go.

He's there, 'Is this true?' actually seeming genuinely *into* the idea.

'All the greats – they can all juggle. Drico. Shaggy. Dorce is like Coco the focking Clown when you get him going.'

He shakes his head in, like, total amazement.

'I'm telling you, spend a week learning how to juggle those balls,' I go, 'then we'll move you onto Coca-Cola bottles. Then you're going to learn to do it blindfolded. See, it's all about trusting your instincts. Do that and you'll never drop another ball again.'

He turns around, roysh, and says something to Conchita in the local jargon. Then he turns to me and goes, 'I just say to Conchita, from this man, in two weeks, I have learned more about rugby than I ever knew. He is a genius.'

Genius? It's a big word. It's not for me to say.

I can feel Conchita smiling at me, like a hundred-watt bulb, out of the corner of my eye.

'Frodo, pull up a pew,' I go, 'and let's get some coffees – *real* ones this time.'

I bell Ro and he immediately answers. 'Rosser,' he goes, 'I'm not in the humour.'

I'm like, 'Not in the humour? To talk to your old man? Where *are* you?'

'In me gaff,' he goes. 'I'm torturing meself here, man. Going troo all me pitchers of me and Bla, wondering should I keep them or should I delete them.'

I'm there, 'Oh – well, look, it's Christmas in another few weeks. Any idea what you want?'

'What I *want*?'

'Yeah, as in present-wise? I mean, I'm obviously going to bring you back a shitload of tobacco because it's, like, cheap as chips over here. But I don't know what to get you for your biggie.'

'I won't be celebrating Christmas,' he goes. 'Look, I've got to split, Rosser. I'm going to delete these pitchers.'

Then he all of a sudden hangs up.

It's snowing. And not just a few flecks either. It's really coming down.

'Don't you facking do it,' Jonny shouts, sort of, like, jabbing his finger at me. 'Don't even fink abaht bringin' us in,' and I'm really beginning to love these goys. Whatever shortcomings they have as, like, players, you can't question their attitude.

'Okay,' I'm giving it, 'backs, keep going. Keep doing the drills. Forwards, let's do an hour on the scrummaging machine. Come on – you've seen focking snow before, haven't you?'

As they're working, I'm talking them up as well, especially the backs, telling them that they have to think like the enemy. In other words, don't just watch the DVDs I show you and decide where the opposition are, like, vulnerable. Think about our own weaknesses as a team and how the opposition are likely to try to exploit them and what we can actually do to, like, counteract that?

I'm already seeing the difference in Frodo's handling. He put on, like, an exhibition of juggling in the dressing-room earlier and he's putting on one out on the pitch now.

At some point, roysh, for some reason I look up and I notice Joseba standing out on the balcony – the first time he's actually seen daylight, I reckon, in the week since the fight. He's standing there in literally nothing except his jockeys and he's just, like, staring up at the grey sky, letting all these flakes just fall onto his face.

No one else seems to notice him for ages, but then all of a sudden – worst possible scenario – Ander does, the little focking lunatic, and he suddenly storts letting rip.

'You fuckeeng tray tare,' he's shouting up at him. 'You dishonour the nem of Andorra. I will strengle you like a cat.'

Everyone suddenly stops what they're doing.

I'm there, 'Ander, chillax,' trying to, like, calm him down. 'He's not doing anyone any horm.'

We all stand and watch Joseba turn and walk back into the aportment. Ander turns to me and, in all seriousness, goes, 'Ross, give me your key. I want to go up there. I will feenish him off like a injured weasel I find on the road, or a elderly relative who piss the bed too much . . .'

I put my orm around his shoulder and go, 'Hey, you've bigger battles than that to fight,' and this obviously means something to him because he goes, 'You are right,' then he goes back to what he was doing, taking only occasional glances up to see if Joseba has dared to show his face again.

Things settle down again pretty quickly and everyone goes back to work.

I'm going, 'Okay, Justo, remember what I told you – absolutely still . . .'

All of a sudden, totally out of the blue, I think I hear a voice shout, 'Your number two's not getting low enough.'

I decide to ignore it.

'Back and bottom,' the voice keeps going. 'Should be absolutely level. Oh, I don't think he can hear me . . .'

I'm sure it's in my focking head. It *must* be.

'Okay,' I go, 'now I want to talk to the rest of you about winning quicker ruck ball . . .'

'Chap's going to dislocate his shoulder engaging like that, Kicker!'

Frodo is suddenly looking over my shoulder, squinting his eyes, going, 'Who is that man?'

I'm there, 'Which one?' trying to bluff it.

'The man with the hat. The cigar?'

'Oh him,' I go, without even looking. 'I've never seen him before in my life. But he's pissing me off in a major way.'

Then I call Ander over and ask him to show him out. He says it'll be a pleasure.

'Tell me about your father,' she goes.

It's obvious we're not going to talk about what happened outside the Lizarran.

I'm there, 'He's here, believe it or not. Turned up yesterday. At training.'

She's like, 'He is free from prison?'

'Apparently.'

'You spoke with him?'

I'm there, 'No. Got one of the goys to fock him out. Put up a bit of a fight, in fairness to him. I was actually pretty impressed, seeing as he's never focking stood up for himself before.'

'What does this mean?'

'Means settling with the Revenue, the Criminal Assets Bureau. I lost everything ... I mean, what's he doing here? This is *my* shit. Why does he have to go sticking his hooter in?'

'Freud tells a story,' she suddenly goes. 'When he was a boy, his father came home and said that a Gentile had knocked his cap into the gutter and told him, "Get off the pavement, Jew." Freud asked his father, "What did you do?"

246

and Jakob shrugged and said, "I picked up my cap – what else?"'

'So what's the moral?'

'Freud was devastated by his father's lack of heroism. It is natural. Every boy wants his father to be a strong role model, is that not so?'

'Whatever.'

'And he disappointed you?'

'Yeah. I'd say big time.'

'But is it also true to say that you would not have been disappointed if you hated your father as much as you say you did?'

The thing about doing this thing is you have to watch every focking word. Shit gets twisted.

I'm there, 'You're getting a bit technical now.'

She's like, 'This is not technical. To be disappointed by him, you would have to have some regard for him in the first place, no?'

'I wouldn't say a major amount . . .'

'*Yes*, a major amount,' she goes. 'I suspect a very major amount. What is the nicest thing you ever saw your father do?'

'Okay, I know I'm going to regret saying this, but there's, like, loads.'

'Loads?'

'Yeah, loads of actual nice things, I mean. Shit like – okay, we were watching TV one night. I was, like, thirteen, fourteen, and there's this kid on the *Late Late* and he's got some shit wrong with him that they can't treat in Ireland – let's just say it's cancer, for argument's sake.

'So he has to go to the States – Chicago, I'm pretty sure – and it's going to cost, like, twenty Ks. The old man just gets up and disappears into his study.'

'He paid for it?'

'I found the cheque stub about a week later. I was rooting through his desk, looking for money to steal. And I could tell you, like, fifty stories just like that one.'

'I think you luff your father very, very much.'

'Maybe. Sometimes. When he's being himself. When he's not trying to do the big pals act.'

'Do you know what kind of relationship your father had with his own father?'

'From what I hear, there wasn't much of one. I never actually knew him – as in my granddad. I think he was pretty hord on the old man, though. All he ever says about him is, "He didn't think very much of me at all."'

'Do you think he craved the relationship with you that he wanted with his own father?'

'I don't know. Maybe. But bear in mind he never had focking time for me. Too busy. Actually, I'll give you an example. Just after we moved to Foxrock, we're in the gorden, just the two of us, and we're cutting the grass. No one had lived in the gaff for, like, a year and the place was in rag order. Anyway, we're hacking our way through this pretty much forest and we end up finding, like, a bomb shelter.'

'A bomb shelter?'

'Yeah, it's actually still there. The dude who lived there before us, he was this, I don't know, mad ortist – totally focking mental supposedly. He was convinced there was going to be, like, a nuclear war any minute? So he had this shelter built, I think in, like, the sixties? You should have seen this thing, it was focking humungous – pretty much the same size as the downstairs of the actual gaff. You went down maybe ten steps and there was, like, a strongroom door.

'So we found the key, went in and there was, like, everything in there – fridge, cooker, TV, beds. You could actually live in it, which I suppose was the idea.

'Anyway, the old man says we'd turn it into a boys' room. Put, like, a pool table in there. Cinema screen. Jukebox. The works. It'd be our little place, he said. Never focking happened, of course.'

'Do you think this is perhaps a source of your anger?'

'Don't know. All I know is I used to go down there every day after school. Supposedly to do my homework. Though what I was really doing was waiting for *him* . . .'

'So where was he?'

'Working. Doing the kind of shit they eventually put him away for.'

'Ross,' she goes, 'I want you to think about this – between now and the next day. Your father was a failure in the eyes of his own father. Is this why he was so driven to succeed in business, something he was good at? Is this also why he was so happy to let it all go?'

I'm there, 'I think you're possibly being a bit *too* fair to him? I'll definitely mull it over, though.'

I get up to go.

I'm like, 'So . . . what are you up to for the weekend?' wondering does she fancy having, I don't know, dinner.

'I am going to Paris to see Bernard,' she goes, totally out of the blue.

'Bernard?'

'Yes – my husband, Ross!'

The way she says husband. With extra, I suppose, emphasis. Which means she's decided that what *almost* happened outside the Lizarran can't be allowed to *almost* happen again.

*

I don't know why I have to keep checking Immaculata's blog. Guess it's like a cor crash – a terrible bloody mess, but at the same time I can't look away. Here's her latest entry.

The city of Dublin is home to 1.7 million people, three hundred thousand of whom are single women, trying to sink their claws into one of the city's two hundred and forty thousand single men. The competition has never been more intense. What can a girl do? Well, she can at least ensure she has *pretty* claws.

Chloe had suggested visiting Nails Inc. for a Saturday afternoon manicure. A nail bar, I discovered, is one of the best portals from which to observe life in this newly prosperous city.

It was while we were in BTs that Sophie spotted someone she remembered from school. 'Oh my God, Alison Bannon – *random?*'

Amie remembered her, too. 'That focking buttermilk bitch – you know who she's, like, engaged to? Zach – as in, *used* to be on the Senior Cup team in Mary's and became, like, a barrister?'

Chloe didn't remember Alison, but she certainly remembered Zach. 'Been there, done *him*,' she goes.

Amie greeted this news as some kind of victory by proxy, while Sophie didn't seem to care one way or the other – as long as she fitted into her new Hervé Léger strapless dress for Jessica Middlebrook's twenty-seventh birthday party, which meant – after weeks of dieting – hitting her target weight at around eight o'clock that night.

Sophie hit two things before then – first her Mastercard limit, then the floor. The nail technician was pushing back her cuticles when, quite unexpectedly, she passed out.

Ten minutes later, she was being loaded into the back of an ambulance. Chloe was full of concern: 'Don't take her to the Mater or any of those shitholes – she's VHI positive.'

The ambulance attendant had some bad news: 'I can only let two of you ride in the back with her.'

But Amie had a solution: 'You guys go – I need to go back in here. Totally forgot to get my TIGI Bed Head Onyx Sparkle Liquid Eye Liner.'

At the hospital, Sophie's problem was quickly diagnosed. Drinking six litres of water in two hours had caused hyper-hydration.

Chloe and I stood at her bedside and listened to her stunningly handsome, stunningly unmarried doctor talk dirty to her: 'If you take it in orally – water, I mean – more quickly than it can be removed, through sweat and urine, your body fluids get diluted and a dangerous shift in the electrolyte balance of the blood occurs. Fainting is the body's way of saying – enough Evian already!'

He handed Sophie a slip of paper and went, 'Take two of these three times a day,' then handed me one and said, 'And *you* take this – any time you like.'

When he'd gone, I opened it – the name Stephen and a mobile phone number. Forward – but very, very cute.

The following Friday, we had dinner in Browne's Brasserie. His credentials were impeccable, having studied medicine at Princeton University. Conversationally, though, this doctor was the original Ivy drip and I would have walked out halfway through my truffle risotto but for this thought – in my search for the ever-elusive female climax, who better to have as a guide than an expert in anatomy and physiology?

Back in his apartment, I submitted to a full physical examin-ation. After tearing each other's clothes off, I lay down on the bed and waited for him to electrolyte my fire. Four minutes of grunting later, the doctor rolled off me. 'I didn't hear your pager,' I went.

He was like, 'My pager? No, you don't understand – I'm finished.'

The following morning, over brunch in Dalkey's In, Sophie

asked the question that was on everyone's MAC Lustred lips: 'How did your date with McDreamy go? Did he give you your medicine?'

I was like, 'Oh my God – three letters. DOA! Departed on Arrival!'

The girls were like, 'No way!'

You know what he had the cheek to tell me – that simultaneous orgasms had *never been his thing*.

'Which is male code,' Chloe goes, 'for, *I'll* have one now and *you* can sort yourself out when I'm gone.'

Amie's like, 'Chloe!'

But Chloe's there, 'I'm sorry, girls, but this is, like, such a déjà screw situation for me. I've been with doctors before. It's well known that they make terrible lovers – it's because the body holds no mystery for them.'

That night I considered this little kidneystone of wisdom. And I couldn't help but ask myself, in the emergency room of love, is my heart now beyond the point of defibrillation? Is there anyone who can prescribe something to send my temperature soaring? And when am I going to have some of what the doctor ordered?

I'm on the old Fiter i Rossell, thinking oh my God, it's, like, Christmas in three weeks, when all of a sudden I'm passing KFC and for some reason – fock knows why – I end up looking through the actual window. *He's* sitting there. On his Tobler. In the hat and the Cole Haan coat he usually wears to Leopardstown, wrapping his face around – of all things – a bucket of popcorn chicken.

Things are obviously bad.

When he sees me, he goes, 'Here he comes – the national rugby coach of Andorra!'

I don't even give him a charity smile, just stare him out of it and go, 'What the fock are you even *doing* here?'

'The chicken,' he goes. 'Can't get enough of it. Seems they marinate it, Ross. Spices and so forth. That's the secret. Will you have something – a plated meal?'

I'm there, 'A what?'

'Two pieces of the Colonel's world-famous chicken, plus two home-style sides – *id est*, if you'll pardon the Latin, rice *et* mashed potato. I had one earlier. This is big news, of course. One of the ways in which prison has marked me – I have my main meal of the day at lunchtime now . . .'

I'm there, 'When I said, what are you doing here, I meant *here*, as in here in Andorra?'

It's the first time I've ever seen him look genuinely, I don't know, hurt. 'Well, *you're* here, Ross. Where else was I going to go?'

'Er, try back to your *wife*? She lost her book deal, you know. Might have taken her down a peg or two.'

He shakes his head, sadly I suppose. 'There's no going back, I'm afraid. Not an option.'

'Because she sold you up the river?'

'Well, I wouldn't use that expression . . .'

'Oh, wouldn't you? She put your entire life and crimes in her stupid focking book. And you're not even, like, pissed off with her about that?'

One of the floor staff arrives over to clear away the leftovers. A dog – no further comment necessary. Of course the old man's already on first-name terms with her.

'*Gràcies*, Mariona,' he's going. '*Gràcies. Deliciósa*,' and she's looking at him as if to say, it's only focking K-Fry – will you get a grip on reality?

'Mariona,' he goes then, 'this is my son – er, *mon fill*. Ross . . .' and she obviously doesn't give two focks. She says something to me, just to be sociable, but I don't understand, so I end up just blanking her.

When she focks off, the old man goes, 'Wonderful girl. Lets me sit over a coffee in here for hours, reading the old bible,' and he waves a copy of, like, *The Economist* at me.

'Are you telling me that *this* is where you've been spending your evenings?'

'Well, the, quote-unquote, guesthouse I'm in – it's not exactly the Conrad. Gets you down, cooped up in that little room, walls closing in and so forth . . .'

I'm almost tempted to tell him he can stay with me. He could have the sofa. He could even have Joseba's bed. I was thinking of putting that focker out anyway. He's bringing me down with his moping around. In the end, I don't mention it.

'I thought we might take a drive,' he all of a sudden goes. 'You haven't lived until you've seen the road to La Massana . . .'

'I'm busy.'

'All these wonderful tunnels through the mountains, then the most extraordinary valley opens up, right in front of your eyes.'

'Hang on,' I go. 'How the fock do you know so much about this place? And jawing away there to the Wreck of the *Kursk* in the local lingo – have you been here before?'

He gives me what I would have to call an embarrassed laugh. 'Ross,' he goes, 'this place is one of the world's most renowned tax havens . . .'

That's a yes.

'Know it like the back of my hand,' he goes. 'Of course, I was a man of more considerable means the last time I was here.'

I'm almost on the point of offering him money – imagine, *me* offering *him* money? – that's how focking pathetic he is. Then I think about him giving away all those sponds and me ending up having to use taxis and public transport for a year.

He's not getting a focking cent out of me.

'All the money in the world couldn't buy what I have now,' he suddenly goes, like he can read my mind. 'An opportunity to spend some – inverted commas – quality time with my son.'

I'm like, 'Yawn!' right in his focking face.

'To see him in his element, as I did the other day, finally doing what he was put on this Earth to do – *ipso facto*, coach. You didn't see me, Ross, but I was at the ground, watching you put the chaps through their paces. Wonderfully inspiring stuff. The way they look at you . . .'

I'm like, 'Yeah, whatever?'

'Of course, I was eventually asked to leave – didn't have the right accreditation. I expect they thought I was one of these spies you read about – dispatched to Andorra la Vella to send back intelligence reports to Michael Bradley himself – God forbid – re. the relative strengths and weaknesses of the national team of Andorra.'

'That's one way prison hasn't changed you – you're still a focking dick.'

'Not that I'd put anything past them. Military-style preparation – that's the new thing. I wouldn't blame you for having the place locked down. Sweep the dressing-room for listening devices if you feel the need. That'd be my advice, Ross.'

'You know what you can do with your advice.'

'What I want to say to you is that if you need any help from me – any help at all . . .'

'I don't.'

'I'm here. And I mean anything – advice on how the front row is engaging in the scrum . . .'

'Eat shit.'

'Wonderful. Now, where's Mariona?' he goes, suddenly looking around him. 'See if she can't furnish us with a couple of their delicious cappuccinos. Did you know this place has outlets all over the world, Ross?'

8. The joke and its relation to the unconscious

When I see Conchita, I end up nearly creaming my Monte Cargos there on the spot – she's a vision in, I don't know, duck down and baby-blue lycra.

Of course I can't help myself flirting. 'You look incredible,' I go and for the first time we actually air-kiss – on both cheeks, as it happens. Then we do it a second time. I'm there, 'Sorry, in Ireland we do it, like, *twice* on each cheek?'

She laughs.

'Hmmm. I was in Cork when I was maybe fifteen,' she goes. 'I don't recall that the Irish do this at all.'

I'm like, 'Cork? Jesus, they're still cleaning their teeth with their own shit down there. No, no – it's, like, a South Dublin thing? I like your Chorm 7s, by the way.'

'Oh,' she goes, slightly surprised, 'thank you.'

'I'm a Salomons man as well,' I go, pointing at the boots I spent nearly four hundred notes on this morning. 'The old Impact 8s. We're talking ergonomic padding, Spaceframe holes, Second Skin shell, ninety-flex rated and loads of other shit I don't understand.'

She thinks that's hilarious as well.

We're standing in the queue for the lift up to Pic d'Arcalis.

'I tell you what,' I go, 'I can't wait to get out there on the actual snow. You're talking to a serious powder addict here. Remind me to show you my Alley Oop Flatspin 540 . . .'

That's when I hear the noise that always sends, like, a shiver right through me.

'Ross! Ross!'

'Ignore it,' I go, but she can't help looking back, curious, I suppose.

I quickly lash on the Oakley Doakleys and pull down my Burton Billboard beanie, but the focker still recognizes me. I suddenly feel his hand on, like, my shoulder.

'*There* you are!' he goes, trying to get his breath back. 'Thought I wasn't going to catch you before you went out on the snow.'

He looks a complete tool, of course, everything red, from head to toe and I'm not even sure it's actual ski gear. He looks like what he is – an old fart in a lagging jacket.

I'm there, 'Er, if it's tickets for the match you're looking for, you're going to have to go through the normal channels,' trying to pass him off as someone who just recognized me from home. 'Now, I don't want to be rude, but the queue storts back there . . .'

'Oh, hello,' he goes to Conchita. 'You must one of Ross's pals, are you? I'm Charles – his *old dad*, as he calls me,' and he's suddenly shaking her hand going, 'Hello – hello, indeed.'

She's only too delighted to meet him, of course.

I'm just shaking my head.

I'm there, 'How the fock did you find us here?' knowing the day is already ruined.

'Serendipity,' he goes, chirpy as you like. 'Called to the apartment, see if you fancied taking that drive we were talking about. Maybe drive to Arinsal, rent some skis, tackle Pic Negre . . .

'That chap you live with – said, you've just missed them, I'm afraid. I'm paraphrasing, of course. They've gone to Ordino-Arcalis, which I knew was only a fifteen-minute drive . . .'

'Joseba?' I go. 'He's got a focking mouth on him like the Port Tunnel.'

And what I don't realize, of couse, is that he's standing right behind the old man.

I don't focking believe this.

'What's *he* doing here?'

'Well,' the old man goes, 'he seemed a bit down in himself. Not surprised either. Stuck indoors on a day like today? With all this wonderful snow? You're coming with us, I said. Yes, you are! Yes, sir!'

Joseba steps forward. He nods at me, then at Conchita. She gives him a smile, but I just blank the focker. Of course the old man's wittering away, roysh, totally oblivious. 'They cycle these hills, you know. Big race every year. Might be the Volta a Catalunya, though I won't swear to it.'

We're suddenly at the top of the queue. I turn to him and go, '*You* can get the Wilsons, you absolute knobhead.'

So the next thing, roysh, we're getting on the chairlifts and it's, like, two to each one and I try to arrange it so that I end up sharing one with Conchita, but she somehow gives me the slip and I end up getting lumbered with Joseba, which is focking awkward, because it's, like, ten or fifteen minutes to the top.

No sooner is the retention bor down than the focker's in my ear. 'Russ,' he goes, 'I did not introduce mayself to you,' and – unbelievable this – he offers me his hand. 'I em Joseba Garmendia.'

I'm like, 'Bit late for that, isn't it? Have you got focking concussion or something?'

'Pulees don't judge, Russ, until you hear what I haff to say. Then you might theenk I am not so bed. But first I haff to say surry to you.'

I'm not even listening to him. I'm just looking down, watching the tops of the trees below our feet.

'Your fathare, he says you are a fair man . . .'

259

I turn and look at him for the first time. 'Why would he have said that?'

'I told heem may story in the car. I tell him, I treat your boy so bed. He says to explen it to you like I explen it to heem.'

'Explain what?'

'You end your fathare, you love each other – thees is ferry clear . . .'

'Could have fooled me.'

'My fathare deed not love me. He was a – how to say – brutal man. He beat me. He beat my muthare. Effery day when I was leetle, this heppened . . .'

It's, like, yadda yadda yadda, until he goes, 'Then one day he keeled her. With hees own hends,' and he suddenly has my attention.

'Are you serious?'

'Yes. And, like a coward, he henged heemself. I haff only one photograph of heem. Taken close to here. In Sant Cerni. He looks so heppy. A smiling basterd.

'Always when I fight, in my mind, I poot hees fess on the fess of my opponent. Then I imagine I em punching my fathare.'

'Jesus!'

'But then some sing heppened. Suddenly I cannot see hees fess any more. The enger is no longer een me. I know I haff lost eet. Then you arrived . . .'

'I actually thought you were going to, like, kill me that night?'

'I was trying to be engry again.'

'Thought you were going to turn my face to mush.'

'But then I see your fess in the light of the door. Your leetle eyes shut tight, waiting for me to heet you, screaming like a leetle girl . . .'

260

'Okay, okay.'

'. . . and I knew I couldn't heet you. I knew eet then. My nerf – it ees gone.'

We're near the actual top now.

'So what are you going to do?' I go.

He shakes his head sadly. 'I cannot stay een Andorra la Vella,' he goes. 'The people, they het me.'

'I don't know if they hate you.'

'They shout at me in the street – cheeken. Tomorrow, I go to Frankfoort. My girlfriend ees there.'

'I saw her picture,' I go. I'm so tempted to add, 'My sympathies,' but I don't.

There's just time enough, before we reach the top, for me to shake his hand, roysh, and tell him there's no hord feelings.

Then it's time to stort giving it loads.

Of course, I'm showing off in front of Conchita in a major way. I'm going, 'Okay, goys, let's corve some serious turns!' and I keep going to the old man, 'Are you sure you wouldn't be more comfortable on, like, the bunny slopes?'

I can't believe it, roysh, when he suddenly digs his poles into the snow and takes off down this trail, we're talking, I don't know, ninety focking Ks an hour here – actually telemorking the entire way down – then at the very bottom he finishes with this unbelievable hop turn.

Conchita and Joseba both cheer, roysh, and of course I straight away take that as a challenge. I'm like, that's it – I'm actually jumping.

So I tear off after him, doing, like, whatever speed he was doing – and *then* some?

I see this huge lip ahead of me and, as I approach it, I give it some serious welly, hit it hord, launch myself into the air, then do the kind of iron cross mute grab that you'd actually spend hours watching on YouTube.

I land and turn, roysh, to try to catch Conchita's reaction – but it turns out she hasn't seen it, too busy helping Joseba with his bindings.

'Bravo!' the old man goes. 'Maximum points from the Foxrock jury!'

I give him a look and go, 'I didn't focking do it for *your* benefit.'

The other two fly down to us then, though, to be honest, there's suddenly more talking than actual skiing going on. Conchita's telling the old man that she hasn't telemorked since two years ago in, like, Val-d'Isère and that prompts a major discussion about the Glacier de Pissaillas, which all focking three of them have skied apparently.

He's an embarrassment, of course.

Believe me, watching your old man spit the G with a bird *you* have the hots for just makes you want to throw your lunch.

'Fitness, that's the key to it,' he's going. 'You keep yourself in great trim, Conchita. I make no apologies for saying it.'

'Are we focking talking or are we skiing?' I go, ending up sounding majorly norked. 'Come on, let's go off-piste.'

But Conchita's there, 'I think I prefer to stay here.'

So the old man, roysh, he obviously sees his opportunity. He's there, 'Off you go, Kicker – show the rest of us up!'

And I'm like, 'Yeah, *you'd* really love that, wouldn't you? Get me off the focking scene so can you can make an even bigger tit of yourself than you're already making.'

'Alas,' he just goes, 'not to mention alack, if you've time, I no longer have the body for those kind of heroics . . .'

'Oh,' Conchita goes, *possibly* flirting with him, 'you are too, too hard on yourself.'

That's it, I think. That is focking *it*.

I jam my poles into the snow, then take off, pretty much like a bat out of hell. I can picture the three of them behind me, watching me disappear into the distance.

I can't believe I'm having to pull something out of the bag here to burn off – of all people – my old man. But I see, like, a humungous lip in front of me and I think, okay, this is it! There's never been a better time to try a Flair in the Pipe, turning into a Lincoln Loop, which I've only ever attempted before on PlayStation.

I'm doing focking warp speed when I hit the lip, roysh, and I'm suddenly thrown into the air, higher than I thought, to be honest.

I manage the full backflip.

And then . . .

I don't actually *remember* what happened then? All I can do is rely on what *they* told me.

I remember waking up and all of a sudden getting that disinfectant smell you associate with hospitals. Then the old man's voice going, 'Aha! How's the patient?'

But it still takes me, like, a good fifteen minutes to get it together and call him a penis.

'Where am I, by the way?'

'The best place,' he goes. 'Didn't know *what* you were trying to do back there. Said to your friends – it's a new one on me.'

'Where *is* Conchita?' I go.

'Working, I expect.'

'Working?'

'She did hang around for a few hours . . .'

'What . . . day is it?'

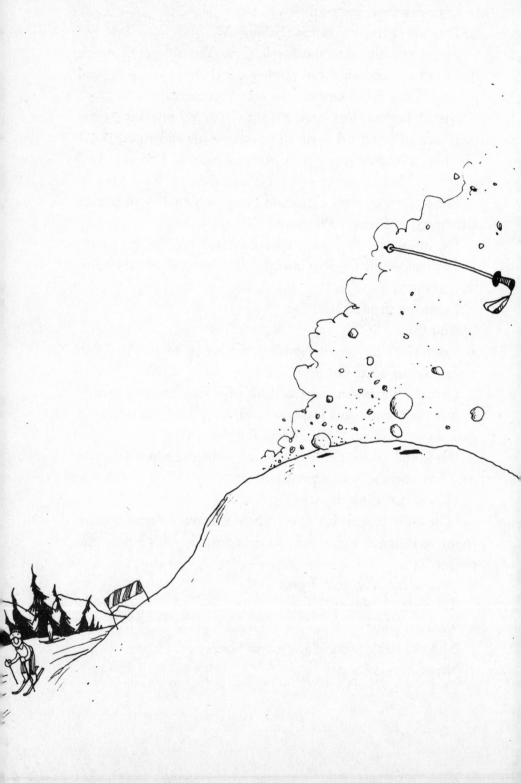

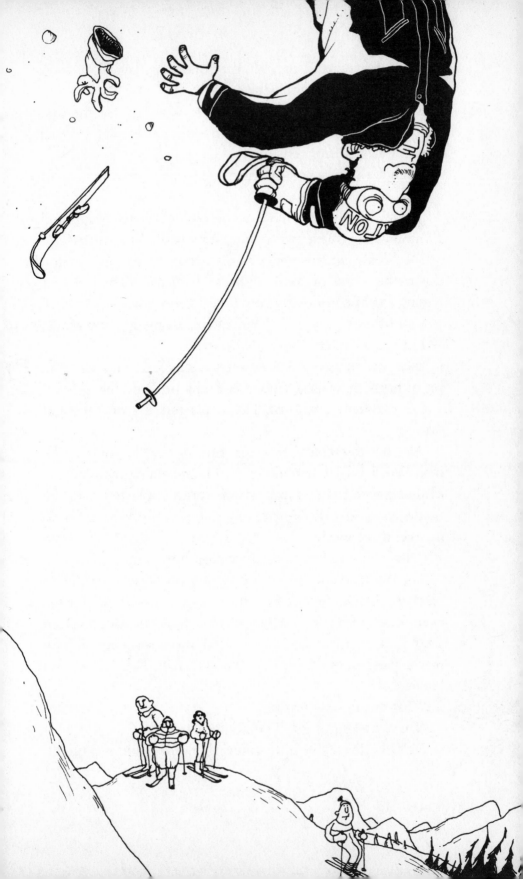

'Well, to you and me, it's the following day. You don't remember the air ambulance at all?'

The following day? I take a long look at him for the first time. He looks wrecked, unshaven – obviously been here all night. Stayed at my bedside.

Then I think – so focking what? Probably only out of guilt.

'Ross,' he goes, 'I have some bad news for you,' and I immediately freeze, wondering how badly I'm hurt.

I suddenly get this image in my head of me going up and down the stairs on one of those banister seats and him having to wipe my orse every time I drop one.

I go to move my toes. They move. So my legs are okay.

I'm there, 'What's wrong with me?'

'Not *you*,' he goes. 'All *you* got was our friend concussion, bit of bruising around your eyes and a broken ulna . . .'

I'm suddenly aware of, like, a plaster cast on my right orm.

'No, it's this chap,' he goes, turning and looking at the next bed. I follow his line of vision and there, lying flat on his back, with his two legs raised – both in plaster – is Rudi Ayala, the man who's *supposed* to be playing hooker for us in, like, three weeks' time?

'Don't tell me I focking landed on him?' I go.

The old man's like, 'No, no – motorcycle accident. Hit a patch of black ice not far from Anyós. Broke just about every bone in his legs. They brought him in about an hour after you. I must say, he seemed more concerned with *your* – quote-unquote – plight than his own. They've sedated him now.'

What am I going to do?

'We're focked,' I go. 'I've no back-up.'

He's like, 'Yes, I've been giving that quite a bit of thought.

266

Well, I didn't sleep much more than an hour – there, in that chair. The rest of the time I put to use considering your dilemma.

'Well, as you know, Kicker, I consider myself something of an authority on forward play – loath as I am to toot my own horn. I might remind our listeners that I was myself the prop on the famous Castlerock dream team of nineteen hundred and sixty-four . . .'

'Yeah,' I go, 'that got pissed on by Pres. Bray in the second round,' because it does no horm to keep reminding him on a regular basis. Keep him grounded. 'Hordly a dream team.'

'Anyway, I have – I might humbly suggest – happened upon a solution. Or, more precisely, a possible replacement . . .'

'Who?' I go, half expecting him to suggest himself.

'Young Joseba.'

I just shake my head.

'He's a monster!' he goes.

I'm there, 'He's too big to play number two.'

'I've seen bigger. And it's not just about size – it's technique.'

'Plus he's a pussy!' I go. 'It's gone – whatever – his nerve. No good to me.'

'Oh, nerve is something you can get back, Ross. I remember old Hennessy lost his once. Playing for Wanderers, of all teams. Nearly broke his neck in a ruck, see. Swore he'd never play again. But he did, Ross – and how!'

'Look, I'm not the focking Wizard of Oz. I don't have time to help him get whatever it is back.'

'But *I* do,' he goes.

I'm like, 'No, fock that.'

'What do you say, Ross? Let this be *my* little project – three weeks to turn this chap into a world-class hooker.'

The answer should be no, but I don't see a whole lot of alternatives.

'Wonderful!' he goes. 'Look at us, Kicker! Like Hooky and Eddie in happier times – spreading the Gospel of rugby around the world!'

'Wait,' I suddenly go, 'he'll be on his way to the airport. He's gone to Germany to see that focking hog he's going out with – a total Muntus Maximus.'

'No, I deed not go,' I hear a voice go and all of a sudden Joseba appears at the old man's shoulder.

'Took the liberty of calling him earlier,' the old man goes. 'Time being of the essence and so forth.'

I check my e-mails.

I've got, like, another one from Sorcha, with about ten or fifteen photographs of Honor attached. It seems she's made her first friends. They're called Kai and Romy and they're, like, twins and I think Cillian works with their old man.

Anyway, Sorcha's good enough to make sure *he's* not in any of the pictures.

Honor's so beautiful. She looks fairer. It pains me to say it, but she's actually looking more like Sorcha and less like me every time I see her. And she must be growing at some rate – that's all brand-new Juicy clobber on her.

I'm thinking, I'm going to get my orse over there the second this match is over. Take a couple of weeks' holidays. Spend some time with her. *He* mightn't be happy, but I know Sorcha wouldn't mind.

I read her mail. She says that whenever she's taking Honor's photograph, she tells her to smile for her daddy and her little face immediately lights up, which is a cool thing for her to say, whether or not it's true.

Then she says she was in Kitson last week and '*Oh my God!* – you will *never* guess who was in there? We're talking Katie Holmes! She actually looked at Honor and she was like, "Wow, what a beautiful baby you have!" And there was, like – *oh my God!* – all these paparazzi outside and I ended up getting in one of the shots! Get *In Touch Weekly* if you get a chance.'

Nothing about Immaculata. I'm thinking she obviously hasn't heard. Then, out of curiosity, I go on to Immaculata's blog again. It's like, holy fock!

For all its prosperity and new wealth, Dublin is a city that bears out the adage that money cannot buy you happiness. Someone should explain this to Mastercard, who seem pretty intent on getting me to pay off my seven thousand euro credit card bill. I've phoned them several times, explaining that I don't have a job – apart from a few hours a week in Sorcha's boutique – and that, anyway, money is the root of all unhappiness. 'That's certainly true in the case of our relationship with you,' the girl said and promptly cancelled my card.

Sophie was sympathetic: 'The problem with living in a city like this is that you'd nearly need a full-time job just to, like, live?'

She was right. I would have to start living within my means – after I'd maxed out my Visa and my MBNA, of course.

I decided that one of my last purchases would be a fitted Ireland rugby jersey. In just a matter of weeks, South Dublin would celebrate the opening of the Six Nations Rugby Championship, when it's customary for women to go to the pub to talk about which players on the screen they find cute, lose interest after twenty minutes, then spend the rest of the evening telling men things like, 'I thought Gordon D'Arcy played – oh my God – *such* a good game.'

269

That Saturday I paid a visit to Elverys on Stephen's Green, where, as it happened, it wasn't just my charge cards that were generating huge interest.

Corrie was an Australian whose eyes, I couldn't help but notice, liked to go walkabout, especially in the region of my Northern Territories. 'I beg your pardon,' I said, 'are you checking out my breasts?'

And with not a hint of embarrassment, he said, 'Yeah, I was – and I've got to tell you, mate, if you don't boy that shirt, I'm gonna boy it for you.'

I gave him what I thought was my best disapproving scowl. 'Are you always this candid?' and he said, 'Nah, I'm just here buying a shirt for meself and I couldn't help but notice that your tits are rippah.'

Corrie, it turned out, was from Canberra and, despite his obvious lack of couth, he was Capital Territory. It turned out he was on a round-the-world trip and was clearly interested in making me his latest stopover.

We exchanged numbers and I went off to celebrate by buying a skinny cinnamon dolce latte and a Fendi weekend getaway bag in maraschino.

That night, as I got dressed for our date, I couldn't help but ask myself: does orgasm always have to be the ultimate goal of sex? Do we get so hung up on the destination that we forget that the real pleasure is in the journey? And while Corrie was an unreconstructed city boy, was he looking forward to visiting my bush?

That night, after dinner and cocktails in Saba, my world traveller and I set out to explore some of the natural delights Down Under.

Thanks to Yogasm, an orgasm through yoga website, I had discovered a technique involving arching your back to achieve better stimulation of the clitoris. So that night, while Corrie removed his navy Brumbies shirt, I presented him with a perfect replica of the Sydney Harbour Bridge.

Unfortunately, his approach to sex was the same as his approach to conversation – namely, blunt and to the point.

The following morning, over waffles in the Mermaid, Chloe was just as abrupt: 'Well, tell us – how did he didgeridoo?'

I went, 'Simple – he didgeri-didn't.'

Amie was like, 'Meaning?' and I was like, 'Meaning that after five minutes, it was dreamtime.'

The girls offered me their support. 'Typical Aussie males,' Chloe went. 'They'll spend all day trying to get up on a wave – but only five minutes getting up on you.'

I was like, 'My life at the moment is like, aaaggghhh! Maxed out when it comes to money – and whatever the opposite of that is when it comes to love.'

That night, I couldn't help but ask myself whether Chloe was right? Is my quest for the ultimate orgasm the female equivalent of the male search for the perfect Bombora? In my search for gratification, should I just stick to plastic? And when it comes to ever enjoying a climax, is it a case – for this particular Sheila – of, You Vegemite, but then again, you Vegemite not?

I'm wondering should I do something, even tell Sorcha? Then I'm thinking, no, she knew best – she delivered her into Chloe's clutches. I'm staying well out.

But at the same time. Holy fock . . .

Fionn rings. It's great to hear from him. He asks me how it's going and I fill him in. The usual. Good *and* bad.

Just broke my orm and lost my hooker. This team of mine isn't as shit as I originally thought they were and there's a bird, a ringer for Eva Green, married but definitely weakening.

Small-talk over, he hits me with a bombshell. Ronan hasn't been in school for, like, a month.

A month? That's pretty much since the day I left.

Fionn, see, is still mates with one or two teachers, who keep him in the loop, even if he *is* a focking labourer these days. 'They'll turn a blind eye up to a point,' he goes, 'but you know how much McGahy hates you, Ross. He'd expel Ronan just to settle old scores with you.'

'I'm going to have to talk to his so-called mother,' I go. 'Hey, Fionn? Thanks.'

It takes Tina ages to answer. She's in the focking hairdressers, getting another council house facelift while her son's up to fock knows what.

'Don't give me *howiya*,' I go. 'What the fock? Ro hasn't been in school for, like, a month?'

'Sure he's little heart's broken,' she goes.

'Oh, that's okay, then. Why don't we take him out of school altogether? Sure he's ten now – there couldn't be much more for him to know.'

'Ex-cuiz me?'

'Yeah, let's just buy him a Vauxhall Corsa, a baseball cap and a load of focking hash, will we? I mean, that's obviously the future you've got in mind for him?'

'Would you ever fook off.'

I lose it then.

I'm there, 'What kind of a mother lets her kid stay off school because he got red-corded? You know how much the fees are costing me?'

'What koynd of a mutter?' she goes. I can't really do the accent. 'What koynd of a mutter? The koynd of a mutter who sits up witter young fella all noit while he's croyin he's lidl heart out, dat's what koynd of a mutter. And where's he's fadder? Off sunnin' heself somewayer?'

I don't even tell her it's focking snowing here. That's how bad I suddenly feel.

'Even me da can't get troo to um. He needs *you* . . .'

'*Me?* Ronan doesn't listen to me. Does he?'

'You're de only one what can talk to um and you're not hee-ur.'

One o'clock, I hit the old Comic Bor, roysh, to grab something to eat before training and maybe a shot of the old racing cor game, if I can manage it with this focking cast on my orm.

The two of them are, like, sat in the corner, shooting the shit.

I'm straight over there, of course.

'So,' I just go, 'this is how you turn him into a world-class hooker, is it?'

The old man's like, 'That's it – starts here. He's going to be a hero again, aren't you, old chap?'

Joseba just nods, big cow eyes on him.

'So,' I go, 'you've explained all about hooking the ball in the scrum, have you? Throwing the ball in at line-outs?'

He's there, 'Not yet, Coach – we'll walk before we can run. Right now, we're working on a way for Joseba here to get back his nerve.'

I look at the glass in front of him. 'What's in that?'

'Is Coca-Cola,' Joseba goes.

I pick it up, have a quick Jonny Bell – he's right.

'You thought it was a brandy,' the old man goes, delighted with himself. 'No, no, that's not the kind of courage we're looking for – not for the job we have ahead of us today.'

He loves the sound of his own voice. I have to ask, though. I end up nearly falling off the focking stool when he tells me that Joseba's going to confront Ander in the cor pork before training.

273

'You're going to be responsible for a man's death,' I tell him, 'and I can tell you, it's not going to be the little goy's.'

Joseba butts in then. 'He call me a tray tare. He say I dishonour my country.'

I'm there, 'Dude, it's not even a proper country. Cheap aftershave and big mountains – you think that's worth dying for? Because it's *actually* not?'

He stands up. 'Now, I will go.'

We follow him out the door, pretty much running to make up the length of his stride. I turn to the old man and I go, 'This is you, this is – what the fock did you say?'

'Just that he should face his fear, to try to imagine it manifest. And he thought of that little fellow, same chap who hustled me out of the ground that day.'

'Hustled you?' I go. 'He threw you on your focking head. I was only pretending not to see you. Oh, well – if there's, like, a silver lining to all this, it's that Rudi's going to have a bit of company in the hospital again.'

'Not a bit of it,' the old man goes, putting on his hat. 'David and Goliath was a once-off. As JP McManus himself told me one Christmas at Leopardstown – the smartest money's *always* on the giant. And he's the Sundance Kid, Ross – not you or me.'

Most of the goys have already arrived. Joseba cops Ander straight away, getting out of a ridiculously large Audi A6. They just stare at each other, roysh, for what seems like ages, like two dogs who are about to go at it, but are, like, sizing each other up first?

Ander makes the first move. '*Pollastre!*' he goes.

'It means chicken,' I hear a voice behind me go. I turn around and there's Frodo and all the rest of the goys as well. They're not going to miss this for the world.

Jonny's there, 'Gonna be a facking sort-out, innit?'

'*Pollastre?*' Joseba goes, walking straight up to where Ander's standing. '*Pollastre*, uh? *Merda!*'

He actually roars the word in Ander's actual face.

'This is a shit,' Frodo goes.

I thank him.

Ander grits his teeth, like he's about to attack him, roysh, but he doesn't. Instead, he reaches inside of himself and goes, '*Gos!*'

'Pretty sure that's a dog,' the old man goes. 'That's one I remember.'

I'm actually pretty surprised at Joseba – he's showing balls. And for the next, like, ten minutes it goes backwards and forwards like that.

'*Gos*, uh? *Rata!*'

'Huh! *Rata? Ratolí!*'

The two of them just, like, circle each other, refusing to break eye contact, both looking like they're ready to kill, the rest of us waiting for this Berlitz language course to turn into a bloodbath at any second.

'*Ruc*,' Ander suddenly goes, then makes, like, a donkey noise?

But Joseba is *not* about to back down here.

He's like, '*Ocell!*' and then he goes, '*Tweet, tweet, tweet . . .*' and I swear to God, roysh, something really weird happens.

Ander suddenly smiles.

I presume at first it's to, like, lull him into a false sense of security before going at him like a knacker's dog – but it's not that at all.

Joseba storts laughing.

Then Ander does as well and at the exact same time he's, like, nodding his head and it's pretty obvious that what he's saying is, dude, you've got it – you've got it back!

Ander sticks out his hand, and Joseba, slowly but

275

eventually, shakes it. The Generalissimo is the first to stort clapping, then everyone else suddenly joins in. I look sideways at the old man, who goes, 'Stewards inquiry calls it a dead heat – not even a photo could separate them.'

That was clever what he did. Sometimes I forget that he learned from the same master as I did.

'That was a focking stupid thing to do,' I tell him.

One by one, the goys all go and shake Joseba's hand.

And it might sound a bit naff, but at the top of my voice, I go, 'Somebody get that man the number two jersey – we've got a game to win!'

I finally get Ro.

Fock knows why he answered his phone to me, but he did.

I'm like, 'Please, don't hang up . . .'

'Go on,' he goes, like he expects me to come up with, I don't know, some magic words to make this all go away.

'Look,' I go, 'not every girl you go out with is going to want to spend the rest of her life with you, kid. You'll be lucky if one does. I know that sounds horsh . . .'

'I love her,' he goes.

Hearing a ten-year-old use that word just, like, breaks my hort.

I'm there, 'I know you love her. But there was no future in it, Ro. You and her – you're different. You're from, I suppose, different worlds. They buy TV licences, not TV licence stamps. They don't go on holidays – they summer and they winter. They go to restaurants where you pay for the food *after* you've eaten it . . .'

'None of that's supposed to matter,' he goes, 'when you love someone.'

The poor kid has so much to learn.

'Her old pair,' I go, 'they don't know what they're letting

go. In a million years, they'll never find anyone like you, Ro. Smort, funny, chip off the old block looks-wise. Look, I know it's hord for you to hear now . . .'

'Don't fooken say I'll meet someone,' he goes. 'Don't say it, Rosser.'

'But you will – you're only ten . . .'

'I won't meet someone because I'm never going outside the fooken door again.'

I tell him not to worry. I'll be home next week for Christmas. I'll sort it – that's a promise.

Of course I haven't a bog *how* I'm going to sort it, just that I'll do literally anything to make this kid happy again. Because, without going into it too deeply, that's what fathers are supposed to do when their kids are hurt or in trouble or in, like, distress about some shit or other.

It's like a knife in my hort when he turns around and says he wishes he'd never been born.

Conchita's in a fouler for some reason. Probably something to do with the stunt I pulled. I rang her, like, five minutes before we were due to meet and suggested, like, a change of venue.

I told her I was outside the Lizarran and I'd ordered us a couple of espressos.

'Ross, we meet in my office,' she goes, trying to be pissed at me. 'Always, we meet in my office.'

I'm there, 'I just find I chillax more when it's, like, coffee. I find it easier to, like, open up and shit?'

'I am not going there – we meet here or we do not meet today,' and she actually slams the phone down on me.

She has all the qualifications, but I haven't bedded the number of beauties I have without knowing a thing or six about the inner workings of the female mind.

Five minutes later, she arrives, with a face as long as a play. 'Ross,' she goes, 'when we are being friends, it is okay to meet here. When you are my patient, we meet at my practice. Is that clear?'

I think she's possibly confused about her feelings for me.

'Sit down,' I go. 'I've something to tell you. I think I'm storting to actually like my old man. How focked up is that?'

She's still not a happy bunny, but she sits down anyway. Takes out her notebook and pen.

'Have you seen this?' I go, holding up my cast. 'He stayed all night at the hospital. Behaving like a real father for once. Genuinely, I think I'm beginning to see things from his POV. Then again, it might be just the painkillers focking with my head . . .'

'Ross,' she goes, laying down her pen, 'we finished the last day talking about your anger . . .'

'See, I was talking to that Joseba, who you know from the day I did this to my orm. He was saying he hated *his* old man and now he's over it. My point is, I don't know if I'm actually *angry* any more?'

'Well, I think there is still very much anger in you and it is important to find the root of it. Before, I spoke to you about narcissism . . .'

'Okay, can we just recap on what that is again? And don't blind me with science.'

Not a smile out of her. Munster are obviously playing at home.

'Narcissus was a character in Greek mythology who fell in luff with his own image. The legend says that falling in luff with oneself is a punishment for being incapable of luffing another.'

'Okay . . .'

'Narcissism is a normal part of our psychological make-up. When we are little babies, it is what helps to build our ego. When we get older, what we call the narcissistic libido is directed outwards, at other people – our friends, our parents, our lovers. But in some cases it is withdrawn from the world. It is still turned back on itself. This is what we call an erotic attachment to one's own ego.'

'And you're saying this is what *I* have?'

'No,' she goes, 'only you can tell me *what you have*, Ross. I am not here to give you answers – just to help *you* find them.'

Our coffees arrive.

She whips out a piece of paper, something she's obviously printed off the internet. 'I want you to take our work seriously, Ross. I don't want to feel it's just a way for you to spend time with me.'

I'm, like, *whatever* at this stage.

'There are, altogether, nine characteristics that are used to support a diagnosis for Narcissistic Personality Disorder. Can you listen to these?'

'Go on,' I go. 'This should be good.'

'A grandiose sense of self-importance . . .'

'Yeah.'

'A preoccupation with fantasies of success, power, brilliance, beauty or ideal luff . . .'

'Yeah.'

'A belief that you are special and understood only by other special people . . .'

'Yeah.'

'A need for admiration . . .'

'Yeah.'

'A sense of entitlement or unreasonable expectations of favourable treatment . . .'

'Yeah.'

'Exploiting and taking advantage of others to achieve your ends . . .'

'Yeah.'

'An unwillingness or inability to connect with the needs of others . . .'

'Yeah.'

'Envy of others or believing others to be envious of you . . .'

'Yeah.'

'And arrogance. Now, do any of these sound like you?'

'*Sound* like me? I thought you were reading my CV there.'

She doesn't even give me that one, just shakes her head, like she doesn't know why she's even orsed.

'Conchita, there doesn't always *have* to be a reason for shit?' I go, although *that's* hordly going to impress her. The girl's probably read more books about the mind than I've had hot women.

Of course she just carries on, like I never even spoke in the first place?

'Often,' she goes, 'narcissism is a means of compensating for problems with self-image. You understand that?'

'Er, yeah?' I go, as in, I'm not *totally* stupid?

'Or sometimes as a defence against feelings or memories so painful to us that we have to bury them. Narcissists shut down their feelings for others while tightening their grip on power. So you expect girls to fall in luff with you without offering any real luff in return . . .'

'Are you asking me or telling me that?'

'I'm *asking* you. What awful feelings or memories are you hiding?'

'I don't know why you're being like this.'

'Can I ask you something, Ross – why do you limp sometimes when you walk?'

I'm like, 'Limp? Where's this coming from?'

'Always when you leave my office, I watch you and you limp out the door. You are not injured because I watch you from the window and you are fine when you are walking from the building. But when you leave the room . . .'

'Okay, it's a habit I have – you're not exactly perfect, in case you haven't noticed.'

'It is interesting. Perhaps it is a simple cry for attention, for luff – a mother's luff, a father's luff . . .'

'I don't know why you've suddenly turned on me.'

'Luff which you felt you did not have. So you seek it from many different places – sex with many different girls, in the form of adulation for playing rugby, even coaching rugby – but emotionally you are blocked for some reason . . .'

I'm there, 'Are we done here, as in time-wise?'

She doesn't answer, roysh, so I just stand up.

I look at her. She's wearing glasses. First time I've ever seen her wearing glasses and, it has to be said, they do fock-all for her.

'I'm out of here,' I go.

She's there, 'Traumatic memories, they do not go away just because we refuse to acknowledge them, Ross.'

I whip out a wad of notes, peel off a hundred yoyos and slap them down on the table in front of her.

'So now,' she goes, 'I am like all the other girls to you, yes? What happened – did I get too close?'

'Babycakes – what's happening?'

That voice can only belong to one man and one man alone.

'Ryle Nugent,' I go, 'how the fock are you?'

He's like, 'Happy to the max, Rossmeister. Was poised to

ask you the same question. Now, I don't need to – you're the talk of the place.'

We're standing outside the Hotel Plaza. 'So what are you doing here?' I go.

He's like, 'Here to do the definitive interview.'

We go and sit in the lobby.

He looks well in fairness to him, suit by HB and a pair of Elizas you could see your face in. RTÉ must be paying him a fortune.

'This game,' he eventually goes, 'talk to me . . .'

I'm there, 'You talk to me. What's everyone saying back home? Presumably I'm the talk of Dublin as well.'

He actually laughs out loud. 'Back up the truck. Everyone's talking about the Six Nations – great chance of winning the Grand Slam next year, good springboard going into the World Cup, blahdy blahdy blah-blah. This match is just a glorified training session, a run-out for one or two players who're coming back from injury.'

'Might be a run-out to you and the IRFU,' I go, 'but we're deadly serious about winning it.'

He's just taken a mouthful of herbal tea and he ends up spitting it all over himself. 'Winning it? It's, what, two weeks to the match and your hooker has never played a rugby match before in his life?'

'Fock. My old man needs to learn to keep his Von Trapp shut. Where'd you meet him?'

'Here,' he goes, flicking his thumb in the direction of the restaurant. 'Five minutes ago. Having dinner with that solicitor of his.'

I'm there, 'Hennessy? What's *he* doing here?'

I don't focking believe it. I get up.

'Give me a ring later,' I go. 'We'll talk.'

Ryle's right. The two of them are in there, casual as you

like, stuffing their faces and milling their way through what turns out to be their third bottle of Château Mouton Rothschild.

You wouldn't focking blame them, would you?

I don't get a chance to open my mouth, roysh, because the second he sees me coming, the old man's going, 'Bet you never thought you'd see your old dad eating *stew*,' and he's shaking his head like he's a wonder to himself.

'Slightly different from the fare we were served up *inside*. *Escudella*, if you don't mind – chicken, sausages and meatballs. Might even be a pinch or two of cinnamon in there.'

'This is very cosy,' I go.

'Yes, it is. Sit down there.'

Which is what I do. There's something about the two of them. An air of something. I need to know what it is.

The waitress arrives with a menu. She's not bad – a little bit like Carrie Underwood.

'Before you even open that,' the old man goes, 'let me recommend the *xai* – roast lamb, every bit as good as your mother's, though you won't catch me repeating that particular blasphemy around Brighton Road or its environs.'

I'm like, 'Whatever.'

The waitress scribbles it down and goes, '*Com li agradaria cuit?*'

'With the blood showing,' the old man goes, 'if I know my boy!'

'*Rar?*' she goes.

He's like, '*Sí, si us plau. Gràcies.*'

Off she goes. The orse isn't great, though.

'So,' I go, knowing damn well that something's going down here. 'What are you two talking about?'

'Hennessy's just popped over,' the old man goes, a little too quickly. 'Your *godfather*, Ross – see if he can't lend us a hand in our hour of need. Played in the front row himself, remember. One of the straightest arrows in rugby – the words of a certain Mr Edmund van Esbeck Esquire.'

'Oh,' I go, at the exact point that my lamb arrives, 'who's paying for this meal, by the way? Just as a matter of interest. Because I know *you're* Keith Flint . . .'

'It's on me,' Hennessy goes. 'About time I honoured all those golf debts, eh, Charles?'

The old man laughs, then cops a sly look at me to see have I bought it. I look at him and I'm suddenly there, 'It's just that I, er, swung into that guesthouse of yours a couple of hours ago. See did you fancy a late lunch. They said you'd checked out. I take it you're staying *here* now?'

I look up at the ceiling for, like, emphasis? It's not exactly a Jurys Inn, if you know what I'm saying.

'Hennessy's given me a, er, loan,' he goes, unable to even look me in the eye.

'Call it a dig-out,' Hennessy goes. 'As the boys said to Bertie, we can't have a man of your stature living rough above a bloody bookies on the Lucan Road.'

Hennessy is the worst liar in history. How he made a living in his line of work, I'll never know.

'So if it's a Lindsay, let me ask you this – what's that you're trying to hide under your orm?'

It looks like a stack of brochures. I make a grab for them, roysh, sending his wine flying.

Turns out they're, like, property prospectuses.

'Look at all this,' the old man's going, mopping at the spilled wine with his napkin and copping a sneaky look at Hennessy, who nods at him, as if to say, the game's up – we're going to have to tell him here.

'We're thinking of buying a ski lodge,' the old man goes.

'You are *taking* the piss.'

'Not at all, Ross. Well, the inspiration – if I could call it such – came from a joke. Hennessy here was visiting me and we happened to be talking about the number of middle-to-low-income families going on winter holidays these days. Tell Ross this funny thing you said, Hennessy? That SSIA stands for . . .'

'Skobies Skiing In Andorra!'

The two of them crack their holes laughing like it's the funniest thing that's ever been said.

'Skobies skiing in Andorra indeed! I thought, wait a minute. You know how prison has changed me, Kicker. Opened my eyes to a whole world of people – good people – I never gave a thought to before. The likes of Lex. We're friends for life . . .'

'Pity he's *in* for life.'

'I told him that when I got out, I was going to dedicate myself to giving something back, inverted commas. And they weren't just words, Ross.

'I remembered the way the chaps inside took to rugby when I introduced it to them. Helped quite a few long-term drug addicts achieve total withdrawal from League of Ireland soccer. So this joke of Hennessy's got me thinking – didn't it, old chap? – what about a skiing academy for Dublin's underprivileged?'

He looks at me like he's expecting a round of applause.

I'm there, 'Sorry, I'm pretty curious it has to be said – the moolah for all of this, I presume it's all Hennessy's? Because I could have sworn at some stage in the past year you said you were broke.'

He doesn't say anything. Doesn't need to. His face says it all.

I end up totally losing it. 'You said you gave them everything!'

He looks around, like *he's* suddenly embarrassed by *my* volume.

'We *had* to say that,' Hennessy suddenly goes. 'Otherwise they'd have taken, well, *everything*,' and he laughs – he *actually* focking laughs.

The old man's there, 'Yes, I didn't tell them about my, er, nest egg.'

'A skiing academy for focking knick-knacks – what kind of nest egg are we talking here?'

He lays his knife and fork down on his plate, then pushes the plate away. 'Forty million,' he goes, trying to say it like it's fock-all – and failing miserably.

'Forty million?'

'Well, yes, you know – *plus* change,' then he asks the waitress, as she's picking up his plate, to bring him a brandy.

'I'm going to need one of those as well,' I go. Then I sit there just, like, staring at him, waiting for an explanation. 'A week ago you were eating popcorn chicken. I actually felt sorry for you. I was going to throw you an Ayrton Senna – can you believe that?'

He's like, 'The money was here all the time, Ross. The problem was, I couldn't get my hands on it until Hennessy got here and he had to leave it a couple of weeks. Would have looked too suspicious, the two of us jetting off together. So I flew into Barcelona, got the bus here. A week later, Hennessy got the Eurostar, then drove down from Calais . . .'

I'm there, 'Sorry, has Kathryn Thomas retired and passed the torch on to you or something? I'm not interested in your focking travel log. You said you were Keith Flint. Have you any *idea* what I've been going through?'

Hennessy sticks his hooter in then, again. 'We didn't want CAB or the Revenue knowing,' he goes. 'We *had* to keep up that appearance.'

'But *me* – why didn't you tell *me*? Tip me off – don't worry, Ross, when Shit Breath there gets out of the slammer, there'll be munjanah coming down the line. Might have been some consolation when I was using public focking transport.'

The old man suddenly clears his throat. He's got something to say. 'We thought it'd be a good idea for you to stand on your own two feet,' he goes, as casual as that.

I'm there, 'Who's *we* – you and him?'

'No,' he goes. 'Your mother thought so as well. It's about the only thing we *have* agreed on since we split. We thought it would be good for you – sharpen up your wits and so forth.'

'Good for me? *I don't know what a tracker mortgage is.* Do you have any idea how many skobies I've heard crack that gag on the Nitelink in the past twelve months? Who knows what diseases I picked up and don't even know about yet.'

'But look at you,' he suddenly goes. 'Take a look at yourself. Because *I* have . . .'

What the fock is he banging on about now?

'That first day I arrived, Ross – watching you take training. Well, it gladdened my heart to see a man doing what he was born to do. Do you think you'd have ended up where you are – the national coach of Andorra, for heaven's sake – if you hadn't been rousted out of your comfort zone?'

'For the first time,' I go, 'I'm beginning to see *why* the old dear stitched you up.'

'*Salut,*' he goes, raising his brandy to me. Hennessy does the same.

I throw mine straight back and go, 'Eat shit.'

I'm in Sal i Pebre, roysh, having a late nosebag and thinking about that old saying about travel broadening the mind. And it's true, roysh. Six weeks ago, if you told me I'd be sitting here with *carnes a la brasa y pescado fresco*, I'd have been drawing up a list of every bird I slept with in the past six months and rubbing cream on my Davinas.

It just shows you.

Anyway, I'm halfway through the old Gunga when all of a sudden the phone rings and even though it's a number I don't recognize, I answer it and I know the voice straight away.

I *should*, of course. I'm still technically married to her.

I'm there, 'Hey, babes,' because things are actually good between us these days.

She sounds like she's been crying.

The first words out of her mouth are, 'Are you anywhere near a computer?'

I'm like, 'Yeah, I'm just opposite Quars – it's, like, *their* Power City? It's closed, though. It's, like, half-ten at night here . . .'

'Did you know Immaculata has her own blog?'

I'm there, 'Yeah – I, er, read one or two.'

She must be on the actual web now, roysh, looking straight at it, because she's suddenly going, 'My new Garda friend told me that anything I said would be taken down. Ten minutes later, in the back of his Ford Fiesta, he was as good as his word . . .'

'Jesus!'

'There's plenty more like that. What about the butcher? He produced his prime cut – then he boned and rolled me . . . Or the pilot? Who better to take me on my first flight into the heavens than my modern-day All-cock?'

For a minute, I think she's actually pissed off at *me* – until she suddenly goes, 'Ross, I owe you an apology . . .'

I'm there, 'Er, okay . . .'

'. . . for thinking that Immaculata would be better off with Chloe and Sophie.'

'Hey, it's Kool G Rap, babes.'

'I should have seen it, Ross – how you are around Honor, how you are around Ronan. You would have looked after her – *oh my God!* – *so* well. You're an amazing father and I never gave you the credit for that . . .'

She's pretty upset, it has to be said.

I'm there, 'Look, if anyone's to blame out of all this, it's that programme, filling women's heads with *all* sort of lies. God, if I ever get my hands on the makers . . .'

'All I keep thinking about is her sweet innocence, Ross. The thank-you letter she sent when I bought that new water pump for her village . . .'

'I know.'

'Now I can't get Chloe on the phone. She's not answering.'

'Are you surprised?'

'Nor are the other two. I've phoned, texted, e-mailed, Facebooked. You know, they didn't even *open* the shop last week?'

I'm like, 'What?'

'For the whole week,' she goes. 'Ross, that shop is my life. If it's not open seven days a week, there're plenty of other shops in the Powerscourt Townhouse Centre that people will go to . . .'

'Is there someone at home you can ring?' I go. 'What about your old pair?'

'Mum and dad are here, Ross. They've come for Christmas. *And* my sister. I can't even bring myself to tell them what's going on. Claire's in a snot with me for not asking her to look after the shop in the first place. Out of all my other really, really good friends, the only one I trust is Erika.'

'And I suppose she's enough on her plate.'

'She's away anyway. Spending Christmas with, like, her birth father . . .'

'Look, as it happens,' I go, 'I'm heading home for a few days for Chrimbo. We're pretty much set here – we're as good as we're going to get in pure rugby terms and I want to catch up with Ro. I'll have a word with Immaculata, see can I persuade her to go home.'

She says thanks and she genuinely means it.

I ask her to give Honor a hug for me and she goes, 'Ross, I can't look at her these days without feeling – *oh my God!* – *so* guilty for taking her away from you. She's changing, like, *so* much every day, Ross. These are really, really precious times and I feel like I've stolen them from you.'

'Don't feel bad about a thing,' I go. 'It was all me – all my doing . . .'

'You sound, I don't know, different . . .'

'I've been doing a lot thinking while I've been away.'

'Ross, you're frightening me.'

'No, no – *good* thinking. Getting shit straight once and for all. I'll tell you about it one day. Look, I'll give you a bell when I get home. And I'll sort it – I promise.'

'Thanks,' she goes. 'And don't forget *In Touch Weekly* if they still have it.'

I'm standing on the old Port de Paris Bridge, looking down at the water. It's, like, the fastest-moving river I've ever seen, faster than even the cors travelling the road to, like, France one way, Spain the other.

It's bent as a focking bedspring to say it, but the moon is huge tonight.

'Don't jump!' I hear a voice behind me go and I turn around to see Conchita standing there, smiling at me. 'If you do, it will not be such a good thing for my career,' and I have to give it to her, roysh, it's a good line.

She rang *me*. Asked me to meet her here. Said she wants to apologize properly before I go home for Christmas.

She leans on the rail, exactly like I'm doing, which is amazing, roysh, because this body language expert in this magazine I'm reading says when someone does that, it's, like, a good thing? They're basically attracted to you.

'You read this?' she goes, nodding at it, rolled up in my hand here.

'Oh, only because Sorcha's in it.'

'She is in this magazine?' she goes, taking it from me. 'Sorcha is a celebrity?'

I'm like, 'No, no – she was just in this shop, buying a pair of Yanuks and, like, Katie Holmes walked in. She's in the background there.'

She looks at the picture very closely. 'She is very pretty. Very thin.'

'Yeah, I thought she'd actually balloon when she went over there. She's a focking demon for the cupcakes.'

She nods like she understands.

'Ross,' she suddenly goes, 'I am so sorry for the way I spoke to you. It was not . . . professional of me . . .'

'Hey, I suppose you were just trying to get me to, like, open up and shit.'

'No,' she goes. 'What you heard in my voice was anger and frustration. But not with you. I was frustrated with myself for not facing up to *my* trauma, *my* wounds. And I projected my anger onto you.'

I'm tempted to ask what she's talking about, roysh, but then I don't know if it's my place.

'Bernard and I have agreed to separate,' she suddenly goes.

My mouth drops open, even though I knew she didn't actually love him. How could she?

'This was the conversation I was preparing to have with him when I met you that day. I am sorry.'

I'm there, 'Are you going be, like, okay?'

She doesn't say yes or no, just goes, 'I am going back to Spain to stay with my mother. But I am sad because I have hurt Bernard and he is someone I care about very much.'

I'm suddenly thinking, if she can tell me that . . .

'I couldn't read.'

I blurt it straight out.

'I couldn't actually read.'

'You couldn't read?' she goes.

Then it's like she's making some kind of, I don't know, calculation in her head.

'Yeah,' I go, 'I knew you'd like that one. You must think I'm thick as a box of rocks,' but she looks at me as if to say, that's not even *worth* a response?

'You *can* read now?' she goes.

I'm there, 'Yeah, no, I've been reading since I was, like, fifteen? Not that that's anything to brag about. But it's like, what the fock – you know?'

'There is no shame in this,' she goes. 'Many, many people have difficulties with reading. Leonardo da Vinci was dys-lexic. Also Picasso . . .'

I'm there, 'I had this teacher for, like, Geography. McGahy was his name – he's, like, the principal now? Hated rugby, so we were never going to get on. I mean, the whole thing about not being able to read is that you're constantly trying to, like, hide the fact? Like, you've got to come up with excuses for not handing in essays, not turning up for exams, not reading in class. You'd be pretty focking exhausted.

'Anyway, this one day, McGahy catches me, I don't know, taking the piss down the back and he puts a piece of chalk in my hand and tells me to stand up in front of the class and write down the difference between a stalactite and a stalagmite on the blackboard. The thing is, I focking knew it. It's one of the few things I *did* know at school . . .'

'But you could not write it?'

'He asked me if I knew what a sea squirt was? I was like, er, no. He said it was this thing that lives in the sea – I don't know if it's, like, a fish or what – but he says all it does is it finds a rock, sits down, eats its own brain, then lives the rest of its life as a vegetable. Of course, everyone's cracking their holes laughing. You're one of life's sea squirts, he goes to me.'

'What about your mother and father?' she goes.

'Exactly. How could they *not* notice that their fourteen-year-old son couldn't write his own name? I'll tell you how – they were too wrapped up in their own shit. Bring this *to* Foxrock. Move that *from* Foxrock. That's all it was. That was their lives. That and making money.'

'So,' she goes, 'who taught you to read?'

'Father Fehily – who else? I mean, he copped it. He was unbelievable like that. He knew I wasn't thick, but at the same time he knew I *acted* thick? So he calls me into his office one day after school and he just goes, "Let's see can we get a handle on this reading thing, shall we?" Nothing more than that. And I didn't say a word. I just went, 'Okay.' And he stayed back with me for, like, two hours, we're talking three days a week for a whole year . . .'

'And you learned to read from him?'

'Pretty much, yeah. And poor Fehily. You know, priests in Ireland get a pretty bad rap – kiddy-fiddling, blah blah blah. But you never hear anything about the ones like him

– the ones who, like, teach you all the shit that makes you, I don't know, a better person. I mean, the worst thing you could have said about Fehily was that he was, like, a Nazi sympathizer . . .'

She nods.

'Ross,' she suddenly goes, 'I think it's unlikely that we will see each other again . . .'

It stops me cold. I hadn't actually thought of that. This is, like, goodbye.

'But you should continue to do your work on yourself. Think about what you have told me and how it may have given shape to your personality. I don't know if you plan to tell your mother and father. But you must forgive them, Ross. Otherwise you will always have anger.

'Merry Christmas,' she suddenly goes.

And I'm like, 'Merry Christmas.'

And it's amazing, roysh, because we both automatically turn at the same time and just, like, fall into this, I suppose, embrace. And we stand there on the bridge like that for ages, roysh, saying goodbye, until I have a quick sniff of her Tony Blair and then try to kiss her, and she pulls away and says she must go.

9. Even a stopped clock tells the right time twice a day

I haven't a bog what I'm going to say to the old dear, but I decide – bearing in mind what Conchita said – that I'm going to try to, like, keep it civil – hord and all as that is. Her cor isn't in the driveway, but I let myself in.

The gaff is freezing and it's like no one's lived in it for ages. There's, like, a mountain of mail piled up underneath the letterbox. I'm thinking, maybe she's focked off to New York, because I know there was talk of some publisher over there being interested in her shit. Septics have *no* taste, of course.

I head straight for the fridge – force of habit – and whip out a corton of milk and I go to knock back a mouthful. I swear to God, roysh, it's full, but whatever's in it doesn't move and the Jonny Bell nearly makes me want to spew my ring. I check the best-by date and it's, like, the ninth of December, which is, like, two weeks ago.

And no Christmas tree, I suddenly notice. No decorations. Weird shit.

I go into the study and the light on the answering-machine is flashing. She's got, like, seventy-something messages. On the desk is her finished manuscript. *My Beautiful Gypsy Mot.* Again, force of habit, I drop it straight in the bin.

I go into the hall and for some reason I stop to look at the photographs she's got hung right the way up the stairs.

Most of them I don't remember, it has to be said. The three of us sitting on some yacht or other – me with a Coke, her with a glass of white wine, him with a brandy big enough to drown a cow in.

I'm six, maybe seven, and we all look actually happy.

Then there's one of, like, the old man collecting the captain's prize at Milltown and me and her looking at him – me proud *as* punch, her pissed *on* punch. And, again, it's all smiles. I'm pretty sure I've been, I don't know, superimposed into these pictures.

'Dog breath,' I shout, 'are you in?' but there's no answer. I stick my head around the door of her room, but it's obvious she's not around.

I head into my own room, just to get some threads, maybe I'll stay *here* for Chrimbo, especially if she's away.

I notice the two stools in a heap in the corner where I left them. I think, before I go back, I might get out the *Golden Pages*, see can I find some focker who could fix them.

My next stop is Blackrock, just to pick up my mail and to check that Immaculata hasn't turned the place into a clip joint.

It's only as I'm whipping out my key that I remember the locks have been changed.

I stick my hand into the mailbox and pull everything out. It's all her newsletters from Friends of the Earth, his back issues of *Business and Finance* and loads and loads of Christmas cords, some of them actually still addressed to Sorcha and me.

I stumble across a letter addressed to Immaculata. It's the stamp that catches my eye. It's got, like, a picture of a black dude on it.

I put all the other shit back, then sit down on the cold doorstep. I tear open the envelope, roysh, and it's exactly as I thought – it's from, like, Mikel.

I won't go into the ins and outs of what was actually in it because it's, like, private between him and Immaculata, but what I will say is that it's one of the most emotional things I've ever read, bent and all as that sounds. He basically pours his hort out to her and it's pretty obvious from the shit he says that, like myself, he's got the big-time gift of the gab, and I'm thinking I might even steal one or two lines, see how they play out for me.

I read it, like, six or seven times, roysh, stick it in my back pocket and then, thinking about my promise to Sorcha, point the rental 5 Series in the direction of town or, more specifically, the Powerscourt Townhouse Centre.

It's, like, half-four on the day before Christmas Eve and – miracle of miracles – the shop is actually open and they're all in there, we're talking Chloe, Sophie, Amie with an ie and – the absolute centre of attention – Immaculata, sipping what turns out to be a grande chai latte with soy and filling everyone in on her latest exploits.

Sorry – sexploits.

They're big-time shocked to see me if the *oh-my-God* count is anything to go by.

'Ross!' Immaculata goes. 'I was just telling the girls. I'm going on, like, a second date tonight with this – *oh! my God!* – amazing goy. He can play, like, José González on the classical guitar . . .'

I'm just standing there in, like, total shock. In the space of, like, five weeks, her voice has totally changed – it's suddenly like she's lived in Donnybrook all her life. But not only that, her clothes have changed, too. She's wearing, like, skinny Sevens and what look very much to me like Sorcha's gold Jessica Simpson Steffi ballet flats that she keeps in here for work.

She looks basically like a black clone of the other three.

Chloe turns to her and goes, 'I wonder what kind of tune this José González goy will play on *your* instrument,' and they all crack their holes laughing.

'What . . . what happened to you?' I go, barely able to get the words out.

Immaculata looks at me like I'm off my cake. '*Duh?*' she goes. 'What are you talking about, Ross?'

'Your clothes, for storters,' I go, looking her up and down.

She's there, 'Oh my God, you're worse than Emer McInally. I met her yesterday in Reiss and she was like, "Oh my God – you're wearing fake Uggs?" and I was like, "*Hello? Fuggs are* the new Uggs?" She was like, "Oh my God, you are, like, *totally* bipolar!" and I was like, *what*-ever?'

I don't *actually* believe this. And bear in mind, roysh, I've watched boggers join UCD and lose their accents before they even had the cellophane off the johnnies in their fresher packs. I've never seen, like, a transformation as complete as this.

Sophie goes, 'Oh my God, Emer McInally – she's, like, *such* a loser,' and Immaculata goes, 'Is it true that when she went on, like, her J1er to, like, Myrtle Beach, they were flying home and the meal was, like, chicken and pasta and Emer asked the air-hostess for, like, Parmesan? That's like, oh-kaaay – *total* weirdo?'

I tell Immaculata that I need to talk to her – in private? She looks at Sophie and rolls her eyes.

Chloe asks me if I've heard. 'Erika's spending Christmas with her new dad on his island – he actually *owns* an island? He's worth, like, billions – can you *imagine* the clothes she's going to be able to buy?'

I point at her and I go, 'You're a focking disgrace. Closing the shop up a week before Christmas. I haven't finished with you,' and she tells me to, like, get *over* myself.

I notice she's eating toilet paper, but I don't even bother asking.

Immaculata follows me outside. I turn to her and I'm like, 'What the fock? I've only been gone, like, five weeks . . .'

'Oh my God,' she goes, 'will you *take* a chill pill? What is your actual problem?'

'*That's* my actual problem – *take a chill pill*, all that. They're not girls to look up to, you know. They're not role models. And it's not cool to be having sex with every second person you meet.'

'*Oh! My God! Hypocrite?* The girls have told me, like, so much shit about you.'

'That's different.'

'How?'

'It just is – I'm a goy. It's different for goys. If you're a bird and you do it, you end up getting a rep. Believe me, no one likes a slapper.'

That's not strictly true, of course. Most people like one every now and again, though I don't say that.

'You were such a lovely girl,' I go. 'What about your, I don't know, culture, blah blah blah?'

She just makes, like, a W with her fingers and thumbs, sort of, like, flexes her Gregory and goes, '*What*-ever?' and then turns around and walks back into the shop.

I'm tempted to tell her about the letter, but I don't. I decide to keep it in the old Eddie Rocket until I come up with, like, a strategy here.

Then I hit, well, Eddie Rocket's, because I'm actually storving.

I order a plate of nachos and that's when – uh-oh, here we go – the old brain kicks into overdrive and I'm suddenly doing some of my world-famous thinking.

Actually, the first thing I'm thinking is that there's an awful lot of hugging going on in here. Young people these days, they're hug-happy, even the goys. At first I thought they must have come from, like, a removal. I'm thinking, whatever happened to the good, old-fashioned high-five? Less gay.

Then I think, okay, now I'm going to try to have some thoughts about the whole Immaculata situation. I think, roysh, what would Father Fehily do?

He'd put on a pair of jackboots and one of his Hitler 45s. That's no good to me.

No, but whenever you had a problem, he always said, stort at the beginning. By the time I've eaten the last soggy jalapeño, I've decided that the answer has to be somewhere on those *Sex and the City* DVDs. So I make up my mind there and then.

There's, like, no other option – I've got to sit down and watch all of them.

First, there's something else I've got to do and it's weird, roysh, because I suddenly feel like a real father for the first time in my actual life.

It's, like, three o'clock on Christmas Eve and I'm standing outside the gaff in Clonskeagh and I'm thinking, this is one of those moments when you don't actually *need* a script?

I just take a deep breath, walk up to the door and ring the bell.

It's Amanda who answers.

There's a nice whiff of spiced beef coming from the kitchen and Mariah Carey singing 'All I Want for Christmas'. It makes me think of Sorcha's granny. The spiced beef obviously, not . . .

At the stort, I don't get a word in edgeways.

'I *know* why you're here,' she goes, 'but we've made our decision. We don't want Blathin to see Ronan and that's the end of the matter.'

But then I go, 'Oh,' giving it plenty of sarcasm, 'because he's from the wrong side of the town? The side where people wear shirts *with* tracksuit bottoms . . .'

'No.'

'. . . trip over things and sue the council . . .'

'That's not it.'

'. . . and stare open-mouthed at the upper deck of buses as they pass by?'

'It has nothing to do with where he comes from.'

'Oh, yeah, I'm sure it doesn't! I saw your sulky face at the sulky race. You *so* didn't want to be there. It's because you're actual snobs . . .'

She suddenly gives me, like, a fake smile. 'We love Ronan,' she goes.

I'm there, 'I'm sure you do.'

'He's a gorgeous, sweet, thoughtful little boy and he was good for Blathin. He really brought her out of her shell. Gave her such confidence in herself . . .'

'But?'

'The reason we don't want him to see our daughter any more,' she goes, looking me up and down, 'is because of you!'

That stops me, like, dead in my tracks.

'Me? As in . . .'

'I couldn't believe it that day you collected them in the car. I said to David, it's *him*. He said it couldn't be – Ronan's a *nice* kid . . .'

I'm like, 'Whoa, whoa, whoa – what's this about? David isn't Clongowes, is he?'

She's suddenly there, 'You wouldn't remember me, Ross, but I certainly remember *you*.'

I immediately get that *uh-oh* feeling.

'My little sister – for reasons known only to herself – had a *thing* for you . . .'

I'm there, 'Okay, that could be anyone.'

'And you really hurt her.'

'Again – I'm embarrassed to say it – doesn't exactly narrow the field.'

She's like, 'Nessa Boyd?'

The name doesn't ring a bell, but it certainly sounds like my MO, so I pull a face like I'm actually remembering her – and remembering her in, like, a good way?

She doesn't buy it.

'There's no reason her name should mean anything to you, Ross. She was just another of those girls who used to follow you around. You told her one night you thought you were falling in love with her? It turned out it was a game that you and your idiot friends were playing . . .'

It has to be Alphabet Forghetti. First you score a bird whose name begins with A, then you move to . . . well, you get the idea.

'She was your N,' she goes.

Yeah, it was definitely Alphabet Forghetti then.

I'm there, 'We were, like, teenagers. Having fun. It was use and abuse in those days.'

'I don't *care* about that. You think we're all heartbroken that she didn't end up with *you*? That she had to settle for a man who treats her really well and has an amazing job with Transamerica International Reinsurance Ireland? She was over you in a week. What I'll never forget is what you said to my mum . . .'

'Your mum?'

'When she rang you up, to give you a piece of her mind? For sending her daughter home in tears like that? You said to her . . .'

'Okay,' I suddenly go, 'don't tell me what I said! I already have a good idea . . .'

'It was disgusting.'

I don't know where the anger comes from, roysh, but I'm all of a sudden jabbing my finger in the air, going, 'But none of this is, like, Ronan's fault. Just because *I'm* his father. Let me tell *you* something now. My old man is a complete and utter dickhead – that didn't necessarily mean I was going to turn out to be a dickhead as well.

'Okay, as it happens, I did. But my sins are *my* sins – not Ronan's . . .'

I'm suddenly aware of the fact that there's, like, tears rolling down my cheeks. What am I like?

'This kid,' I go, 'he's ten times the person I am or ever *will* be. And you're never going to know that and I pity you for it,' and I turn to walk away, stopping only to shout, 'Pity you,' again, really just for effect.

That's when the door suddenly opens wider and David is stood there.

'Quite a speech,' he goes, but it's, like, he actually *means* it?

In fairness, I can be a bit of a wordsmith when the moment takes me.

'Look,' I go, trying to get them to see reason, 'yeah, I was a bit of a player in my day. Still am, I like to think. I'll probably never change. But Ronan and Blathin, they're just kids. They're, like, playmates. You can't use them just to get at someone who happens to be an orsehole.'

David looks at *her*. I've definitely won *him* over. She folds her orms and sort of, like, purses her lips, like she's thinking.

I'm there, 'Honestly, he's nothing like me.'

When she looks at David, he gives her, I suppose, this little nod.

Then she goes, 'Okay.'

I'm there, 'Okay?'

'We'll, er, give Ronan a call,' David goes.

I'm there, 'Hey, I am so grateful . . .' but before I can say another word, the door is just, like, slammed in my face.

An hour later, I'm back in Foxrock and I get a text from Tina. It's just like, 'Thnx ross. Mery xmas x.'

Six focking series. It's, like, ninety-four half-hour episodes. There's no point in me even attempting to do the maths. Instead, I ring the only man I know who could, and he says he'll be over to me in twenty.

'Merry Christmas,' he goes, giving me the high-five. 'Welcome home.'

I'm like, 'Fionn, you're good at, like, sums. How long is, like, ninety-four half-hours?'

Of course I should have known better than to expect a straight answer out of him.

'Ross, were you even mildly curious about what the rest of us were doing in school?'

I'm there, 'All I know is, you didn't get your Billy Joel until a good five years after you left – so who's the fool now?'

He laughs, roysh, and it's great to hear it because I've been treating him with kid gloves since Aoife died and I think what we've both really missed is hammering each other.

'How the hell are you?' I go.

He's like, 'I'm good. Well – you know . . .'

And I do. First Christmas and everything . . .

'Anyway,' he goes, 'since you've made me drive out here, I have to admit, you have me intrigued. Ninety-four half-hours – what's it about?'

I sit down. I tell him to as well. 'I'm about to watch every single episode of *Sex and the City* . . . back to back.'

'Jesus!'

'Look, you may or may not know, but Immaculata's gone totally off the rails and I pretty much blame myself for letting her at Sorcha's boxset collection in the first place. I'm pretty sure that the answer to the problem's in those DVDs.'

'Well, the answer to your question,' he goes, 'is forty-seven hours.'

I'm like, 'What's that in days?'

'Well, if you don't eat, drink or sleep, it's an hour short of two full days and nights. Ross, are you sure this is safe?'

I'm there, 'I don't know, Fionn. All I know is that it's got to be done.'

'Forty-seven hours of women's TV,' he goes. 'It's going to be a serious shock to the system. Are you sure you're ready for it?'

'Hey, I'm ready all right. I've got the old dear's Super Turbo Sole Therapy Foot Spa, six bottles of Prosecco, a box of Kleenex and a tub of Häagen-Dazs so big I ended up nearly herniating myself taking it out of the focking fridge.'

'But, Ross,' he goes, 'it's Christmas.'

I'm like, 'Well, how else am I going to spend it? The old man's in Andorra. The old dear's God knows where. I'd spend it with Ro, but I don't fancy watching Tina spend Christmas morning trying to squeeze the turkey into the deep-fat fryer.'

'Come to mine,' he goes. 'They all love you in my house.'

I'm like, 'Dude, you didn't actually *have* to say that, which means it's doubly appreciated. But this is something I've just got to do.'

'I'll tell you what,' he goes, obviously still worried about me. 'I'll ring Oisinn and JP. We'll call around at different stages, keep you company,' and of course I'm left thinking, with friends like these . . .

Series one is, like, six hours long, roysh, and for me the highlight has to be when Charlotte gets her clunge out for some painter she's never even met before. But then I have to keep reminding myself to forget about the actual storylines and keep looking for the message.

It finishes just before eleven o'clock and I straight away lash in series two, which storts with something I can actually identify with – sport. Turns out that Miranda's a massive Yankees fan, like myself.

Well, I have the actual shirt.

The second series passes by in a blur of small mickeys, lesbians, blue movies, Viagra, love at first sight, circumcision, drag queens, S & M, foot fetishists and crabs. And of course the running joke throughout the whole thing is that Samantha just so happens to have an orgasm every time she has Posh and Becks with someone – and it's suddenly easy to see how you could get, I suppose, confused if you weren't in on the gag.

It's, like, eight o'cock – sorry, I mean *clock* – the following morning when the second series ends.

They definitely get inside your head, these four birds.

I'm even thinking in Sarah Jessica Porker's voice – that morning, I asked myself, am I any closer to finding the key to unlocking the spell that Immaculata's under? And if this gang of New York birds is so hot, how come I'd ride the ginger before any of them?

I crack my hole laughing at that, but of course there's no one there to, like, share the joke with?

I go out to the kitchen and grab another bottle of Prosecco – my third – and all of a sudden realize that it's, like, actually Christmas morning.

Totally out of the blue, roysh, I suppose in the spirit of the season, I decide to ring Conchita, but it ends up going straight through to her message-minder. I leave this message, roysh, which I regret immediately, telling her I can't stop thinking about her, think I've fallen for her in a major way, blahdy blahdy blah.

Then I'm back in front of the TV again. I'm a good three or four hours into series three when there's, like, a knock at the door. I answer it, roysh, and it's, like, Oisinn, who says he's called around to wish me a Merry Christmas and to see have I sprouted tits yet.

It's good to see the focker.

From behind his back he produces a bor of Galaxy the size of a focking door and I'm thinking, friends-wise, I'm actually every bit as lucky as Carrie Bradshaw.

He asks me if I'm okay and I tell him I'm cool and that I'm going to go right the way through – as in no sleep, like we used to do in the old days.

So he sits down with me, roysh, and everything's fine until around, I suppose, midday, when the weirdest focking thing happens.

Totally out of the blue, I burst into tears, which is something I'm making a focking habit of.

But I also turn around to Oisinn and go, 'Do we *really* treat women this badly?'

Of course, Oisinn doesn't know how to react.

I'm there, 'Dude, we play with their horts, like it's all just a focking game.'

Oisinn goes to put his orm around me, roysh, but I just, like, swat it away.

I'm there, 'No! Why can't Big just leave her alone? He only wants her because she's with somebody else!'

He picks up the remote and presses pause.

'Dude,' he goes, 'you've got to get some sleep.'

I'm not listening, though. 'I mean, she's got this new

thing going on with Aidan. The poor goy's just nipped out for coffee, then that big . . . focking grinning goon shows up . . .'

'I know – the timing couldn't be worse,' Oisinn goes, basically humouring me. 'But even if you got just a couple of hours' kip, Ross . . .'

I'm there, 'No,' literally grabbing the remote from him.

I press play again and Oisinn slips out of the room, roysh, saying he's going for a Forrest, though I know he's really gone to ring either Fionn or JP.

It must be Fionn, because an hour later he shows up again, just as Big's telling Carrie that he's leaving Natasha.

When he walks in, I turn to him and go, 'The goy has got – *oh my God* – serious commitment issues,' and Fionn's all of a sudden ripping off his jacket, throwing it on the ground and going, 'Oisinn, how did you let it get this far?'

He grabs my head in his two hands and looks straight into my eyes.

I'm going, 'Okay, Aidan's not exactly Mr Spontaneity – but he's reliable . . .'

'His body's producing too much oestrogen,' Fionn goes. 'Oisinn, what's he taken?' but before he gets an answer he scans the living-room floor and sees the empty Prosecco bottles and the wrapper from the Galaxy.

I must have eaten my own focking body weight in chocolate.

In fairness to him, Fionn is, like, calmness personified, if that's the word?

'Oisinn,' he goes, 'we need to get this goy's testosterone level back up and we need to do it fast. Go out to my car – there's ten cans of Red Bull in a Superquinn bag. Make it quick. I'll stay here and talk to him about women and rugby.'

Which is exactly what happens. Oisinn gets me to take

big gulps of Red Bull, while Fionn asks me if I think Rob Kearney will make the step up next year and keeps mentioning the names of birds I like – Amy Smort, Rachel Weisz, Vanessa Hudgens.

Eventually, roysh, despite the focking gallon of Red Bull they've put into me, I somehow manage to drift off to sleep and I end up having the weirdest focking dream, where I'm tied to a spit and I've got, like, an apple in my mouth and I'm being slowly turned, roysh, over this humungous fire and then I realize I'm in, like, Bubby's in TriBeCa, roysh, and Carrie and her crew are sitting there, basically slavering over me and arguing over who's having a leg.

I can actually smell burning flesh and then I suddenly wake up and what I'm actually smelling is, like, Christmas dinner, as in a *full* Christmas dinner? We're talking turkey, we're talking ham, we're talking two types of stuffing, we're talking potatoes roasted in duck fat . . .

It's unbelievable.

'Eat up,' Oisinn goes, putting the plate in my hands.

I'm there, 'Goys, I can't believe you . . .'

'My old dear dropped it around,' Fionn goes. 'She always makes way too much.'

Then he's like, 'Ross, you're not doing this on your own. One of us is going to stay with you from now on. Oisinn's going to head home for his dinner. I'll head off later, then JP's offered to come around.'

Without these goys, I don't know where I'd be.

I lash on the rest of series three. I'm actually okay after that. Fionn rations the chocolate, giving me, like, four squares an hour and I lay totally off the Prosecco. He stays until midnight, when JP arrives to relieve him. Fionn has to confiscate a humungous box of Lily O'Brien's off him at the front door and tell him the rules.

JP's in cracking form. He said he was at a lovely Mass on Christmas morning, the first one he really enjoyed in a long time. He cops my worried reaction, but says he's honestly fine.

Stephen's Day flies by, with me totally engrossed in, like, series four and five, but at the same time no closer to finding the answer.

But at half-three the following day, nearly three days after the first episode, the smell of BO only focking Padraig, with a five-kilo Galaxy orse on me and more zits than the mosh-pit at an Avril Lavigne concert, I watch the last episode of series six and – it's incredible – it suddenly all becomes clear to me.

It's one of those, like, *eureka* moments.

It's hilarious, roysh. The goys are all, like, fast asleep in various corners of the room. They wake up just as the final credits roll.

'Now,' Fionn goes, 'I'm bringing you up to bed.'

I stand up and I'm like, 'No, I've got to see Immaculata while this is still fresh in my mind.'

The shop is closed, even though the sales are all storting today, but, after a trawl through their usual brunch spots, I find them in The Unicorn, picking through the antipasti buffet and the bones of last night.

'Ross,' Chloe goes, the first one to see me standing there, 'you look terrible. And – *oh my God* – you stink. What happened?' but before I get a chance to answer, Sophie mentions that Immaculata went home last night with a goy who owns, like, a *real* Steve Kaufman, who was, like, an apprentice to, like, Andy Warhol? And then she turns to Immaculata and goes, 'What was it of, by the way?' and Immaculata says she can't remember, maybe Marilyn Monroe. Or Mickey Mouse.

I go, 'Will you all just shut the fock up for a minute – I've got something to say,' and that gets their immediate attention. 'I've just sat through every focking episode of *Sex and the City . . .*'

All of a sudden, roysh, everyone in the restaurant stops talking and every set of mince pies in the place is suddenly on *me*.

'Oh, yeah,' I go, looking around, 'the weirdest focking Christmas ever. I've been to some pretty dork places over the last two and a half days. You know what I learned, though, by the final episode? Those four birds that you're all so keen to, like, model yourselves on – they all believed in love.

'I mean, yeah, they all banged like a focking shithouse door, I'll grant you that – but, in the end, Carrie ended up with Big. Miranda ended up with . . .'

'Steve,' someone from another table goes. They know their shit in The Unicorn.

I'm like, 'Yeah – Steve. Samantha ended up with Smith and Charlotte ended up with the weird-looking one. My point is, at the end of the day, they all believed in, like, one girl, one goy . . .'

I see Immaculata sort of, like, nodding her head, like I'm slowly convincing her.

'In other words, they were all obsessed with, like, work and shoes and – dare I say it – orgasms, but eventually they all discovered that what they were really looking for was, like, staring them in the face all along . . .'

I know I sound like a focking movie trailer, but I'm pretty sure I see, like, a tear trickle from Immaculata's eye and run down her boat race. So I stick my hand in the old Eddie and I whip out the letter.

'This came for you in the post,' I go. 'I took the liberty of opening it . . .'

'Mikel!' she goes, maybe recognizing the writing, or maybe taking, like, a guess.

'That's right,' I go. 'And the dude's hort is, like, breaking. Have a listen to this,' and I give them a little taster. '*You are my lifeblood. You are my food. My love for you is bigger than Chappal Waddi.*'

I look up at everyone and go, 'I Googled that – it's, like, a mountain? *Without you my life is empty. I don't care why you ran away – I just want you back here with me. Please, Immaculata, when you have found what you are looking for, come home to my arms, come home to where you are loved . . .*'

It's unbelievable, roysh, because all of a sudden she just, like, bursts into tears. And it's not just her either. Chloe, Sophie and Amie with an ie stort bawling their eyes out as well.

In fact, pretty much everyone in The Unicorn is wiping away tears.

Immaculata all of a sudden jumps out of her seat and just, like, hugs me and then there's, like, a round of applause.

'I will go home,' she goes, even her accent suddenly back to normal. 'Mikel is my true love . . .'

I go back to the old dear's and sleep for, like, twenty-four hours straight.

The lock is, like, stuck solid. It must be rust. It's years since it's been opened. I'm jiggling the key in it and lashing on the old WD-40, but it's fock-all use and eventually Ronan pushes me to one side and belts it a few times with a bit of rock.

It breaks off and suddenly we're in.

I flick on the lights, which still work, and it lights up. So does Ro's face.

'Look at this fooken place,' he goes. 'I'll tell you what,

Rosser, you were blessed I didn't know about this before –
lot of storage space in here, man. Might have had to lean
on you once or twice, know what I'm saying?'

I laugh.

I'm there, 'Yeah, I can't think why I didn't mention it to
you . . .'

'And what is it,' Ronan goes, 'a bomb shelter?'

I'm like, 'Used to be. Do you know what you and me are
going to do, though? As soon as this match is over? We're
going to turn it into a boys' room.'

He points at me. 'I like your fooken style, Rosser . . .'

'We can come here and hang out.'

'Like the Bada Bing.'

'Yeah,' I go. He's a little comedian in fairness to him.
'Maybe a few less strippers. I was thinking we could get,
like, proper wooden floors laid. Then we could get, like, a
pool table, plasma screen, jukebox . . .'

'A jacuzzi?'

'Yeah, whatever you want.'

He runs his hand along the wall. 'Cost a few bob, but.'

'Don't worry,' I go. 'The old man's paying for it. And
believe me, he's focking good for it.'

'Some fooken workmanship in these walls,' he goes,
sounding like a man five times his age. 'Not a crack in that
plaster. Needs a lick of paint, but. Here, Buckets of Blood's
after going into decorating – you might thrun a bit of work
his way.'

I'm there, 'I thought he was, like, a debt collector?'

'Sure he was never much use at that,' he goes. 'It was
always buckets of *his* blood got spilt. Nah, painting's his new
thing.'

I'm there, 'So what does he call himself now? Buckets of
Emulsion?'

Ronan cracks his hole laughing at that one, in fairness to him.

'Ah, you're a funny fooker, Rosser, so you are,' he goes.

And even, like, twenty minutes later, you can still hear him repeating the name to himself and, like, shaking his head, laughing.

'We'll get Buckets to do it, then,' I go. 'Can't wait to see the old dear's face when she gets a load of him. Speaking of which, you haven't heard from her, have you?'

It's actually a touchy subject. She's never had a focking conversation with Ronan in her life.

He just shakes his head, then moves a box of her shit that she's got stored down here and storts searching the walls for the electrical points.

I'm there, 'Yeah, no, it's weird. Both her mobiles are switched off . . .'

There's, like, four pretty decent-sized bedrooms in the place and we decide to move all of *her* shit out of the main living area into one of them, to make way for all the new stuff.

Just as we're about to lift a Laura Ashley occasional table, Ronan turns around to me, totally out of the blue, and goes, 'Here, thanks by the way.'

I'm like, 'For?'

'For having a word with Blathin's pardents.'

I'm there, 'Hey, it's cool.'

'I heard you made a right fooken arse of yourself.'

'I wouldn't say that.'

'Bla said she heard you.'

'Oh.'

'*I pity you for it! Pity you!*'

'Yeah, I might have said something along those lines.'

'State of you.'

'Thanks, Ro.'

'I appreciate it, but. End of.'

It's great to have him back.

We spend, like, an hour clearing out the big room, then wiping away all the cobwebs and dust and finally, like, sweeping the place out. When we're finished, I tell Ro that we should give Buckets a bell now – he might have it, like, finished by the time I get back from Andorra.

There's no signal down there, of course, so we have to go outside and it's then I notice that I've got, like, a missed call from Oisinn.

When I ring him back, roysh, his opening line is one of the weirdest focking questions I've ever been asked. He's like, 'Ross, you haven't bought the *Evening Herald* yet, have you?'

I'm like, '*Yet?* Er, try *ever?*' and then I'm like, 'What's this about anyway?'

'They've got a story,' he goes, 'about your old dear,' and at the same time, roysh, I can hear sniggers and I immediately know it's Fionn and JP.

I'm like, 'What's she done now? Bear in mind, roysh, I don't give a fock about her one way or the other.'

'No, you have to see this yourself,' Oisinn goes. 'I don't want to spoil the surprise.'

I tell Ronan we need to go for a drive. We hit the petrol station opposite the Stillorgan Pork Hotel and I swing in, roysh, and ask Ro to go in and get me one of those *Heddild*s.

Obviously, I wouldn't know how to order it.

So in he goes and I watch him walk back across the forecourt to the cor, staring at the front page of the paper and I'm trying to, like, read from his face how bad the news is – but his expression is, like, neutral?

He gets back in and drops the paper on my lap. It's the lead story.

The headline is like, FIONNUALA'S SEX TAPE SHOCK.

I swear to God, roysh, my blood actually storts to boil.

'Millionaire author Fionnuala O'Carroll-Kelly was said to be outraged last night after video footage of her engaged in an apparent sex act with her former agent found its way onto the internet.

'The seven-minute X-rated clip appeared on the web just weeks after a video tape – described as being of a private nature – was stolen from her locker in Carrickmines Croquet and Lawn Tennis Club . . .'

I'm thinking, stolen my orse. She focking *put* it out there.

'O'Carroll-Kelly, the South Dublin housewife behind bestselling bodice-rippers *Criminal Assets* and *Legal Affairs*, told friends of her embarrassment from New York, where she is negotiating with a number of major US publishers for the rights to her next book after splitting with her previous publisher, Penguin.'

It's focking typical. No sooner have I sorted out the problem of one raving nympho than along comes another.

I turn to the next page.

'Last night, one friend, who didn't wish to be named, dismissed suggestions that it was all a publicity stunt to attract the kind of global media attention that catapulted Paris Hilton to fame.

'The footage, posted on the popular YouPorn website, is catch-lined "One Night in Foxrock" and appears to show O'Carroll-Kelly, 52, making love to literary agent Lance Rogan.'

Well, Angela warned me she was going to do something drastic. And here it focking is.

'Rogan, who recently announced plans to wed chick-lit

sensation Charlotte McNeel, 26, admitted last night he was "highly embarrassed", but refused to comment further.

'As in the famous sex tape involving Hilton, O'Carroll-Kelly answers her phone midway through proceedings and can clearly be heard giving out recipe advice, telling the caller, "Pistachios are a wonderful complement to penne."'

Her flight is, like, two hours before mine, so I hit the airport early, just to, like, say my goodbyes? And also to make sure she gets on the actual plane. Of course, there's no real worry there.

I lent her the old Wolfe in the M1 last night to ring Mikel and she was on to him for, like, an hour? Whatever it ends up costing my old man, though, was worth it for the thank you message Sorcha left me this morning.

She looks great. No baby-doll clothes, no heavy eye make-up, just the traditional, I suppose, African clothes she arrived in.

'Ross,' she goes, as we're sitting over a couple of farewell lattes, 'Mikel and I cannot thank you enough for what you have done for us. I hope you will come to Nigeria for the wedding?'

Wedding? It's like, whoa, Mikel – bit drastic.

She goes, 'I would also like to apologize to you for my behaviour. I know that I caused you a lot of worry and for that I am truly sorry.'

I'm there, 'Hey – it's not a thing,' which it isn't.

The next thing, roysh, my phone rings and I can see from my caller ID that it's, like, Gerry Thornley.

I tell her I have to take it. It's someone who's been pretty good to me over the years.

I answer it by going, 'I wondered when you were going

to ring. One F's been all over the story for weeks. Even the *Indo* had it two weeks ago . . .'

He's there, 'I'm just doing six or seven pars for Saturday. Okay, give it to me quickly – what are your hopes for the game?'

I'm there, 'I suppose the question you're asking is, are there any similarities between my coaching psychology and Eddie O'Sullivan's . . .'

'Ross,' he goes, 'don't give me any of that guff you gave Ryle Nugent. Win, lose or draw? Well, you can't win. You're highly unlikely to draw. So, what? Keep the score down? Keep it to, what, forty points? Fifty?'

I'm like, 'Dude, shut the fock up for a second, will you?' because I'm thinking.

I'm thinking about everything I've been through in the last few days. We're talking good shit, we're talking bad shit – Ronan, Immaculata, *Sex and the City*, my old dear – and I end up getting suddenly emotional and all this amazing stuff storts, like, pouring out of my mouth.

'Stick this in your notebook,' I go. 'Rugby is like life in many ways. You can do all the wrong things and win. You can do all the right things and lose. I actually don't care if we lose or how much we lose by – as long as we can look each other in the eye afterwards and say, yeah, we did the best we could with what we had at our disposal.'

I've known the dude for, like, ten years and I swear to God, roysh, he's never heard me talk about deep shit like this before.

'Will I just put *fifty* points?' he goes.

I'm there, 'Yeah, put fifty. When are you flying out?'

He's like, 'What?'

I'm there, 'When are you flying out? The game's on Saturday. That's, like, the day after tomorrow.'

'I'm not *going*,' he goes.

I'm there, 'What?'

'None of the papers are sending. Ross, it's Ireland *A*. Hardly a big deal. Anyway, I better shoot. I've a Six Nations preview to write.'

We go through deportures and I walk Immaculata down to her gate. 'So,' I go, when we get there, 'looks like this is it.'

Her eyes fill up with tears. 'I will miss you,' she goes. 'I will never forget my time in Ireland,' and then she throws her orms around me. 'And I have not given up hope of ever having an orgasm.'

An elderly couple overhear her and I roll my eyes at them.

'Sure,' I go, rubbing her back. 'It might well happen – just never stop believing,' at the same time hating myself for setting Mikel up like that.

10. In the wee small hours

Today is one of those days when everything suddenly clicks into place. One of those days when you think, there's nothing more I can do with this team.

Or I should say, nothing more *we* can do with this team.

Because even though I wouldn't be his number-one fan, there're two of us in this – me and the old man – and he has done an unbelievable job with Joseba. He must have been working with him every day over Christmas because the goy actually looks like he's been playing in the position his whole life.

Our final training session has me feeling unbelievably confident about tomorrow.

They could change Frodo's name to Velcro – that's how sure his hands are, while Jonny can't miss with his kicking. He'll win no prizes for, like, ortistic merit, but he'd actually be good enough for the AIL.

Without blowing my own trumpet, I can safely say that this team is, like, twice the team they were a few weeks ago. And they know it.

The only one of them I need to have a word with is Ander, and I know exactly what I'm going to say to him.

Just after I got the job, roysh, Fionn gave me a book on the history of Andorra, with a Post-it stuck on the cover – ripping the piss, of course – saying basically, *in emergency, please open*.

I was flicking through it last night, reading mostly the

captions on the photographs, when I saw something about Hitler and straight away thought, holy fock, Fehily's sending me a message. So I read it and I thought, that's it – I've found a way to connect with this little nutter.

So after training, roysh, when everyone else is gone for a shower, I call him to one side and I go, 'Ander, I'm all for passion, wearing your hort on your sleeve, blahdy blahdy blah. But all that waving your fist at the crowd, giving it loads, it's wearing you out . . .'

He looks at me like he's just caught me beasting his dog. 'You have somesing against my love for my country?'

'Absolutely not – whatever you're into. I just think you could be, I don't know, cleverer about it. Okay, I've a question for you – did the Germans ever invade Andorra?'

'No,' he goes straight away, like I've seriously wounded his pride. 'We stopped the Wehrmacht at the Port d'Envalira.'

I'm there, 'Who did? The ormy?'

'No, no – we had no army. The Beeshop, he spoke to Franco and Franco spoke to Heetlah. He stop the advance.'

'So what would you call that?' I go. 'Diplomacy? Getting what you want by using your brains instead of anything else?'

He smiles, a huge focking smile, and he points at me, going, 'Aha! Aha! You! You! You are ferry goot, meester!'

I walk over to where the old man is standing with Hennessy, the two of them deep in conversation. 'It, er, pains me to say it,' I go, 'but you've done an unbelievable job with Joseba. I mean, he's no Keith Wood, but he'll do.'

'Always a pleasure to pass on knowledge,' he goes.

I ask him how his Christmas was and he sort of, like, looks at Hennessy, then goes, 'Oh, you know, Ross – up and down. I might need to, er, have a little chat with you after the game.'

Don't worry, I tell him. I saw it in the *Heddild*. The woman's a focking disgrace.

Autographs? I *don't* focking believe it.

Here I am, roysh, about to deliver a seriously kick-orse speech, telling them not to show Ireland A even the slightest bit of respect, when I see them standing around the so-say, asking them to, like, sign shit as they're getting off and going into the ground.

They're all there. We're talking Frodo. We're talking English Jonny. We're talking The Generalissimo.

Johnny O'Connor. Jeremy Staunton. Roger Wilson. They must be thinking, what the fock – we're, like, heroes to these goys.

Of course, I totally flip. We're actually *talking* Conniption City, Idaho, here. I'm, like, straight over there, ripping the pens out of their hands and the little pieces of paper and stamping them into the ground.

One of the Ulster players, who I don't recognize, tells me to catch myself on, which is Northern Irish for cop yourself on. And I immediately tell him, hey, we'll do our catching ourselves on out on the field, which is South Dublin for, well, nothing really, but it sounds good in the heat of the moment.

I sort of, like, herd our players into the dressing-room and then I let rip, as in seriously let rip. I'm going, 'I don't actually believe what I saw out there. What kind of psychological edge do you think you've just handed them? Do you think Keith Earls is kacking himself in there now? Do you think Johnny Sexton's shitting his pants?'

I shake my head like I'm disappointed. None of them will even look at me. I'm there, 'You know, I was back home for Christmas and people were coming up to me in the street, going, "Andorra? Oh, they don't play rugby, do they?"'

One or two heads look up.

'"The people there – they're backward, aren't they?"'

A few more go up.

'"The sun never shines. They eat with their hands and shit in the street and they have sex with donkeys because their women are mongs."'

Of course, this is *actually* stuff we say about Limerick, but I've, like, tailored it to suit the occasion?

'"They smell like rotten liver."'

'Thees ees not right!' Ander suddenly goes. Then he turns to the others and goes, 'Thees ees not right!' and suddenly the goys are all going focking ballistic and I see the kind of attitude from them that I want to see out there on the field.

It's at that exact point that, like, Bernard walks in? He looks like shit, it has to be said, even in a suit that probably cost two or three Ks. Probably hasn't had a proper night's kip since him and Conchita split up.

He looks around the dressing-room, catches my eye and then smiles, but it's not, like, a warm smile? It's, like, a major effort for him.

I just block him out and I go, 'Today is the day we let the world know what Andorra is all about. From this day onwards, no one, anywhere in the four corners of the globe, will ever have to go, "Andorra? Do they play rugby?" because believe me, they will know.

'Goys, when Bernard there gave me some DVDs to watch of some of your past performances, my first reaction, being honest, was, what the fock have I let myself in for here? That lot couldn't beat indigestion.

'But I'm proud to say I was wrong. I saw pretty quickly

that you had the ability. All you actually lacked was the belief . . .'

Frodo shouts, 'You gave that to us, Ross – because *you* believed in *us*!'

I'm there, 'I still believe in you. Now, let's go put this crowd to bed.'

They're pumped after that, we're talking totally pumped. They all stort spilling out. Bernard waits at the door of the dressing-room for me. 'I want to weesh you gude luck today,' he goes.

I'm there, 'Er, cool.'

'Obviously, you and I need to hev a conversation,' he goes, 'but we weel do eet efter the game,' and naturally I'm thinking, what the fock is this about?

I queue up in the tunnel with the players and then we walk out onto the pitch. I'm, like, waiting for the roar. Of course, there isn't one. There's only about a thousand people in the ground, half of them locals who are here out of curiosity, the other half Irish knackers who wouldn't know a rugby ball if they focking sat on one.

We line up for the anthems – Ireland's two and then our own, which is pretty emotional. When it's over, I cop the old man. He's standing in the crowd with Hennessy, the two of them in their match-day coats and hats, each with a Cohiba the size of a butcher's orm clamped between his teeth.

I tip over and I'm like, 'I thought you'd show your face in the dressing-room . . .'

'No, no,' he goes, 'it's *your* team, Ross. *Your* day. I expect Brads is trembling in his boots.'

I'm there, 'You don't want to have, like, a last word with Joseba even?'

'Said all that needs to be said,' he goes. 'Now, I'm happy to just fade into the background.'

Then he goes, 'I've, er, booked a table in the Plaza for nine, Ross. Need to talk to you about something. It's rather delicate.'

It's like, what the fock is going on here? There's no time to think about it now, though.

I have a quick last word with Jonny. 'Remember – want it,' I tell him. Then I tell Joseba that this is going to be the day he rediscovers the man he used to be.

I've got an incredible feeling about the next eighty minutes. We're going to do something today that shocks the world.

Half-time. We've conceded thirteen tries and it probably doesn't need saying that we're playing shit.

Johnny O'Connor's having one of those games most have only dreamt of. He's scored, like, four tries and it's exhibition stuff.

You could say we're making an exhibition of ourselves as well. Missed tackles. Knock-ons. Handling errors. The stats are a nightmare. If you laid our two second rows end to end, they'd be, like, two or three feet taller than theirs – and we still haven't won a line-out. And they're tossing our scrum around like an old rag doll.

I give them dog's abuse in the dressing-room. I'm going, 'I thought we were going to make history out there today? I didn't think it'd be the biggest tonking in rugby *ever* – because that's what we're looking at here . . .'

'They are too goot,' The Generalissimo goes. You'd never know he played basketball for Spain from the way he's, like, struggling for breath. 'Too sthrong, too fest, too skeelfool.'

I'm there, 'So what – you just want to go home? You don't think you can win a single line-out against these goys?'

'We are honly hamateurs.'

327

So I hit him with one of Fehily's old lines. 'Check the label on your jersey there . . .'

He looks at me like I'm off my cake.

I'm there, 'Seriously, dude – take it off and check the label,' and that's exactly what he does. He's looking at the label, then he's, like, looking at me.

I'm there, 'Does it say anywhere that these colours run?'

It takes a few seconds for the ones who speak English to get it. Then they translate it for the rest and it's, like, the whole atmosphere of the dressing-room suddenly changes.

That's when Joseba – by far our best player so far – stands up and goes, 'I know what eet ees to breeng shem on the name of Andorra. I let my country down and I haff leefed weeth that. After today I wheel not leef with eet any more! What about ollof you?'

'No!' everyone suddenly goes.

'Again!'

'No!'

Ander pipes up then. 'We can steel ween thees fucking game . . .'

I'm like, 'Er, ninety points down, I think it's pretty much gone away from us actually. If Brads took them back to the hotel now, I'm still not sure we'd score ninety focking points in the second half. But, goys, what about this – let's stop *them* scoring any more. What about that? Let's, I suppose, reset our priorities – stop them putting a hundred points on us.'

They like the sound of that.

I'm there, 'Let's defend like our lives basically depend on it. Ander, remember I told you to be a bit lower key? Forget it, dude. Go out there and tear them aport.'

They all let out a roar and I swear to God, roysh, you can feel the floor of the dressing-room shake.

The second half, roysh, is a totally different matter. Jeremy Staunton knocks over three penalties, but they can't find a way over our line. It's like war out there. We've still got a big focking zero on the scoreboard, but the goys are, like, throwing themselves into tackles and I wouldn't be too surprised if two or three of ours have to head straight from here to the hospital.

At the end, roysh, the two minutes of injury time are up and it's, like, the next time the ball goes dead, it's over. But they need one more score, roysh, to get the hundred points and they're, like, battering our line. It's like a focking battle-field out there, bodies lying everywhere in the mud.

All of a sudden, roysh – and I have to rely on Frodo's account because he was one of probably only a few who saw what happened in the actual confusion – the ball comes loose, drops in front of him and he just, like, randomly boots it.

The ball wobbles through the air and lands like a shot duck just inside their half. The nearest man to it is probably the man you'd fancy least in a sprint.

It's Joseba.

Time slows up. It seems to take forever for him to reach the ball. When he does, roysh, he whips it up with, like, a grace – I suppose – that I never thought he possessed.

The crowd goes focking mental, our five hundred, for the first time, suddenly making the noise of five thousand. There's a clatter of green jerseys chasing after him, but he's got a ten-, maybe fifteen-yord stort on them.

Like everyone else, I'm giving it, 'Run! *Run!* Run like your legs are on fire and your orse is catching!'

Joseba's focked, though. He's been our best player out there today – a man who never played the game until a few weeks ago – but it's taken its toll. His legs are like jelly, but on he goes, like a cor with the handbrake off rolling slowly down a hill.

Six Irish players are almost on him and it's only a matter of seconds before he disappears under a mountain of green. Fifteen yords from the line, Chris Keane goes to take him down with, like, an ankle tap, but somehow slips in the mud at the last minute and takes Jeremy Staunton down with him.

On he goes, not so much running as, like, stumbling forward. The crowd is going ballistic.

'Go on, Joseba! *Go on!*'

I'm thinking, he's going to score! He's going to score a focking try against Ireland.

A.

Just before the line, roysh, Keith Earls launches himself at him, throws his two orms around Joseba's thighs and brings him crashing to the ground no more than a metre from the line. Two more players are immediately on top of him.

I put my head in my hands. I'm thinking, so close. *So* focking close.

And then I watch as, almost in slow motion, Joseba's orms suddenly emerge from this pile of bodies, the ball wobbling in his two hands.

I'm still pretty sure he's going to spill it.

But he doesn't. He slams it down into the mud, no more than an inch over the Irish line.

The place just erupts. No one notices Jonny kick a perfect conversion and no one hears the final whistle. A couple of hundred of our fans just, like, flood the field. Several efforts are made to lift Joseba up onto their shoulders, but without a JCB, it's useless. Instead, they pick me up and carry me in, like, a king's chair around the pitch.

You honestly wouldn't know which team actually won here. Not even just won, but blew the other off the face of the actual Earth. The Irish players are, like, standing around, clapping us and you've got to say fair focks to them.

I notice English Jonny crying his eyes out, hugging someone who I presume to be his wife, going, 'We facking done it! We only gone and facking done it!'

Then I see Frodo. He's crying as well. I tell him I'm proud of him. I couldn't have asked for a better general going into battle and he tells me that the second the final whistle blew he looked for his girlfriend and when he found her, he asked her to marry him.

And do you know what she said?

She said yes.

It hits me all of a sudden. Joseba's try. It was identical in almost every detail to the one the old man claims to have scored against Blackrock College in, like, a friendly back in the sixties. Last minute. Defending their lines. The kick downfield. The slowest man on the field off in chase. Just enough pitch left – we're talking millimetres here – to get the ball over the line.

I realize all of a sudden that it was no fluke. He told Joseba something. What, I can't even begin to know. Where to stand? How to anticipate the spill?

All I do know is that the try was down to him.

I have to, like, fight my way through the fans and the other players to get to the section where the old man and Hennessy were standing, but they've gone. Disappeared in a puff of Esplendido smoke.

I feel, like, a hand on my shoulder. I immediately go, 'Dad!' but it's not him. It's Joseba. I think he's the only Andorran player on the field who isn't in tears.

He did his crying in the ring, I suppose.

We just, like, embrace each other. I tell him I'm proud of him. I tell him that, more importantly, Andorra is proud of him.

He says thank you. He says I have helped him to rediscover what it means to be a hero . . . and a man.

I'm suddenly brought back to Earth with a bang when I remember that Bernard wants to talk to me, and already I've got the feeling that it's not good news.

But I have to face it, just like every one of those players faced up to forty minutes of, like, constant pressure from Ireland A.

In that moment, Frodo, Joseba, Ander and the rest of the goys are, like, an inspiration to me.

They probably always will be.

I go back to the dressing-room, stick my head around the door and it's, like, total mayhem in there – we're talking players, their families, fans, making easy work of the crate of champagne that Brads sent in to them.

He's a class act in fairness to him.

I duck out again and end up running straight into Bernard in the corridor. He catches me totally on the hop when the first thing he does is reach out and, like, hug me.

'Today, I em a proud, proud men,' he goes, pretty much dribbling down the back of my blue Hugo Boss blazer. Then he suddenly holds me at orm's length and goes, 'Where shell we heff zees conversation?'

I'm there, 'Er, let's do it here?'

'Here ees not so gude,' he goes because there's people milling in and out of the dressing-room and making an unbelievable noise. He takes me instead into a little kitchen that I didn't even know was there before.

'Tonight,' he goes, 'you wheel say goodbye to ze players.'

I'm there, 'Excuse me?'

'Conchita, as you know, has gone beck to Spain. When she left ze apartment, she forgot to breeng her phone weeth her. Zat phone call you made on Creestmus Day . . .'

'You listened to the message?'

'Yes, I leestened to ze messarge.'

'Dude, you've got to understand, nothing happened between us.'

'I know zis,' he goes, as if the idea was, like, totally focking ridiculous. 'I cannot blem you for ze failure of my merridge. But you tell my wife you haff all zees feelings for her. Zat is not right. You understend – we cannot work togezzare any more . . .'

I know he's right. Me and my big . . .

'Ross,' he goes, 'you are an outstending coach. Beeg theengs weel heppen for you. One day, in perheps eight, twelve, sixteen years, Andorra weel qualify for ze World Cup and we weel remember zis day as ze start of eet. Ze day when we started to heff belief een ourselves. And we weel remembare you, Ross.'

I suddenly feel like a piece of shit.

I'm thinking back to that day we met in Paris, how I was convinced – and still am – that Fehily somehow brought us together. Without even knowing me, Bernard took a chance on me. He's been like an uncle to me. And I let him down.

'Of course we weel pay out ze remainder of your contrect,' he goes. 'Eighteen months. You weel be een great demand efter today. Liechtenstein needs a new coach right now. So too Malta. It ees a compliment to you to say zat I hope zey do not get you.'

Then he sort of, like, grips the top of my orm and gives me a kind of half-smile. His way of saying goodbye.

*

I'm asked three times by three different waiters if I want, like, a table, but I tell them no. For some reason I just want to stand here for now, watching him. He pours himself another glass of Coteaux du Languedoc, checks his watch, then goes back to reading the menu. The unsung hero of the hour.

The truth is, roysh, I don't know how to tell him that I've just got the bullet. The second coaching job I've lost for being too much of a Johnny Big Potatoes.

So I stand and watch him for a little bit longer, then I decide to tell him that I quit over money. He'll understand that.

He sees me across the restaurant and he's immediately on his feet, going, 'Here he comes! Ross Kyle Gibson McBride O'Carroll-Kelly. King of the Pyrenees!' and for once I don't call him a penis or a dickhead or anything.

I just, like, point at him and smile. 'That try, I don't know what happened, but don't even *try* to tell me it was a fluke . . .'

He gives me this big wink, then shakes my hand, at the same time gripping my elbow. 'Sit, sit,' he goes and I suddenly remember the reason I'm here, roysh, is because *he* has something to tell *me*.

He clears his throat. 'Today,' he goes, 'I'm a proud, proud man. Happily, you, too, are a father, Ross, so you'll know a little of how that feels.'

I'm suddenly remembering Ro on the day of the sulky race. 'I know *exactly* how it feels,' I go.

He smiles at me. 'Of course you do. Young Ronan. He's a credit to you, Ross.'

'I kind of feel about twenty per cent more *alive* when I'm around him, if that doesn't sound too weird? He's amazing.

I get sort of, like, giddy – as in *drunk* giddy? – whenever I hear his voice, even when I know he's up to no good.'

He gives me a wink. 'I know *that* feeling,' and I suddenly feel guilty for being so hord on him down through the years. 'The older I get,' he suddenly goes, 'the more I realize that passing on the genes isn't the most important reason we're here – it's the *only* reason.'

He's actually right.

I'm there, 'It doesn't matter how much of a fock-up I am, I look at Ro and I look at Honor and I think, well, there's *something* I got right.'

'Prison gives you a lot of time for reflection,' he goes. 'Doesn't matter if you don't so much as crack the spine of a book while you're in there – everyone comes out wiser. Maybe not better, but certainly wiser, because of the time to think.

'I told John Lonergan when he shook my hand to see me out. John, I said, I've finally found my moral compass. Charles, he said to me, you're one of the lucky ones. And that's a direct quote.

'I haven't been a good father, Ross. I've made terrible, terrible mistakes. I've a lot of atoning to do. A lot of making up.'

I'm there, 'Well, I haven't exactly been, like, a *model* son? But I'm certainly a lot wiser, too. And I'm prepared to give it, like, a *proper* go between us? In fact, I actually bought you those stools.'

'What stools?'

'Your and Hennessy's stools – from, like, the Berkeley Court?'

His face lights up. 'Ross,' he goes, 'I don't know what to say.'

'You don't have to say jack shit. I knew how much they meant to you, so I picked them up at the auction.'

'What a wonderfully thoughtful thing to do.'

'Well, don't get carried away. I smashed the focking things off the wall one night. The good news is, though, that Buckets of Blood is going to fix them. He's a decorator slash DIY man these days.'

'Well, thank you, Ross.'

'It's not a thing. You'll probably have to wait for them, though, till I get back from the States. I've decided to go. To see Honor mostly.'

He's like, 'You must really miss her.'

'Like you wouldn't actually believe. And of course I want to make sure she never forgets this face. I don't want her growing up thinking that other tool's her old man.'

'There's a very special bond between a father and son,' he goes, suddenly all misty-eyed. 'And you and I have borne that out down through the years, Ross. But there's another type of bond – different, but equally special – between a father and his daughter.'

I'm there, 'You're not wrong there.'

And it's then that I notice, like, the extra place-setting. And the lit candle in the middle of the table.

I turn to him, in all innocence, and I'm like, 'Who's this for?'

And then I hear it – a girl's voice.

'It's for me,' she goes.

It's like I've suddenly been dropped into an ice bath. Every muscle in my body freezes up. It takes me a good ten seconds to look up at her.

To look up at . . . Erika.

I can suddenly hear that my breathing is faster. 'No,' I go. 'No no no no no . . .'

The old man stands up and pulls the chair out for her, then signals to the waiter for another menu.

She's like, 'Thank you, Charles,' and I'm thinking, how are they like this around each other already?

I end up totally losing it with Erika, like it's somehow *her* actual fault?

'*Him?*' I go. 'Of all the focking people. I thought it was some Greek goy, supposed to be rolling in it . . .'

'Do you think I'd tell those stupid girls the truth?' she goes, equally losing it with me. 'Do you think I'd tell those stupid girls anything?'

I'm there, 'So, like, you were here for Christmas? With *him?*'

The old man goes, 'It's called getting to know each other, Ross. Look, you're not the only who's in shock over this.'

Shock doesn't even begin to cover it. This scene is, like, too focked up for words.

I look at the old man. 'So how long have you known?'

'Years,' he goes, sounding pretty ashamed, and rightly so.

'So, hang on. That thing you said – you and Frank Sinatra in the Berkeley Court – about us only having one true love . . .'

I flick my thumb at Erika and go, 'It was *her* old dear?'

'Helen, yes,' he goes, 'we were in love.'

He smiles sort of, like, sweetly at Erika, who's wearing the black Dolce & Gabbana satin bustier that Sorcha wanted and ended up having a total freak attack when she bought it first.

'We met at a dinner dance in Pembroke Cricket Club . . .'

Erika smiles back at him. It's like she already knows the story, but wouldn't care if she heard it a hundred times more.

'She was like a young Elizabeth Taylor. Alas, I was no Richard Burton . . .' and he laughs – he *actually* focking laughs.

'So, come on,' I go, 'gimme the sordid details. I was no whizz at maths in school, but, given that me and *her* are pretty much the same age, you must have been seeing her old dear while you were actually married?'

He suddenly loses the rag with me, which is something he never does. 'I'll thank you *not* to use words like "sordid",' he goes. 'You're talking about Erika's mother . . .'

He smiles at Erika again.

'We were in love. I mean, this was years *before* I met Fionnuala. You could say Helen and I were soulmates. But then she went away, to Chicago. Oh, we tried to make it work, but the distance and so forth . . . impossible. Especially when you've been that close. I was broken-hearted, of course – we both were . . .'

Out of the corner of my eye, I can see Erika nodding – approvingly, I suppose is the word. It's a good focking story, I'll give him that.

'But we both resolved to move on with our lives. Then – it was a few years later – Helen came back. Bumped into her one day, just like that, in Switzers. You wouldn't remember Switzers, either of you. Well, I was married by then, to Fionnuala. And Helen was married, too. To Tim . . .'

'I don't even want to hear *how* you two got it on,' I go, then I turn to Erika and I'm like, 'Are you not even embarrassed by this?'

That's when *she* totally rips me.

'It's not all about *you*!' she screams, which sort of, like, stuns me into silence. 'It doesn't always *have* to be about *you!*'

Then she goes back to her menu.

The old man eventually breaks the silence. 'What are you going to have, Erika?'

She says she really enjoyed the supreme of corn-fed chicken with Morteau sausage stuffing last night. I don't know how they can even *think* about eating.

I stare at the old man. 'I can't believe you told Frank Sinatra and you didn't tell me . . .' which is a line I basically never thought I'd hear myself say.

It's suddenly all becoming clearer now.

'So that's why the old dear stitched you up,' I go, 'as, like, revenge?'

The old man nods.

'I won't try to understand her motives, but, yes, she – as you put it – stitched me up. The thing is, she *knew*, Ross. She knew about Erika, even before she was born. And she was fine with it, once there was no contact, once it wasn't acknowledged. But then – I don't know what happened – she went a bit funny when she went through that, well, menopause thing of hers . . .'

I can't think about that on top of all the rest of it. I'm like, 'Whoa! TMI, already? TMI.'

I'm sitting there, looking at the two of them, trying to see resemblances between them and at the same time just shaking my head, hoping this is all just, like, a nightmare.

Then I suddenly remember something else and it's like someone's just jabbed me in the head with a fork. I stare at Erika until she eventually looks up from her menu.

'What about that time we . . .'

She just, like, shakes her head at me, as if to say, do not even *go* there, Ross?

I'm there, 'The *two* times we . . .'

She tells me to shut the fock up. She doesn't even want

to think about it. Says it's like something from *Hollyoaks*, or the West of Ireland.

The old man looks up at us, over the top of his reading glasses, and says the *cunillo* is wonderful.

Erika lifts her glass and goes, 'Happy New Year,' but I'm too in shock to return the toast. So her and the old man end up just clinking glasses.

'It will be,' he goes. 'It will be now.'

Acknowledgements

Rachel Pierce is so much more than a great editor. She is Ross O'Carroll-Kelly's surrogate mum. She has been there since the very first book and still refuses to let me write a lazy sentence. She has also come up with an embarrassing number of storylines for me. Thank you, Rachel. Thanks also to Faith O'Grady, my wonderful, wonderful agent, who makes all things possible. Thank you to Michael McLoughlin, Patricia Deevy, Brian Walker, Patricia McVeigh, Cliona Lewis and everyone at Penguin for the privilege of working with the best. Thank you to all my editors, past and present, especially Ger Siggins and Paddy Murray, who saw a future for Ross when I didn't. Thanks to my dad, my late mother and my brothers for the laughter that always pervaded our home, even if most of it was at my expense. And finally, most of all, thanks to the lovely Mary. I go quite mad while I'm writing these books and it's she who reminds me, every day, what really matters and what really doesn't. I love you, Mary. And the rest of you, too.